INNOCENCE LOST

A notorious rake, the Marquis of Bradstone stole young Olivia Sutton's heart . . . and then ruined her life. For seven years she has been forced to hide her past behind a false identity. And now the dashing scoundrel has returned a different man: more handsome, more serious, more desirable . . . and far more dangerous than the cad who brought scandal and shame into Olivia's world.

RAPTURE FOUND

Major Robert Danvers is living a lie—but for a noble cause. Masquerading as his cousin, the late marquis, Robert's secret mission for the crown has led him straight to the beautiful, scheming seductress he believes was responsible for his brother's death. But there is a gentle innocence about this Olivia that belies her murderous reputation—and a passionate sensuality that makes him yearn to hold her forever in his arms. His loyalty to his mission tells him that surrender would be the worst sort of betrayal—yet once tempted, how can a man resist, when his heart tells him here is his one true love?

Other Avon Romantic Treasures by
Elizabeth Boyle

NO MARRIAGE OF CONVENIENCE

If You've Enjoyed This Book,
Be Sure to Read These Other
AVON ROMANTIC TREASURES

ELIZABETH BOYLE

Once Tempted

An Avon Romantic Treasure

AVON BOOKS

An Imprint of HarperCollinsPublishers

This is a work of fiction. Names, characters, places, and incidents are products of the author's imagination or are used fictitiously and are not to be construed as real. Any resemblance to actual events, locales, organizations, or persons, living or dead, is entirely coincidental.

AVON BOOKS
An Imprint of HarperCollins*Publishers*
10 East 53rd Street
New York, New York 10022-5299

Copyright © 2001 by Elizabeth Boyle
ISBN: 0-380-81535-4
www.avonromance.com

First Avon Books paperback printing: July 2001

Avon Trademark Reg. U.S. Pat. Off. and in Other Countries, Marca Registrada, Hecho en U.S.A.
HarperCollins ® is a trademark of HarperCollins Publishers Inc.

Printed in the U.S.A.

10 9 8 7 6 5 4 3 2 1

To the memory of my grandmother,
Patricia Lantow

She was one of the few people I've ever known who wel-
comed each day and explored it with unbridled enthusi-
asm. May her spirit live on forever in the gardens she loved
and tended, and in the hearts of her family who will miss
her always.

Prologue

London, 1805

The sharp pain and darkness that had carried Orlando into unconsciousness began to lift. He fought the urge to moan, to groan, to rub his throbbing skull. Instead he did as he'd been taught and remained as still as a corpse.

After all, that was what the Marquis of Bradstone, the man who'd just finished rifling his pockets and stealing the missive he carried, thought—that Orlando was dead.

And Orlando had no doubt that if his assailant knew he still lived, he wouldn't remain that way for very long.

So what was he to do?

In another part of the house, the ball being thrown by their host, Lord Chambley, sounded as if it had reached its height. Music competed with conversations, and the jovial din reached even this secluded part of the elegant and spacious town house.

Ignoring that distraction, Orlando focused instead on the muttered curses and rustle of parchment rising from the other corner of the library, where the Marquis of Bradstone was attempting to decipher the coded missive.

A missive that, in the right hands, would enable the English to unhinge Napoleon's tight grasp on Spain—or just make Bradstone a very rich man.

Madre de Dios, he thought. *I can't let this happen.*

With the other man occupied, Orlando did a furtive and silent inventory. His pistol, once tucked into his waistband, was gone, but that much he expected.

His hand slid down to his boot top, his fingers closing over the silver hilt of the stiletto he kept tucked inside.

Orlando would have grinned if he wasn't supposed to be dead. Instead he stole another glance at the marquis.

The man looked about to have a fit, his face contorted with frustration.

The code had obviously proven harder than the man had expected.

Keep trying, you greedy bastard, Orlando thought, *then you'll not notice when I slit your throat.*

Just as he was about to take his revenge, the door to the library sprang open.

"There you are. I've been waiting," Bradstone said, with his usual smooth charm.

Orlando cursed his foul luck, easing back into his spot behind the desk. Now he had two opponents to dispatch instead of just one. That is, until he heard the voice of this newest arrival.

"I'm so sorry, my lord." The soft whisper of a woman stopped Orlando's next breath.

A woman? Bradstone was in the midst of stealing a fortune and he was taking the time to have a midnight assignation?

Apparently so, for her footsteps padded lightly across the carpet as she swept past the desk. In her wake fell the delicate scent of perfume. Roses, he thought, drifting over him like a feminine rain.

"I couldn't slip away until my mother's attention was completely diverted," the woman said. "How thoughtful of you to send someone to play cards with her, especially when you know she is unable to refuse a good hand."

Her voice surprised Orlando with its youthful innocence. She sounded young, far too young to be alone with the likes of Bradstone, or any man, for that matter.

Bradstone was laughing. "Anything to be with you." The sound of kissing followed.

Orlando had no compunction about killing his enemy, but the man's mistress, now that was an entirely different matter.

"Oh, Robert, I have missed you so," she said breathlessly.

"And I you, my dearest Olivia." More kissing ensued.

Orlando took this opportune moment to peer through his lashes.

Bradstone's "dearest Olivia" was hardly what he expected. The girl in his arms was no Cyprian, no Haymarket bird. She wasn't even some ingenue belle, the pretty, breathtaking kind of innocent femininity the *ton* liked to call an Original.

No, Bradstone's paramour could hardly even be called that—she was, in Orlando's humble estimation, a rather plain little sparrow of a miss. Sure enough, her auburn hair fell in the requisite cascade of ringlets down over her shoulders, but its coppery luster seemed like a handful of dull farthings rather than some fiery silken mane to inspire such heated passion.

When she tipped her face toward him and Orlando could make out her features, again he found himself astounded. The girl was young, there was no doubt there, but her features were not the kind that would make a man sit up and take notice when she entered the room.

Even her gown was rather dull, a soft yellow muslin that only made her hair look more orange than red and did nothing to add color to her already pale cheeks and brow.

Orlando's gut filled with ill-ease. Something was not right. Not at all.

What the devil was Bradstone doing summoning some innocent into his treasonous scheme?

"Come, my dear," Bradstone was saying to her, his hands brushing back her wayward curls. "You know I find you irresistible."

"You are too kind, my lord," she said, a hint of wistfulness to her words. She paused for a moment. "Did I decipher your note correctly? Did you really mean what you said? That you love me? That you have something special to ask me this night?"

Most of her astounding disclosure was lost on Orlando for one word had caught and held his attention.

Decipher.

"Of course you read my note correctly," Bradstone

told her. Again the sound of kissing filled the room. "You always do, my little bluestocking."

Bluestocking? Orlando thought it an odd endearment between lovers, but the girl didn't seem to mind, for she laid her head on the marquis's shoulder and sighed.

Something unfathomable began forming in Orlando's mind. Could Bradstone possibly intend to use this girl to decipher the code?

Impossible. It was the throbbing in his head that was giving him such crazy notions.

Very quickly he realized that he'd once again underestimated his adversary.

"I promise tonight will be like no other for you," Bradstone began. "That is, if you can do this one thing for me."

Orlando heard the familiar rustle of parchment. The missive. He couldn't keep his eyes shut. To his shock, Bradstone handed the future of the Peninsula and Britain to this mere slip of a girl.

"Oh, Robert," the girl said breathlessly. "Anything." She clutched the most coveted secret in the history of Spain to her bosom as if it were nothing more than a bit of heartfelt verse dashed off by an earnest lover.

The pair kissed again, while Orlando tried to fathom how Bradstone could believe this girl was capable of deciphering what eleven hundred years of learned men and treasure hunters had found unintelligible.

"Come, now, we mustn't," Bradstone told her. "We cannot succumb to this madness. *Not again.*" The Marquis purred those words like a triumphant alley cat, sure of his success and position.

Orlando's noble-bound honor bristled at the thought.

She may not be comely, she may not even be of high and lofty rank, but it was obvious she was gently bred and innocent of heart—and her now inevitable fall from grace would destroy her.

English society wasn't so unlike the strict rules of his homeland. Once tempted into a man's arms, a young woman could give up any hope of living a respectable life.

And if what Bradstone implied was true, Olivia was thus tainted. Irretrievably so.

"No more," Robert was saying, the kissing finally coming to a stop. "Not until you tell me what this says."

The girl sighed. "If you insist."

Orlando heard her gown rustle again and then her footsteps as she padded toward him.

He held his breath for what he knew was coming.

Sure enough, a shrill gasp began and was quickly muffled.

"Yes, I was going to warn you about that bit of business," Bradstone said. "Now, if I take my hand away from your mouth, will you promise not to scream?"

She must have agreed, for a moment later, she asked in a soft, tenuous whisper, "Is he—" Her question faltered.

"Dead?" Bradstone finished. "I fear so."

Yes, you go on believing that, you arrogant dog, Orlando mused silently.

"Who is he?" she asked.

"A French agent. Here on Napoleon's devilish business."

French? Orlando bristled. The blood of seventeen generations of Castilian grandees flowed though his veins and enough English blood for him to be thoroughly indignant. Then he spied the girl moving closer to him, so he held his indignation and breathing in check.

"He doesn't look French to me," the girl said. "More likely Spanish."

"Yes, well, he's one of the Corsican's Spanish lackeys," Bradstone declared impatiently, pulling his unwitting accomplice away from Orlando and back into his arms. The marquis lowered his voice. "The man was a Napoleon lackey come here to bedevil our good King and country. It was up to me to stop him."

The girl glanced back at Orlando. "He looks rather young to be as nefarious as you say."

"Yes, so I thought, until he tried to kill me with this," Bradstone said, brandishing Orlando's pistol. "Thankfully, I was able to surprise him before he could carry out his plot."

"Oh, Robert, how brave you are," she said, wrapping her arms around his neck. "But what were his plans? Don't keep this from me. If I am to be your . . . wife"—she said the word with a soft little sigh before continuing—"then you must tell me."

"And so I shall," her lover said, disentangling himself from her embrace.

Once again Orlando heard the rustle of the missive.

The marquis continued, "He carried these instructions. They are in an ancient code, and you my dearest girl, being as extraordinarily skilled as you are at deciphering, I knew you could help me."

" 'Twas your good fortune and a happy coincidence that we met at Lady Bloomberg's puzzle party in May," she said.

"Yes, quite," Bradstone said, but to Orlando's way of thinking the man didn't sound so truthful. "You left me astounded by your superior intelligence, for Lady Bloomberg fancies herself quite the encryption expert." He held the note out to her. "Now I ask you to use your remarkable talent for me and for your King."

Orlando's heart hammered in his chest at these disclosures. But how could he stop this madness while Bradstone still held the pistol in his hand and this innocent girl remained in the room? Orlando suffered no doubts that if he made a move, she may be harmed as well.

One thought cheered him though. They had yet to unravel the code. Perhaps all he needed to do was to wait and see what Bradstone's bluestocking would make of it.

Then he would decide if her life was worth placing in such jeopardy.

He didn't have to wait long.

"Someone went to a lot of work to make sure no one could read this," she said. "It appears each pair of words uses a different cipher. The first uses a displacement of Greek and replaces it with the corresponding sequence in Spanish. You see here and here," she offered, pointing at the note before her.

"Yes, yes, that is quite brilliant, but can you get the message?"

"I don't know," she said. "But I can try, especially if this is as important as you say."

"The message in this note is a matter of life and death."

Life and death, Orlando mused. As if Bradstone cared one whit for the lives he would cost England by stealing this information. But in this he'd fail. For Orlando still would have bet a shipload of gold that this snip of a schoolgirl couldn't unravel the key.

And then to his horror she did.

"Oh, I see what they've done," she declared. *"El Rescate del Rey* it starts out." She turned her face toward Bradstone, who shrugged at her use of Spanish. "The King's Ransom," she translated. "Does that make sense?"

"The King's Ransom," he whispered in an awestruck voice. "Yes. Yes. Go on. Go on."

While Olivia struggled with the next section of the message, Orlando scrambled to control his shock at what had just happened.

This chit had grasped the first part of the missive. Something no one had done in eleven centuries. If she got the rest of it . . . Orlando didn't even want to consider the consequences.

But the evening went from nightmarish to horrific as Bradstone slowly and silently cocked the pistol he'd stolen and held it behind the girl's back.

A matter of life and death. A matter of life and death.

The marquis's previous words sang like an unholy refrain in Orlando's throbbing skull.

Now he knew what the man had truly meant. Bradstone intended to kill her as well.

Silently Orlando rose to his feet.

"Oh, here it is," she sang out, innocently unaware that every refrain she provided her lover was one step closer to her demise.

"What does it say?" Avarice laced Bradstone's demand, filling the room with the man's insatiable greed.

Orlando steadied himself on the edge of the desk.

His senses reeled and swayed at having to stand, and he used every ounce of strength he possessed not to draw any attention to his movements.

Meanwhile the little bluestocking continued. "This line reads, 'In the Tomb of the Virgin.' " She bit her lip. "I've never heard of such a place. Certainly not here in London."

Bradstone nodded in agreement. "Then try the last word—that one should reveal everything." To urge her on, he kissed the top of her head, while behind her back Orlando's pistol rose until it was pointed at the base of her skull.

For a moment it brushed over the hairs there. She flinched ever so slightly, as if she sensed the nearness of death.

Life and death. Life and death. The words urged Orlando forward. His hand flexed over the hilt of his stiletto, and he took another silent step.

"I think I have it!" she said, slowly and deliberately. "The last word is . . . 'Madrid.' " She held it up for him. "The King's Ransom. In the Tomb of the Virgin. Madrid." Her lips pursed in concentration. "But it makes no sense. Why would a ransom for King George be in a tomb in Spain?"

"It doesn't need to make sense to you," Bradstone told her, his fingers curling around the trigger.

"Kill her, you bastard, and you shall be next," Orlando told him. Both the girl and the marquis whirled around.

Orlando took advantage of their surprise and leaped forward. He plunged the stiletto at Bradstone, but the man saw it coming and deflected the worst of the blade's intent, sending it skittering across the library floor.

Now locked in a deadly battle with the man, Orlando struggled to gain control of the pistol wavering between them.

Out of the corner of his eye, he spied the girl standing near the fireplace. "Run. He means to kill us both," he told her in Spanish, since it was apparent she had a good grasp of the language.

He saw a flash of yellow silk and thought she was heeding his advice, but suddenly he found her coming at Bradstone with his lost stiletto. Bradstone saw her as well and yanked the pistol free of Orlando's grip and turned to aim it at her.

"No," Orlando cried out, reaching for the muzzle and yanking it in a different direction, hoping to turn it finally on the marquis.

And then a shot rang out. At first Orlando thought he had succeeded, that he had stopped Bradstone—but in that next moment, a hot, burning flame of lead passed through his gut. It tore at his senses until all he knew was a wretched tangle of pain.

Her piteous cry pierced his thoughts, a mourning keen to comfort his last few seconds.

Sinking to the floor, he landed at her slippered feet. Her horrified gaze locked with his, her hand covering her mouth.

Down the hall, footsteps and shouts pierced the sudden, deadly silence of the room.

Bradstone wasted no time. He shoved the still smoking pistol into Olivia's hand and went for the door.

"In here. Come quickly. There has been a murder," he called out.

Orlando struggled to hold on, to hear what was being said, in case, just in case he lived, so he could tell Hobbe . . .

But he wasn't going to live, for the pain spread throughout his chest, his body convulsing with wrenching finality. His eyelids grew too heavy to remain open, while a mixture of darkness and comforting light began blotting out his senses. As he started to drift away, a soft, warm hand cradled his, pulling him back.

Over the buzzing in his ears, he heard Bradstone's voice saying, "Miss Sutton has committed a murder. That man there. She shot him."

There were gasps and shouts but not from the lady herself.

No, Orlando tried to tell the growing crowd of witnesses. *She didn't do this.*

"*¿Cómo podría ayudarle?*" she whispered in his native tongue. How can I help you?

He fumbled to free his hand and with the last ounce of strength he possessed he pulled the ring from his finger. She still held the note in her hand, so he set the gold band atop it and crushed his fingers over hers, tightening her grasp on his two most precious belongings.

The bright light now filled the room. It distracted his thoughts and strangely eased his pain. As much as he wanted to abandon himself to its comforting warmth, he couldn't leave this girl behind to pay for his mistakes.

"Run, now," he managed to say. "Go as far as you can. Hide where they cannot find you. Give this to no one but—" The pain overcame him, and he stumbled over the name that should have come so easily to him.

"Who?" she pleaded. "Who should I give it to?"

"Hobbe," he managed to whisper before he finally relented his life to what he could only hope were angels overhead.

Chapter 1

London, 1812

"**H**ow was your trip to the solicitor, my lady?" Carlyle asked as he helped his mistress, the Marchioness of Bradstone, down from her carriage.

"Wretched!" she complained. "The incompetent man says there is nothing we can do. Nothing in the least. He is certain that next month the House of Lords will pronounce Robert dead and allow the title to revert to the Crown."

Carlyle shook his head. "I feared as much, madame."

Her ladyship fluttered her handkerchief. "A month, Carlyle! A month!" she wailed. "Where will I live? Where will I go? Everything that matters is entailed with the estate."

Where will we all go? Carlyle would have liked to

add to her lament. The Bradstone staff had just as much at stake as their mistress in the Parnell family keeping the title—their livelihoods depended upon it as well.

Lady Bradstone drew her handkerchief to her nose and sniffed. "If only my dearest boy would come home and prevent all this. Surely he must know the fits and tremblings his continued absence causes me, let alone this newest injustice."

"If his lordship were aware, my lady, I am sure he would hasten home without further delay," Carlyle said very diplomatically. He had tried on any number of occasions to explain to her that it was highly unlikely her son would ever come home.

For seven long years she'd denied that her son had fled the scandalous scene and sought passage on the doomed *Bon Venture*. Seven years of refusing to believe her son had been on that ship when it was attacked and sunk by the French off the coast of Portugal. The papers had been filled with the sad tale of how all hands and passengers had been lost.

Including the Marquis of Bradstone.

In the ensuing years, the marquis's estate had been cast in turmoil—first from a lack of heirs and now because of the Prince Regent's maneuvering to see the title revert back to the Crown.

Apparently Prinny wanted to reward one of his favorites with the prestigious title and the accompanying rich estates.

But the greatest impediment to disposing of the Bradstone legacy turned out to be the marquis's mother. Lady Bradstone refused to believe her son had perished. Not even the eyewitness account provided by the captain of a nearby packet ship swayed her from her unshakeable belief that her son had escaped death's watery trap.

A mother would know, she often told her pragmatic butler. *If Robert were dead, I would know.*

"This is all that Sutton creature's fault," her ladyship was saying, causing any number of her staff to look away, some of the cheekier footmen to roll their gaze heavenward.

Carlyle sent one and all his most severe stare. If their mistress wanted to blame the infamous debutante for the marquis's hasty and fatal departure from London, who were they to question her?

"If that horrible jade hadn't led my poor, sensitive boy astray, he wouldn't have had to flee town in such a confused state." The marchioness paused for a moment, her lips pursed, her jaw set with long held rage. "I shudder to think of him all those years ago, lost and undone over that wretched affair, prey to who knows what sort of fiends and villainy. I told Mr. Hawthorne-Waite this very morning that I am convinced Robert was most likely kidnapped and taken aboard some other villainous ship against his will. For he would never have gone off voluntarily on that awful *Bon Venture*." She paused again.

Carlyle waited for her final refrain. It hadn't changed a word in seven years.

And after the requisite pause, she finished her vehement rail. "Lisbon, indeed! My Robert would never have gone to such a heathen place by choice."

"Yes, indeed, ma'am," Carlyle replied.

Her ladyship sighed. "And so I told Mr. Hawthorne-Waite. Though I am starting to doubt that man's qualifications as a solicitor." She turned her watery blue eyes on the butler. "He is of the opinion that kidnapping is not reason enough to keep one's son from being declared dead."

"A terrible injustice, ma'am."

She smiled bravely and began to take the steps again up to the front door. "And he also refused to find and bring that jade to justice. She murdered that poor Spaniard. Who's to say she didn't harm my Robert as well? And can you imagine my shock, Carlyle, when that odious little solicitor had the audacity to intimate that she more than likely died with my Robert! Can you fathom such a thing? My Robert taking a murderess with him to Lisbon? I think not."

"Yes, my lady," Carlyle said, while silently agreeing with the solicitor's tactless assessment of the situation. Why shouldn't he?

Witnesses had seen Miss Sutton crouched over the body of the dead Spanish agent, a smoking pistol in her hand. Lord Bradstone had told several of the gathered crowd that Miss Sutton had committed the crime. Then in the hubbub and panic, Lord Bradstone had disappeared. Slipped away and fled London in the dark of night aboard the *Bon Venture*. And to make the entire scandal even more lurid, the next morning Miss Sutton was also gone.

After a brief investigation, letters found in Miss Sutton's room linked her and the marquis romantically. Several of them had been reprinted in the press, telling the sordid tale of their secret affair.

Yet through it all, Lady Bradstone refused to believe anything that tainted her son's reputation. With each year, her remembrances of the man had grown and risen to such proportions it was hard to believe that such a paragon had ever existed.

"Oh, Carlyle, what will I tell Robert when he comes home and finds I have lost his title and estates?" The lady's lip quivered, her eyes welling up with familiar tears.

He directed her toward the door. Once inside, he'd settle her in her favorite drawing room with a large pot of tea and a tray of her favorite cakes. Perhaps then he could broach the truth of the matter one more time and see if he could convince her ladyship to take a more constructive view of their situation.

It was about time the lady believed what everyone else knew to be true.

The Marquis of Bradstone was not coming home.

As Carlyle turned to take the overly familiar step of telling her ladyship that she ought to heed the solicitor's advice and start planning for a less than secure future, he noticed the lady's gaze was fixed on the street, and she'd gone an unearthly shade of white.

Her mouth fell open in a wide O, her shocked, unblinking gaze trance-like as if she were seeing a ghost.

Carlyle turned in that direction and felt his heart still with cold shock. He tried to breathe, tried to say something, but his voice failed him, his reserved and steady nature fleeing at the sight of the lone figure crossing the street.

"Oh my," Lady Bradstone managed to sputter as she collapsed in a swoon worthy of the London stage.

But luckily for the lady, her landing on the cold stone was cushioned by a prone Carlyle, who had fainted dead away at the sight of a very much alive Marquis of Bradstone striding across the street.

London, a sennight later

"Well, if it isn't the infamous Lord *Bradstone*," said the man seated in the dark, shadowed corner of the pub. "You look well for a dead man."

Robert frowned at him before settling into the other vacant seat. "Don't call me that, Pymm. Not here. I'm in no humor for it. Or for trouble." Already his entrance had brought more than one quizzical stare from the rough-hewn patrons of The Rose and Lion.

This Seven Dials crowd may not have cared that in the week since his miraculous return from the dead he had become the current *on dit*, but knowing he had a title and perhaps some measure of wealth would make him a perfect target for getting his throat slit and his pockets picked.

"You're late," Pymm said, holding up his watch for a moment, then settling it back into the deepest pocket of his shabby vest. He sniffed and then sneezed, bringing out a soiled handkerchief from his pocket and sloppily wiping his red nose.

"Hard to get a hackney to bring one to this part of town," Robert replied. "That, and my *mother* had other plans for me this morning." He nodded to the serving girl, who looked like she'd left more than just her youth behind in the last century. "Whatever he is having," he told her, nodding at the short glass in front of Pymm and laying a coin in her outstretched hand.

Pymm grinned at her. "Make that two." When she paused and waited for his coins as well, the man nodded to Robert. "Do you mind? I seem to be a bit short."

Robert frowned, then reluctantly added another coin to the girl's palm.

She stared down at the meager offering as if it were

an insult, obviously having expected more, before stomping off to the bar.

Meanwhile they waited for their drinks in silence. Apparently he wasn't that late—for Pymm had only one empty glass before him and therefore was in no mood to talk. Robert knew from experience that Pymm never talked until he was settled into his accustomed routine—two drinks, then business.

But that was Pymm for you. Disrespectful of rank, most often apparently in a state of drunken *dishabille*, and always just plain ornery, he was also one of the few men in London Robert trusted.

And one of only a handful who knew he wasn't the real Marquis of Bradstone.

Major Robert Danvers, late of His Majesty's army in the Peninsula, settled back in his chair and considered how much his life had changed so quickly. If the truth were told, he'd rather be facing French canon than sitting in Seven Dials.

Or London, for that matter.

No, if he'd had his way, he'd be back in Portugal or Spain, doing what he loved—spying for Wellington.

Damn, if he hadn't intercepted that French courier and rushed to Lisbon with the information three months earlier, he wouldn't have stumbled into one of Wellington's newly arrived aides-de-camp—the man who'd mistaken him for Robert's cousin, the Marquis of Bradstone.

"Parnell!" the man had uttered in a shocked and choked voice, using his deceased cousin's family name. "What the devil are you doing alive?"

Once the entire episode had been sorted out, all the men had laughed. Even the usually taciturn Wellington had managed a short but concise nod to the humor

of the situation. And yet at the same time, Robert had
seen the man's meticulous mind whirling as to how
best he could put this oddity to work for his cause.

Two days later Wellington had come up with a plan.
There, behind closed doors, the commander of the Allied forces in the Peninsula had issued his extraordi-
nary orders.

Robert was to report to London and masquerade as
the Marquis of Bradstone.

A military man through and through, having risen
to the rank of major through his service on the battlefield and behind enemy lines, Robert had balked at the
very notion. But a cagey Wellington had dangled an
enticement before his objections that left him little
choice.

"If you go, I suspect you will be able to uncover the
location of The King's Ransom," Wellington had said.

El Rescate del Rey. The name burned through Robert's
heart like a brand. How he hated the very mention of
it. A legendary treasure, gathered eleven centuries earlier by a Spanish queen to help ward off the Moorish
invaders. It hadn't stopped the Moors then—and
Robert doubted that even if it did exist, it wouldn't
stop the French now.

As far as he was concerned, the English army
would do that.

And so he had argued with Wellington. But his
commander held a different opinion, and so did their
Spanish allies—who regarded The King's Ransom as
real as the sparkling English regalia locked in the
Tower of London. And the last known person to possess information as to its whereabouts was his cousin.

The man to whom he now knew he held an un-
canny resemblance.

Damn his cousin, and damn the treasure.

If his cousin's involvement wasn't enough, Robert had other reasons to hate *El Rescate del Rey* and its siren's call of wealth. It had also caught a very good man in its trap that night seven years earlier.

An innocent man who shouldn't have died in its pursuit.

It was that thought that made Robert realize that what Wellington was offering him was an opportunity to finally uncover the past. A chance to gain that final bit of retribution that had lingered as hatred in the back of Robert's mind all these years over the treasure's insatiable lure.

A chance he couldn't turn down, despite his misgivings over impersonating a cousin he'd never met.

The aide who'd known Bradstone had been brought in to help with the deception, detailing the man's haunts, habits and associates. At first he'd been reluctant to be forthright, but eventually he'd become quite honest about the marquis's reputation as a rake and a gambler.

Considering what Robert had learned about his late relation, it had probably been for the better that their family connections had been severed when Robert's mother, the daughter of the Duke of Setchfield, had eloped with his father, Lucius Danvers, a minor baron with little in the way of property and income, who'd sought his fortune in the service of his King. Robert had grown up with his parents, spending his life wandering the courts of Europe, far from the dulcet scene of England and kindred ties.

Over the past few years, as Robert had crisscrossed Portugal, Spain, France and Italy, tracking Napoleon's movements for Wellington, he'd played any number of deceptions—but he'd never played a man who had actually existed, a man with a living past, with friends and family who would be able to recall his likes and dislikes.

To cover for his deficiencies in these regards, he claimed to have suffered a head injury from his fall overboard when the *Bon Venture* was sunk. An excuse about as likely as his return to London, but one that he soon discovered was taken without question—smoothing his transition into the dangerous course of his cousin's reckless existence.

And so it was that he was in London, here in one of its worst neighborhoods meeting with Pymm, a man Wellington trusted implicitly, and one Robert knew his father had held in high regard, the two men having worked together for years in the Foreign Office.

The surly serving girl tromped over with their drinks, setting them down on the table with a negligent slosh. "Anything else?"

"No, that will be all," Robert told her.

She shrugged, then left.

Robert took one sip of the whiskey and immediately set the glass down. Whatever it was before him, it tasted as if it had been distilled straight from the Thames.

Pymm didn't seem to notice. He tossed it back in one swallow, sputtered for a moment, and then launched right into the matters at hand. "What have you found?"

"Nothing," Robert told him. "Absolutely nothing."

Pymm cursed. "I had thought that once you got in the house you could recover everything we need."

"Yes, your plan was quite sound, wasn't it?" For once it was Robert's turn to tweak Pymm. "Though it hinged on the idea that there was something there to find."

Pymm had the effrontery to look insulted for a moment before he continued on, ignoring Robert's obvious doubts, "Anyone approach you? Give any hint that they were looking for their share of your good fortune?"

Robert knew what he meant was a stake in The King's Ransom.

"Not the way you'd like," he told him. "But it seems I left town with a number of outstanding vowels. Shall I bill your office for my expenses on those counts?"

Pymm snorted and reached across the table for Robert's neglected glass. Like most in the Foreign Office, Pymm regarded those in the military as lesser cousins in the same cause, a notion Robert found amusing if not a bit insulting.

Still, Pymm's next words came as a complete shock to him, leaving him in awe of the man's prowess in the duplicitous world of intelligence. "Hmm," he was saying. "I would have thought by now *she* would have come forward."

"She?" Robert asked, not all that sure he wanted to hear the answer. He'd had enough women throwing themselves at him in the last week to last him a lifetime. Not only had his cousin left a few outstanding gambling debts, but also a string of tawdry and blowsy mistresses who weren't averse to renewing their old ties.

"The girl," Pymm said, as if any fool should know this. "Perhaps she would be able to solve your problems."

"Who? What girl?"

"Miss Sutton."

Robert knew one thing, the cheap whiskey was obviously getting to his companion. "Pymm, Miss Sutton is sharing my cousin's grave at the bottom of the Atlantic. I doubt she is in any shape to be paying a social call."

The man shook his head. "Oh, she may well be dead, but her grave wouldn't be anywhere near your cousin's."

Robert eyed him. "Miss Sutton died with her lover. Everyone knows that. She boarded the *Bon Venture* with him before it sailed."

Pymm squinted down at Robert's now nearly empty glass. "Yes, that was the official decision, but it wasn't the truth."

"What do you mean, 'wasn't the truth'?"

"I'll deny any of this if you ever try to bring it to light." Pymm leaned forward and whispered, "Olivia Sutton didn't board the *Bon Venture*. She was taken to her mother's house, where she later effected an escape."

"Yes," Robert said. "And boarded the ship with her lover later."

Pymm's gaze narrowed. "No. She was never there. The woman aboard with Bradstone was Sally Callahan, an opera dancer he'd taken up with in the weeks before."

Robert took a deep breath, letting this bombshell rewrite all the facts he'd thought he'd known. "Why the lies?"

"It was felt by those handling that bungled mess that if it was common knowledge that a murderess was on the loose, public opinion would be rather dire. That, and it would have ruined an already tenuous situation with the exiled Spanish government. We'd lost both the missive and our agent's murderer. The political ramifications at that point would have been—"

Robert held up his hand to stave off any further explanations. "Let me guess who masterminded that plan—Chambley."

Pymm tipped his empty glass at the serving girl and then gave a barely discernible nod.

Lord Chambley. Damn the man and his blind ambition. The King's representative in the Foreign Office, Chambley's ineffective bumbling and desire for personal glory had once again cost the lives of British agents and military personnel alike.

Robert's father had always maintained that there was more to Chambley's blunderings than met the eye, and perhaps now Robert would have a chance to topple the King's personal advisor, before the man could switch his allegiance to the rising power of the Prince of Wales.

There still remained one obvious question. "So if this girl still lives, why hasn't anyone tried to find her?"

Pymm shoved his empty glasses forward and waved again to the serving woman. "Don't you think I've tried? As has Chambley, mark my words. But the minx up and disappeared. Like smoke into fog."

"So all these years she's lived, while so many lives have been lost on the Peninsula." While Robert didn't necessarily believe in the legend of the King's Ransom, he knew the Spanish guerrillas who were waging their own deadly war against Napoleon did. And Wellington wanted to be the one who made every effort to deliver it to them. To unite them under his flag, his cause, and defeat the French once and for all.

And for a time, a few years ago, it had seemed that this remarkable dream was possible. An aged and patriotic priest had discovered the sealed and coded message in a dusty tomb, and believing it to contain the ransom's whereabouts, had carried the ancient scrap through enemy lines, to be seen by Wellington's eyes only. He had made Wellington vow to find someone to unravel its ancient mysteries, for none of the priests could untangle their ancient predecessor's code.

And so the missive had been carried to London by a young agent, and the rest had become yet another sad chapter in the tragic history of the treasure.

The serving girl arrived with Pymm's drink and waited until Robert provided adequate payment before she set the overpriced liquor before them.

Robert glanced across the worn wooden table at his companion. "So I gather when you heard about Wellington's plan, you thought she would come out of hiding to welcome me home."

Pymm nodded. "Though you did treat her rather shabbily the last time around. She'll probably want more than her half as recompense."

"Her half," Robert scoffed. "Why would she think she deserves half of any of it?"

"Because in all likelihood she was the one who decoded the message for your cousin."

"Pymm, you've had too much of that wretched swill." Robert sat back in his seat. "You're telling me some seventeen-year-old miss just out of the schoolroom deciphered the most important document in the course of Spanish history? Those directions were written by one of the most brilliant and learned minds of the eighth century, not the gossip columnist of the *Morning Post*."

"That probably only made it easier for her to understand," Pymm insisted. When still faced with Robert's disbelief, he continued, "Miss Sutton had been decoding messages for the Foreign Office for years—albeit unwittingly. Her father was Sir John Sutton."

Robert knew that name. "The linguist?" he asked. "The one who hanged himself after he was caught selling secrets to the Dutch?"

"The very same," Pymm said. "His daughter learned everything at his knee. And she was a damn sight better at it than he was. Sutton thought it quite a lark that she could decode what the so-called experts in the Foreign Office found unintelligible."

"And Bradstone learned of her talents and . . ." Robert's statement trailed off as he put together the obvious conclusion to the story. She'd thrown her lot in with his nefarious cousin to gain a measure of the legendary ransom for herself. And then she'd murdered the agent who'd tried to stop them.

No wonder Pymm had such a keen interest in finding her.

"Wellington knew all this?" Robert asked.

Pymm nodded. "Now you see why you were chosen."

Wellington had known that once Robert learned Miss Sutton lived, nothing would stand in the way of his finding her and bringing her to justice. "Damn her traitorous hide." Robert slammed his fist down on the table.

Pymm scrambled to right his tottering drink. "Yes, like father, like daughter," he said in what could be called companionable agreement, but there was an underlying tone to the man's words that suggested he wasn't quite sure.

Robert eyed him but decided not to press his suspicions. "What do you suggest?"

"The same tack that worked the last time," Pymm said, his words sharp and sure for a man who looked well into his cups. "You join forces with the girl."

"And how will I do that, when no one knows where she is?"

"My suspicion is that she'll find you. And when she does, court the girl, lull her once again into your confidence. Seduce her if you have to, just get what we need."

"Seduce *her?*" Robert shook his head. "Are you mad?"

Pymm rose from his seat. "No, just practical."

Robert followed suit, and the two men went to the door. Once outside, Robert asked the other man, "Suppose I do find her and get what we need from her. Then what do I do with her?"

Pymm smiled, a cold, bitter twist to his mouth. "Whatever you consider fair revenge."

Chapter 2

Finch Manor
The Kent countryside

"**K**eates! Keates, where are you, you faithless girl?" Lady Finch clamored and bellowed from her wheelchair, the one she'd confined herself to for over twenty years and honestly didn't need. "I want to see those London papers Jemmy brought down from town this morning before Lord Finch carts them off to his potting shed."

Her ladyship's tirade was punctuated by the clanging of a cowbell she kept at the ready for those trying situations when it seemed the entire house ignored her.

Keates, the target of Lady Finch's tirade and her hired companion, hurried down the front staircase in answer to her mistress's strident cries.

Most of the servants felt it a cursed shame that such

a kindly woman had not only been widowed at such a young age but had been left with no choice but to work for such a harridan.

But then again, they all felt much that way about their own positions in the Finch household.

At the bottom of the stairs, Mrs. Keates was met by Lord and Lady Finch's only child and heir, Mr. James Reyburn. The pride and joy of Finch Manor, Jemmy, as he was affectionately called by one and all, cast a furtive glance down the hall toward the room where his mother held court and was currently bellowing out another chorus of demands for the newly arrived papers.

"The old bird is in rare form this morning," he whispered as loudly as he dared. Even at nineteen, Jemmy still regarded his mother with an unholy terror. That probably explained why the young man hightailed it back to London every chance he could. "Got to warn you, she's in one of her moods. She's been calling for you and the papers ever since she heard me ride up."

Mrs. Keates sighed. "And why didn't you just deliver them?"

"Me?" Jemmy asked in mock disbelief. "And face the dragon before dinner? Not bloody likely." The cowbell clamored again. He winked at her and held up the bundle of posts, newspapers and cards he'd brought down from town, while in his other hand a pair of pistols dangled. "Why not ignore her and come shooting with me? For old times' sake."

Mrs. Keates smiled at the handsome young man. When she had first arrived at Finch Manor, Jemmy had been only twelve, and such outings had been quite acceptable. But in the last few years, she had tried to put a distance on their once chummy relationship.

It was better for both of them, she knew, especially when she saw the fond light in Jemmy's eyes sparkling at her in invitation.

"They're brand new," the young man explained, "and all the rage with the Royal Fuzileer officers I met last month in town. When mother relents and allows me to buy my commission in the Seventh, I will be ready for those demmed Frogs." His gaze filled with youthful passion for his dream of making a military career. "But for now, come out and see how accurate they are. I'll even let you have the first round—much more fun than spending your day with her dragonship."

"Keates!" Lady Finch bellowed.

"Yes, your ladyship," a resigned Mrs. Keates answered. "I'll be right there."

"What is holding you up, girl? Is that miscreant son of mine out there? If he is, bring him in. I will have an accounting for this bill I received from his tailor."

Jemmy blanched at his mother's wrath. He put a finger to his lips and shook his head furiously at Mrs. Keates.

"I haven't seen Jemmy, my lady," Mrs. Keates told her, "but he left the papers and letters here in the hall for you."

"Harumph," the old girl sputtered. "Well, what are you lolling about for? Bring them in."

Smiling at his savior, Jemmy put one of the pistols on the highboy and whispered, "In case you get a chance to escape. Come join me in the east meadow." He winked and then retreated down the corridor toward the kitchen, where she knew he would hide out until the coast was clear.

Picking up the bundle, Mrs. Keates sighed. Once the London news was delivered to her ladyship, she knew the rest of her day would be spent listening to her ladyship's outrage and utter dismay at the moral decay of good society.

There would be letters written to editors regarding their blatant disregard for the truth, notes dashed off to friends chastising them for their latest follies, and of course, inquiries made as to who exactly the "Lady S." or "Mr. L." in the gossip columns might be.

All of which was dutifully and patiently penned by Mrs. Keates.

"There you are," the lady huffed, as Mrs. Keates entered the room. "I think this entire house has gone deaf."

She smiled at her employer and laid the papers down on the table next to her ladyship's chair. Picking up the cowbell, she held it aloft. "If that is so, then I can only guess as to the cause."

The lady harrumphed again. "You've too much cheek. I should fire you, Keates."

Mrs. Keates grinned. "Should I write my notice before your correspondence or after?"

"You'd more than likely demand your full day's pay since it is almost noon, so you might as well earn it before you start packing your bags."

Mrs. Keates nodded in agreement, knowing full well Lady Finch wouldn't dismiss her for any amount of cheek. Catching the edge of the lady's chair, she wheeled her over to the window so she would have better light by which to read. "What shall it be first? *The Times* or the *Morning Post*?"

The lady fluttered her hand. "The *Morning Post*. I want to see if they printed my letter."

Sorting through the stack, Mrs. Keates organized the collected fortnight's worth of copies into chronological order, handing the first one to Lady Finch. Then she settled into her chair at the desk nearby, taking up a pen and waiting for her ladyship's first order of business.

It didn't take long.

"Keates, will you listen to this! Lady Bennington has gone and delivered a son! And at her age. How unseemly." The lady made several clucking noises that were harbingers of a long letter and a healthy dose of unwanted advice. "I suppose Lord Bennington is strutting about town, taking credit for the entire business himself. Why Miranda married that tiresome goat I'll never understand."

"How old were you when you had Jemmy?" Mrs. Keates asked, knowing full well Lady Finch had been at least five years older when the Finch heir had made his unexpected arrival into the world.

"Harumph! That is none of your business." Lady Finch's lips puckered with vexation, and Mrs. Keates knew only too well her employer was considering how she could at least convey some portion of her displeasure with the situation.

Eventually her eyes lit with triumph. "Send Miranda a note of congratulations on the child's safe deliverance along with that layette set we stitched last winter." The lady glanced up at the hallway where Jemmy was in the process of sneaking out to go shooting. "Goodness knows, I'll never live long enough to see my grandchildren wear any of these things," she said, waving her hand over the basket of sewing that she always had at the ready.

Mrs. Keates smiled, as the sound of Jemmy's pace doubled at the mention of setting up his own nursery.

"And don't forget," Lady Finch said, turning back

to the paper at hand, "to make a copy of my instructions on the hiring of a suitable wet nurse and nanny, so that child is properly cared for."

Mrs. Keates paused, knowing full well that wasn't all the lady would be sending.

And of course, it wasn't.

"And add to the note a word of caution," Lady Finch said in an offhand manner. "Counsel Miranda that now she's provided that no-account husband of hers with an heir, a separate bedroom with a good lock is entirely in order."

Mrs. Keates nodded, holding back the smile that threatened to turn her lips.

Lord and Lady Finch still shared a bed, but Mrs. Keates thought better of mentioning that point of fact.

For the rest of the morning and afternoon, through a hasty tea and well past supper, Lady Finch continued to scour her papers. From her chair, she directed Mrs. Keates to send the necessary notes to the various acquaintances she read about, to copy instructions from Lady Finch's vast repertoire of advice for those in need and to prepare admonishments for those whose deeds necessitated her immediate intervention.

Finally the lady drew to a close with the most recent paper Jemmy had brought up from town. Usually she skipped immediately to the gossip page, but this time she stopped at the front page.

" 'Tis remarkable," she finally muttered. "The man's alive. And here I thought he was rotting in hell all these years."

Mrs. Keates yawned, exhausted by a long day of unrelenting work, her head throbbing and her hand aching and stiff from all the copying and scribbling she'd done. She didn't care if it was Nelson himself returned from the grave, all she wanted to do was to find a cold compress for her head and seek the quiet comfort of her bed.

"Listen to this, Keates," Lady Finch said, before she began to read aloud: "It is said that miracles do not occur in these modern times, but one has to be astounded to hear the tale of the latest arrival in London. Declared a hero and being given a fête in his honor this Saturday, it is a story that will be oft repeated for months to come."

Nodding, Mrs. Keates tried to force a smile and wondered if she shouldn't order another brace of candles. She could see her correspondence spreading into the wee hours just by the glint of excitement in Lady Finch's eyes.

"Oh, here comes the good part," her ladyship declared. "After surviving a sea battle off the coast of Portugal and days adrift, our brave son of Britannia—" The lady stopped her narrative. "Brave son of Britannia, that has a nice ring to it, don't you think, Keates?"

"Yes, quite," Keates acknowledged without even knowing what it was she was agreeing to. Her mind was caught by the first part of the tale.

A sea battle off the coast of Portugal . . .

The remembrance of just such another story filled the pit of her stomach with cold dread.

"Now here's the rest," her ladyship said, drawing the paper closer to her nose. "Our brave son of Britannia endured nearly seven years—"

Seven years? No, it couldn't be. Disbelief rose in Mrs. Keates's chest, leaving her unable to breathe. *He was dead. Dead all these years. All these seven long years.*

"—as a prisoner of the French. Two months ago, our hero effected a daring escape from a garrison in Spain—"

Spain. The very name left her heart hammering. Memories of that word, of that night filled her mind.

"Keates! Keates! Are you listening to me?" Lady Finch's agitation cut through the shock clouding her ears. "Why, you look terrible! Call for Mercy to get you a tincture of my megrims cure."

Shaking her head and hoping that her trembling didn't show, Mrs. Keates braved a smile. "No, that won't be necessary. Pray, go on, my lady."

"Yes, well, if you say so." Lady Finch straightened her paper, glanced one more time over the top of it, studying her companion with a keen and penetrating stare.

For her part, Mrs. Keates sat up straight and nodded for her ladyship to continue.

"Where was I?"

"Spain," Mrs. Keates prompted, the word like a brand on her tongue.

"Yes, Spain." Lady Finch scanned down the column. "Oh, yes, here it is. Escaped from a garrison in Spain and made it to the English lines in Portugal with the help of Spanish guerrillas." Her ladyship shuddered. "The poor boy. How glad he must have been to see our noble colors flying from a standard."

Mrs. Keates nodded, only too afraid to speak. For fear she'd show too much interest. For fear the sick feeling in her chest would spill out and she'd disgrace herself by tossing up her tea on the carpet.

It couldn't be him. It just couldn't be.

"From Lisbon, where he was much honored by Wellington, he set forth on the *Archimedes* and arrived in London this Tuesday past, sending his mother into a fit of delight. The brave lady, her fight to save his title and inheritance well known to these readers, is hosting a fête in honor of his return." Lady Finch shook her head. "And here I have been writing to Sarah all these years to forget about that scandalous scalawag she called a son and find another distraction other than pestering the House of Lords about his estate. I do say, those Parnells are a determined lot."

Parnell. The only too familiar name hammered at her unwillingness to believe.

Her ladyship set the paper aside. "Well, well, the Marquis of Bradstone returned from the dead. And a hero to boot. I wonder if anyone remembers why he left. Now, there's a story that bears repeating, more than this taradiddle about him escaping the French. That was just before you came here, Keates. I don't suppose you've heard it, though if you had, you surely wouldn't forget it." Lady Finch waved to her maid, who had arrived to help take the lady to bed.

Mrs. Keates managed to draw a slow, even breath. "Yes, my lady, I recall the tale," she whispered as the maid rolled Lady Finch's chair out of the room.

Mrs. Keates, née Olivia Sutton, hadn't just heard it. She had managed to live through it.

As she made her way to her modest bedchamber, the events of that night played through her thoughts.

After Robert had pointed her out as the young Spaniard's murderer, her life had turned upside down. One minute he was there, accusing her of murder, and the next moment he was gone, having slipped into the crowd.

Hours later, locked in her own room and under house arrest, she still couldn't fathom how everything had gone so wrong. Even the blood-soaked note and band of gold she still held clenched in her hand seemed unreal.

She'd looked around the darkened room and tried to find the words to voice her anguish. Yet all she could think of was what the Spaniard had told her.

Run, he had warned. *Go as far as you can.*

But to where and how? she had wanted to cry out.

No, running wasn't the answer. But Lord Bradstone was.

Yes, that was it, she would go to him. He would see her name cleared.

Luckily for Olivia, the locks in her mother's house had been in ill-repair, like the rest of their family fortunes since her father's death, so it was only too easy to pry the tumblers loose with a hairpin. Having packed all her jewelry and the pin money she'd been hoarding for her planned elopement with Robert, she'd made her escape past the sleeping guard who'd been placed in their house.

From there she'd gone to Robert's house, where a post boy had told her of overhearing his lordship ordering his driver to take him to the docks, for a ship called the *Bon Venture.* Olivia passed the boy's directions to the hackney driver she'd engaged and in no time found herself at the gangway of a merchantman. But it had just slipped free of its moorings, and with it all her hopes, all her dreams.

Worse still, just then she saw Robert on deck, extending his hand to a woman nearby and drawing her into his embrace.

"Come, my love, let us go below," he was saying, his voice carrying over the water. "Now that I am well rid of that boring baggage, we have much catching up to do."

Olivia could only stare after them as they made their way out of sight. She'd staggered away from the docks, stunned and in shock, and only hours later did she find herself on the coach to Kent without any real memory of how she'd gotten there.

But as luck would have it, there she had met Lord Finch. The poor man was returning home from London without the lady's companion his wife had sent him to fetch. Apparently the real Mrs. Keates had learned about her future employer's unpleasant nature and begged off the position, leaving Lord Finch empty-handed.

And so Olivia had offered herself for the post, taking the lady's name so that Lady Finch would be none the wiser.

It had seemed the only thing to do at the time.

So she'd done exactly as the dying stranger had advised. *Hide.* Hidden from her ruination, hidden from the scandal that rocked London for weeks with the publication of her letters to Lord Bradstone and the mad speculation as to the dead man's identity.

Then her precarious position had been made easier by the sinking of the *Bon Venture*. Since Lord Bradstone had been seen in the company of a woman aboard ship, everyone assumed it was her—so the search for the murderess had been given up.

And so for seven years, Olivia Sutton had lived as Mrs. Keates, poor widow of a mythical army officer and companion to Lady Finch. Really, how could she leave? She was wanted for murder, and even if she told the truth, that she hadn't killed that man, who would believe her, when the only other witness was also dead?

Now the question remained, how would she live

with the memory of that horrendous night, knowing that the Marquis of Bradstone, the man who'd brought about her ruin and murdered that innocent man, still breathed?

She glanced over at her narrow bed, where underneath she still kept stashed the small valise in which she'd carried away her meager possessions that night. Pulling it free from its hiding place, she slid her hand into the lining until her fingers wrapped around the ancient bit of bloodstained parchment there.

Then there was his gold ring. She wore it on the silver chain her father had given her for her sixteenth birthday. The ring dangled over her heart, her personal talisman and remembrance of what that brave stranger had lost and what she owed him.

Give this to no one but Hobbe.

Hobbe.

She had thought of this mysterious man every day since, prayed for a way to find him, scoured Lady Finch's newspapers for any hint of his existence and had found nothing. She didn't even know if Hobbe was a man, but something told her he was.

For if the boy had trusted this Hobbe so implicitly, he must be a man of impeccable honor and integrity.

And in her mind he'd become her own personal knight in shining armor. Her hero. A man of action and decisive power. Hobbe was handsome, darkly so. Not with Bradstone's black-hearted nature but with a rakish appeal. The kind of man who would sweep her off her feet and carry her to safety.

There were days when she believed that if Hobbe were to walk into a room, her heart would know him without a moment's hesitation, so long had she spent dreaming of him.

Now if only she could find him, then she and Hobbe could exact their revenge for the young man's life—together they'd make Bradstone pay.

Bradstone. She shuddered at the very thought of him.

A hero. Being celebrated and fêted. Living with all the rewards society poured at his feet, while she remained trapped in this—her own personal prison for a crime she hadn't committed. Her only crime had been trusting Bradstone. A man with whom she'd believed herself in love. Well, she wouldn't make that mistake again.

She glanced out her bedroom window into the darkness of the January night and shivered.

On a cold night like this, how could she believe there was a Hobbe? For a bleak moment, she knew she'd never find him in time.

So the task fell to her shoulders. To make damn sure the Marquis of Bradstone wished he'd stayed in that French prison. She finished packing her bag and set out to complete the vow she had made all those years ago. Not the one to the dying man, the one she'd made to herself.

Revenge.

And as she passed through the dark shadows of Finch Manor, she took only one thing.

The pistol Jemmy had left for her on the highboy in the hall.

London

Lady Bradstone's welcome-home fête for her son had the entire house in chaos.

As Robert hazarded his way through the confusion of delivery wagons out front and the battalion of servants rushing about inside, he would have liked nothing more than to turn and run in a direct line back to Portugal.

He had spent the last week chasing after Pymm's unbelievable revelations. Yet locating Olivia Sutton proved to be as elusive as finding a decent drink in Seven Dials. Since everyone believed the girl dead, it was hard to start an investigation.

Her scandalous affair with Bradstone and her connection to the murder had left her reputation in tatters, ruined forever in the eyes of polite society. Everyone he'd questioned, albeit casually, had felt that even if she was living, she was better off dead.

Avoiding his aunt and Carlyle, who would both have a list of requirements that needed his attention, he sought refuge in the marquis's luxurious and spacious bedchamber, where perhaps he could find some peace and quiet in which to sort out the mystery of finding the infamous Miss Sutton.

But an undisturbed corner wasn't to be found there, for glowering in the middle of the room stood his batman, Aquiles.

"Ach," the man said, scowling as another servant brought in more pressed clothes, "they would drown you in all this."

Robert agreed wholeheartedly. If the dirt and stench of London wasn't bad enough, the clothes he was expected to wear as a peer of the realm made a French prison look cozy.

Ridiculous cravats designed to choke a man. Breeches and jackets so tight he could barely move. Orders and regulations he understood, having spent most of his life in the army, but the strict rules that made up the good society of London left him as unsteady as if a cannonball had just landed at his feet.

"*Yer mother*," Aquiles said with a short, gruff snort, "and that conceited coxcomb she hired said you should wear this one." He held up a green ensemble that looked more befitting as funeral regalia for a toad. Grimacing, he tossed the expensive suit on the bed and turned on Robert. "*Yer mother's* been in a regular state since you left, especially when I wouldn't tell 'er where you went. She's been badgering me right awful. You're supposed to be front and center and on display when the first guests arrive. And *yer mother* also said—"

"Please stop calling her that," Robert told him. His memories of his real mother seemed almost tarnished when she was compared to her blowsy and social-climbing sister. "When we are alone, you can drop the act."

"Fine with me." Aquiles shrugged. "Guess you should be thankful she isn't *yer* mother. Egads, no wonder yer cousin lit out of London like he did. That woman frets more than a Lisbon whore at confession."

Though Robert wholeheartedly agreed with Aquiles' rather forthright assessment of his aunt, he didn't feel quite comfortable giving the man's statement credence. "You should have more patience with her," he said. "She loved her son very much."

"Then she was the only one," Aquiles muttered, as he went about his task of setting out Robert's shaving accessories. "Dishonorable bastard."

Robert didn't feel all that honorable himself impersonating his cousin and leading his aunt to believe that her only child was still alive.

"Will you look at this bit?" Aquiles was saying as he

held up a long, starched and laced cravat. "Better get that fancy-boy maid of yours up here to tie this around your neck—I might slip and hang you with it." The man laughed at his own rough humor.

"Do you mean Babbit?" Robert asked, referring to the rather flamboyant valet his aunt had hired for him.

"Bah! Rabbit would be a better name for that useless one. He couldn't start a fire if he was up to his arse in kindling and holding a lighted torch." Aquiles eyed once again the perfectly pressed cravat.

Robert knew his old servant was quite disdainful of the other man's talents and place in their life. "I doubt we will be calling on Babbit for anything other than ironing and polishing."

"Fancy that," Aquiles said, mocking the man's accent and manners.

Robert laughed. To Wellington's plans for the Bradstone deception Aquiles had been a last-minute addition. He'd been a servant-cum-bodyguard in the constantly-moving Danvers household for as long as Robert could remember. And when the middle Danvers' son had announced his intention to take a commission in the army, Aquiles had packed his bag and followed Robert.

"Not about to let him get his arse shot off," the half-Irish, half-Spanish blackguard had been heard to mutter. And so he'd become Robert's unofficial batman. As it turned out, Aquiles's rather colorful past, fluency in the languages of the Peninsula, and Catholic leanings often paved a smooth course on Robert's forays into enemy territory.

Aquiles leaned forward and asked, "Did you find anything out about her?"

"No," Robert said. "Like Pymm said—it's as if she vanished that night."

"Women!" Aquiles huffed, his arms crossed over his chest, his back against the door. While his stance looked like one of indifference, Robert knew the man had one ear finely tuned to the hallway beyond, listening for anyone who might interrupt their discussion. "What will you do now?"

Robert was about to say he hadn't the vaguest notion, when in the hallway a chattering group of maids passed by, busy with their final preparations for the fête. Both men stilled until the noisy prattle died away.

"I hate this place," Aquiles muttered. "Too many interfering females."

"If we could just find that one female, we'd be bound back to Wellington on the first ship, my friend," Robert told him.

"Don't see how that little bit o' muslin could disappear like that and for all these years. What if she met with foul play? Given what we've learned about that cousin of yers, he may well have done that poor—" Aquiles's assessment ended abruptly when suddenly the door to the room burst open, sending the man staggering forward.

In his floundering wake hustled Lady Bradstone. She glanced first at Aquiles, whom she spared a disapproving sniff, and then at Robert.

"Gracious heavens!" she announced, her hands going to her ample hips. "Robert, you aren't dressed. The first guests will be arriving in less than an hour, and you must be ready to greet all our friends."

"My apologies," Robert told her, bowing his head slightly. "I'm afraid I lost track of the time."

"I can't imagine why." She sent another annoyed glance toward Aquiles, as if she blamed him for Robert's tardiness. "But do hurry. Lady Colyer is bringing her daughter, and it would be so nice if you would make a good impression."

At this blatant matchmaking, Aquiles started to chortle.

"Don't you have some work to mind?" she shot at Robert's batman. "Perhaps something useful?"

The man grinned. "I probably do." He bobbed his head at her. "My lord. My lady," he said, sending Lady Bradstone a saucy wink.

"That man is odious," Lady Bradstone started in before Aquiles was even out of earshot. "He slinks about the house like a cat. I never know when he is going to turn up. It quite unnerves me. And I don't like the way he leers at the younger maids. He should have been dismissed the day you returned and sent back to that Papist country of his."

"He is in my employ," Robert told her. They'd had this discussion before. "I will remind you again that he saved my life."

She sighed loudly. "I suppose I should be grateful for that. Just see that he remembers his place." Her hands, moving in nervous flutters, fussed over his still undonned evening clothes. "I'll send Babbit in immediately. I don't see how you thought you were going to get dressed with that pirate helping you."

Robert forced a smile on his face. "Thank you, madam," he told her, unable to drive the word "mother" past his lips. It was the one part of this deception he couldn't condone. He only hoped she wouldn't notice.

She did.

"Oh, Robert, you needn't be so formal with me!" she scolded, hustling across the room and wrapping him into her soft embrace. "I am your mother." She looked up at him, her brows creasing with a hint of worry. Reaching up, she brushed a stray lock of his hair out of his face. "You've changed. I blame those horrible Frenchies for locking you away all these years. But you're home now, and you'll be your old self in no time, my dearest boy." She released him and left the room as she had arrived in a blowsy breeze of violet scent and fluttering lace.

Robert forced a more sincere smile on his face as she departed. Even if the lady wasn't his mother, she was still his aunt and as such deserved a modicum of consideration.

He quickly set about getting himself dressed as best he could before Babbit arrived and went into a state over the condition of his now wrinkled shirt—a garment that would barely be seen beneath the acres of lace in his cravat and his waistcoat.

As he struggled into his coat, a garment that more resembled a strait jacket than what he would consider fashion, his thoughts turned back to finding Miss Sutton. Pymm's description of the girl had been rather vague, fitting half the misses in London. Not overly pretty, plain features, hair the color of a farthing.

Still, despite this less than distinguishing description, someone had to know where the chit was—women didn't just disappear into thin air. A man, now, that was entirely different—but a seventeen-year-old girl with no experience in the world? It was unfathomable that she could just vanish.

Then again, perhaps Aquiles was right. She might have met with foul play. There wasn't any reason to believe that Bradstone wasn't capable of having her removed from his path as well.

Behind him the door opened and closed quietly.

He paused for a moment, awaiting the impending explosion from his volatile valet, but none came.

"I'm almost ready, Babbit. You needn't have bothered," he told the man.

Then came a sound that Robert had heard too many times in his military career not to have it leave every hair on the back of his neck standing on end.

It was the defiant snap of a pistol being cocked.

It hadn't been hard for Olivia to find Robert's bedchamber.

Robert had sneaked her up to this very room at the height of a ball his mother had thrown not a month after their secret courtship had begun. She'd only too willingly allowed him to steal her away from the propriety of the crowded ballroom and into the solitude of his private sanctuary.

How foolish and headstrong she'd been that night. Believing his lies as he'd carried her across the threshold and set her down in a rush of silk and lace onto his bed. It had been there atop his downy coverlet that he'd declared his undying devotion for her. That since he'd met her, he'd spent nothing but lonely nights dreaming of her in that very bed . . . and longing for the day when she would share it with him.

His earnest declaration, softly whispered endearments and a long, slow kiss had left Olivia believing in his dreams, and a few of her own.

And they all had to do with sharing his bed.

He'd kissed her again, this time, he confessed, to seal their love. And then he had done oh-so-much more. Not that she hadn't been only too willing. She'd have given him anything that magical night.

And in a sense she had. They'd played a game of decoding and seduction. He'd given her a paper with an undecipherable message, and with each word she discovered, he rewarded her with kisses and promises until she'd untangled the entire message and he'd removed all her clothing.

Breathless from his touch and dizzy with his heady promises that one day very soon she'd be sharing this chamber with him as his marchioness, their ruinous play had continued until they were interrupted by his valet.

The memory of her idiotic indiscretion brought a blush of shame and regret to her cheeks. If only she'd seen through his deceptions. If only she'd realized that the Marquis of Bradstone had no intention of making her his bride.

Certainly not her, the bluestocking daughter of a disgraced knight.

If only she'd known that he'd had no intention of doing anything other than using her intellectual prowess and her oh-too-willing body for his nefarious purposes.

She shook off her memories and focused on the here and now. 'Twas time for the two things she'd been dreaming of since she'd learned Bradstone was alive.

Revenge and redemption.

Robert stood on the other side of the spacious room with what seemed like an acre of Turkish carpet between them. He remained in the shadows, outside the ring of light from the brace of candles on the desk, with his back to her.

She hadn't remembered him being so tall or his shoulders as imposing.

When she'd cocked the pistol, he'd flinched. But now his stance seemed poised and ready—for death or action, she couldn't tell.

Like Hobbe.

Egads, where had that stray thought come from? The marquis and Hobbe sharing any similarity? Never.

"Can I help you?" he asked.

That smooth voice. She'd heard it in her dreams, whispering to her from his watery grave. Now it called to her in real life, bringing forth the memory of that long-ago time when she'd fancied herself in love with him. And believed that he loved her. And trying now to edge its traitorous way back into her shuttered heart.

Remembering Robert's true feelings for her, she steadied Jemmy's wavering pistol, aiming it at his head.

She would have preferred to direct her shot at his heart, but she knew from experience he hadn't one.

"Are you going to shoot, or must I die of boredom waiting for you to get your aim correct?" He stood there for another moment or so, then he slowly turned around in an easy, fluid motion.

His features remained much as the rest of him, concealed in the obscurity of his lair.

"Yes?" he asked, his tone almost blasé about finding a pistol bearing woman gracing his bedchamber.

Then again, this was the Marquis of Bradstone. Unrepentant rake. Despoiler of the innocent. Scenes like this probably happened on a regular basis.

He took a step toward her, bringing himself into the light and out of the darkness that had all but enveloped his face.

One elegant brow rose as he gazed at her. The sight of him after all these years caught her unawares. It was as if she were seventeen again, standing off to one side at Lady Bloomberg's, a debutante of negligible connections and presence. And then he'd singled her out with just that look.

And yet this time there was something very different about the man. Something that left her breathless and trembling for reasons that had nothing to do with their tarnished past.

Before she could put a finger on what was so very wrong, in the blink of an eye, his features masked themselves with a practiced air, closing her off from any further scrutiny.

Though Olivia had seen much in that unguarded moment. Appraisal. A fleeting hint of appreciation. A startling maleness to his bold, raking assessment of her.

And something else. A revelation that hit her with a hot, searing shock, as if she'd been shot herself. He didn't know who she was. He didn't remember her.

Oh, she'd heard of his head injury, but she'd never thought that he wouldn't remember *her*.

It stung more handily than she cared to admit.

"Well?" His question hung in the air. And she knew what he wanted to know.

Was she going to kill him or not? Her finger trembled over the trigger. She should pull it. She should send him back to his grave. She should repay the debt she owed that poor Spaniard for giving his life to save hers.

But for some unfathomable reason, her finger refused to move. Something about this entire situation, about the man before her seemed dead wrong.

And, she reasoned, she at least wanted him to know who was sending him back to hell.

"It's been a long time, my lord." Involuntarily she took a step toward him.

He didn't move. "Am I supposed to know you?"

Of all the incredible gall. She took another step closer so she stood completely within the circle of light that now entwined them both. "Does that help?"

She wanted him to see that she wasn't the same naive girl he'd used for his own ruinous ends.

What she hadn't expected to discover by coming this close to him was that he had changed as well. Utterly. Completely.

If it was possible, his years of captivity had only made him that much more handsome. When she was seventeen, she'd been taken with his smooth, polished looks and elegant manners, but now, at four and twenty, she found herself breathless at the man he'd become.

The mocking and handsome features of her dreams were now hardened—there was even a jagged scar running along his jawline. The healed wound gave him a wicked, bounder type of mien. His black hair, before so meticulously coifed, was now styled in a restless sort of way that lent him a mysterious, careless quality that would draw women to him to untangle his secrets.

Including her.

No, don't even think that, Olivia told herself, taking a cautious step back into the safety of the shadows. *Don't look at him*. There was something alluringly haphazard about this newfound Marquis of Bradstone that set warning bells clamoring in her heart.

As if he'd actually become the dangerous man of mystery and foreign intrigues she'd thought him to be all those years ago.

"Do I know you?" he asked again, this time the acrid annoyance in his voice all Bradstone, jarring her out of her unsettling reverie. "Because if you haven't noticed, I will be required downstairs very soon, so if you are here to kill me, then aim straight and sure." He paused, then opened his waistcoat and pushed aside his mangled cravat, clearing a path to his mythical heart. "Consider it a favor, for a bullet is certainly more humane than the torture her ladyship has planned for me and that mob of hers." A lazy grin spread over his lips.

He chose a time like this to tease her? The Marquis of Bradstone she remembered had been cynical, sarcastic, even at times ironic, his witty remarks known to cut to the quick.

But teasing? Never.

A strange whisper of foreboding stole over her. She shook it off, telling herself that time changed everyone. Even the incorrigible.

With lazy, languid movements, he pulled his immaculate white shirt free so she could see clearly the muscled plains of his chest that was now her target. He patted his left breast and nodded at the pistol in her hand. "You've got it a little high. Try lowering it a bit, or you're likely· just to take off my ear, Miss . . . Miss . . ."

Olivia's anger seethed. This was all a joke to him! "How dare you—" she started to say, not sure what piqued her more—that he didn't remember her or that he found the idea of a woman about to shoot him worthy of some bad jest. "I've spent the last seven years waiting for this moment, and I'll not let you white-wash me with your newfound sense of ill humor."

Seven years.

Her words hit their mark, for suddenly a hot, furious light blazed to life in his gaze.

Recognition . . . and something else.

As if her need for revenge now belonged to him.

"Miss Sutton," he breathed, his shoulders once again straightening into a taut line.

She cocked a brow at this sudden formality.

"Olivia," he corrected himself.

"How kind of you to remember."

"How could I forget *you*?" He smoothed his shirt back over his chest. "How have you been?"

The strained intimacy behind his question whispered over her. It was as if they had never met at all, and yet they had. More to the matter, Olivia certainly didn't want to start trading reminiscences with him—he didn't fare all that well in her version, and she certainly had no desire to hear his.

Instead she changed the subject. "I take it you never found your treasure?"

He cocked his head and eyed her anew. "Why do you say that?"

"You're still alive."

"Why wouldn't I be?" he asked.

She smiled at him. Since the French hadn't killed him, she'd half hoped that *El Rescate del Rey* would. That is, if he'd been able to find it. She hadn't been completely disconnected from learned society at Finch Manor and had discovered a few scant bits about the ancient Spanish treasure from the texts she'd obtained through Lord Finch's membership at a London lending library.

What had the Moorish tract read?

Only those pure of heart and intent can claim the King's Ransom.

Pure of heart and intent. Robert counted on neither measure.

And unfit as he was to claim the ancient treasure, according to the twelfth century Moor who'd done the most thorough investigation into the missing ransom, then his manhood and limbs would soon be withering.

She slanted a glance at his arms and legs and even at the tight fit of his breeches.

Much to her chagrin, she found no signs of dissipation in any direction. Instead she did her best to ignore what was probably the best example of potent male physique in the entire *ton*. "In your rush to the Peninsula, you forgot to do a little more research on your prize. It is guarded by a curse."

He gave a dismissive wave and continued straightening his clothes. "I don't believe in curses. And I doubt you do either."

She shrugged, for in fact she didn't believe in ancient myths or hexes, though it didn't stop her from wishing that perhaps this one held some small bit of validity.

Robert casually retrieved his discarded coat. She followed his lithe movements with the pistol.

He glanced over his shoulder, his expression seeming to say that he was surprised to see she still bothered. "So have you come for your share?"

She'd been wrong to think him changed. Oh, this was Robert, all right. Already his greed ascended over any good sense he may have possessed.

She waved the pistol at him in what she hoped was a derisive gesture—and to remind him that she was in charge. "What makes you think I would want any part of your blood money?"

"You're here. With a pistol." He nodded toward the piece in her hand. "I presume that thing is loaded."

She nodded.

"Then do be careful. Those models have a question-able trigger."

"Now you know why I chose it."

His lips turned in a rather appreciative smile. "In-telligent and beautiful." He paused, then added as if it were an afterthought, "Just as I remember."

Beautiful! He had the nerve to call her that now? He'd said those words before, but she knew he hadn't meant them. She'd never been considered a beauty by anyone's standards. Too tall. Her hair too red. Her fea-tures hardly noteworthy.

But when he had said the words just now, there had been a ring of genuineness behind them that made a small, long-buried part of her wish that they were in-deed true.

Oh, dear God, what was the matter with her? A few minutes in his company, and all of a sudden she was falling prey to his false praise.

"It won't work this time, Robert," she told him. "I haven't forgotten your old lies as yet."

"Still thinking about them, though," he noted.

Her cheeks flushed hot, but she ignored their sting-ing admission. "Go over there," she told him, waving the pistol at a writing table that stood against the far wall.

"And what would you like me to do there?" he asked.

"Write your confession."

He just stared at her. "You expect me to condemn myself?"

"Yes." Olivia pointed the pistol back at him.

Robert chuckled. "And what will you do with this confession, Miss Sutton? Clear your name and repudiate your involvement in all this? Who will believe it?" He laughed again, as if that notion was quite ridiculous.

She bit her tongue to keep from telling him exactly what she would like to do with it. Even if he was probably right.

As a peer of the land, his word would always supersede hers.

Still, she clung to a small hope that his confession was a start toward exonerating herself and ending her years of hiding. It just had to be.

She shook the pistol at him. "Just do as I say."

He shrugged and made his way to the desk.

"What do you propose I write this confession on?" he asked, after he had sat down. "I seem to be out of writing paper."

Olivia ground her teeth together to keep from using one of Jemmy's more colorful expressions. Then she remembered that while packing to leave Finch Manor, she'd brought along some of her ladyship's instruction sheets on traveling, along with some blank sheets of her ladyship's stationery.

It had been nothing more than habit at the time, but now she could see why Lady Finch insisted a lady always carry proper writing materials on her travels.

Olivia knelt down beside her valise, and with one eye and the pistol still aimed at Bradstone, fished out a piece of paper from her bag and handed it to him.

"Write," she ordered, nudging him toward the seat with the muzzle of the gun.

He shrugged, then took up the quill. "What would you have me confess to?"

A hundred things, she thought. *How you lied about loving me. That you had no intention of calling on my mother and asking for my hand in marriage. That you intended to ruin my reputation and my life.*

Instead she told him, "Why don't you start with the most important part and explain that I had nothing to do with the murder of that man."

His head swung around, his eyes narrow, the force of hatred and anger pouring from them startling her with its intensity. "And you don't think you did?"

His accusation hit at the heart of her guilt.

He has the right of it, a nagging voice in the back of her conscience chimed in. *If you hadn't been there, that young man might still be alive.*

It was an indictment that had plagued her on more sleepless nights than she cared to count.

"Well?" he was asking. "Do you really think anyone is going to believe that man's death was *my* fault? Especially when you were found over his body with the murder weapon in your hand?"

How dare he continue this vilifying charade! Her hand tightened around the grip of the pistol. In a dark moment her anger got the better of her, and she wanted nothing more than to kill him, here and now.

"If I have to go to the gallows for murder, then perhaps I should go for having actually committed the crime," she told him.

Robert smiled at her. "If ever you intended to kill me, you would have done so five minutes ago."

The pistol wavered. "How do you know I won't do it now?"

He nodded over her shoulder. "Because it is too late."

Olivia twisted slightly only to discover a giant of a man looming over her.

Before she could even utter a yelp of protest, Robert

quickly stripped the pistol from her hand, but in the process, the sensitive weapon discharged.

In an explosion of powder, the bullet whizzed past his ear and tore a hole through the expensive gilt paper covering the wall behind him.

"Damn you, Robert," she cursed, as his henchman pinned her arms behind her back and held her as one might pin a butterfly to a display case at the British Museum. "Damn your nine lives. You won't do this to me again."

Robert crumpled up the piece of paper on the desk and tossed it aside. He stalked toward her until they were nose to nose. "It appears, Miss Sutton, I already have."

Chapter 3

Miss Sutton let loose with a rather eye-opening curse, the type one might expect from an unrepentant young rake about town but certainly not from the lips of a young lady of good breeding.

Then again, Robert was fast coming to his own conclusions as to Miss Sutton's qualifications on that point.

There was a lot about the lady that left him dumbfounded. The Olivia Sutton of Pymm's rather unflattering description and the intelligence he'd gathered had in his mind looked like all the other boring English misses he'd met. With their pale complexions and mincing manners, they caught his attention about as much as he paid heed to his morning meal—and there were only so many ways to serve kippers, and that seemed to be true of London misses.

Certainly he hadn't expected this tempestuous handful.

While she had the look of a bookish scribbler, with her black, boring dress and ink-stained fingers, the rest of her defied that stereotype.

For one thing, her coloring was all wrong. A fiery mane of rich, thick auburn hair fell free from its half-hearted attempt at a matronly chignon.

Even her widow's weeds, a hideous dress designed to put a man at arm's length, hinted that beneath the black silk lay hidden a lush body. For the bleak gown could not conceal the fullness of her breasts straining the front buttons or how the skirt fell over the seductive curves of her hips. She might hide behind her weeds and books, but he doubted even a Spanish mantuamaker could conceal such a ripe body.

A paphian hidden beneath a bluestocking's guise.

And her eyes. Wherever had that color come from? No demure blue for this one. More like the Spanish sky over the high plains of Castile—rich and azure, so clear and deep that one almost thought one was looking at the heavens.

And right now they burned at him as if she furiously wished she hadn't hesitated to pull the trigger of her pistol and send him to his just reward.

Preferably one where he stayed dead.

"Ouch!" Aquiles cried out, shaking one hand and hanging on for dear life to the little wildcat with his other. "She bit me."

To make matters worse, she connected the heel of her sensibly shod foot with the poor man's shin. Aquiles appealed silently to Robert to do something, anything—for Robert knew only too well, his batman held all women in high esteem, even when they were robbing him blind or leaving him battered and bruised, as Miss Sutton seemed intent on doing.

"Enough of that," he told her. His sharp reproach stilled her—for the time being.

In the tense silence of the room, Robert heard the aftermath from the pistol shot—the house had gone into a state of alarm. Downstairs Carlyle shouted orders over the pealing shrieks of the maids, while the pounding feet of the footmen indicated they were searching the house. Rising above it all, his aunt's histrionics pierced the clamor and din.

Any minute now, someone would barrel through the door and discover him with Miss Sutton along with her smoking pistol.

He could imagine the scandal and gossip that would follow—and hinder his investigation. Robert's gaze swung around the room, looking for somewhere to stow her until the furor had died down.

She seemed to follow his intentions. "It is too late, my lord," she told him. "You are about to be caught."

"Not yet," he told her, catching up the horrendous length of his cravat. He ripped off an end, wadded it up in a ball and shoved it in her mouth. With the remaining length, he tied the gag firmly in place.

Her protests continued, though muffled, punctuated with more shots from her thick and sturdy heel—no delicate silken slippers for this miss.

"Get her in the dressing room," he told Aquiles, opening the door to the chamber off his bedroom. "Tie her up. Hang her from the shelving, if you must. Just make sure she can't get loose and that she remains silent. Then post yourself outside this door and make sure no one goes in there until I return." He went back and grabbed the lady's valise, which she'd left in the middle of the room, and tossed it in behind his friend and their squirming and twisting captive.

Just as Aquiles disappeared into the adjoining chamber, Carlyle and Lady Bradstone burst into his room. "Robert! Did you hear?" she asked. "Carlyle says that horrible noise was a pistol. How can that be? Shots fired in our house? Are you all right?"

"I'm fine," he told her.

"I feared the French were coming to take you away from me," she said between big tearful sniffs into her handkerchief.

"No, madame. Nothing like that," he said, holding up the weapon. "Aquiles found this in my dressing room. I had forgotten all about winning this piece in a card game from Lord Potter, or was it that Bingham fellow?" He shrugged and tried to effect a lazy grin. "Not that it matters now. Still, imagine my surprise when I discovered the damned thing was loaded after all this time." He nodded at the hole in the wallpaper. "My apologies, madame."

For once, his aunt didn't notice his formality, for she was staring in wide-eyed shock at the wall. "Goodness!" she exclaimed. "You could have been killed."

"Not this time," he muttered as he wrapped a comforting arm around her and led her from the room. "Not this time."

The fête downstairs was in full swing by the time Olivia was able to wiggle her hands free from Aquiles's knotted restraints. With her fingers loose, she plucked off the lacy gag and took a deep, freeing breath.

Damn the man, she seethed, as she felt her way to the door of the tiny chamber. She had half a mind to march down to his welcome home festivities and tell one and all about his nefarious deeds.

"Yes, Olivia," she grumbled to herself. "And just who will believe you?"

What she needed was proof that Robert had been the one who'd murdered that man, not her.

But how to get it?

What would Hobbe do? she wondered. Her hero wouldn't have gotten himself in this entanglement. Of that, she was certain.

Well, first things first, she thought. *I need to get out of this prison.*

With her ear pressed to the door, she could hear the even, steady snoring of Robert's henchman close by. And as she tried to push the door open, she found it barred by some great weight.

Probably the big oaf himself, she realized.

She turned around and leaned against the door, vexed and angry at herself for getting caught by Bradstone this second time.

If only he wasn't still so . . .

She stopped herself before she even dared finish that thought. *Still so handsome,* was what her wayward imagination had been about to admit.

And yet, there was something fundamentally different about the Marquis of Bradstone.

Oh, there were the superficial things. Take the scar on his jaw, for instance. Or his plebian hairstyle.

But what had stopped her was the light in his eyes as he stared down the barrel of Jemmy's pistol. A black-hearted gaze that held a courage of character she'd never thought Robert Parnell, Marquis of Bradstone, could ever possess.

Olivia closed her eyes and let out a long, frustrated sigh. How could a man have changed so much? Didn't anyone else notice? She'd heard of his head injuries, but she suspected there was more to his changes than a good rap on the head could have provided.

And if that wasn't enough, he had changed physically. His shoulders had broadened, his stance matured. There was something compelling about him, something that lit the ashes of her imagination as if they were dry kindling instead of cold dreams.

If it was possible, Robert had become even more masculine, more attractive, more desirable.

Desirable?

Her lashes sprang open, and she was about to borrow another of Jemmy's expressions when she spied a small stain of light creeping through the racks of clothing.

Following it like a beacon, she pushed aside a selection of heavy, winter wool cloaks and found herself staring at what appeared to be the outline of another door. Catching up her valise with one hand, she felt around until she found the latch and ever so slowly twisted it.

The door opened, and inside the adjoining room a man let out a surprised squawk. Unlike the formidable Aquiles, this fellow was like a whisper of wind on a calm day. Spry, short, with thinning gray twists of oiled hair, he sprang from his chair, where he had been reading a book. "Dear me! Oh my!" he exclaimed. "Who are you?"

"Hired I was for the night," she said, using her best country accent. "Got lost on the stairs looking for the necessary and a place to change into my workin' apron. Don't know how I ended up in the wrong place." For effect, she hugged her small valise as if it contained the most valuable apron ever to grace Bradstone House.

The man frowned, then hustled forward. Grabbing her by the elbow, he shoved her toward a similar door on the other side of the narrow room. "Lost, indeed," he said, propelling her out into the hallway. "That was his lordship's room you so carelessly wandered into. He would be incensed if he discovered you in there."

He'll be even more angry when he finds me gone, Olivia wanted to add.

Her unwitting rescuer shoved her out into the dark hallway. "Down this corridor are stairs that will lead you to the kitchen. Ask one of the girls there to show you the servants' area." He stuck his nose in the air and shut the door in her face.

Olivia smiled and followed the man's instructions almost to the letter. When she got to the kitchens, she continued on by walking out the back door.

"You aren't the only one with nine lives, my lord," Olivia mused as she slipped into the darkness of the garden behind the house.

Grinning at the ease of her escape, she continued until she found herself on a nearby street corner. There she paused and looked out into the lonely and dangerous darkness of London, a single question begging to be answered.

What do I do now?

"Robert, do come here," his aunt said, interrupting his conversation with a rather inane woman and her equally stupid daughter.

Lady Bradstone smiled broadly at his companions. "Lady Colyer, Miss Colyer, I see you have met my dearest son. I hope you are conspiring to steal his heart." She patted the blushing girl on her arm with her fan.

Miss Colyer tittered nervously at such an intimation, while her mother beamed as if her daughter's elevation to marchioness was nothing more than a formality at this point.

For a moment it struck him that the woman locked in his closet would never make such a nit of herself. Olivia Sutton captured a man's attention with her vivacity, with her fierce independence, with her uncommon beauty. The *ton* might not have appreciated her lively coloring, but Robert had always had a weakness for redheads.

Besides, it was hard to forget a woman who would boldly enter your bedchamber and threaten to kill you. And that she hadn't killed him made her all that much more a study in contradictions, unlike this transparent little fortune hunter before him.

"Do excuse me, ladies," Robert said, offering a short bow and taking his aunt's arm. "Duty calls."

Lady Colyer tapped her fan on his other arm. "Perhaps my daughter and I can call on you later this week, my lord, so we can finish recounting for you our recent visit to Gravesly Manor. We haven't even gotten to the description of the second drawing room yet."

"I will be breathless until I hear all of it," Robert told her. For a moment he almost wished Miss Sutton had finished him off. At least it would have given him a viable excuse for never having to listen to Lady Colyer's shrill voice ever again. But given that he had Miss Sutton in his possession, he would soon be free of London and the Lady Colyers of the world.

With the other woman now out of earshot, his aunt added her own grating complaint. "Robert, didn't we discuss this problem not four hours ago, and now here he is again."

"Who, madame?"

"That pirate of yours. He is lurking about the ball-room in the most unfashionable manner." She pointed her fan toward one of the doorways, where Aquiles towered over the guests like a draft horse amongst a herd of ponies. And by the way he was hopping from one foot to the other, he looked about as comfortable as one as well.

Something must be damned wrong for him to leave that chit alone, he thought. He could only imagine what trouble Miss Sutton was causing now.

"I thought I explained that it was imperative he be kept out of sight." She shook her head. "He is frightening some of our more refined guests."

Robert wanted to ask her who those might be, as he hadn't met anyone who qualified for that distinction.

"Oh, please do something about him, Robert," his aunt said in her most plaintive and trying voice. "You promised."

"So I did, madame," he told her. "And I will see to this indiscretion immediately."

He crossed the room as quickly as he could, nodding to those who called out greetings or well-wishes and avoiding those who sought a more lengthy dialogue.

But one guest did manage to stop him.

Lord Chambley.

"Bradstone," he said in greeting, as he stepped into Robert's path and stopped his course cold. "We have unfinished business, you and I. You can't continue to avoid me for much longer."

Robert wasn't too sure what he'd been doing to avoid the man, so he nodded in acknowledgment and said nothing.

"I will have an explanation," Chambley said, his voice low and menacing.

"Now is neither the time nor the place," Robert told him, adeptly sidestepping him and wondering at the man's "business" interests with his cousin.

"Soon, Bradstone. Soon," Lord Chambley called out after him.

When he reached Aquiles's side, Robert asked, "Why aren't you upstairs?"

Aquiles stared at the ground, his lips moving but no words coming out.

"Out with it, man. What has happened?"

"She's vanished," Aquiles stammered.

"What do you mean 'vanished'?"

"Poof. Gone. Perhaps by the angels, I think," he said.

Aquiles always liked to attribute anything that on the surface did not make sense to the mischievous actions of angels.

Robert sincerely doubted angels would dare meddle with that termagant they had corralled upstairs.

Leaning forward, Robert sniffed at Aquiles's breath. Angels had a way of appearing to his servant when he'd been imbibing too much Madeira.

"I haven't been drinking, if that is what you think," the man protested. "I opened the door to check on the poor little thing because she had grown so quiet, and she was no more. You can come see for yourself."

Robert did just that, and to his dismay discovered that Aquiles was right.

Miss Sutton had vanished.

As he stared into the empty dressing room, he used the same colorful oath she'd used earlier in the evening.

To his surprise, Babbitt poked his head out from between a pair of heavy winter cloaks. "My lord? Is that you?"

Robert strode forward, pulling the hapless valet out of his path, and stared at the second opening which led to Babbitt's spartan quarters. "Where the hell did that door come from?"

"I believe, my lord, it has always been there," a rather subdued Babbitt replied. The man paused for a moment, then suggested, "Perhaps with your injuries you forgot about it."

"Yes, my injuries," Robert answered as he retraced his steps back into his room, glancing this way and that.

He'd had her in his grasp and now he'd lost her. "Dammit!"

He'd all but forgotten about the valet when the man said in an anxious voice, "Is this about the girl?"

Robert swung around, his gaze pinning the little man to where he stood. "You saw her?"

"Yes," Babbitt replied. He glanced nervously at Robert, then at Aquiles, then bucking up his thin shoulders, he made his report. "Cheeky thing. Irish most likely. Claiming she got lost on her way to the necessary. I suspect she was looking for items to supplement her wages for the evening. Those kind always do, steal that is. I doubt you'd find a trustworthy one in the entire country."

Aquiles made a low, rude noise in the back of his throat.

Babbitt's gaze fluttered over to the man. "Did I say something wrong?"

"My batman is half Irish."

"Oh, my deepest regrets, Mr. Aquiles," Babbitt

squeaked. "Had I known about your unfortunate parentage, I wouldn't have been so bold."

Robert glanced away so as not to laugh out loud as Aquiles's face turned a mottled shade of red.

Babbit, obviously sensing his apology hadn't made the right impression, tactfully changed the subject. "Did that wretched girl steal something, my lord? Did she disturb your belongings? For if she did, I blame myself. I should have searched her bag. I should have held her for the authorities. I should have—"

"Yes, Babbitt, duly noted," Robert told the man. "I doubt she committed any nefarious deeds on your watch."

The man preened at what he obviously perceived as a compliment from his employer.

Robert hadn't meant it as one.

"Oh dear," the valet exclaimed. "This room is quite disorderly. Allow me, sir." He crossed the room and retrieved the crumpled sheet of paper Robert had begun to pen his confession on.

"Wait," Robert told him. "I need that."

The valet flinched at the sharp demand, then handed over the piece of paper with a martyred air about him.

"That will be all, Babbitt."

The man left, albeit reluctantly, casting more than one speculative glance over his shoulder as he left the way he had arrived, through the closet.

Once he heard the second door pulled firmly closed, Robert began the task of smoothing out the paper. He recalled that when Miss Sutton had been ordering him to write his confession on the sheet, he had noticed something unusual about it. Now that he had it flat, he held it up to the candle still burning on his desk. "Look at this," he said to Aquiles. "What do you make of that?"

The giant bent over and peered at the sheet. "A watermark?"

"Aye. A family crest of some kind. Could be a clue as to where that banshee has been hiding."

"More like roosting," Aquiles said, his eyes squinting to get a closer look. "It looks like a little sparrow, maybe?"

"That," Robert said, "is a finch."

With little money of her own and nowhere else to turn, Olivia hailed a hackney and set out for the Finch town house. With the family in the country, she could probably give the housekeeper, Mrs. Delaney, some believable excuse about coming to town for the night on an errand for her ladyship. She spent the ride over to the Mayfair address fashioning a reasonable one.

But her knock on the door was not answered by the housekeeper but by Addison, the butler from Finch Manor.

"Addison, what are you doing here?" she asked, almost afraid to enter the house.

"Awaiting you, Mrs. Keates."

She stared at him, still stunned by his sudden appearance in town. The loyal family retainer would never leave her ladyship, let alone Finch Manor, not unless . . .

"Is that her, Addison?" Lady Finch's voice called out from somewhere close by. "Bring that impossible girl to me immediately. And don't let her get away."

Olivia would have liked nothing more than to back down the steps and run, but Addison, true to his mistress's edict, caught Olivia by the arm and pulled her into the house.

She couldn't help wondering if perhaps she'd been a little too hasty in making her escape from Bradstone.

"There you are!" her ladyship said. "Do you know the fright you have given me?" She sat in a high-backed chair, not unlike the one she had at Finch Manor and used for interviewing—or rather, chastising the servants, Jemmy when he overspent his allowance, or Lord Finch when he spent too much time in his orchid house. Next to her, Jemmy sat in an equally formidable chair, his features pale and drawn.

"My lady, what are you doing here?" Olivia still couldn't believe her employer had followed her to town—a place Evaline Reyburn, Lady Finch, hadn't set foot in twenty years.

"Concern for me?" Lady Finch said. "Isn't it a little too late for that when you nearly put me in my grave with vexation over your disappearance? How could you do this to me?"

Olivia shuffled a bit under the lady's emotional outburst. "I'm sorry, my lady. It was just a bit of urgent business that came up. I didn't want to worry you with my poor concerns."

"Your poor concerns? Since when is confronting Lord Bradstone a poor concern?"

Olivia's mouth dropped open at this, but she snapped it shut quickly and tried to brazen out a falsehood. "I don't know what you mean. I have a cousin. Yes, a cousin. She is in dire financial circumstances. A widow, like me, without—"

"Olivia Sutton," Lady Finch blurted out, halting the stumbling tale. "You have always been a poor liar. You were the first day you arrived with Lord Finch. A widow, indeed! When the entire town was talking of the murder at the Chambley ball and the disappearance of both Lord Bradstone and his paramour, Miss Sutton. How coincidental then that you turn up on my doorstep not two days later, calling yourself Juliet Keates, and claiming to be the woman I'd sent Lord Finch to fetch from town. *Her* name was Mary."

Olivia shook her head as she watched her secrets and lies unravel before her.

Lady Finch continued, "That you were able to convince Lord Finch to help you, I have no doubts. The man knew better than to return home empty-handed."

"You're confused, my lady," Olivia told her. "Everyone knows that poor girl died aboard the *Bon Venture* with Lord Bradstone. I couldn't be her." Olivia sent a withering smile to Jemmy, hoping the young man would rise to her defense as he did when his mother became too overbearing.

But this time Jemmy shook his head, the disappointment in his eyes sending a river of guilt through Olivia's heart. "Is it as mother claims? Is your real name Olivia Sutton?"

She bit her lip, unable to tell the truth but unwilling to lie to the young man who was like a beloved brother.

"Olivia," Lady Finch said, in a voice so soft and maternal that it made both Jemmy and Olivia turn and stare. "When you came to my house, I wrote to your mother to confirm who you were." The lady reached for her reticule, which was lying on the small Queen Anne table beside her. Opening the silk strings, she pulled out a letter and handed it to her.

Olivia's fingers trembled as she took the missive,

the tight, perfect handwriting which addressed it to *Evaline, Lady Finch, Finch Manor, Kent* only too familiar.

"You can read it or not."

Olivia could well imagine what her mother had said. "I'd rather not. But if you knew who I was, why didn't you turn me in?"

Lady Finch snorted. "You? A murderess? I hardly think so. These fools in town might have been chow headed enough to believe such rubbish, but not me. The facts never added up. My guess is Bradstone did it and left you to take the blame." The lady paused. "So that is it—I can see it plainly on your face. That, my dear Olivia, is why you would never make a good murderess." She sighed and brushed her hands over her skirt. "Now that we have that settled, why don't you tell me what happened with that man? Does the bastard still live, or did your kind heart let him slip free once again?"

The watermark on the sheet of writing paper, Robert discovered the next morning, turned out to be the crest of the Finch family. Lord Finch and his invalid wife, he learned from his aunt, resided in a rambling manor a half-day's ride from London.

According to Lady Bradstone, Lady Finch spent her time in the country doling out advice, wanted or not. Why, it was considered quite a boon to receive a letter of admonishment from the lady.

"I pity her abigail, though," Lady Bradstone had confided over breakfast. "Mrs. Keates, I believe her name is. The poor woman is most likely chained to a desk day and night, copying and composing Evaline's epistles." Lady Bradstone sighed. "But I suppose for a widow there are worse ways to earn a living than writing a bitter old woman's correspondence and listening to her endless nattering."

Widow. Correspondence. The words stabbed at his memory.

Suddenly Miss Sutton's drab dress and ink-stained fingers made sense. Where better for an educated lady to hide than behind the weeds of a widow and in the secluded country house of an invalid lady whose company was sought by few?

Robert reasoned that his quarry couldn't have returned to Finch Manor overnight, so that meant she had stayed in town. His aunt readily supplied the directions to the Finch's London residence and then finished with an admonishment to avoid the young Mr. Reyburn—apparently he had turned out quite wild, and Lady Bradstone didn't think he was appropriate company for a man of Robert's rank and standing.

Unsuitable sons notwithstanding, Robert set out for the place at once.

Still, when he arrived at the fashionable address, he found himself at a loss as to what to do next.

The Marquis of Bradstone could hardly knock on the door and demand an audience with a lady's companion. Nor could he do what he would do in Spain— break in and corner the unsuspecting girl and get the information he needed. If he were caught before he accomplished his mission, he would have a hard time explaining what a peer of the realm was doing housebreaking on a lark.

But he had to find some way to confirm that the Mrs. Keates who served Lady Finch was indeed Olivia Sutton.

Waving away his carriage, he set out on foot to make a survey of the perimeter of the house, eyeing the windows and various entrances and exits to gauge how many people it would take to watch the residence. Then he settled against a wall near the mews, hidden out of sight but within spying distance of what appeared to be the servants' entrance.

Now all he needed was an informant. A greedy or indiscreet maid or footman he could bribe to give him more information about their mistress's hired companion. And as luck would have it, a likely tattler came sneaking out the door.

A maid, he guessed, and from her furtive posture, obviously shirking her duties to run off on a clandestine rendezvous.

Just the perfect snitch. Guilt-ridden and afraid of being caught. And only too willing to share information to keep from being dismissed without references.

As he started after her, planning on catching the girl just out of sight of the house, he realized he'd been right all along that this was the perfect person to tell him about Mrs. Keates.

For as the woman turned the first corner, Robert caught a glimpse of red-gold hair peeking out from beneath her hood.

He smiled. If only his work in Iberia was this easy.

Olivia didn't realize she'd been followed until she'd made it about halfway across the small park in the middle of the square and someone caught her by the arm. She first thought it was Jemmy, up and after her to offer his valiant assistance, but the moment her assailant spoke, she knew how wrong she'd been to leave the red-brick sanctuary of Lady Finch's town house.

"Just a moment, Miss Sutton," teased a deep, rich, all too haunting voice.

Robert. How had he found her?

She froze for only a second, then whirled on him, her hand balled into a tight fist and aimed for his chin, while her foot went careening at his shin.

But to her dismay, the once fussy marquis easily sidestepped her booted assault and managed to catch her hand as it pummeled toward him. He moved so quickly and without so much as a ruffle to his badly tied cravat, that before she could blink, Olivia found herself trapped in his embrace, breathless and stunned by his fluid, graceful defense—as if he'd trained at Gentleman Jim's side all his life.

The arms that now held her captive did so with a steely, taut certitude. She felt the unforgiving, stalwart muscles in his arm wound tightly around her back, while his hand rested just beneath her breast. He used neither hold to take advantage of his superior position, but at the same time he left her almost breathless with anticipation.

She was close enough to feel the heat of his body, the hammering of his heart. He might have moved with a languid, almost bored motion, but his body was responding with a very male awareness—as if being awakened from a long sleep and finding itself ravenous and only too willing to be sated with the nearest morsel.

And yet, he only held her, keeping whatever illicit desires he might have been feeling in check, maintaining his control with an exacting, almost noble reserve.

How could this be the same man she'd known?

Olivia tried once or twice to shrug herself free, but Robert's unrelenting grasp told her he was not about to let go. Not yet.

Not until he gets what he wants.

Some things, she knew, *never* changed about a man.

Well, he was about to find out she had. The once innocent girl he'd taken advantage of wasn't about to help him. Never again. Not to find his treasure. And certainly not to kill someone else.

One man's blood on her hands was enough.

She struggled anew, though she knew her efforts were futile. His potent will wasn't going to be conquered by her feeble attempts. And besides, it only made him tighten his grasp, pull their bodies closer together. Which, Olivia discovered, as her body brushed against his with an appreciation that verged on sinfulness, wasn't a good thing.

"Are you done making a scene?" he asked.

She nodded and remained silent as he towed her over to a secluded corner, where thick rhododendrons grew to conceal anyone who wandered there. It was a romantic spot even in the dead of winter, with the smell of dew and grass competing with the dank London air, offering the illusion that one was standing in a romantic country glen.

A place designed for lovers.

But not for Olivia. And not with this man.

"Let me go," she said, finally mustering the strength to shake him off. "You have no right to manhandle me so."

"You tried to kill me last night, isn't that reason enough?"

"Well, I missed. Consider it my coming home gift to you. Now leave me be."

"I can't. I need your help, Miss Sutton."

There it was again. That formal tone to his voice.

Miss Sutton. He said it as if they had just been introduced at an assembly and he was getting up the nerve to ask her to dance.

"If you think I will help you again, my lord, you are mistaken." She started to step away.

His hand caught her again. "This time it is different."

Different. That was an understatment. The urgency of his touch sent shock waves through her senses. He had never affected her thusly—the warmth of his fingers easily penetrating the wool of her sleeve, a heat filled with temptation. Before his touch had left her giddy and dizzy, but this man evoked nothing but the deepest, most alarming sense of longing within her.

How could he affect her so?

It certainly wasn't something she hadn't expected, to a certain degree, to feel in his presence—but this was an altogether new awareness of what it meant to be a woman alone with a man. A niggling sense that twisted inside her, begging to be released from that sheltered place in her heart, from the heat growing indecently between her thighs.

"Miss Sutton, countless lives are at stake."

Even as she closed her eyes and struggled to ignore the way his voice curled around her shadowed feelings, he continued his appeal. "It is a matter of national importance. Only you can help. Please, I beg this one favor."

Olivia's lashes flung open. He'd have been better off if he'd left out the plea for King and country. She'd heard that lie from his lips before. Heard it and believed it.

But what stopped her was the fact that Robert, the Marquis of Bradstone, had just used the words "please" and "beg" in the same sentence.

Please?

Life in a French prison must have changed him more than she thought possible. Or made him a better liar.

She chose to believe the latter.

"You must help me . . . again," he added hastily.

"Help you?" she managed to sputter through her outrage. "I would rather help the French."

He let out an exasperated sigh. "If you refuse to tell me what I need to know, you will be."

"I doubt it is as dire as all that," she shot back. "You probably dangled some enormous boon before that toady Corsican to let you go, and now you must provide it and hence your need once again for me." She paused, waiting for him to admit the real truth behind his fervent appeals.

Yet as she stared at the set of his strong, scarred jaw, the hard gaze of his flint-green eyes, she found her breath stolen away. He wasn't Bradstone anymore, certainly nothing like the man she remembered. This man was someone different, someone she wanted to trust, a man she wanted to believe in—with her heart and soul.

Like she'd always imagined she'd feel when she met Hobbe.

Oh, bloody hell, she thought, using one of Jemmy's more egregious curses. What the devil was she thinking? The man before her was the same greedy, evil fiend who'd taken the very heart of her innocence and trust as well as taken that poor boy's life right before her eyes—not her mythical hero.

He wasn't the man of her dreams. Certainly not her Hobbe.

"Tell me, my lord," she asked, "what would you do

with The King's Ransom? Line your already rich pockets with the gold of the dead? Or would you return it to the Spanish people? See that it was used to free the Peninsula from tyranny, as it was originally intended?"

"And what if I said that is exactly what I intend to do with it?" His grip softened. "Since the look on your face clearly says you don't believe me, then come with me and see for yourself."

Come with me . . . The invitation whispered at her soul and frightened her anew at his ability to so easily seduce her away from her chosen path.

Gone were his flowery declarations, the whispered devotions of love that sidestepped the truth. Olivia found herself almost welcoming his new approach, the open bluntness of his offer called to her in a way that his previous wordy and feigned professions had never stirred.

Go with him, indeed! What the devil was she thinking? She'd rather go to hell. And she told him just that.

His jaw tightened at her rather forthright refusal, and his grip intensified. Then he yarded her into his grasp, pulling her close, so close she could smell the tang of his soap. No expensive perfumes for the marquis anymore, just plain bay rum soap.

The clean, masculine scent suited this new man only too well.

And even as her nose twitched with awareness, the rest of her senses awoke to him as well. Her legs were pressed to his, her breasts against his chest. He held her so intimately she found herself just inches from those mesmerizing eyes, those tantalizing lips.

Yet she didn't remember feeling so eager in the marquis's arms. It was as if someone else was holding her, awakening her heart for the first time, inflaming her senses with his understated, yet overwhelming, seductive charm.

Someone like Hobbe. But even as she tried to tell herself this new Bradstone, this very different man, was no knight in shining armor, she couldn't help but lean closer to him—to discover what other secrets he was hiding.

He'd told her he needed her, and all she wanted to do was believe him. That he needed her. That he wanted to seal his new vows with a kiss from those lips.

"Do you remember what the missive said?" he asked, his mouth moving and her eyes unable to look away.

Before she could stop herself, she whispered, "Yes."

His lips brushed over the edge of her ear with the merest touch, yet it sent a bolt of lightning down her spine. "Then tell me," he urged her, this time his tongue flicking lightly over her skin, leaving a warm, hot trail. "Tell me again."

The words, the truth came bubbling up, lured by the heated passion behind his smoky words. What was he doing? she thought, as her knees started to buckle under his expert assault. He may be utterly and completely different, the type of man she'd always dreamt of, but when all was said and done, he was still the Marquis of Bradstone. Her mouth snapped shut, leaving the words he so wanted to hear as trapped and hidden as the treasure itself. He was working his magic on her again, and she was falling for it like the innocent schoolgirl she'd once been.

To ward off his intoxicating spell, she struggled to remember why she was in London. To fill her thoughts and overwrought senses not with him but with memories. Of the pistol firing. The endless report ringing for what seemed like an eternity. The face of the young man as he lay dying, the dark stain of blood spreading across his stark white shirt.

His last words ringing through her mind like a funeral bell.

Give this to no one but Hobbe.

Hobbe.

The boy's trusted hero. The one man honorable enough to save her, to save the treasure from the greedy hands that sought to steal it. Not this sorcerer of seduction, this faithless rake bemuddling her common sense.

"Well, will you or won't you?" he was asking. "I must know what the missive said."

Olivia mustered her resolve and shook off her body's treasonous longing for this man. "Tell you?" She shook her head. "Never."

"You did before," he whispered in her ear, his smooth tones breaching once again her newfound, albeit shaky, determination, like that niggle down her spine still clamoring for her to listen to him.

This is not the same man, this is a man you can trust, it seemed to say.

No, he wasn't the same man, she'd agree. But neither was a snake when it shed its skin. Though it was still a snake, no matter what coat it chose to wear.

Whatever her doubts about him, seven years of exile had left her clear concerning one thing: she would never help the Marquis of Bradstone again. Unless it was into the nearest unmarked grave.

She struggled out of his grasp. "Yes, but I was a fool

then," she told him. *And I won't be one again.* "I'll not help you, Robert. Not ever. You might as well kill me here and now, for I won't reveal one word of that missive to you."

He ran an impatient hand through his hair. "Miss Sutton, whatever our relationship was in the past, it is in the past. But rest assured I will not relent until I have your help." He caught her arm again in his vise-like grip and held on with what she supposed was his attempt at brute force—though in her heart she just knew he wouldn't kill her this time, despite the fact that he'd had every intention of doing so that long-ago night.

"I need to know what was in that missive—the one you translated for me—and I need to know now."

Olivia's nose tipped upward. "Considering that you thought that information worth killing for, I'm surprised you've forgotten it."

His brows furrowed. "My head injury," he said, with a hint of falter to his voice. "It has left some of my memories in pieces. I recall some things but not others."

"How convenient."

"No, not really," he told her. "Especially when it comes to *El Rescate del Rey*."

Olivia's gaze narrowed. His words once again hammered at her doubts. What had he said? *El Rescate del Rey.* The King's Ransom, and in Spanish no less. He'd even said it with the pitch and nuance of a native—not with the stumbling arrogance of the Englishman she remembered.

That small voice inside her roared to life anew, crying out that something was very wrong. All of this was wrong.

He shook her again. "If I have to rattle it out of you, you blasted little termagant, I will."

That was it? He was just going to shake it out of her? No pistol to her head? No brute force?

It was all so absurd, she couldn't help laughing. "Really, Robert, you did much better with seduction and charm than this feigned attempt at savagery. Whatever happened to 'Olivia, my dearest love?' Or 'Olivia, you make my heart weep at the sight of you'? Granted they were rather trite and you hardly meant them, but they did work better than trying to shake my acquiescence out of me."

His gaze narrowed and then swept over her again in that appraising way she found so disconcerting. "So that is how it is to be." There was no question in his words, just a statement.

He caught her in his arms, this time like a lover, eager and only too willing.

"Nooo—" she managed to stutter. "It won't work."

He paused for only a moment before his lips claimed hers in a demanding kiss, a kiss that turned her body traitor in a matter of a heartbeat.

Nooo—she continued to cry silently as he deepened the kiss. His tongue swept past her sputtering lips, taming her unspoken protests with his touch. She found herself welcoming his invasion, opening herself to him, as he caressed and soothed her objections to only a breathless sigh.

Still she fought him. Fought her own body's elated response to him. *No, I won't do this . . . No, this isn't . . .*

It wasn't . . . The realization hit her hard, even as he continued to kiss her senseless, her body awakening to his ever growing demands.

If she'd had doubts about the man before her, he'd kissed them all away.

Because he wasn't Robert.

Chills coursed down her spine. She wasn't kissing the Marquis of Bradstone but an imposter.

Not Robert? How could that be? And what was even worse was the way her heart sang this recognition with a burst of joy.

So if he wasn't Bradstone, who, then, was blazing her checked passions alive with his sensuous kiss?

Egads, she was kissing a total stranger.

That was enough to give her the strength of will to push the man in her arms away.

She struggled to catch her breath until finally she managed to ask, "Who are you?"

Her hand went to her swollen, and still tingling lips, lips that had been branded by a man who had the face of her enemy but the soul of another.

"Who are you?"

Chapter 4

Before Olivia could repeat her question a third time, she heard her name being called from a distance.

"Olivia? Olivia? Oh, where the deuce are you?"

Jemmy! She turned in the direction of his voice. What was he doing out here, and at this early hour?

"It appears you are about to make another timely escape, Miss Sutton," said the man she'd thought, up until a few moments ago, was Lord Bradstone.

She glanced back at him, the differences between her enemy and this stranger now only too glaring. His unpolished veneer lent him a rakish, tangled look, a dangerous air, whereas Robert, the man she remembered, was nothing but smooth manners and cultured wit.

Having spent too many years dreaming of her own knight errant, her only too noble Hobbe, she was shocked to discover that this imposter captured her heart with something akin to that same dark passion.

A deep heat of longing and desire that was only too unfathomable to understand. One she had banished from her life.

And yet, as she glanced at him again, the lines between Robert and this man blurred—he wanted her help, just as Robert had—and for what reasons it was anyone's guess.

He must have sensed her suspicions, because he said, "I haven't time to explain. I need your help and I need it now. Tell me what you know about *El Rescate del Rey* before that puppy of yours arrives. I must know what Lord Bradstone discovered the night of the Chambley ball."

"No!" She hadn't been about to give it to the likes of Bradstone again, so she certainly wasn't going to give it to a complete stranger.

No matter how compelling she found him.

"Oh, dash it, Olivia, there you are!" Jemmy called out, his boots stomping through the wet grass, his arms pushing aside the thick branches of rhododendron. "What the devil are you doing back here in the brambles on such a—" His footsteps and inquiry came to an abrupt halt as he spotted her companion.

Olivia had never seen Jemmy's affable features take on such a mottled color of rage.

"Step away from her, sir," the young man said with deadly calm.

Her startled gaze flew to Robert. *He's not Robert*, she corrected herself. The Robert she knew would have had no compunction about seeing Jemmy dispatched for his impertinence and interference—removed permanently—but this man only sent a look of cool amusement toward her eager champion.

Olivia turned back to her would-be rescuer to see

that he was now brandishing one of his new pistols, the hair-triggered match to the one she had stolen.

"I said step away," Jemmy repeated. "You won't be harming her, not without killing me first."

This imposter found Jemmy's threats amusing?

Recalling the way he'd so coolly stared down her own denunciation last night, Olivia sensed that this man was used to facing death straight on.

And winning every time.

"Jemmy, put that away," she told the Finch heir. "Put it away immediately. This isn't Lord—"

"This isn't the time to settle our differences," the man beside her said, his commanding tone and clipped words bringing her disclosure to a sharp halt. "I've no quarrel with you, sir, nor with the lady."

"That's not up to you to decide," Jemmy told him. "Olivia, has he hurt you? Threatened you? Just say the word, and I'll—"

"You'll do nothing, Jemmy. Now put that pistol down." She stared at him much as she had done when he was twelve and she'd caught him in one or another infraction. It worked to some extent, for he let the muzzle drop, but he did not relax his stance. "His lordship and I were just parting company." She turned to the man beside her. "Isn't that correct, *my lord*?"

Olivia let the dare behind her words challenge him to contradict her. It hadn't escaped her that she had the upper hand on this Bradstone look-alike.

At least for the time being.

"My apologies for detaining you," the man murmured, though the predatory light in his eyes told her only too clearly that her advantage wouldn't last for long.

Jemmy grumbled something under his breath about

overbearing blackguards, which both Olivia and the imposter chose to ignore.

"Come on then, Olivia," Jemmy said, stalking out of the bushes toward the path. "Mother is in rare form this morning and sent me out to find you before you came to a *bad end*." His final words he shot directly at her companion.

"Until we meet again, Miss Sutton," the *faux* marquis said, with a polite nod. As he passed her, he added one last warning, low enough to exclude Jemmy from its hearing. "Don't think this is finished." His hand shot out and caught her by the arm, holding her in place. "I will have what I came to London for—one way or another."

"We shall see, sir," she told him as tartly as she could muster, shaking off his grasp and her own reaction to his touch.

The heat of his fingers seared her skin with the memory of the passionate fire his lips had kindled to life.

So lost in the remembrance of it, she almost didn't hear him say, "My name is Danvers. Robert Danvers."

Danvers. The name whispered over her ear, teasing her to try it out with her own lips.

"I don't care who you are," she said instead. "I won't help you."

His brows arched over his cold green eyes, lending him a wicked, unforgiving air, while his gaze raked over her as if he was once again assessing her like some great conundrum. "We'll see about that."

Olivia had the uneasy feeling that there was more to his quest than just the treasure, something deeply personal that had to do with her and her alone. Something that should leave her fearful and wary of his wrath.

But for now, she did the only thing she could—she fled from his side.

He's not so different from Robert after all, she tried telling herself as she retreated to where Jemmy stood waiting impatiently. *No, he's not that different whatsoever.*

Oh, but he was. Very different. Her hand went once again to her lips, where the heat of his kiss still lingered, one that had burned away everything she'd known about men and women and kissing.

She redoubled her flight toward Jemmy, who stood, boot tapping on the grass, his jaw set with a determination that rivaled his mother's well-known obstinacy. With every hurried step, she did her best to forget that she'd kissed this stranger—this Robert Danvers.

"What the devil were you thinking, coming out alone?" Jemmy began. "That bastard could have killed you, or worse." His tone implied all kinds of ominous occurrences that she as a lady could never imagine.

But Olivia wasn't a lady, not in that sheltered oh-so-proper sense, and she knew only too well what happened in the world Jemmy was so darkly hinting around the fences about.

"And to think I let him go," he continued blustering. "I should have done the world a favor and just—" He held the pistol out and trained it on a hapless squirrel dashing across the green. "Why, I'd have just—"

"You would have done no such thing." She took the pistol away from him and continued toward the house.

Robert Danvers could be just as murderous as the man he was impersonating and Jemmy would end up losing his life protecting her long-lost honor.

But do you really believe that? The question haunted

her with memories of his kiss and her body's betrayal under his touch.

Then an even worse thought hit her, leaving Olivia quaking in her boots.

What if *she* had killed him last night?

She would have sent an innocent man to his grave.

The guilt that assailed her passed quickly. For truly, how innocent was a man who was impersonating a peer of the realm and obviously out to steal a king's ransom?

Robert Danvers returned to Bradstone House with more questions than answers.

And with the realization that perhaps he'd made an error in kissing Miss Sutton.

And it wasn't the fact that she'd then been able to determine that he wasn't the marquis but what it had done to his carefully wrought plans.

Instead of being able to coerce her into revealing the information she held, he'd given himself away and in the bargain had found himself entangled with a tempting handful.

He'd kissed women in the line of duty before—a ravishing countess in Madrid, whose husband was a French collaborator, a seductively practiced Italian woman, who'd been deserted in Portugal by one of Bonaparte's cronies and was only too willing to trade her secrets—but none of their traitorous lips had ever coaxed him into forgetting his own *raison d'être*.

But Olivia Sutton's lips teased his mind to forget and his body to react with a primitive heat that burned away his usual cool detachment. This fire went far deeper than her chestnut hair and flashing eyes.

Never had poison tasted so fine.

How had this chit taken him so unawares? So utterly and completely in one kiss that he'd nearly overlooked the true reason he'd come to London?

Then again, the little wench had known exactly what she'd been doing, he told himself. He'd sensed her confusion and then recognition immediately—and yet it had taken her nearly a minute more to wrench herself from his arms. And yet . . .

There had been something completely innocent in her kiss—resistant, tentative, almost afraid. And her eyes, while they had flared with an untamed and heedless anger, they had also told him more than her indignation could—they'd also been relieved, stunned and only too curious as to who he was.

That curiosity, he knew, was what he should fear the most. For a curious miss, especially one as intelligent as Miss Sutton, could prove dangerous. If she started asking questions, making inquiries, his deception would be ruined.

But before he'd let that happen, he'd find a way to pry the secret of *El Rescate del Rey* from her lips, no matter what method of coercion he had to take.

He could imagine what Pymm would suggest. *Take the wench to your bed and be done with it.*

Robert shook off that thought immediately. Kissing the little termagant was one thing.

Bedding her was an entirely different matter.

One that appealed to him more than he cared to admit.

"Damn her," he muttered, as he marched down the street in a worse mood than he had been in last night when he'd discovered her missing from his room.

"I beg your pardon," huffed a matronly lady who was in the process of hustling her string of wide-eyed charges out of his foul path.

Robert doffed his hat in a short bow, muttering a quick apology. If this were the Peninsula, he wouldn't have any need for all these wretched formalities and deceptions. He'd haul the traitorous lady before a board of inquiry and wrench the information out of her.

Unfortunately, the situation called for a slightly different tack. And if he was to play on an even field with Miss Sutton, then he needed to know a little more about her.

And Robert knew exactly who could provide this invaluable intelligence.

Striding up the steps of the Bradstone town house, he nodded at Carlyle and asked him, "Can you tell me where her ladyship is?"

The man glanced over his shoulder at the clock ticking away on a shelf in the alcove. "Your mother should just be getting her morning repast in her suite," he answered. He glanced at Robert's wrinkled coat and neckerchief and then back out the door as if trying to determine if his eyes were deceiving him—that the Marquis of Bradstone had truly ventured out into London wearing such a poor ensemble.

"Out taking a morning stroll," Robert told him. Heading for the stairs, he made a parting comment before heading up to his aunt's suite. "Never fear, Carlyle. I doubt anyone saw me."

"One can only hope, my lord," the poor guardian of the Bradstone portals muttered.

Robert had never ventured into his aunt's private rooms and didn't quite know what to expect as he tapped on the half-open door.

"Robert, darling!" she cried out, waving her hand at him to enter. "You're just in time to join me." Dressed in a ruffled morning gown, she sat on a comfortable looking sofa. Before her a silver tray with a basket of rolls and a pot of tea sat on an ornate low table.

He smiled and walked slowly into this foreign territory. Lady Bradstone's private sitting room, unlike the rest of the staid and elegant house, was filled with frippery. Lacy curtains and delicately carved chairs added to the dainty appeal of the room. Baskets of needlework sat awaiting attention, as did numerous books and the scattered pieces of correspondence, invitations and calling cards littering a delicate looking desk in the far corner.

The room and its accoutrements, much like his flighty aunt, seemed destined to accomplish many things and nothing at all.

He took the seat next to her on the yellow and white striped sofa. "Good morning, my lady."

"Robert, you must get over this formality you've brought back with you. It is very disconcerting." She took up the teapot and poured him a cup, adding a lump of sugar and giving it an agitated stir before handing it over to him. "Now, what are you doing up at this hour and in that wretched coat? Certainly Mr. Babbit didn't suggest this . . . this *ensemble*?"

"Never fear," Robert told her. "I chose it myself."

"Harumph," she sputtered as she poured herself another cup of tea. "Looks more like something you borrowed from that Papist pirate you insist we keep about the house."

Robert suppressed a smile. Leave it to his aunt not to pass up an opportunity to cast aspersions on Aquiles. "I was out for an early stroll," he explained. "I didn't think Babbit's services were all that necessary for such a minor outing."

His aunt's brows rose a bit, as if to say that his valet's services were more than necessary for every occasion. Then she sighed and reached for a roll, buttering it with the same air of despair that she had used when stirring his tea.

Wisely Robert adhered to the one rule of spying he'd learned early on. When faced with an impossible situation, one learned more by saying nothing than by chattering mindlessly.

So he sipped his tea in chastised silence and let his gaze wander around the room, passing over the gilt pieces and the female frippery until it landed on a small portrait hung next to his aunt's secretary.

"Mother," he whispered, before even realizing he'd spoken.

"Yes?" Lady Bradstone answered. "What is it, my dear?"

He shook his head and turned to her. "Um, oh, nothing." But against his own volition, his gaze turned back to the sight of the face he hadn't seen in years, not since his childhood.

Her ladyship rose from her chair, followed his line of sight and pulled the small painting from the wall. "My sister, Susannah."

"She was lovely," he managed to say, as his aunt returned to the sofa and handed him the portrait.

"Yes, Susannah was the real beauty of our family. Though I had my own legions of *beaux*, my sister claimed the heart of every man in the *ton*." His aunt sighed. "I miss her ever so much. More each year. Why, she's been gone, for . . . oh, bother, too many years to count."

Twenty-two years, Robert thought. And he'd counted every single one since he'd been four years old and his

father had come into the room he shared with his
older brother Colin early one morning to tell them
their mother was gone. That the fever that had kept
her in bed for most of the week had taken her life.

"Oh, aren't we a melancholy pair," his aunt said,
bubbling once again. "Susannah would never have
stood for anyone weeping over her portrait. She loved
life too much. 'Twas her folly, I suppose."

"Why do you say that?" he asked, suddenly curious
about the woman of whom he held only a few cher-
ished and blurred memories.

"She could have had her pick of husbands. Father
quite indulged her in the matter. But then again I suppose he never assumed she wouldn't choose someone
equal to her in rank. And when she didn't, making the
most unsuitable match, it was disastrous."

"How so?" All Robert knew of his parents' marriage was happy times. His mother smiling over the
table at his father. The light in his father's eyes when
he entered a room and looked at his wife. Their marriage, short as it was, seemed to Robert to have been
ideal—a perfect match of love and friendship.

Apparently his aunt did not see it that way.

"She married for love." His aunt set the portrait
facedown on the table before them. "Promise me,
Robert, you will never marry for love. It is a horrible
proposition if ever there was one." She took his hand.
"Promise me you will marry some sensible, eligible
parti, not one of these flighty cits' daughters who seem
so popular these days."

"Madame," Robert said, "I can promise you, marriage is the furthest thing from my mind at the present
moment."

This proved not to be the response her ladyship was looking for. He might as well have said he had planned to return to his French prison.

"Oh, Robert, you can't mean such a thing. You must secure the estate with an heir." She let out a breathy sigh. "I won't go through another dispute with that wretched Prinny again. He wants your title something dreadful for one of his odious favorites, and I will not let him have it. Now, you must start seriously considering marriage. Perhaps Miss Colyer, though I realized last night her features are far more coarse than I remember."

"I doubt Miss Colyer and I would suit," he told her quite plainly. He could well imagine Miss Colyer on a covert mission in Spain—he doubted she'd last the first mile.

But then unbidden came an image of another woman, a woman he suspected would make not only the first mile but every one after that. He could see her quite plainly, astride a Portuguese donkey, her skirts hitched up, the wind tousling her fiery red hair, her eyes alive with mischief as they crossed enemy territory.

What the devil was he thinking?

"Miss Sutton," he muttered, shaking the errant thought aside.

"Miss Sutton!" his aunt repeated. "Oh, Robert, don't tell me you still have a *tendré* for that murderess? Tell me you haven't seen her." She paused for a moment and peered into his face. Whatever she saw there he couldn't guess, but only too quickly her eyes grew wide and she paled to a ghostly white. "Oh, dear God, you have!" she exclaimed, rising to her feet, her hands clutched to her breast. "I can see it. That scandalous little jade. She won't rest until she's utterly ruined you and our family. Oh, you can't marry *her!*"

"You know she's alive?" he asked.

"Of course I knew she lived. I never believed a word of that tarradiddle about you taking her with you. What nonsense!" She flopped down on the sofa and reached for her cup, taking a much needed sip. "I've suspected for years that she was lurking about awaiting her chance to ruin our lives once again."

Robert smiled at her. "Never fear, madame, I have no plans to marry Miss Sutton. Believe me."

His aunt sniffed, her skepticism clearly etched in her features. "Well, at least tell Lord Chambley that you've seen her. He promised me years ago that if I was able to locate her, he would see to it that she was brought to justice for that poor boy's murder and that your name would be cleared of any wrongdoing."

"Lord Chambley?" Robert asked.

"Why, yes," Lady Bradstone said. "He has been most solicitous of me over the years. My champion, I declare. After you were thought lost on that wretched little ship, he took all your papers and went through them for me, looking for any indication as to where you might have headed so he could send agents there to find you for me. A most thoughtful gentleman, Lord Chambley."

Robert took a moment to consider this bit of news.

According to Chambley's report at the time, there had been no papers found in Bradstone's possessions.

First his deceptions about Miss Sutton's alleged demise on the *Bon Venture* and now this.

Orlando had been slated to meet Chambley the night he died. Could it have been just bad luck that Orlando ran afoul before their arranged meeting, or a series of unlikely coincidences that all ended with one man—*Chambley*?

"What else has his lordship done for you?" he asked her. Then he added, "So I can properly thank him when next we meet."

Lady Bradstone set aside her cup. "Funny you should mention that, but I was rather expecting him to call this morning." She glanced over at the clock on the mantel. "I can't imagine what is detaining him."

"Lord Chambley call here? What for?"

"Oh, he's been after me ever since you returned to let him call on you. He has some questions for his reports, or whatever it is that department of his likes to record. A mere formality, he assures me, that won't take up more than a few moments of your time." She sighed and glanced at the clock again. "He's been sending around notes nearly every day since you returned, requesting an audience, but I told Carlyle not to let him in and not to bother you until you were ready to start receiving company." She looked at him expectantly.

That explained, Robert mused, Chambley's odd remarks the night before.

"Oh, I can see you are vexed with me," his aunt was saying. "I shouldn't have done that, should I? But Robert, please don't be angry with me. I know you and Lord Chambley were thick as thieves before you left—"

"Chambley? We were friends?"

"Well, yes. Don't you remember?" She studied him for a moment. "I can see that you don't. You and he spent any number of hours locked away in your study before your unfortunate incident."

"I seem to have forgotten," Robert said. "Do you recall what we were doing?"

"Oh, some business venture or other. Not that I have the wits for such matters."

Finally, all the pieces fell into place. "Chambley," he muttered. "He was involved the whole time."

His aunt's sharp ears picked up his words immediately. "Of course he was—that is why I thought nothing of letting him take your papers. And it is exactly why I held him at abeyance. I wanted to make sure you had gathered your wits about you before you started mixing with your old friends. Don't frown at me so. I did it for your sake, so you wouldn't have one of your *moments* in front of someone besides myself or Carlyle."

"That was probably for the best," he told her. "Perhaps I will pay Lord Chambley a call and settle this business once and for all, so it will no longer weigh so heavily on your mind."

She smiled at this and poured him another cup of tea.

Yet what weighed on Robert's mind wasn't Chambley's involvement with the King's Ransom but his aunt's other disclosure—of Chambley's vow to see Miss Sutton brought to justice if she were ever found. It foretold an ominous future for the chit if Chambley managed to find her before Robert could extract what he needed from her.

And he doubted it would have anything to do with justice.

"My dearest Miss Sutton, it is good to see you well and alive. I had quite given up hope of ever seeing you again." Lord Chambley sat well ensconced on the best chair in Lady Finch's parlor. With his hands folded over his ample belly, he looked more like a concerned and relieved grandfather speaking to an errant child than the angry and belligerent government official she remembered.

"Thank you, my lord," Olivia said. She hadn't been convinced that approaching Lord Chambley, as Lady Finch had insisted, was the best course of action, but now, seeing his evident concern and sincerity, she felt almost foolish for having waited so long to divulge what she knew.

Yet the dying man's words rang in her ears like a warning bell. *Give this to no one but Hobbe.*

There is no damn Hobbe, she told herself. He never existed. Not anywhere but in her imagination.

So then why did Robert Danvers's face suddenly come to mind? His forceful presence, his cool reserve, his only too strong and masculine embrace—just exactly as she'd always envisioned Hobbe.

Oh, she was going mad when she started seeing heroes in men like Danvers—the conniving imposter!

"It is a miracle and a testament to your innocence and intelligence that you are hale and hearty," Lord Chambley was saying. "But the keenest part is that you've finally come to your senses and are seeking my guidance."

Olivia tried to set aside the niggling feelings of doubt creeping down her spine at his overly familiar sentiments. Shaking them off, she decided she'd become far too suspicious.

Lord Chambley was a highly placed official in the Foreign Office. He was a peer of the realm, regarded as a leading member of the House of Lords.

But then again, you were right to suspect something was amiss with that phony Bradstone, that nagging little voice reminded her.

Olivia forced a smile on her face and tried to look contrite. "I am so sorry for any inconvenience I have caused you, my lord, or your office."

He nodded at her and turned to Lady Finch. "This really is all my fault. I was far too severe with her that night. Probably frightened the poor girl out of her wits. Obviously left her with the wrong impression. Bravo to you, Lady Finch, for finally setting her to rights and bringing her back into the sanctity of society."

"Yes, that is all well and good, Lord Chambley," Lady Finch told him. "But what is to be done about the murder charge?"

Olivia held back a grin. Lady Finch wasn't one to be bothered with the winding path of Lord Chambley's political niceties. Leave it to her employer to get straight to the point.

Lord Chambley blustered for a moment at such a blunt and forthright request, then said, "If she can provide me with the information I want—I mean, that the Foreign Office is most desirous to obtain, then the gel can go free. I'll see to it personally that all the charges are handled appropriately."

Lady Finch nodded.

He turned to Olivia. "You do know what I mean by *the information*, don't you?"

Something stayed her head from nodding, her lips from forming a "yes."

Don't tell him. Don't give him any indication that you have any clue as to what he is asking. Save it for him.

She nearly ground her teeth.

Him. Hobbe. Where was he? Her knight errant? Not sitting before her offering her amnesty. So why was she hesitating? Not even that *faux* Bradstone Robert Danvers had dangled such a boon before her.

Knights errant and phantom marquises. These were who she was trusting her life to. Ridiculous.

She took a deep breath. "I believe I can tell you everything you need to know, my lord," she said. "In fact, I've even been able to do a little more research into this and have learned that *El—*"

"Ah, thorough to a fault, I see," Lord Chambley chuckled, cutting her off. "Just like your father."

This diverted Olivia's attention utterly. Her father? No one ever mentioned him. Not since . . . "You knew my father?"

"Yes, quite well. Sir John's work was invaluable to his country—that is, until . . ."

She knew how the sentence was to be finished.

Until your father sold his talents to the Dutch and then hanged himself to avoid public censure.

Everyone sat for a few moments in uncomfortable silence until Lord Chambley brushed his hands over his lapels and said, "Now, there, let's get on with our business. No need to dwell on the unhappy events of the past." He drew a large breath into his barrel chest and let it out in a wheezy rush. "Now, what would you say to coming down to the Foreign Office with me and telling all this to my secretary. He can transcribe it into a working document for me to pass along to the correct authorities."

"The Foreign Office," Jemmy said in awed tones, finally unable to keep in line with his mother's edict to remain silent. "I'd be more than happy to escort you, Olivia."

"Completely unnecessary, young man," Lord Chambley said. "Highly confidential matters of state. Besides, Miss Sutton will be more than safe with me. As if she were my own daughter."

* * *

Aquiles rushed through the front door of the Bradstone town house coming face to face with Carlyle's blustered objections at his not using the servants' entrance.

Robert, having just come down from his aunt's suite, stepped into the middle of the fray—Carlyle insisting Aquiles leave and enter the house properly, and Aquiles telling the stiff English butler where he could go in his most colorful Spanish.

"It won't happen again," Robert promised Carlyle, while he hauled a spitting mad Aquiles off to a corner.

"Why aren't you over at the Finches'?" he asked his servant in a low whisper.

Aquiles spat in Carlyle's general direction and continued cursing in rapid Spanish until finally he said a coherent set of words that caught Robert's attention.

"Chambley se hizo con ella." Chambley's got her.

Robert's hand balled into a fist.

The bastard had found her. And now he had her.

So it was only a matter of time before the unscrupulous man relieved the young woman of the information she possessed. And Robert doubted Lord Chambley had any qualms about how to carry out that deed.

Miss Sutton would be lucky to see another day.

Then again, he was talking about the same woman who had quite possibly murdered a Foreign Office agent. The same woman who'd allied herself with his treasonous cousin and attempted to steal a fortune in Spanish gold. The woman who not eighteen hours earlier had trained a pistol on him and vowed to shoot him if he didn't do her bidding.

For a moment, Robert thought perhaps he should

rush to warn Chambley what he was getting himself into.

Robert wasn't too sure he knew himself what he was doing as he stalked out of the house—saving the vexing little minx from who knows what dangers—or saving her from herself.

Upstairs, Lady Bradstone watched Robert and his servant depart the house in a great hurry, as if the world depended upon their next course of action. A small sigh slipped from her lips as Robert's tall figure finally strode out of sight. For a moment she stood in silence, her lips pursed and her thoughts taking a direction she didn't want to hazard.

Robert will be fine, she told herself. He is an intelligent man—very much like Papa. Yes, the Duke of Setchfield would have been proud of such a grandson, proud of his long lost namesake, she mused—that is, if he had lived long enough to find the forgiveness in his heart that it would have taken to bridge the family rifts.

The thought should have given her comfort, but instead it filled her with sadness. There were few who remembered her father as she did—unforgiving, cold, hard to please. Most chose instead to ignore those qualities, regarding his demeanor and extreme eccentricities as the right of nobility, just as they did with the obvious changes in Robert.

But then again, perhaps the alterations in Robert's character weren't as glaring to others as they were to a mother.

Her gaze fell on Susannah's overturned portrait and she reached down to right it. Her sister's lively eyes, dark hair and imperious airs stared forth. Reverently Lady Bradstone carried the portrait back to its place of honor beside her desk. She hung it and for a moment studied the smiling face before her.

"How like you, little sister, to send him to me when I needed him." She reached out and brushed her fingertips over the oil and canvas version of her sister's once soft cheek. "I'll watch over him, Susannah. As if he were my own dear Robert. For you have given me something I have always dreamt of—a son I can be proud of. Your son."

Chapter 5

Olivia strained against the ropes binding her to the straight-backed chair in Lord Chambley's guest room.

Some guest room, she thought, looking around the bare chamber. The only furnishings were the chair to which she was bound, a small desk and two other similarly uncomfortable chairs. She had no illusions about how the room had been used in the past, for a bloodstain partially covered by a thin rug revealed that she wasn't the only one who found the room inhospitable.

She paused for a moment and tried to reason what she should do. Screaming would be useless—the servants were probably well paid to ignore such cries, and the next house was far enough away and separated by a high wall and a spacious garden that her laments would go unheard.

For the hundredth time, Olivia cursed herself for not listening to her instincts about Lord Chambley.

Having packed up her notes about The King's Ransom, she and Lord Chambley had left in his carriage for the Foreign Office. When she alighted in the mews of Lord Chambley's town house and not their intended destination, his burly footman, Milo, had quickly and efficiently caught her by the arms and dragged her up a set of backstairs before she could utter a complaint.

Chambley had planned his little guest suite well. Tucked up on the third floor of the house, it was high enough to preclude escape through the window and bare enough not to offer any aids in arming oneself against the formidable Milo, whom she now referred to as Ox.

As if she could have stopped him—it would have taken a cannon to bring the behemoth down. And apparently the man knew how to restrain a prisoner, for the ropes he'd tied around her wrists and feet resisted any efforts to wriggle a hand or foot loose.

The only bit of luck she'd gained in this latest tangle was that moments after Ox had hauled her up the numerous flights of stairs to the guest suite, another servant had come to fetch Lord Chambley.

"I've been directed to attend Lord Castlereagh immediately and will regrettably have to leave you, Miss Sutton," he'd said, with his usual pompous air, snapping the note closed and tucking it into his waistcoat pocket. "Matters of state and all. I fear I might be a while, so you'll have plenty of time to consider your fate. For when I return, I'll be anxious to see if you are as forthcoming with the information I want as you were willing to give Bradstone all your charms— linguistically and otherwise." His lips moved to a leer, and his gaze flitted over her as if he were considering whether or not to sample her charms.

"I won't tell you anything," she'd replied. "I'd rather die first."

He'd come within a hair's breadth of her, then his hand caught her hair and yanked her head back until she thought he meant to snap her neck. "You'll tell me what I want to know, if only to die and release yourself from the pain my associate here is infamous for providing. That is unless you decide to become more willing and obliging with your information and favors . . ."

And with that ominous threat hanging like a storm cloud over the room, Chambley and Ox had left her alone. Well, not entirely alone. His lordship had been kind enough to leave one of his watchdogs curled up on the rug to keep an eye on her.

Every time she moved so much as to shiver in the freezing room, the ugly-looking wretch would curl its lips and growl at her. Olivia was no expert on hounds, but this brindled, wiry-haired fiend looked capable of chewing off her leg.

Cold, frightened and just plain mad at herself, Olivia gave her bindings a good tug and pull.

"Blast and drat," she muttered, trying to find a way to free at least one of her hands. The ropes burned into her wrists, her skin raw from her exertions.

The dog sat up and looked at her, his eyes narrowed. He was large enough to be nearly eye to eye with her.

"Oh, go ahead. Take my toes or my ankles," she told the great beast. "But I warn you they are as cold as ice and won't give you much in the way of a warm meal."

He cocked his head at her again and then trotted across the room, circling around her as if gauging which part of her would be the most tasty.

Olivia closed her eyes and braced herself for the first chomp, but instead all she got was the warm, wet slurp of his tongue over her hands.

"Blah," she said, as the dog's slobbery tongue bathed her aching hands, making her bindings a drooling, slippery mess.

Slippery? Her hands, now all covered in the beast's saliva, felt as if they had been greased. With a mighty tug, she pulled one of her hands free from the bindings.

"Perhaps you wanted to even the score before you bit me," she said to the dog, who sat looking at her with what she thought might be a smile.

Now all she had to do was find a way out of Chambley's fortress and to get . . .

To get where? Olivia nearly swore again when the only thought that came to her was *to get to Robert*.

To that scoundrel, indeed!

Not all that desirous of another encounter with Milo the Ox, she went to the window and opened the sash. Glancing down, she realized a trellis came all the way up to her window and would make her escape, while difficult, not impossible.

Holding her breath, since she hated heights, she swung her leg over the sill and then looked down to gauge the descent before her. The garden below swayed in a dizzy circle, nearly sending her tumbling out the window. It was enough for her to pull her leg back in as quickly as she could to consider another option.

She backed away from the open window and collapsed into the chair. Her heart hammered at her chest, and she could barely catch her breath. The dog came over and settled his head in her lap, looking up at her as if to say he was glad she was back.

"And so am I," she told him absently, scratching at his ears. "I'm not cut out for scaling walls."

For some reason her wayward imagination saw Robert Danvers making such a dangerous ascent to save his ladylove. Knife clenched in his teeth, dressed in black, his hair tied back in a pirate's queue, he'd probably consider such a climb beneath his talents.

Well, it wasn't like he, or any hero for that matter, was going to be coming after her, she thought. If she was going to be rescued, she'd have to do it herself. After several minutes of considering all her options, she decided that perhaps she could risk facing Milo if her only alternative was climbing down the side of Lord Chambley's stately and all too tall town house.

Besides, how could she get down with her valise in hand? Olivia picked up her old, battered bag and gave it a slight hug, glad for the excuse it afforded her not to attempt such an escape.

She made her way to the door, her companion trotting companionably after her. "Oh, you want out as well?"

The dog wagged his tail.

Olivia went to put her hand on the door but found the latch turning by itself.

Egads! Someone was coming in! Her newfound protector started to growl, and Olivia glanced again around the room for something with which to protect herself and realized she had nothing but her own wits and the window.

Robert smiled to himself at Chambley's hasty exit. He'd taken the bait with the note they'd bribed a young boy to deliver to the house.

"Castlereagh will be surprised to see him," Aquiles chuckled.

"No more so than Chambley after he's done bowing and scraping and then is dismissed," Robert said, watching the coach wheel away. "Hopefully he'll be kept waiting long enough for us to borrow back Miss Sutton and leave unnoticed."

Getting into Chambley's house might have posed a problem for someone with less experience than Robert and Aquiles, but the pair of them had been sneaking out of inns, houses and even French garrisons for the past two years, usually with the local dragoons hot on their tail, so they had confidently approached Chambley's London residence with little doubt they'd be able to gain entry.

"This place is a bleedin' fortress," Aquiles grumbled after their fourth attempt to get into the house failed.

Chambley's home was proving more difficult than either of them would have imagined. For one thing, his lordship kept most of his windows locked and barred, and those that were loose had the unwelcome addition of a dog or some other mongrel lounging before the hearth inside that threatened to set up an unholy racket every time they tried to enter the room.

They had found a poorly maintained trellis that led to a fourth-story room, but on Robert's first attempt to climb it, the rotted wood crumbled between his hands and snapped beneath his boot.

There would be no entry or escape via that route.

As he searched for another route in, a window above them slid open. Robert and Aquiles ducked into an old hedge growing up against the house, concealing themselves from view.

As they watched, a face surrounded by a tangle of

red curls peered out the window, as if gauging her surroundings.

Miss Sutton.

"Seems we've found Lord Chambley's guest," Robert whispered to Aquiles. "And she doesn't look too happy about her accommodations."

Just then a leg came dangling out the window, not only revealing a shapely and trim calf and ankle but indicating that the lady attached to it had no idea that the trellis she was about to climb down would never hold her.

Robert's breath froze in his throat. Was she crazy? When he finally found his voice, ready to call out to stop her, even as her foot teetered inches above the first rail, she paused, then quickly plucked her leg back inside. The curtains settled back into place, hiding her once again.

While he wanted to strangle her for taking such a dangerous risk, a small part of him had to admire her aplomb for even considering such a daring escape.

"We could fight our way in," Aquiles suggested. Robert's servant did love a good brawl with a worthy opponent. And the large, burly footman they'd spied lounging about the front door promised to give the contentious Aquiles a good round or two.

"No, it's too risky," Robert said, shaking his head. "By the time we got to her, the watch would be on us, and then where would we be? It would only be our word against Chambley's that he, the King's own representative, is a traitor and his houseguest holds the very fate of the Peninsula. No, we need to take the lady without witnesses." Robert glanced back up at the window so high above them.

What the devil had she been thinking aligning herself with Chambley? That she'd changed her mind was obvious, but that still didn't explain why she'd gone with him in the first place.

Part of him wanted to believe her claim of noble duty to the Spanish treasure—the same part that found her kisses intoxicating and her spirited manners a challenging delight.

But her arrival at Chambley's house only gave further evidence against her, and that, coupled with her treasonous and murderous past, made it hard for him to believe that the lady's lips were nothing more than the product of a skilled liar.

That didn't, however, preclude him from gaining her back from Chambley, whether willingly or not.

When they started out of the hedge, Robert's jacket got caught on a branch. As he turned to free himself, he spied a set of stairs, nearly hidden amongst the overgrown tangle, leading down to the cellar. They broke their way through the shrubbery, and as luck would have it, the long-forgotten entrance was not only unlocked but unguarded.

Finally inside the house, they discovered Chambley kept a minimal staff, for they saw only one or two housemaids as they dashed quietly through the halls.

In one of the rooms they ducked into to hide from a maid, they found it already occupied by one of Chambley's more fierce looking dogs. The great creature opened one lazy eye and growled.

That was enough for Aquiles. "Get me out of here," the man whispered, nearly climbing up Robert like a ladder. For a man who could bring down his enemy with one fist, Aquiles held an unequaled fear of dogs.

Robert nearly growled himself. "Pretend it's a cat."

"Bah!" Aquiles spat. "We should have fought our way in. Or called the Guard to help."

"Because of a pack of overfed hounds? You've been away from the front for too long." Robert peeked out the door into the hallway. "It's clear, we can go."

Aquiles barreled out of the room, nearly running down Robert in the process.

Very quickly, they found themselves in front of the door to the room Robert suspected held Miss Sutton.

"On the count of three," Robert whispered, his hand on the latch. He held up his fingers and as he counted them off, he started to turn the handle.

On three they burst through the door, only to see a flash of muslin going toward the window.

"Dammit," Robert cursed, as he dashed into the room. Before he could stop her, Miss Sutton flung herself over the sill and out the window.

"Aaahh," came her terrified cry, followed by the splintering crash of wood. "Oh, help!"

Robert made it to the window only to find Miss Sutton dangling by one hand. Beneath her, the trellis had crumbled and she had nothing nearby to use as a footing or a handhold.

He caught her by the wrist immediately and held on with all his might. Although she appeared to be a slight thing, hanging four floors above the garden, she felt as if she could rival Aquiles.

Glancing over his shoulder, he called out to his servant, "I need a hand here."

Aquiles only shook his head, pointing at the monstrous dog seated in the middle of the room, its tail wagging invitingly.

"Oh, come on," Robert said, leaning out the window and catching her other arm. Aquiles's head shuddered back and forth, his eyes never leaving his brindled nemesis.

Olivia's hand slipped, and he held on tighter. "I don't think I can get her inside by myself," he told his servant.

It probably wasn't the best thing he could have said, for she only struggled harder now, making it that much more difficult to hold onto her. Her eyes had grown wider than a pair of his aunt's best dinner platters.

"Hold still," he told her.

"You've got to get me up," she sputtered, her feet peddling against the bricks, trying to find a toehold anywhere.

"It would have helped if you hadn't decided to jump out the window," he shot back, tugging at her and making some progress in lifting her.

"This is hardly my fault," Olivia told him as he finally managed to hoist her up and through the window. She fell against him, her body molding to his, her chest heaving as she tried to catch her breath. He steadied her as he found his own.

"I would have been just as happy . . ." she sputtered, "to escape out the door . . . if you hadn't come bursting in here . . . scaring me out of my wits."

"Scaring you?" Robert shot back, trying to ignore the heated response his body was having to her in his arms. She would have looked thoroughly scared and innocent, like someone in over her head, if it hadn't been for her righteous indignation. But fury and Miss Sutton seemed to agree with each other, and he found it a compelling mixture. He couldn't help provoking her a little further. "Look what you've done to my servant."

She swiped at her errant curls and looked over his

shoulder at his still cowering batman. "This is who you bring to rescue me?" When she glanced back at him, her mouth twisted into a wry smile, surprising him with the intimacy of it—as if it were meant to share some secret just for them.

For a moment it was like it had been earlier in the park, just before he'd stolen that fateful kiss. But this time they both knew what awaited them, and it seemed to Robert that the lady was not only waiting for him but more than willing.

Then suddenly she seemed to grow only too aware of her proximity to him and the heated sparks between them, for she pushed away from him, a blush coming to her face.

"I didn't need rescuing, thank you very much," she said, the annoyance returning to her voice.

"I didn't exactly come here to rescue you," he told her. "Rather to borrow you back."

Her mouth closed tightly, and she promptly bustled past him to her discarded valise. "I should have suspected as much from the likes of you."

She made it sound as if he were some Seven Dials shyster and not Wellington's representative. But then again, he realized, she didn't know he was here as the general's handpicked agent.

"Now, if you are done making matters worse," she was saying, "I'll be leaving." With a pat of her hand to her hip, the dog trotted obediently to her side and followed her out the door.

Aquiles scrambled atop the nearest chair to get out of the beast's path. And Robert had to wonder if it was the dog or the click of Miss Sutton's determined heels that sent the man skittering for higher ground.

Robert stared after her. He couldn't quite believe

her audacity. He'd just plucked her off a ledge, and she blamed him for the entire incident. More than that, she had a way of tangling with his senses, leaving him wavering between kissing her and strangling her.

Well, there was one thing he could say about her, she was a determined chit, there was no arguing that.

"Come on," he barked at Aquiles as he went off after her.

She'd made it to the landing by the time they caught up with her. She glanced back at them, her gaze rolling upward, and then after a disgusted shake of her head, she continued down the stairs.

"You aren't going anywhere without me," he told her, catching her by the elbow.

She whirled around and leveled another one of those damned pistols of hers at him. How many firearms could one woman possess?

"I wouldn't be so sure, if I were you," she said.

He vowed right there and then, the first chance he got, he was going to get every blasted one of them away from her once and for all and toss them all into the Thames. He had half a mind to dunk her a couple of times as well, just for good measure.

So off she went, with Robert and Aquiles trailing after her.

"How do you know which way to go?" he asked her.

"I don't," she whispered back.

"Then you'll get us all caught," he told her. "If you would for just one moment trust me, let me explain everything, I'd have you out of here and somewhere safe—on my word as a gentleman."

"Bah," she told him. "Lord Chambley made much the same offer earlier. I've had enough *gentlemanly* promises for one day."

She continued on but was forced to stop at the next landing as two maids on the floor below passed by.

Her apparent disbelief that he possessed not an iota of honor stung. For a man who regarded his honor as impeccable, his integrity, his life blood, to have someone, especially a woman surrounded by treasonous circumstances, scoff at his intentions as anything less than noble was inconceivable. Her chiding tones got the better of him.

"What is the matter, Miss Sutton, wouldn't Chambley cut you in for your fair share?" he asked, sidling up to her and ignoring her scowl at his unwanted presence.

"No." She shoved her way past him and continued down the stairs. "He wants the entire thing for himself."

"So Chambley intends to cheat you."

"Cheat me—bah! He means to kill me."

"Kill you?" He grinned at her. "What did you do? Shoot at him as well?"

She didn't say a word at first. Then she cast a disgruntled look over her shoulder at him. "It seems his lordship is not so unlike everyone else who is mad to have *El Rescate*." Her glance said only too clearly she included him in that greedy lot.

It tweaked his pride anew to have her think so little of his motives, but he had to admit he hadn't given her any evidence to think otherwise.

They turned down another hall, only to find Lord Chambley's burliest servant lounging near a doorway.

"Milo," she whispered, obviously having met the brute earlier. Her softly muttered utterance carried louder than Robert was comfortable hearing, and Milo raised his lolling head to determine the source.

Damnation, he'd had enough of letting her lead the way, pistol or no. He caught her in his arms, one hand over her mouth and the other around her waist, and yanked her back around the corner and into the nearest room.

Her canine friend followed obediently, settling himself down on the nearest rug and looking at the pair of them expectantly, as if he couldn't wait for the inevitable fireworks at this turn of events.

When Aquiles got the door closed behind them, Robert released his hand from her mouth.

"Unhand me!" she snapped, wrestling out of his arms and once again aiming her confounded pistol at him.

"You are going to listen to me," he told her. "Whether you like it or not."

She cocked one brow, as if to say whatever his case, she would find it sadly lacking in truth.

"Oh, let me guess," she said. "You are here on a secret mission to recover The King's Ransom. Probably sent by Wellington himself to see the treasure recovered for the good of the Spanish people and for the glory of England."

"Well, yes, that's exactly it," he said, feeling a little let down to have his plans so completely exposed.

She threw up her hands. "Do you think I am such a simpleton to fall for such an idiotic story?"

"But it's true," he sputtered.

"Harumph!" she said, dismissing him with a wave of the pistol. "You can tell me whatever lies you like, Mr. Danvers, but at a time that is a little more convenient for me. Lord Chambley was called away, but there is no telling how long he will be gone. And I have every intention of being quite a ways from this house before he returns. . . ." She let out a long sigh which seemed to end her sentence with one very adamant thought.

And I'll be gone from here without you.

"Oh, I have a feeling Lord Chambley will be delayed for some time," he said as she beat a retreat toward the door.

She stopped and whirled around, pointing the pistol at him like an accusing finger. "You sent the note."

He would have smiled if he hadn't been staring down the barrel of that infernal piece. "And unfortunately Lord Chambley's carriage is about to lose a wheel. Someone should have warned him before he got into such an unsafe conveyance."

His self-satisfied answer obviously didn't offer much merit for his case in her court as she set off again, muttering an expletive about his parentage that no decent lady should have ever been able to put together.

Somehow it only made him admire her more.

Outside the room, the house suddenly bustled with activity. And only too quickly they discovered why.

"Where is Milo?" Lord Chambley's question boomed through the house. "Find him immediately. I want him to attend me upstairs with our guest."

"So much for your note," she shot over her shoulder at him.

Olivia counted silently to ten. How had she gotten into this mess? While her heart told her that Robert was the hero she'd been waiting for, experience made her wary of trusting him—no matter that he'd single-handedly saved her life by pulling her to safety from the window ledge. Or that he'd come to rescue her.

Honestly, she wasn't convinced he'd come to rescue her at all. He'd probably just done all this because she was the key to finding *El Rescate del Rey*.

Oh, he was no better than Bradstone—or Chambley, for that matter.

But her heart clamored a different argument, especially when he took her hand in his.

"Come along," he told her. "We're getting out of here."

She turned around to find Robert's servant already out the window, the pair having devised an impromptu rope with the window hangings.

Olivia backed away from him. There was no way she was going out another window.

"I think you are forgetting I have this." She held up the pistol. If she was going out of this house, she'd make her escape in a more conventional route—like a highwayman, not like a chimney sweep.

"Would you put that fool thing away before you shoot yourself, or worse, me." He reached out so quickly, she barely saw his arm move. And in a flash, he'd stripped the pistol from her hand and had it stuffed back into her valise. Taking up her battered bag, he pointed a finger at the open window. "Now quit being foolish and come along. It's the only way." He turned toward the window, as if she was just going to follow him because he'd said so.

'Twas almost laughable, but this was the way she'd always imagined Hobbe would sweep into her life—commanding and direct. Yet, while her heart hammered that this was the rescue she'd imagined and she should be throwing herself into his worthy and oh so capable arms, her previous experience with Lord Chambley's windows and her cowardice over heights was too much for her to just give in to her foolish fantasies.

Racing to the door, she listened for half a second,

and hearing nothing beyond the portal, she swung the door open.

From behind her came an outraged protest. "Olivia! No!"

As it turned out, her hero had been right and her escape turned out to be short-lived.

"Well, what a surprise to find you here, Bradstone," Chambley drawled at Robert. "I should have recognized your ill-conceived bumbling on that wild-goose chase to Castlereagh. Lucky for me, I ended up going past his carriage not far from here, and we were able to complete our business without me having to go all the way over to his office." Chambley pulled a pistol from his pocket and pointed it at Robert. "*Partners* should trust one another, I've always thought, but apparently we don't share that philosophy."

He cocked the hammer back, aiming the weapon at Robert's chest.

Before she realized what she was doing, Olivia surged between them. "Don't kill him. I'll give you what you want, just don't kill him." What the devil was she saying? Why was she protecting this man when Chambley had just said they were partners?

Chambley glanced over her shoulder at Robert, his lips curled in a sneer. "How do you keep convincing this chit that you care about her?" He then turned his gaze back to Olivia. "*Still* falling for his charms, my dear? Don't you know he doesn't care a whit for you? Never did, never will. Isn't that right, Bradstone?" He took a step closer to her so that the muzzle of the gun rested between her breasts. "You've only been important to us for one thing—providing the whereabouts of the King's Ransom."

Olivia's gaze narrowed. Chambley truly thought the

man before him was the Marquis of Bradstone. The real Lord Bradstone. *So what if this Robert was telling the truth?*

"Let us go, and I'll give you what you want," she said, her mind awhirl.

"You'll give me what I want? How kind of you," he mocked. "But you don't seem to realize I'm in no mood for bargaining. And as long as I hold this gun, you are in no position to do anything other than to tell me what I want."

She stood her ground. "I won't tell you a thing until you release him," she said, nodding at Robert.

"Olivia—" Robert began to protest.

"Silence, Bradstone," Chambley ordered. "You'd do well to remember Sir Sutton's fate."

"My father?" Olivia asked, an ominous chill running down her spine. "What has he to do with this?"

Chambley's thick lips spread into a malevolent smile. "Your lover over there and I approached your father about joining our little venture, but he refused. Quite adamantly. Wouldn't hear of stealing the missive, though it would have made him a wealthy man instead of the poor, misguided scholar that he was. How unfortunate for him that he didn't see our offer as the opportunity that it was, eh, Bradstone?"

Robert said nothing.

"Perhaps if he'd agreed, those damning letters from the Dutch wouldn't have been found in his possession."

"You did that," Olivia said. "*You* set him up as a traitor."

"Of course I did. We both did," Chambley said, nodding at Robert. "And still your sire refused to help us."

Robert surged forward. "You bastard."

Chambley swung the pistol toward him. "What, Bradstone? Don't you want your little bit of muslin here to know your part in her father's unfortunate demise? I don't think she'll mind much. After all, she did come running back to you like a bitch in heat. She appears to be as eager for you now as she was back then, eh, my good man?"

Olivia had never believed her father had committed the treasonous acts he'd been accused of, no more than she had thought him capable of such an unholy act as suicide.

"He didn't hang himself," she whispered. "You did it."

"I had help," he replied. "Didn't I, Bradstone?"

Olivia struggled to catch her breath. Her father had been murdered. Betrayed by Bradstone and Chambley because he'd refused to aid them.

Suddenly her entire past was rewritten, and Bradstone's betrayal became only that much more poisonous. It hadn't been some twist of fate that had led the marquis to court her but part of a calculated plan.

And when they'd failed to gain her father's support, they'd taken advantage of her naiveté and grief by sending the handsome and only too eligible Bradstone to ensnare her. While her mother had welcomed his advances toward her daughter because he was rich and titled, Olivia had been too inexperienced and blindly smitten to see the devilish truth.

But it was time for a measure of retribution. Bradstone may have already received his just due, but Chambley still lived. So she would give him what he so desperately wanted—The King's Ransom. It was her only bargaining chip and a gamble she was willing to take. Not that any of her notes or the coded missive would be of help. For by the time he could find anyone to decipher her research—that is, if there was anyone capable of doing so—she and Robert would be well gone from here.

She hoped the riddle of *El Rescate* drove Chambley mad.

In the meantime, her plan would buy her life and time to determine whom she could trust. Or if she would ever trust another man again.

She snatched her satchel free from Robert's grasp and tossed it down on the floor between her feet and Chambley's. "Take it. All my notes are inside. Everything you want. The directions to the treasure, where it is buried, everything. They are yours, if you let us leave."

Chambley eyed her. "You still want him? Didn't you hear me, you numb-witted little fool? The man killed your father."

She shrugged. "I don't care. Just let us leave."

Silence descended around them as Chambley considered her offer. Then he bent over and snatched up the bag and as he rose, he pointed the pistol at Olivia.

The next few moments replayed like the past. In an instant she thought she was back in the library with Bradstone and it was another man leaping forward to save her.

Even the voice sounded eerily the same.

"No!" Robert shouted, as he grabbed her, throwing her out of harm's way.

The report sounded just the same to her ears, ringing forever and then suddenly stilled as she hit the floor hard, Robert's body covering hers, shielding her from harm, sheltering her from Chambley's evil intentions.

The dog that had followed her barked wildly, running in circles and howling at Chambley as if he were the devil himself.

"Shut up," Chambley told it, stepping here and there away from its snapping teeth. "Shut up." In his hasty movements, he kicked her valise toward her, and now it lay open, the butt of Jemmy's other pistol poised and waiting for her.

Olivia took advantage of the man's distracted attention and groped wildly for it, but Robert's inert body held her pinned to the ground.

The gun was just a hair's breadth out of reach, but still she struggled to get it, for she could see Chambley reaching into his coat.

Then as her hand closed over the butt, she saw out of the corner of her eye Chambley pulling out a second pistol and taking aim at them.

She didn't think, rather she reacted, this time out of instinct more than the hatred burning through her. Her arm came up, her finger tugged the trigger, and a second shot exploded, this time felling Chambley.

She watched him whirl back and land in a heap at the base of the stairs.

The blast seemed to bring Robert to life. He struggled to his feet, sparing a glance at Chambley, then down at Olivia. "Are you hurt?" he asked her.

She shook her head, unable to take her eyes off Chambley. Her blazing need for revenge fled in the face of what she'd just done.

Dear God, she'd shot a man.

Chambley lay howling and writhing on the floor, clutching at his arm and cursing everyone in sight.

"We must get to the carriage," Robert said, grabbing first her valise, then her hand, and towing her from the frightful scene.

"Not with you," she protested, trying to dig in her heels.

Robert appeared unmoved and didn't stop his forward momentum down the stairs and out of the maze that comprised Chambley's house. "A few minutes ago you couldn't wait to leave and now you want to stay?"

"That was before I killed a man," she offered, coming up with the only excuse she could think of other than the truth.

"You didn't kill anyone. You only winged him."

"Are you sure?"

"Yes."

She glanced back up the stairs, where even now a tide of servants was rushing to the aid of their master. "I think his injury will be grave, for I've never missed."

Robert made a disgruntled sound in the back of his throat and reached over and took the still smoking weapon from her hand. "Unfortunately for us, you chose today to start. Now he'll be able to raise the Watch, probably even the dead with all his caterwauling."

"Still, perhaps we should call for a surgeon," she said, trying to delay what she now saw was inevitable.

She'd tumbled out of Chambley's prison into another.

"You're coming with me," he told her.

They ran out the front door, Robert brandishing her pistol at anyone who stepped in their path. Down into the street they went, where a carriage lurched forward to meet them.

Olivia looked up to see Aquiles's grim face.

"I heard the shots. Is that bastard dead?" he asked.

Robert shook his head. "No."

His servant uttered a curse in Spanish, the translation of which brought a blush to Olivia's already flushed cheeks.

Without any ceremony, Olivia found herself hoisted inside and tossed into the nearest seat. Robert was no more than a hair's breadth behind her, when Aquiles shouted at the horses and the carriage careened forward. The abrupt departure sent Olivia crashing into Robert.

Everywhere Olivia tried to find a handhold, she found nothing but the hard, unforgiving muscle of Robert's body.

The man who had just saved her from death.

"Thank you," she murmured as she righted herself by catching hold of his arm. His closeness made her breathe a little faster, her heart beat with an irrational flutter. "Thank you, sir, for saving my life," she whispered.

He glanced down at her hand still resting on his arm. "You may not thank me later," he said, with a wave of his hand that shook off her touch.

Feeling embarrassed by her heated response to him, she scrambled to the other side of the carriage, staring down at her tingling hands now primly folded in her lap.

Only then did she realize they were covered in blood.

Robert's blood.

Her gaze flew up to him. Her mouth opened in a wide O at the red stain now spilling from his sleeve and soaking his jacket.

Obviously Chambley hadn't missed his target.

"You're hurt," she managed to gasp, clambering

back across the swaying carriage until she sat beside him.

His face was set in a granite fortitude. "It's nothing." He nodded at the ragged portion of his coat. "I'll be fine, though this coat is probably done for." His hard green eyes sparkled for a moment.

Despite his poor attempt at a jest, Olivia could see a wildness behind his gaze, an animal rage fighting against what must be searing pain. "You've been shot. You need to see a surgeon, a doctor."

"If you've forgotten, you've just shot a man. A rather important one. The Watch, Bow Street, everyone will be looking for us. A doctor is a luxury we can ill-afford at the moment." He made a couple of attempts to shrug out of his coat, but to no avail.

Olivia reached forward to help him, her heart hammering as she gently tried to ease off the tight-fitting coat without causing him any more pain than was necessary.

Once it was free, she saw only too clearly the ugly hole in his upper arm. She'd only seen one other such injury—on that night in Chambley's library—and that experience hadn't given her any better stomach for the horrors that a bullet could inflict on a man's flesh.

She looked away for a moment, calming the rolling tide in her gut. Swallowing back the bile threatening to rise, she took a deep breath and ripped his shirt further, exposing his arm, which was bleeding at an alarming rate.

"Oh, dear," she managed to whisper. "I'll need to bind it."

He was already tugging at his neckcloth. "Use this."

She reached up and started to unwind the cloth. Her efforts brought her face to face with this stranger.

This wary hero. She paused for a moment, staring into his pain-filled gaze. "Who are you?"

"Robert Danvers." He looked down at the gaping wound in his arm. "Well, actually Major Robert Danvers, of Wellington's private staff."

"Still joking," she said, trying to make light of the moment, as she finished unwinding the cravat. Carefully she wrapped the injury with the length of silk.

"This is no joke, madame," he said through gritted teeth as she made another pass. "I truly am here at the behest of Wellington."

For a moment Olivia said nothing. Even if he was telling the truth, it was all so unbelievable. "You look just like him," she said, breaking the strained silence between them.

"Bind it tighter," he told her, nodding at her work. As she did his bidding and pulled the ends together, he said, "He was my cousin."

"Distant, I would guess. Lord Bradstone would never have saved my life over his. But it does explain the differences between the two of you." She finished the job by tying the ends into a sturdy knot and smiled weakly.

He studied her for a moment, his gaze searching. "What differences?"

What could she tell him—that his kiss had given him away? That it had touched her heart in a way she'd never thought possible? That he'd come to her rescue like the hero she'd spent countless nights imagining?

"The scar," she said quickly, now wishing she hadn't said anything. "Your hair. Your clothes. Lord Bradstone wouldn't have been caught dead in that jacket or badly tied neckerchief."

"You could say he almost was," he joked. "A couple

of inches more to the right, and Chambley would have put that bullet through my heart. My poor valet, he would never have been able to find work ever again after my disgraceful appearance at my demise."

Olivia laughed despite herself. Though she didn't see how he could make jokes, especially given how gray he was turning. His eyes started to close, and he leaned heavily against her. Oh, dear, what if he were to . . . Her heart lurched at the thought of him dying. Of him leaving her alone . . . once again.

He may not be her Hobbe, but he was the closest thing to a hero she'd ever found.

"We need to find you a surgeon," she said.

"I need to find that blasted treasure," he told her.

"It won't do you any good if you are dead."

He took a deep breath, as if trying to hold onto his composure. "Madame, without it, you and I are surely dead."

Chapter 6

"What the devil were you thinking, bringing her here?" Pymm asked, after his servant, a scrawny lad by the name of Cochrane, had been dispatched to fetch the local surgeon. "The Watch, Bow Street and every citizen in between is on the lookout for her and you."

Robert held his ground, shaky though it was—his shoulder throbbing and his control wavering because of the tremendous loss of blood from Chambley's poorly aimed shot.

"Look at you!" Pymm complained. "You know how much it is going to cost me to get everyone around here who's seen you to forget this . . . this . . . sight." He flapped his arms in despair.

So his coat and shirt were soaked in blood—he probably wasn't the first poor sot to come slinking into Pymm's neighborhood, battered and bleeding. And it hadn't been his first choice to bring Olivia to Seven Dials either, but he knew of no other place where he could take the woman. Or any other place where his injuries could be tended without anyone asking for more than a handful of coins to look the other way.

"What would you have suggested I do?" he asked his unwilling host. "Go to Bradstone House, where the Watch was probably waiting for me? Or better yet, leave her at Chambley's?"

Pymm nodded emphatically at this idea. "Yes. That's it. You should have left her behind." He glanced again at the closet door, where Olivia had started kicking the panel and calling out an ugly assortment of invectives. "We wouldn't be in this mess if she weren't such an uncooperative bit o' muslin. This just proves my theory she's a danger to every man she meets. She probably set the French after the *Bon Venture* after your cousin deserted her."

Having seen the lady in action, Robert wouldn't put it past her. But right now he needed Pymm's help, and there was one sure way to guarantee it. "She knows where *it* is."

Robert didn't have to say what *it* was, for the light that blazed to life in Pymm's beady gaze said only too clearly that they both understood what this meant.

The King's Ransom.

"Where?" Pymm managed to whisper.

"I don't know. She won't say."

"Why not? What does she want? Money? Amnesty? A nice cold dark cell in Newgate?" Pymm's indignation that anyone would not immediately help their cause was almost comical, considering the first thing he'd done when his unwanted guests had arrived was demand that Olivia be locked in a windowless closet attached to the main room. And there she had remained secured for the past hour.

Of course, the *first* thing Robert had done before putting her in there had been to check within to make sure there were no other avenues of escape.

Olivia hadn't gone in willingly, and even with the heavy door barred shut, she'd pounded and complained and cursed at her imprisonment without any sign of letting up—though in the last few minutes her tirade had dwindled to a muttering stream of curses as to his likely parentage.

"She claims she will not divulge a word," Robert said.

Pymm sniffed at this. "I have some associates who could convince her to talk."

He could well imagine Pymm's associates and doubted even these masters of persuasion could get the lady to reveal anything.

Olivia Sutton was the most stubborn woman alive.

Just then the door to Pymm's apartment sprang open.

Aquiles, who had until now appeared to be slumbering on a chair against the door to Olivia's prison, sprang to life, pistol in hand, his black eyes blazing with the fury of Blackbeard's ghost.

Cochrane's eyes widened with fright, and his lips flapped with words they couldn't summon forth.

Pymm shooed Aquiles back to his post. "What is it, boy? Where is Becker?"

The boy's gaze never left Aquiles when he answered. "Sorry, sir, but Mr. Becker can't come. Too many of the Watch and Runners skulking about, looking to find 'im," he said, nodding toward Robert. The boy had not arrived entirely empty-handed though.

He reached inside his ragged jacket and pulled out a packet. "Mr. Becker, sir, says this ought to set the gentleman to rights, iffin you can find someone to sew 'im up."

Aquiles opened the boy's offering. Inside lay clean linen cloths, a needle and black thread, along with a packet of some foul-smelling concoction.

" 'E says you're to make a poultice out of those," the little urchin said, pointing at the folded paper. "And to bind it to the wound after yer done stitching the hole shut." The boy rubbed at his nose. "Oh, and he wanted to know iffin you'd got the lead out of there."

"Passed clean through," Robert told him.

The boy nodded. "Good. 'E said iffin you hadn't and couldn't get it out, not to tell you that you'd likely die." Cochrane shrugged and took up his post on a stool near the fireplace.

Pymm didn't so much as take another breath before continuing his protest. "Runners? I detest those drunken sots. I won't have them lurking about my business! Do you realize what this may cost me?" The man fidgeted about the small, cluttered apartment, adroitly sliding through the maze that made up the room—a couple of chairs scattered around a battered table, a long sideboard against the wall, topped with several half-filled or nearly empty decanters, an assortment of chipped cups and glasses, a plate and some cutlery. The far wall, if it could be called that considering the small space his apartment afforded, featured a fireplace and a small trundle bed tucked nearby. And everywhere there were piles of papers and notes and maps, as if all the secrets of the British Empire lay rotting in this godforsaken corner of Seven Dials.

Pymm, glass in hand, the contents slopping over

the side and onto the much-stained carpet, stopped his pacing in front of Robert. "I can't protect you now," he said. "I won't protect *her*."

"No one is asking you to protect her," Robert told him. *That was his job.*

The ferocity of his conviction stopped him cold. He tried telling himself that Miss Sutton's welfare was a matter of national importance—but in the last few hours he'd almost forgotten that. Forgotten the *real* reason he'd come to London. His resolve, his intentions, lost in the wake of her kiss and his own traitorous response to it.

"It's not like she murdered Chambley," he heard himself saying, defending the very woman he suspected of the worst kind of treachery. "Besides, you should be thankful. She stopped him from killing me."

Pymm didn't look all that indebted. "Shooting Chambley might have been a favor to those of us on the right side. Unfortunately there are too many people who view him as one of our allies. I wouldn't be surprised if the Prince Regent has called for her arrest and following that, he'll demand that you be brought to justice as well for your hand in all this." Pymm eyed his nearly empty glass and frowned.

Ambling over to the battered sideboard, he poured himself a glass of the dark liquid. He tossed back his newly poured drink in one hearty gulp. Then, as if he finally remembered he had guests, he poured another glass and held it out for Aquiles, who paused in his ministrations to Robert's shoulder long enough to partake of Pymm's poor fare.

When Pymm held up another glass for Robert, he waved the offer off, his stomach turning at what he guessed were the contents of the decanter. Knowing their host and his parsimonious ways, he guessed that Pymm probably bought his private stock from the Rose and Lion.

Robert shuddered.

Aquiles paused, needle in hand. "I haven't even started yet. What are you shaking about for?" He nodded toward the decanter. "Take some of that. It will make you forget what I am about to do."

Robert looked over at the needle and the black thread and then down at the ragged hole in his arm. He could barely think through the searing pain. And yet Olivia's words rang in his ears, rising through the excruciating din.

I've never missed.

Hardly the confession of an innocent miss. But also the first bit of evidence he'd been looking for in what he considered his true reason for coming to London.

To finish the mission started by that ill-fated agent seven years ago—Orlando Danvers.

His brother.

Dead and gone these past seven years, but never forgotten. Robert's youngest brother, the serious one, the one who'd longed to show his elder brothers that he too could carry out the family legacy of adventure.

He'd certainly had the bloodlines for it.

After Robert's mother, Susannah, had died, his father, Lord Danvers, had been assigned to a posting in Spain. There he had met and eloped (once again) with Maria Elena, the fiery and outspoken daughter of a highly placed Spanish grandee who'd made a fortune in the New World in his youth. Once the scandal at this impetuous and impossible marriage had died down, Maria Elena's relations had welcomed the Danvers children into their warm fold and given Robert and

Colin the only family they had ever known, especially since the Danvers brood had grown to include two more sons, Raphael and Orlando.

Robert glanced over at the door to the closet, where Miss Sutton continued to pound and protest at her imprisonment.

The only witness to his brother's murder and very possibly the one who pulled the trigger.

I've never missed.

Oh, if she only knew how those words damned her in his eyes.

But leave it to his canny servant to know exactly what he was thinking. "Bah!" Aquiles said. "She's no killer." The man stopped threading his needle for a moment. "Considering what that man told her about her father, yer lucky she didn't shoot you first."

Robert shook his head. "She didn't kill me because she knows I'm not Bradstone."

At this Pymm sputtered over his drink. "She knows what?" he managed to choke out.

"She guessed it this morning," Robert admitted.

Pymm's already ruddy face went to a mottled color of rage. "Oh, this is most impossible. Ruinous. How did she find out?" He paused for a moment. "You didn't take her to your bed, did you?"

Robert flinched, less from Aquiles's rough stitching than from Pymm's perceptive inquiry.

"Does it matter?" He wasn't about to confess that he had been kissing the woman suspected of murdering his brother. And worse still, that he'd enjoyed her traitorous lips more than he cared to admit.

"This might hurt ye a bit," Aquiles warned.

A bit? Robert hadn't even a second to brace himself as his devil of a servant pulled and knotted the thread, a hot blinding pain shooting through his chest and down his arm to his very fingertips.

For a moment, he sputtered over a curse, until Aquiles finished his work by pushing a glass of Pymm's bitter brew into his hand and forcing him to take the measure in one hearty toss.

"There you are, lad," his servant said, as he finished his work by adding the surgeon's foul-smelling poultice to Robert's shoulder and binding it there with a clean linen cloth. "Good as new."

From the door of the closet, Miss Sutton's pounding took on a new immediacy. "Let me out. I say, let me out immediately. There is something in here." This was followed by a loud shriek and even more frantic hammering on the wooden panels.

"Damn rats," Pymm muttered.

"She's in there with rats?" Robert asked.

Pymm shrugged. "Better in there than out here."

Robert turned to Aquiles. "Get her out."

The moment the door opened, Miss Sutton came hauling into the dimly lit apartment as if her skirt were on fire. Inside the closet, a lone rat sat cowering in the corner.

Apparently even rodents feared the woman. And with good reason. She was a bossy shrew.

And she started right in. "How dare you lock me in that wretched hole, you—" Her harangue halted as her gaze locked onto the bandage over his shoulder. Her features whitened for a moment before she set her mouth in a grim line and marched over to his side. "Who tied this?" It was no mere question but an imperious demand.

"Well, I did, miss," Aquiles said sheepishly.

"It will never stay put like this." Without even so

much as a by your leave, she set to work unwrapping Aquiles's handiwork.

"Do you mind?" Robert asked her. "What do you know of dressing wounds?"

"Enough," she said through gritted teeth.

It was not the answer he wanted to hear. His hand shot up and caught her wrist. "Aquiles's work is good enough for me."

She stared at him for a moment with those compelling blue eyes of hers. Beneath his fingers, her pulse beat a wild tattoo, so alive and yet so fragile.

In a blink of an eye he wanted to trust her—trust her as he'd never trusted another human being. Yes, he trusted Aquiles, he even trusted Pymm, even if they didn't see eye to eye on everything.

But this woman wanted him to trust her on a level that touched his heart. A connection born out of a kiss and pulling them together with intangible ribbons of fate.

Somewhere in between kissing her and watching her strike into action today at Chambley's had left him intrigued.

More than intrigued, and damned if he understood the half of it. Her impassioned demeanor, the unending contradictions that encircled her, her fierce independence—they'd cast a net around him, ensnaring him. But there was also something about this woman that he'd never encountered before, like a far-off campfire on a moonless night. She offered both hope and a terrifying unknown.

Then, as if she too felt the strange bond between them and was unwilling to bind herself in its tangled web, she wrenched her arm free.

He had to wonder whether if he'd had the strength

to stop her, if he would have let her go. He shook off the unthinkable notion and said curtly, "I've had worse injuries. I'll be fine."

She took another disdainful glance at Aquiles's doctoring. "Good enough if you want to die from infection," she sniffed. "I know what I am doing. I've tended more grievous injuries than this."

Part of him wanted her to say she'd never seen anything so bad in her life, she'd never witnessed anything as foul as she'd seen today. He didn't know why, barely understood it, but he wanted to believe this woman innocent of Orlando's murder.

But he couldn't stop replaying in his head what had happened just a few hours ago.

The report of Chambley's pistol. The searing hot burn of lead as it passed through his shoulder.

He'd lain there, stunned and unable to move, seeing only Chambley's wry grin as the man had reached for his second weapon. But beneath him, Olivia Sutton had struggled forth. She'd fought and clawed her way to her pistol, and once it had found its way into her capable grasp, she'd taken her shot at Chambley even as the man sought to consign Robert to hell.

She'd saved his life. This wanted murderess had saved his life as steadfastly and unhesitantly as it was said she killed his brother.

Now this woman was carefully unwinding the bandages over his wound with a practiced, gentle touch. When she got to the poultice, she dispatched the foul-smelling concoction without a second glance.

Her lips pursed as she eyed Aquiles's needlework. "The stitching looks well enough." She turned to his servant. "Is this your handiwork?"

Aquiles nodded.

"Did you heat the needle before you stitched him up?"

The man shook his head.

Olivia followed suit, shaking hers. "Fools. I wouldn't be surprised if you had a fever before morning. Lady Finch insists a heated needle makes a better stitch and doesn't get infected as often." She sighed. "You, there," she said, snapping at Cochrane, who so far had remained tucked in a corner, taking in the proceedings with a practiced ear. "Go to the apothecary's and fetch me the following items." She ticked off a long list and turned to Robert. "From the looks of this place, he'll need money."

Robert nearly laughed at Pymm's rather affronted look. He nodded toward his money pouch lying on the table. "Give him what he'll need as long as you promise not to poison me with that witch's brew."

Now it was Olivia's turn to look insulted. "If I wanted you dead, don't you think I would have done it by now?"

Exactly his own question. Why had she saved him? But instead of asking, he shot back. "Oh, yes, better to let me live so you can prolong my misery."

Olivia ignored him as she counted out the coins, adding a few more as an afterthought. "Tell the man you want fresh supplies," she told the boy. "Nothing with mildew or dust. Tell him I'll come down and discuss the matter if he sends inferior samples."

The boy nodded, his eyes wide and his fingers clenched over the coins.

"Well, get on with you," she told him.

Cochrane scrambled out of the apartment in the wake of her feminine tyranny.

"Now see here," Pymm said, finally summoning up the words to confront her. "You are not in charge of this establishment. Quite the contrary, Miss Sutton. I'd say you'd be well served right back in the closet if you don't—"

The man's lofty orders came to a fast halt when the lady turned in his direction, her hard gaze seeming to pin him to the spot where he had once stood with such rabid assurance. "Who is this?" she asked Robert.

"An associate of mine," he told her.

"Harumph." She cast another skeptical glance at Pymm. "Does he have a name?"

Robert nodded. "Miss Olivia Sutton, may I introduce to you Mr. Pymm. He may not be the most affectionate or gracious of hosts, but he is highly regarded in some circles."

She made another skeptical noise. "And you expect me to trust him? I've seen weasels in henhouses with more apparent character."

Robert eased himself up in his chair and grinned at Pymm. "Most would probably agree with you. But Wellington wouldn't. He rather likes Mr. Pymm here."

"Then I have to agree with Lady Finch," Olivia said, her arms crossed over her chest, her scathing gaze flicking between Pymm and Robert.

"How's that?" he asked.

"Arthur Wellesley is a horse's ass."

Olivia could tell that Lady Finch's sentiment about Wellington was not shared by any of the other occupants in the room.

She was being bossy and outspoken in the extreme.

A lesson she'd learned from Lady Finch in how to keep men off balance. Especially when she felt her own life had tipped upside down.

She'd quite possibly killed a man today and most likely would hang for her crime. At least this time she could comfort herself that she actually deserved the hangman's noose.

Her stomach rolled again, and she struggled to remain calm. If there was one thing she was certain of, it was that she had to keep her wits about her and determine whose company she'd fallen into—and how she could escape them.

She was in a poor tenement, she knew that much, somewhere in a part of London she'd never seen before. Seven Dials, she guessed. With a trio of men she had no idea if she could trust.

But you can, a small voice whispered to her.

The same voice that had urged her to stop Chambley from killing this enigmatic man before her.

Robert's hand took hers again. "You reacted as Aquiles or I might have if we hadn't been otherwise occupied. You did the right thing."

"The right thing?" Pymm blustered. "What are you nattering about?"

Robert didn't let go of her hand, his warm assurance compelling her to trust him. "She's a little overwrought about Chambley."

"Piffle," Pymm declared. "The man should have been shot years ago. Too bad he still lives. You would have saved the Crown a pretty penny, what with not having to try and hang the bastard for treason."

"My apologies," she shot back. "That would have been quite a consolation when I was hanging at Tyburn to know I saved the Treasury money."

"Both of you," Robert said, "stop this useless bickering. Right now it matters not that Chambley was shot. What matters most is the information you have regarding *El Rescate del Rey*."

Pymm's hands fluttered up and down like a hapless conductor. "Keep your voice down, you fool. Someone might hear you."

Olivia watched them both and wondered not for the first time what their stake was in all this.

If only she knew who to trust.

Trust him.

This time she recognized the voice whispering to her. An echo from the past. The boy she'd held as he died reaching out over the years, with the same insistence in his voice as he'd had that night when he'd begged her to save his mission.

Find Hobbe, he'd said. And yet she was no closer now to finding the elusive man than she had been that night.

"You can tell us where *it* is?" Mr. Pymm was asking.

Olivia held her tongue. She wasn't about to divulge a word until she had a few matters straight with them. And even then she wasn't convinced she'd reveal a word of what she knew. Especially since she wasn't convinced any of them was capable of keeping any promise.

"I will not say a word to either of you while I am imprisoned in this house. When I am free and safe, then I may share what I might know."

Pymm's gaze rolled upward, and he made a rather rude noise in the back of his throat.

She ignored him. "There is one other condition."

"Go on," Robert said, over the choking and blustering noise emanating from Mr. Pymm.

"I must find someone. A man I heard mentioned that night. When I find him, then I will be able to finish all this business."

"Now see here," Pymm said, waggling his finger under her nose. "You are in no position to start bartering with us. Do you know who you're speaking to?"

Olivia tried to keep her animosity in check. "From where I stand, I happen to be looking at a weasel of a man who locked me in a closet with rats and another who is parading about London pretending to be a man he isn't, in the company of a pirate who looks capable of slitting throats for the fun of it." She put her hands on her hips. "Not much to inspire confidence in a lady."

"That is, if she is one," she heard Pymm mutter into his cup.

"This is getting us nowhere," Robert told them. "Who is it that you seek? If anyone can find him, you can count on Pymm to be able to ferret out your confidant."

Olivia paused. She had never mentioned Hobbe to another living soul, and now her throat seemed to close around her attempt to utter his name.

Trust him, the voice urged again.

Taking a deep breath, she pushed the name past her reluctant lips. "Hobbe. I am looking for a man named Hobbe. Do you know him?"

"Hobbe, you say?" Pymm's hands fluttered again, this time in dismissal. "Never heard of him. Are you sure that is the name?"

"Yes," she said. "Hobbe. I heard the name quite clearly."

While some of the memories from that night had faded and changed in her mind, the boy's claim that

Hobbe would help her had never wavered in her recollection.

Stroking his chin, Pymm sighed, then shook his head. "Never heard of anyone with such a name. He's not in the Foreign Office, I assure you, and definitely not part of the Home Office." The man turned to Robert. "Does it sound familiar to you? An officer in the Guards, perhaps even the Dragoons?"

Olivia's gaze followed Pymm's to face Robert. For the briefest moment, she caught something in his eyes—anger, betrayal, and most importantly, recognition.

Chills spilled down her arm, leaving goose flesh in their wake.

He knew. He knew who Hobbe was. She would have bet her life on it.

But as quickly as she came to her elated conclusion, his eyes darkened and her confidence faded as the look she'd spied flashed away and was replaced with a practiced nonchalance.

But then she happened to glance at Aquiles, who looked about to chime in until an almost imperceptible flick of Robert's fingers stopped the man. Aquiles's lips closed as expeditiously as his master had hidden his own recognition.

Robert shook his head. "No, I have never heard of the man."

His every word held a quiet fury, and she wondered at this sudden transformation in him.

More rightly, this change between them. Whatever thread had found a way to tangle them together it was suddenly yanked loose—broken and frayed by her admission.

He knew Hobbe and didn't want her to find the man. But why?

One thing for certain, she was as far over her head as she imagined her innocent and scholarly-minded father had been with Bradstone and Chambley. And look where that had left him.

The chills now ran down her spine, like the fingers of death prodding her forward, leaving her heart beating a wild tattoo.

It was all she could do not to bolt out of there. And fast.

"Then I don't believe we can strike a deal, gentlemen," she finally told them, after she'd caught her breath and calmed her pounding heart. If she'd learned anything in the last few days, it was that the information she carried in her head was too valuable for them to kill her outright. As long as she clung to her secret, her life was safe. It was her only hope and buoyed her shaken confidence.

"Miss Sutton, these games are costing men their lives. You will help us," Mr. Pymm told her, his biting impatience blotting out her momentary sense of security and assurance.

"Why should I?" she asked. "Lord Chambley gave me much the same assurances, in fact he even promised me amnesty, and look where that very nearly got me."

Robert flinched as he shifted in his chair to face her. From the look of his wound it was already seeping. It tweaked at her conscience—he'd put his life at risk for her. But then again, many more had risked just as much to get their greedy hands on The King's Ransom.

Despite what her heart was telling her, she knew that this man might not be any different.

"Rest assured, Miss Sutton, you are in good hands," Pymm was saying. "We mean you no harm. We only seek information on Wellington's behalf."

Whatever she thought of Robert Danvers, she thought even less of his friend Mr. Pymm. "Wellington?" She laughed. "You expect me to believe that Lord Wellington is behind this noble endeavor?" Olivia waved her hand at his shabby apartment.

"There is nothing to laugh at," Pymm told her. "While your experiences with Chambley were regrettable, rest assured, *we* are the side of right. I work for the Foreign Office, and Robert works on Wellington's personal staff. Our credentials are impeccable. A far cry from Chambley's shady dealings."

"Yes, I can see that," she said, glancing around the poor rat's nest in which they were hiding. "Tell me, then, Mr. Pymm, exactly when did the Foreign Office and the Army take offices in this part of London?" When neither of them answered her, she continued, "Major Danvers, why don't we go down to the Army offices and you can introduce me to the Duke of York. Perhaps he can instill the measure of conviction in your claims that I find lacking."

The man let out an exasperated breath. "Very few are privy to my orders. I doubt anyone here knows about my mission."

Olivia sniffed. "How convenient." She turned to Pymm. "I suppose the Foreign Office would disavow any knowledge of you as well."

Pymm frowned. "My connections are highly confidential, my business not commonly discussed. It would be most irregular and highly inadvisable."

She nodded. "Why am I not surprised? And you shouldn't be either, when I say that if you want answers from me, you are going to have to do better than this. In fact, at this point, I can assure you that the only man I would tell about The King's Ransom is Wellington. You take me to him, and I'll dig up your treasure myself."

Pymm threw up his hands and paced the length of his apartment, stopping in front of his fireplace, muttering with each step about "impertinent and impossible females." For a moment he stared into the flames and then glanced over his shoulder back at her. "And this is your final decision, Miss Sutton?"

"Yes," she said. "So if you don't mind, I'd like to leave."

Pymm nodded and said, "As you wish, Miss Sutton. I can see you are a lady of integrity and I have to respect that. My apologies about the closet. Old habits die hard."

She nodded her acceptance but couldn't help wondering at his easy acquiescence to her refusal. The little weasel had a plan behind those beady eyes, but she couldn't fathom what it was—not yet.

The door opened, and Cochrane came hustling in like a house afire. "I got the things but don't see that there's time for them now. There's trouble brewing outside."

"What kind of trouble?" Robert asked.

"Someone asking questions about her ladyship here," the boy said, shooting Olivia a wary glance even as he set the packets of herbs and supplies she'd asked for before her on the table. "He's offering gold for any information."

"Chambley," Robert said, as if the man's name were the foulest curse.

"You might as well settle in, Miss Sutton," Pymm

said. "I can promise you that you are safe as long as you stay here."

She glanced at Robert.

"I can't protect you if you leave," he told her. "You'll be on your own."

As much as Olivia wanted nothing more to do with them, she wasn't foolish enough to think she'd find help in the Dials. Not with Lord Chambley's gold whetting the appetite of every thief and snitch within the district.

"Well, I'll stay for a bit, at least long enough to dress this wound." She turned to Pymm. "Do you have any hot water in that kettle?" she asked, nodding at the pot hung over the coals. He nodded. "Good. I'll also need something in which to steep these herbs. A clean basin or bowl."

"Anything to help," he said, far too cordial for Olivia's comfort. "Cochrane, fetch the lady whatever she needs, then go keep watch. I want no more unexpected guests." He opened the sideboard. "Oh, where are my manners? It is a good two hours past tea, and I haven't made the least offer of hospitality." The man rummaged around. "Ah, yes. A nice cup of tea to while away the time, eh, Miss Sutton?"

"That would be nice," she said, setting to work sorting the herbs Cochrane had secured. Moments later, Pymm set a cup of tea before her, the sweet distinctive odor rising from a delicate china cup sitting on a matching saucer. She suspected these were the only two items in the place that weren't chipped or dirty.

" 'Twas my mother's favorite blend and her dearest cup," he said, taking a momentary sniff into his filthy handkerchief.

With such a sentiment, Olivia could hardly refuse,

besides she hadn't had anything to eat or drink all day. She took several sips and found the brew to be surprisingly pleasant. "Hmm, this is good," she told him.

"Oh, drink up," Pymm urged her, bringing a faded teapot forward and topping off her cup. "My mother would be pleased. She said a single cup was quite restorative."

Olivia drank down the entire contents and set back to work on the herbs Cochrane had purchased.

But suddenly the careful piles she'd divided up began to blur and move. Her eyelids grew so heavy she could barely lift them. She sank to her chair and clung to the edge of the table. From a distance, she could hear Robert's outraged voice, feel his hand on her shoulder supporting her.

"Dammit, what have you done to her, Pymm?"

Funny, he sounds so far away, she thought. And yet hadn't he been right next to her?

And even as Olivia felt herself slipping into a soft, dark abyss, she distinctly heard Mr. Pymm tell Robert, "Nothing much. Just seen to it we won't be getting any more objections from the lady."

She would have argued with the man if she hadn't finally fallen prey to the comfort of oblivion.

Robert cursed again as he cradled Olivia's limp figure in his lap. "What the devil is in that brew?"

"Just a little concoction my mother used to make," Pymm said, carefully pouring the remaining contents of the teapot into a chamber pot. "She's just asleep and should remain so until morning."

"And she'll be more inclined to talk then, after you've poisoned her?"

"Of course," Pymm replied. "Because by then, you

and Miss Sutton will be well out into the Channel and on your way to Lisbon."

"Lisbon?" Robert exploded. "Are you daft?"

"It was her idea," Pymm said, pointing an accusing finger at Olivia. "I quote: 'The only man I would tell about The King's Ransom is Wellington. You take me to him.' Those were her exact words, not mine. And now it is your job to see this done."

Robert's next words were a string of oaths that left even Aquiles blushing. When he came to the end of his tirade, he took a deep breath.

Dammit if Pymm wasn't right. What else could he do? He could continue to hope she'd finally trust him and tell him what he needed to know, or he could take her to Wellington and let his commander deal with her.

Then he remembered what she'd told Chambley about her notes in her valise.

"Perhaps I won't have to," he said, reaching for her battered case. Digging around inside it, he plucked out a worn journal and started paging through it. But to his even greater frustration the entire volume was written in a language he didn't recognize. "Do you know what this is?" he asked Pymm.

The man peered down at it. "Code. Not likely any of us could break it. Or any of my best men. I'm afraid there is only one way to get what we need out of her, and you know what it is."

Take her to the Peninsula. Robert glanced over at her prone form. Damn her stubborn hide.

Cochrane stuck his head in. "I don't know how long I can hold this feller off. He's getting mighty persistent."

"You'll have to take her now," Pymm said, shoving Olivia's journal back in her valise and pushing it into

Robert's unwelcoming embrace. "There is a ship leaving on the evening tide for Lisbon. I can get you passage quite easily. The captain owes me a favor." He picked up a sheet of paper and dashed off the directions and handed them to Aquiles. "Cochrane, show our guests out the back entrance."

Aquiles hoisted Olivia over his shoulder while Robert gathered up the herbs she'd asked Cochrane to purchase. While he still suspected she'd probably ordered a pestilent potion to kill him, the way his shoulder throbbed, it didn't hurt to err on the side of caution.

Pymm's capable assistant was already one step ahead of all of them and had ordered a carriage brought around.

As they were climbing in, someone shouted from the corner, "Hey there, stop right this minute."

Aquiles took the reins from the driver and immediately set the horses flying down the street.

As they made their way out of London's most notorious neighborhood toward the docklands, Robert came to only one good conclusion about sailing to Lisbon with Olivia.

He could find out what the hell she knew about Hobbe.

And more importantly, Orlando.

Chapter 7

Robert's enthusiasm for returning to the Peninsula came to an abrupt halt when they got to the ship on which Pymm had directed them to take passage.

He stood on the gangway looking at the painted name on the side of the tidy and swift merchantman, the *Sybaris*. He should have known. How like Pymm and his perverse sense of humor to send him to his brother Colin's ship. But before he could back away, a familiar voice hailed him from the rail. "Robert? Is that you, lad?"

"Livett?" Robert looked up to see the weathered face of the ship's master staring down at him.

"Aye, sir. Good to see you. Come to see yer brother, I suppose. 'Bout time the two of you made amends."

"I'm not here for a visit," Robert told him. "I need passage. For me and my companions."

Livett took only a cursory glance at Aquiles, but when

his gaze fell on the pair of slippers and muslin hem sticking out of the blanket they'd used to bundle up Olivia, his face turned stormy. "Cap'n won't like that. He's not even lettin' her ladyship sail with us this time, so I doubt he'll be all that pleased with your *companion* there."

Robert didn't doubt in the least that his brother would find Olivia's presence aboard ship highly objectionable, but what his brother didn't know wouldn't hurt him. At least, not until they were well out into the Channel.

"Livett, I was sent by a mutual friend, who said you were sailing for Lisbon."

The master's wrinkled brow furrowed like a set of deep waves. "In mutual friend, you don't be meaning that wretched Pymm?"

"One and the same."

A string of curses followed worthy of a man who'd spent more time at sea than on land. When he finished his colorful rendition of Mr. Pymm's virtues, Livett spat over the rail and then said, "Well, come on then. Bring the lass aboard. But don't think I'll be the one to tell the Cap'n."

Robert stepped back and allowed Aquiles and his armload up the gangway first. It wasn't that he was hesitant to board his brother's ship, despite the fact that they rarely saw eye-to-eye on any matter, but this wounded shoulder and loss of blood were finally exacting their toll on his usually iron constitution. And the last thing he wanted to do was to pass out in front of his brother's crew.

As it was, he was swaying from side to side by the time he got to the top of the gangway, and if it hadn't been for Livett's steadying grasp, he would have fallen back into the murky depths of the river.

"Easy there, lad," Livett said. "Why, you've got the legs of a—" The man's teasing words came to a halt as Robert's coat fell open and revealed the blood-soaked bandages beneath. "Jesus, Joseph and Mary, lad. What have you got there?"

" 'Tis just a scratch, Livett. Nothing to worry about. But I think it would be best if we got aboard and below without any further delay. I'd prefer no one noticed our departure."

Livett whistled low and sharp, and a boy came running along the deck. "Take these folks down below. Put the lady in yer mother's cabin and tuck these other fellows in mine. Then fetch yer uncle here a measure of rum. Tell Cook I told him to get it from the Cap'n's own stores."

Robert took a second glance at the lad and immediately recognized Colin's wife's dark eyes staring up at him from the boy's keen features. "You must be Gavin," he said. "We've never met. I'm your Uncle Robert."

"I've always wanted to meet you, sir." Gavin's face lit with a mischievous light. "Father says I take after you."

"That can't be good," Robert told him, swaying again and this time reaching out for the railing to keep himself from pitching to the deck.

"Well, it really isn't meant as a compliment, I suppose. I tend to get in trouble quite a bit." The boy's keen gaze took in Robert's condition and the bulge of wadding at his shoulder. Intelligent little monkey that he was, he didn't ask any questions but offered Robert a helping hand along the deck and toward the hatch and ladder that led to the cabins below.

"I still do . . . Tend to find trouble, that is," Robert said, glad for the help.

"So I noticed," Gavin replied, his grin coming back.

Olivia was stowed in a tiny, well-fashioned room off Colin's spacious cabin in the stern of the *Sybaris*. With her snoring away on the narrow berth, Robert finally gave in to his own pain and collapsed into his brother's large berth in the main room.

He told himself it would be just for a moment. Just until he gathered his strength to get to Livett's cabin on the next deck below.

"Is there anything else I can do for you, Uncle?" Gavin asked, when he returned moments later, bringing with him the measure of rum Livett had told him to deliver.

"Don't mention my arrival to your father. Or the whiskey." Robert tipped the glass to the boy and then took an appreciative sip of his brother's finest stock. It warmed his chilled bones. "How fares my batman?"

Gavin's gaze rolled heavenward. "He's been sick twice and begged me to lead him back above deck and push him overboard." The boy leaned forward and whispered, "Is he always such a lubber?"

Robert laughed. "Oh, aye. And it will get worse before it gets better."

The lad's nose pinched in disgust. "Do you want some help to your cabin, Uncle?"

He shook his head. "No, lad. I know the way. You get on with your duties, while I rest a bit longer. I'll be gone from here before your father returns."

Gavin winked and clambered out of the cabin in a flash.

While he knew he should go see to Aquiles, Robert hadn't the strength to rise from Colin's well-appointed berth. Aquiles was like a lion on land—nothing could conquer him—but at sea, his prowess and strength toppled in the face of his worst enemy: *mal de mer*. The only thing the man could do was weather his first few days in the haven of a bunk with a bucket at his side. Then shakily he'd finally come forth like a newborn colt, and by the end of the voyage his strength and vigor would be back.

Robert's eyes rocked shut with the sway of the ship. He would have sworn they closed only for a few moments, but when he came to the cabin was dark. What had awakened him was the sound of hasty, hard footsteps stomping down a ladder and getting closer by the moment.

A lamp swung into the room, leaving Robert all but blinded by the brilliant light.

He rolled out of the bunk but found he hadn't the strength to stand. His knees buckled beneath him, so that all he could do was cradle his shoulder to keep from jarring it until he found his footing. It wasn't very easy, for his injury burned with an uncontrollable fire, as hot and fatal as the light swinging before him like a hangman's noose.

And when his eyes adjusted to it, he found the cabin's source of illumination was held aloft by none other than a very angry Captain Colin Danvers.

"I don't believe my eyes," Colin said, sweeping past Robert and hanging the lamp from a nearby hook.

The lamp continued its haphazard sway, casting a harsh light to and fro, leaving Robert dizzy and nauseous in its wake. His entire body seemed gripped by the clammy, cold hand of sweat, leaving him shivering with a strange chill that challenged the rush of burning heat leaping from his wounded shoulder. He tried to concentrate on what Colin was saying and ignore the dangerous, throbbing pain where Aquiles had stitched him together.

What had Olivia said?

Oh, yes, he recalled it now.

I wouldn't be surprised if you had a fever before morning.

For once the astute lady had been wrong. His fever had set in before dawn.

He took a deep breath and rose before his brother, staying outside the circle of light offered by the lamp and keeping his shoulder turned so it wasn't as visible.

"Good to see you, Colin," Robert offered.

"I wish I could say the same," his brother replied. "What the devil are you doing here?"

"I needed passage to Lisbon and Pymm sent me."

Colin shrugged his answer off. "What were you doing in London in the first place and out of uniform?" he asked, nodding at Robert's dark coat.

He pulled the wool serge tighter around him. " 'Tis complicated."

"Why doesn't that surprise me?" Colin muttered.

From the adjoining cabin, a small snore erupted.

His brother swore, caught up the lantern and crossed the room to the partition before Robert could stop him. "Georgie, damn you, I told you not to—" His voice halted as he held the lantern aloft. "What the—" He swung back to Robert.

"That's part of the complication," he told him.

"And is there more?" Colin asked through a firmly clenched jaw.

"Oh, aye," Robert told him, as his fever surged through his limbs, leaving him unable to stand for another moment. He slumped to the ground, hitting the oak plank floor hard. "Get her to Wellington. No matter what," he said, before the fever overtook his senses.

Colin rushed to his brother's side, setting the lantern on the table. He'd been in enough battles to recognize a dying man. Pale from loss of blood and hot with fever, his brother showed all the signs. Gingerly he searched Robert, until he found the wad of bandages at his shoulder. Carefully opening his coat and unwrapping the linen cloths, he saw the beginnings of infection streaking across Robert's shoulder.

"Dammit, Hobbe," Colin said. "What have you gotten yourself into now?"

Olivia tossed in and out of a dreamless sleep, trying to claw her way back to consciousness. At one point, she heard muffled voices in the darkness.

"Hobbe," a man was saying, his voice thick with emotion.

She too tried to cry out. *Hobbe, Hobbe, I'm here.*

But her tongue was thick and dry, lodging over the words, leaving her able to make only a low croaking sound. Yet even as she struggled to say the words again, she fell back into the strange sleep that seemed to hold her in a prison of lethargy.

When she finally awoke, she blinked at the light peering in from the small window beside her bunk and coming from a doorway that she could only guess where it led to.

The world around her rose and fell in a gentle cadence she'd never felt before. But it took only a moment for the fresh tang of salty air to assail her drugged senses and awaken them to her surroundings.

She was at sea. And she didn't need to guess twice as to where she was headed or with whom.

Robert.

Damn him, she thought, as she tried to remember how she had gotten aboard this ship.

Her memory of the past week came in strange flashes of remembrance. She closed her eyes, her hands cradling her pounding temples.

She could see it as if it had happened to someone else.

Lady Finch reading the paper . . . Bradstone's return . . . Revenge, she'd wanted revenge. Going to London in the mail coach . . . and then on to Mayfair . . . Robert, and yet not Robert. The images of the man she'd known separated into two. Two parts of the same man. One she'd loved with regrets, the other she'd kissed and regretted not. . . .

Blushing at the memory of Robert's kiss, of his hands touching her with such rough assurance, Olivia struggled to remember the rest. Not the kissing but the other things that danced just out of range.

And it all came back like a crack of gunshot.

Chambley. Threatening her. Gloating about her father's "suicide." Of him aiming a gun at Robert and pulling the trigger. Of her own blind rage and unfathomable reaction.

She'd shot him.

Olivia sat straight up and gasped. She'd shot a man.

Shakily she rose from the berth, her slippered feet touching the floor gingerly. Holding on to the berth, she stood there for a moment, trying to accustom herself to the rocking of the ship. She still couldn't account for how she'd gotten there. That part of her memory seemed lost in a fog as thick as the haze that could roll up from the Thames in January.

Putting one foot out in front of her, her toe nudged something. She looked down to find her valise. Kneeling down beside it, she opened it and found that her journal and notes were still there, as well as some other items she couldn't place. Bundles of pungent herbs, carefully wrapped in blue apothecary papers. Closing the valise back up, she slid it out of sight and began edging along the wall until she came to a doorway. There she took a deep breath and peered out.

The room before her was wide and brightly lit. A long row of windows made up the back wall. Beyond them lay the sea, with nothing visible but the vast, blue breadth of waves and sky, confirming her worst suspicion that she was far from land. She blinked a few times, her eyes finally adjusting to the light, and then her gaze moved over the room to an unlit lantern swaying over a wide, wooden table that took up most of the middle of the room. Seated there, a man was working at a large book, his pen scratching at the thick sheets and pausing every few moments while he considered his next choice of words. She couldn't see his face as he bent to his work, only a shock of dark hair and his tanned hands.

She glanced around and realized they were alone. There was no sign of Robert or even his ever present servant, Aquiles.

Damn him, she thought. He'd probably just cast her aboard the nearest southbound vessel and washed his hands of her.

"Hello, there," the man at the desk said, setting aside his pen and rising to his feet. He was tall, his head nearly scraping the ceiling. There wasn't anything in his simple coat and breeches that told her who he was, but his stance and features spoke of well-earned command. His features were craggy and tanned, giving further evidence that this was a man who'd spent years at sea.

But his face—it was so familiar. The green eyes, the hair, the same rugged jaw.

He was related to Robert and Bradstone, more than likely. As if that should reassure her.

His lips spread in a warm, cozy smile, edging away at her wariness. "Glad to see Pymm's potion has finally worn off. I was starting to think you'd never wake up."

Pymm! The mention of his name cleared away her hazy memories. "That tea!"

The man nodded. "Oh, is that how he did it? You obviously haven't spent much time with him or else you'd have known never to take anything that man offers you. His mother was Louis the Fifteenth's personal poisoner."

Olivia's hands went to her throat.

"Oh, gad, I've frightened you. Don't worry, if you aren't dead now, you've more than likely nothing to fear." He swiped his hand through his wayward locks. "Suppose that's of little comfort either. My wife says I am far too blunt for my own good." Awkwardly he gestured at a nearby chair. "Please sit down, and I'll call for some refreshments. You must be famished."

"Where am I? And who are you?" she asked, still holding onto the partition that divided her small chamber from his vast cabin.

"You're aboard the *Sybaris*, and I'm her captain, Colin Danvers. At your service." He bowed low and then crossed the room to the main doorway. "Gavin? Lad, where the devil are you?"

"You're related to Robert?" she asked.

"Brothers, actually," he said.

How handy, she thought. To keep all their nefarious deeds within the family. She wondered what other robbers and thieves and pirates Robert had dangling from his family tree.

"Right here, Cap'n," a perky young boy said, as he came bustling into the cabin. He turned to Olivia and bobbed a short bow. "Ma'am."

"Fetch our guest a tray of bread and cheese." Captain Danvers glanced over his shoulder at her. "Tea, perhaps?" He grinned at her and waggled his brows. "I promise it's not the same blend as Pymm's."

Olivia found herself smiling back, despite her resolve not to trust him. "Yes, thank you. I'd appreciate that." She crossed the room and took the chair he had offered before.

"Now that's all settled, perhaps you can tell me how you got mixed up with my rapscallion brother and the rather infamous Mr. Pymm."

She shifted slightly. "I'd prefer not to discuss it, if you don't mind."

"I see," he said, retaking his seat in front of his log book.

"What I'd like is to be returned to London," she told him. Why she'd asked for that she didn't know. London didn't seem any safer than being marooned in the middle of the Atlantic with a shipful of strangers.

Captain Danvers was shaking his head. "I regret I'm unable to put you ashore."

"What if I told you I was possibly wanted for murder in London? That the authorities would reward you handsomely for returning me?" She hoped he might be a greedy sort, tempted by gold. If she could convince him to turn his ship around, she'd make her escape the moment they docked.

But the captain appeared to be neither concerned nor alarmed that he was carrying a wanted passenger. He merely laughed. "So is half my crew, Miss—?"

Olivia didn't know if she should be relieved or unnerved to be traveling in such nefarious, albeit fellow company. "Mrs. Keates," she said, using her former *nom de guerre.*

"Mrs. Keates, then. My apologies, but I didn't learn of your presence until we were well out in the Channel, and I can't possibly take you back now. I have . . . *business matters* that cannot be delayed."

Business matters. By the way he said it, it hardly sounded like he engaged in the tea trade or woolen shipping. So she'd been right on one count. Secrets were a Danvers family trait. "Where are we bound?"

"Lisbon."

Olivia let out a long, slow breath. Lisbon. And one step closer to *El Rescate del Rey.* Goose bumps fluttered over her arms.

Still, it was a long way to Portugal, and in between here, wherever here was, and that fabled land, she was alone on what was most likely a pirate ship, with a crew wanted for a menagerie of heinous crimes, and all because of one man . . .

"Damn him," she muttered between gritted teeth. Damn that Robert Danvers for dragging her into this mess.

"I assume you are referring to my brother," Colin commented, leaning back in his chair. "He does have that effect on people."

"This is all his doing. I'll see him in hell for this."

"Actually, you may have your wish sooner than you think. He's in the first mate's cabin gone with fever. I doubt he'll live through the night."

If anything, Olivia discovered, Robert Danvers was a hard man to kill.

"This fever has to break," she muttered to herself, as she reached for the linen cloth soaking in the basin of water and mopped his sweaty brow for probably the thousandth time.

Robert twisted and turned in the narrow berth, and Olivia struggled to hold him still. She'd restitched his wound twice—for he'd pulled the threads loose in his imaginary battles against the foes he fought in his fever-soaked brain.

"Lando! Lando!" he called out. "Don't go there. Don't trust anyone."

"There, there," she whispered, trying to soothe the worries from his brow with the cool cloth. "All is well, you must rest."

He caught her hand, the desperate strength in his fingers belying the fact that he had been ill all these days. "Warn him. Tell him what she'll do to him," he begged her.

"Yes, I'll tell him. But first you must rest or you'll be of no use to him."

He did not let go but pinned her with a wild gaze, his eyes focused for a moment on hers and his piercing stare cutting through her. "You're lying. You aren't going to warn him."

She'd been through this with him countless times already, so she knew what he wanted to hear. "I have already warned him. He's safe. He's on his way home."

Her words, once again, eased the demons raging within him. He slumped back into the berth, his eyes closed and his restless movements ceased.

At least, for the time being.

In his latest struggles, his blanket had fallen away, and she went to cover him before he got chilled. Even as she started to pull the frayed woolen length over him, she paused for a moment, magnetized by the sight of his body.

The scars and imperfections she'd become intimate with over the last few days of caring for him, she now looked upon as old friends and landmarks. And yet it was the maleness of him, the unrelenting strength that even in illness he would not give up, that took her breath away.

The corded muscles in his shoulders. The lithe, lean shape of his torso. The small patch of dark, curly hair forming a triangle on the upper part of his chest. Unbidden, her hand went there. She ran her fingers through the curls, the warmth of his body coursing into hers, the cadence of his heart beating a refrain into her own.

Something had changed her heart as she'd cared for him—softened her toward him. He wasn't the arrogant beast who'd kidnapped her, the man who'd so rakishly kissed her in the park.

But a man in need of her touch. Of her faith. Of her hope.

His fierce devotion to this Lando made her almost jealous. He fought and fought with every ounce of his meager store of strength for this unknown man or woman, not unlike how she imagined her Hobbe might.

With unswerving dedication.

Could a man out only for the promised wealth of a lost treasure also hold such unselfish loyalties?

She thought not. And so she found herself looking at him differently, and late one night, in a blinding moment of realization as he'd clung to her hand and begged her to warn Lando of some impending danger, she'd wished Robert held the self-same feelings for her.

Her passion for Hobbe found a new life in the dying embers of this man. And if anything, she wanted more than ever for him to live, if only to prove her right. If only to discover that her heart wasn't betraying her this time.

"You've spent another night with him, haven't you?" Colin called out from the door.

Olivia snatched her hand back and hastily covered her patient. Smoothing her damp palms over her skirt, she turned to face Robert's brother. "His fever needed tending."

"So I see," he said, stepping into the small chamber and taking a look at his brother. His sharp gaze turned and studied her. "I don't need any more patients on this ship. Aquiles and my brother are bad enough. You need rest." The underlying order in his voice brooked no disobedience.

But it had been this way each morning for the last three days. And she ignored him just as stubbornly today. "He needs me more. He wouldn't be in these circumstances if it hadn't been for . . ."

If he hadn't stepped in front of Chambley's pistol and saved her life. Now she owed him a life in return.

"I'll have Gavin bring you up some food and a hot pot of tea," Colin offered, his mouth set in a line of frustration. He turned to leave, but then stopped and turned back to her. "Olivia, I've seen men linger like this too many times not to know the outcome. You've done a lot to keep him from dying, but if his fever doesn't break soon, I fear for his mind. He may never recover."

Olivia smiled weakly at him and nodded. "He's had a busy night, what with evading the French, begging me to hide his maps and asking for someone named Lando. Do you know who he is talking about? This Lando?"

She swore Colin's eyes flickered with some bit of recognition, but the man, as cagey as his brother, refused to offer her any help in piecing together Robert Danvers's identity—or his past.

"No, 'tis just the fever speaking. Men say all kinds of odd things when their blood is infected."

Olivia didn't believe him but hadn't the strength to argue the point. Still, she couldn't help asking, "Captain Danvers, who is your brother?"

The man smiled, an odd, wry twist to his lips. "That is a good question and one better left for him to answer."

"And if he dies?" she managed to ask, glancing at Robert's flushed features and fever ravaged body.

"Then I suppose neither of us will ever know the answer." With that he turned and left.

A few moments later she heard a shuffling in the gangway, and assumed it was Gavin with her tray. "You can just set it on the trunk there," she said, without looking up from her work. When the boy didn't say anything, she turned and discovered someone entirely different in the doorway, the last person she'd ever expected to see here, so far away from England and her former life.

Jemmy Reyburn.

Chapter 8

"Olivia!" Jemmy said. "There you are! I've had a devil of a time slipping up here to find you."

She managed to find the words to get past her shock. "Jemmy?"

He ducked into the room, glancing back to make sure he hadn't been seen. When he straightened and looked at her, his face split in a wide smile, a grin surrounded by four days of youthful and uneven beard. His clothes, once the pride of Bond Street, were a filthy, disheveled mess, and he stank as if he'd been bathing in bilge water.

"Hail, Queen Mab," he said, using his pet name from childhood for her.

"What are you doing here?" She hustled past him and closed the door.

"Rescuing you, if you must know."

"Rescuing me? How did you ever get here? Where have you been?" She plucked at his coat. "Don't answer that last question. I'd rather not know."

"As for how I got here, it is a rather adventurous tale. Mother and I decided it wasn't proper for you to go to the Foreign Office without someone to lend you support, so I volunteered to go, but when I got there, no one knew anything about Chambley bringing you in. Not even the fellow's secretary. Impertinent fellow, that one."

"Yes, yes," Olivia said, "but how did you end up here, on the *Sybaris*?"

"After I left the Foreign Office, I headed straight to Chambley's. Never liked the fellow. Heavy-handed and all." He shot a glance over her shoulder at Robert. "Going to live, do you think? The crew has quite a pool on the matter. Most think he'll heave up anchor before the day is out." He paused for a moment. "I believe that means they don't think he has much of a chance."

"He'll live," she said, more to convince herself. "He and I have some unfinished matters."

"Then if I get the chance, I'll put my money on you. Mayhap I'll win enough to pay my passage."

"Speaking of passage, how did you end up on this ship?" she asked, determined to see Jemmy to the end of his story.

"Oh, yes, my arrival here, I was getting to that," he said. "After I got to Chambley's, there you were with Bradstone barreling out of the place, with the entire house in uproar. I had a devil of a time following you. That fellow of Bradstone's is quite the deft whip." He stopped and scratched at his sleeve. "I don't even want to know what is crawling inside this coat."

Neither did Olivia.

"Well," Jemmy said, continuing his long-winded tale. "I got lost in the Dials looking for you until I offered a rather cheeky lad most of my pocketbook to help me locate you. When I did, that bastard Bradstone had you bundled up and into another carriage before I could stop him." Jemmy shot an aggrieved glance over at her patient. "Hope he lives. I've got a bit of a score to settle with him on your account. Demmed if he is a marquis, he can't treat you like this."

"Jemmy, before you go issuing any challenges, you should know that man isn't the Marquis of Bradstone."

"Isn't Bradstone? How can you be sure?" Jemmy shook his head, unconvinced by her assurance. "His own mother took him in."

Just then Robert shifted in his berth, the blanket covering him falling free, exposing his bare buttocks and legs.

Olivia blushed and pulled the woolen length to cover him. "Rest assured, I would know the difference."

"Suppose you would," he muttered, blushing as well. Finally he hastened to finish his story. "I followed you all the way to the docks and watched them cart you aboard. I knew I needed to get you off before they sailed, but I had a devil of a time getting on without being seen, and when I finally did, they were just about to set sail. The problem was I couldn't find you, and the next thing I knew, we were off and away down the Thames."

"And you've been aboard ever since," Olivia said, finishing his story.

"Sadly, yes. I tried at night to find you, and I've spent the rest of the time dodging the crew and trying to find a safe place to hide out." Jemmy drew in a long breath and then sighed. "I suppose if he isn't Brad-stone, you really didn't need rescuing."

"Oh, Jemmy, you are the dearest boy, but look what you've done! Your mother is going to be beside herself wondering where you've gotten to."

He nodded, hanging his head in false contriteness, as he had when he was twelve and she'd catch him stealing tarts in the pantry. Then, just as suddenly, he brightened. "Is it true we are bound for Lisbon?"

"Aye," she nodded.

His face glowed in excitement. "Wellington! This will be my chance!"

"Not if I have anything to say in the matter," she told him. "You'll be on the first ship homebound and back to your mother. She'll never forgive me for drag-ging you into this. That is, if you aren't pitched over-board first."

"You think they would?" he asked. "They are a rather bloodthirsty looking lot, aren't they?"

"I think you may have something there. The captain claims to be a simple merchantman, but I have my doubts."

"A simple merchantman?" Jemmy laughed. "Not likely! Not unless arms and munitions are considered regular cargo. If what I've seen is any evidence, there's enough powder and shot down in the hold to sink half the fleet."

Before Olivia could reply, the door bumped into Jemmy's back.

"Pardon, miss," came Gavin's voice through the closed door. He pushed it open and barged in. "Brought your tray along, like the Cap'n ordered." The boy's eyes widened at the sight of Jemmy.

"Gavin, this is my friend, Mr. James Reyburn," Olivia

said, pulling the boy into the already crowded cabin. "I was wondering if you would risk a bit of trouble for my sake."

At the very mention of the word, Gavin grinned, and she knew she had a co-conspirator.

Olivia spent the rest of the day and well into the night with Robert, his fever taking a turn for the worse. She'd given up hope that he would survive. She stopped believing that he intended to take her to Wellington. Rather, she spent the night cursing her heart for caring as she watched Robert Danvers slip deeper and deeper into his fever.

What time she fell asleep she didn't know. The last bells she'd heard had been at the second dogwatch.

In her dreams she found no relief. Like the other nights when she'd fallen asleep at Robert's side, his presence stole into her slumber like a thief.

But this time the dreams were not the wild images that had plagued her since she'd first laid eyes on the imposter marquis; they were different.

No longer was his love fierce, demanding and rough, but rather the gentle ministrations of someone who held her heart.

His fingers stroked her hair, plying the loose tendrils slowly, tentatively. Somewhere in her drowsy state, she heard him calling to her.

"There, now, my little termagant, what have you done to me?"

Those same fingers that had tenderly combed her hair now coaxed her awake, slowly tracing a line along her jaw and over her lips, teasing them to open, leaving them longing for a kiss.

Her lashes fluttered open, and for a drowsy second

she tried to remember where she was. All she could see before her was the expanse of a man's bare chest and her own fingers toying with the dark curls resting there.

As she blinked again and pulled herself up, her hand came down on his thigh and a hard, throbbing warmth that told her only too clearly that Robert Danvers had lived through the night.

Not only lived, thrived.

Her head spun toward the top of the berth. She guessed it was near dawn, for the first warm fingers of light crept in at the tiny window. This morning a red-gold shaft of light cast over his dark head like a halo. His eyes were closed, his face almost serene, as if he'd finally found peace from all his feverborn fury.

For a moment she thought she'd been mistaken, he wasn't alive but dead, but then his lashes fluttered open and those green eyes, the color of the waves beyond the window, sparkled with life.

"Hello," she managed to whisper, swiping at the tangled locks of her hair that he'd freed from the loose chignon she'd taken to wearing in the last few days.

He glanced around the cabin, obviously assessing where he was and trying to remember the events that had led him there. She knew how he felt. His hand went unconsciously to his shoulder, and he flinched for a moment as he plucked at the poultice she'd placed over the inflamed wound. "So you missed another opportunity to do me in."

"So it seems," she said.

"How long?"

She knew what he meant. "Five days."

He sucked in a breath and tried to rise, but she stopped him by doing the same thing she'd done all week—her hands on his bare chest and using all her weight to force him back.

But holding down a man who was fully aware was an entirely different matter from one gone with fever, she discovered.

This time she realized how her breasts pressed against his chest, how his body offered a solid resistance to hers. Perhaps resistance wasn't the right word—more like a welcoming embrace.

When she glanced up, there was a wry smile on his lips, while one brow arched at her.

She struggled up from his chest. "Stay still," she told him. "You'll tear your stitches again."

"Again?"

"Yes, you've torn them twice." She edged away from the bed, away from this man who had gone from helpless patient to unnerving male in the blink of an eye.

"I suppose I should be grateful that I agreed with Pymm's advice and let you tag along," he teased.

"Tag along! You kidnapped me!" she snapped back, before she saw the flash of tantalizing challenge in his eyes.

"A matter of linguistics," he said with an indifferent shrug, then a flinch of pain. "You're the expert, I'd think you'd know the difference."

"Harrumph!" she muttered.

He smiled at her. "So why did you save my life?"

She hemmed for a moment. Her pride wasn't about to let her admit the truth, so she offered the next best plausible excuse. "Because you saved mine."

"Oh, you mean this scrape from Chambley. Don't read too much into that. I had no choice. You carry valuable information. Saving you was a matter of duty." He said it with a bored air of indifference.

"*Duty!*" Why, she'd never been so insulted. So much for her fantasies about a hero, about a man who'd put her life before his out of undying loyalties. How had she been so foolish to think him capable of the same honorable, noble intentions Hobbe would have extended to her. Not out of duty . . . but out of something she doubted this man would *ever* understand.

"I suppose I should be grateful," he said. "I have no doubt you've been most attentive to my needs." He rolled a bit in the berth, a grin spreading across his face. Lifting up his blanket, he peeked beneath, then over the edge at her. "Was this your idea?"

Olivia blushed. "It was necessary."

"Did you do the honors?"

"I did not!" she told him. "Your brother undressed you. My dealings with you have been quite . . . quite . . . decorous."

"You? Decorous?" He laughed. "Perhaps you sought to confirm once and for all I'm not Bradstone."

Olivia tipped her nose in the air. Of all the insulting insinuations. And after she'd worn herself ragged saving his miserable life. The leering waggle of his brows and his mocking gaze seemed to see right through her veneer of indignation. But a wicked bit of her decided the man could use a dose of his own medicine, even if it was a lie.

"Yes, I did discover some inadequacies between you and your cousin. But on those regards, your secret is safe with me."

* * *

Any hint of a truce between them ended the next morning. Olivia awoke at dawn and went to check on her patient. She found him halfway out of his berth, a blanket wrapped around his waist.

"What do you think you are doing?" she asked.

"Getting out of this confounded bed, if you must know," he told her. "Where have you put my clothes?"

She should have been warned immediately by the crotchety tone in his voice, but she hadn't just spent the last week nursing this man back to life only to have him throw it away by getting out of bed too soon. Hands on her hips, she faced him. "I threw them overboard."

"You tossed my clothes overboard?"

"Well, at least your hearing wasn't addled by your fever, but your mind obviously was if you think you are well enough to get dressed and start stalking about this ship."

His face turned murderous, but it was hard to fear a man whose legs were shaking like a foal's and whose jaw was quivering in a painful line of determination.

She could only guess how much it had hurt him to inch his way out of his berth, let alone continue to stand there arguing with her.

He wavered for a moment, his grip on the berth tightening, leaving his knuckles a deathly white.

"I should fetch you some broth," she told him, turning to leave.

"Damn the broth, you termagant! Get me some clothes."

"That is hardly the way to address someone who saved your life."

"Might I remind you, you owed me one." He

slumped onto the side of the bed in defeat, letting out an enormous frustrated sigh. "Consider us even now."

"Even?" she sputtered. "I hardly think so."

He looked up. "And how is that?"

"Have you forgotten you kidnapped me? Hauled me aboard this ship against my will and in a sack, no less?"

His answer was an arrogant shrug. "As a point of record, I don't remember you making any protests as we boarded this ship."

"I might have been able to express myself if you hadn't poisoned me."

He slumped back into the bunk, finally giving in to the pain that must have cost him all his meager stores of strength. "That was Pymm's idea, truly not my first choice. But really you left us no other means."

She took the two steps across the room to help him, but he brushed her away. "You most certainly had other means," she told him gently, setting aside her more strident tones and trying to take a more calm approach. "And the obvious one was to leave me be."

"Leave you be?" He laughed. "I hardly think so. I have my orders where *El Rescate* is concerned. I wasn't to return to the Peninsula without its whereabouts, and according to you, now I have them. Such as it is—and what good it will do is a fool's notion." He gazed out the window, but Olivia knew what his mind saw was far away, far from the endless waves, to the well-worn tracks of Portugal, to the high, hard plains of Spain. "Legends and dust—they have much in common with the death and dying that happens every day there."

The bitter chill of his hopeless conviction stopped her. It had never occurred to her that of all the men who had sought her help discovering *El Rescate del Rey*, this one would be so different.

So completely different.

"You don't believe," she whispered, her own shock sending ripples of gooseflesh down her arms. In the seven years since she had learned of the King's Ransom, it had never occurred to her that it might not exist. That he didn't believe left her scandalized. "It is real. It has to be."

He shook his head. "Do you know how many people have spent their lifetime searching for it? Most of the idiots hadn't even a notion where to start, much less what they were looking for. Eleven centuries of men chasing its shadow." He scratched at the dark whiskers that had grown with abandon during his illness and made him look like he truly belonged on this pirate ship. "A ransom for a king no one remembers. 'Tis pure folly and a waste of time," he muttered.

"Wellington obviously doesn't believe so." Olivia stepped into the circle of his anger and cynicism, wanting with all her heart to vanquish his disbelief. "My father said that all legends have a basis in truth somewhere, even if it's just a small measure."

"Yes, well whatever the measure, I doubt this ransom will save the Peninsula from the French. It certainly didn't save it from the Moors all those years ago."

It was Olivia's turn to shake her head. The King's Ransom did exist. It had to. For if it were just folly, as Robert believed, then her father, that poor boy Bradstone had murdered, and even Bradstone himself, had all died in vain.

The last seven years of her life had been in vain.

And that she couldn't, wouldn't believe. "*El Rescate del Rey* is real."

"You aren't the first to believe so," he said. "And you probably won't be the last. All I care is that you tell what you know to Wellington. Then let him do with it what he will."

"You really intend to take me to him?" She still hadn't shaken free her more pressing doubts that he, like all the others, was chasing her only to gain the treasure for himself.

"Of course. Why else would I go to this trouble?" He nodded down at the blanket covering his lower half. "But if I am to do that, I will need my clothes."

It was Olivia's turn to smile at him. "You are a persistent devil. I think it might be better if you remain as you are until you are strong enough to get out of bed."

"I'm strong enough," he told her, throwing his legs over the edge and tugging the blanket free from the middle of his torso.

"Keep that blanket on," she told him, backing out of the room.

"Why?" he asked, his eyes wide with mock innocence. "It isn't like there isn't anything there you haven't seen before."

Olivia colored. Whether from embarrassment at being caught or from his insinuation. "I did no such thing," she lied.

"Five days with me tossing about this bed, and this blanket *never* fell off?"

"I'm too much of a lady to answer that question," she said, taking the high road.

"You, Miss Sutton, are no such thing."

At this Olivia's color deepened, but this time with indignation. "How dare you!"

"You forget, your letters to Bradstone were published in the *Morning Post*," he countered. "I don't need to dare when all of London knows your past." He leaned forward. "What I don't understand is how you were so duped by Bradstone."

She turned away. It was a question she'd asked herself too many times to count. "I was very young. I believed myself in love."

He shook his head. "That might be. But I suspect, Miss Sutton, if you'd been given the chance, you would have outfoxed him at his own game."

Olivia drew a deep breath and looked away.

"Aha!" he said. "I believe I'm on to something. Do tell—your secret is safe with me."

He was coming too close to the truth for her comfort, so she used an old trick of Lady Finch's and turned the tables right back on him. "You're a fine one to be accusing me of keeping secrets. Parading about London claiming to be the Marquis of Bradstone, skulking about with the likes of that dreadful Mr. Pymm and finally kidnapping me with some grandiose claim that you are doing it for King and country. You must admit, it is all a bit far-fetched."

"Not really," he told her. "I think it all makes sense. Now, you, on the other hand, were at the scene of murder, fled the crime and hid for seven years. Why is that?"

"I had nothing to hide," she declared. "I was innocent."

"Then why disappear?"

She chose to ignore him. "Do you want some broth or not?"

"I want my clothes and some answers."

"You're getting broth," she told him, leaving the

cabin before his questions became too persistent. Behind her, she heard his muttered complaints, but she chose to ignore those as well.

Just down the hallway, Jemmy stepped out of the shadows, causing her to start in fright.

"Sorry there, Olivia," he said, as she tried to catch her breath. "I didn't mean to scare you. I was just so glad to see you."

With Gavin's help, Olivia had been able so far to shield Jemmy from detection. They'd done this by keeping him stowed during the daylight hours and letting him up out of the hold only at night during the wee hours. It had worked so far, but Olivia knew it was only a matter of time before someone discovered the stowaway's presence aboard the *Sybaris*.

"What are you doing out here? Someone could see you," she scolded quietly, glancing back over her shoulder to make sure she'd closed the door to Robert's cabin tightly.

"I'm starving," he complained. "I'm also demmed tired of all this darkness and lurking about. I want to see the sun and I want to own up to the Captain."

"I don't know, Jemmy. It could be dangerous."

"All this slinking about is hardly honorable, I'd say." He crossed his arms over his chest. "I need to stand up and take whatever fate deals me."

"Jemmy, I think it's better if we keep your presence a secret right now, at least until I can speak to Captain Danvers first."

"No secrets, eh?" a voice from the end of the hallway asked.

Olivia turned and found Robert leaning in the doorway of his cabin, the blanket around his midsection, his face white from the exertion.

"I'd say you are hiding more than you bargained for, Miss Sutton."

Robert found the warmth and brilliance of sunlight on his face more rejuvenating than any pot of broth. After more than a week of being kept in his berth until Olivia declared him well enough to venture above deck, he was glad to finally be free of his prison. A fortnight, all told, of being cooped up had nearly been his undoing.

It was a good lesson to him not to get caught by the French—for he imagined he'd go mad in a prison cell. Especially if his gaoler was as strict as Miss Sutton.

He'd conned Gavin into stealing a pair of breeches and a shirt from his brother's trunks, and to his surprise Gavin had produced Robert's boots, cleaned and polished.

Once he'd gotten dressed, he'd checked on Aquiles, who'd also been at Miss Sutton's tender mercies. The poor sot had practically begged Robert to pitch him overboard, and Robert couldn't help wondering if it was the *mal de mer* or the ocean of broth and Miss Sutton's cheerful nursing that had Aquiles longing for death's welcoming embrace.

As for himself, while he was glad for the opportunity to get out of his blasted bunk, a part of him had to admit he'd miss the lady's bossy attentions.

Olivia had spent hours trying to keep him amused, reading to him, testing his skills in languages and asking him endless questions about Spain and his life there, before and after Napoleon's occupation. She obviously had an insatiable curiosity, and he enjoyed having such an avid audience with whom to share his love of his adopted homeland.

She was certainly a woman of many facets, and he found each one intriguing. Yet he knew she carried some long-held secrets. And he suspected they all dealt with the night of Orlando's murder. A point he couldn't help puzzling over.

What had happened in those last minutes? And how deeply had she been involved?

"Hey there," his brother called out from the poop deck. "Do you have permission to be up here?"

Robert glared up at his elder sibling.

Colin only laughed. But it annoyed Robert even further when he watched Colin glance over at Olivia to see her nod in agreement to his arrival above deck.

The wretched woman! His brother had better watch out, or the next thing they'd know, she'd be directing course corrections.

Robert took the ladder to the upper deck as swiftly as he could, but his shoulder was stiff and his arm weak. When he got to the top, he was sweating and his muscles burned, but he'd be damned if he'd admit it in front of her.

She'd have him at her mercy for another sennight, trapped in his berth and drinking endless cups of broth.

"Good to see you up and about," Colin said, a grin teasing at his serious expression.

"Would have been up sooner, if I'd had my way," he grumbled. "Sorry about dragging you into this mess." Robert nodded at where Jemmy Reyburn stood with one of the crew, getting a lesson in knot tying.

"I'm not complaining. The boy is a hard worker. It's like having an extra hand on board. And we are short this trip. Besides, he feels so bad about stowing away, he's working twice as hard as my crew—he's putting them all to shame." Colin grinned.

"What about your other passenger?"

Both of them glanced over at where Olivia sat curled up on a coil of rope, a basket of sewing beside her and a length of cloth in her hands, her needle swiftly plying a long seam.

Sitting on her perch, she sat with her head cocked as she continued her task at hand. The salty breeze curled and whispered around her hair, sending lazy red tendrils dancing around her face. Not even her strict attempt to bind her hair in some matronly design could keep the fiery and wayward strands in place.

The southern sun was starting to kiss her once fair cheeks, for now they were starting to hail a rich glow. Most women would have shunned the warmth of the sun, but Olivia seemed to bloom beneath it like a wild, unkempt rose.

And just as tempting to pick, he thought, despite the threat of thorns.

"What is she doing now?" Robert asked. "Dressing the crew in more respectable uniforms?"

"Actually she is refitting some of my clothes so that you'll have something to wear. But I see you've already had a hand in that yourself," Colin said, glancing first at the breeches and then at the shirt. "Let me guess, Gavin picked the lock on my trunk?"

Robert hated to see his nephew get in any more trouble, since he'd been assigned to scrubbing decks from dawn to dusk since the discovery of Jemmy Reyburn aboard. "No, this was all my own doing," he said.

Colin appeared unconvinced but didn't say anything more on the subject.

Robert glanced again over at Olivia. Whereas most women would have taken an indignant stand of protest over their situation and locked themselves in their room, she had not. He knew from what Colin had told him earlier that she'd pitched in wherever she was needed, in the galley, chatting with the sailors in their native languages and quoting the now infamous Lady Finch's advice on any number of subjects. She had turned a disastrous situation into a great lark.

He had to admire her adaptability.

"I'm surprised she's not making me restraints to keep me locked in my sick bed until we reach Lisbon," Robert joked.

"You should be in restraints," Colin said. "What were you thinking kidnapping a woman and hauling her to Portugal? Aren't there enough dulcineas there to keep you happy?"

"It isn't like that," Robert said. "This is a military matter, pure and simple."

"The war going so bad that Arthur is taking to recruiting widowed women into his ranks?"

Robert didn't see any way of avoiding the issue. "She's no mere widow. That woman could be the key to ending the war or the most treasonous threat yet."

"Mrs. Keates? A treasonous threat? Are you sure that bullet didn't rattle more than your shoulder? She's an army widow who works as a lady's companion."

"Mrs. Keates is the name she took after she left London seven years ago. Before that she was known as Miss Olivia Sutton."

Colin paled and turned to survey anew the woman he'd so easily given sanctuary on his ship. "Olivia Sutton." He shook his head. "It can't be."

"Mark my words, the lady over there is none other than Olivia Sutton. She was there, Colin. She was with Lando when he died."

"She didn't have anything to do with it." Colin made his statement with such firmness, such finality that it left Robert stunned.

"Of course she had something to do with it," he shot back. "Chambley's been hunting for her ever since that night. And our cousin went to great personal lengths to secure her aid. She has a hand in this, mark my words."

"That means nothing," Colin told him. "That woman is no more capable of murder than Gavin is of keeping out of mischief."

"She shot Chambley. You should have seen her. She took aim and shot him. If she hadn't been so blind with rage at the time, she would have put that bullet straight through the man's heart."

"And why, may I ask, was the lady blind with rage?"

Robert paused. "Chambley had told her that he was behind her father's death. Apparently Sir Sutton didn't commit suicide; he was murdered by him and Bradstone."

Colin's mouth fell open. "Eh gads. That puts an entirely different light on things. You'd have done the same thing."

Colin had a good point there. But that still didn't explain what happened the night Orlando died. Or why she was found at the murder scene, the pistol in her hand.

"I know what you are thinking," Colin said, "she was involved in Lando's death. You're wrong."

"And you aren't listening," Robert said. "She may well have fired the shot that killed Lando. She is certainly capable of having done it."

Colin shook his head. "No, Hobbe. That woman did not murder our brother. She is no more than an unwitting pawn in all this. Mark my words on it. Why don't you just ask her?"

Ask her? Robert had never heard anything so stupid in his life. *Excuse me, Miss Sutton, did you murder my brother?*

As if the chit would tell the truth.

He shook his head. "I wish I could claim your assurance on the matter, but I don't trust her. She's holding something back. She hasn't been entirely honest. Why, she even—"

"Perhaps if you weren't half in love with her, your judgment wouldn't be so clouded," Colin remarked, then turned to answer a question Livett had on their course.

Half in love? With Olivia Sutton? He'd never heard of such a stupid notion. Obviously, Colin had finally gone mad after all these years aboard ship. And yet, even as Robert tried to form the words that would deny his brother's assessment of the situation, they died in his throat as he gazed across the deck at Olivia Sutton.

Her hands worked nimbly with the needle, but it appeared her thoughts were elsewhere, because suddenly she pricked herself. When she brought her finger to her lips, she caught sight of him watching her and offered a tentative smile.

It caught his heart unawares and nearly knocked

him off his already unsteady feet. Like her kiss in the park.

If Napoleon wanted to win the Peninsula, Robert thought, he should just send a battalion of Miss Suttons to Spain. They would turn the entire English army as traitorous as his own once stalwart heart.

"She thinks you are taking her to Wellington," Colin said, as he rejoined Robert and followed the direction of his brother's intense gaze.

"I intend to."

"Whatever for?"

"She claims to know where The King's Ransom is buried."

"Mother of God," Colin sputtered. "Does she know what that means?"

"I think so, but not the entire extent of it." Of this Robert was certain. Only someone raised in Spain would understand the almost mystical sway of *El Rescate del Rey*.

A treasure powerful enough to unite a country. Or leave it in ruins.

"If anyone knew—"

"Exactly," Robert said. "She'd be prey to every opportunist, every spy Napoleon has loose in the Peninsula and England. Not to mention the Chambleys of the world."

"No wonder you hauled her out of London so fast. I would have done the same thing." Colin rubbed his chin. "Do you really think she knows where it is?"

"She believes she does, and I suppose that's all that matters. I'll deliver her to Wellington and then she'll be his problem, not mine." Robert turned and left, as if with that said, he could just as easily walk away from Olivia Sutton.

Colin watched him stalk across the deck and smiled.

His brother was about to learn a hard lesson in matters of the heart.

Chapter 9

Robert thought about Colin's advice for two days before he got up the nerve to approach Olivia.

Just ask her, his brother had said.

Seemed simple enough, once he got right down to it, until he found himself crossing the deck to where she stood chatting amiably with one of Colin's crew—and in a language he'd never heard.

As Robert came up to them, the sailor bobbed his head, said something to Olivia that left her laughing and went back to his work.

"What language was that?" he asked.

"Slavic," she said, her eyes alight. "The man is most fascinating. He was kidnapped as a child from his village and hasn't spoken his native tongue in years."

"How did he know you spoke Slavic?"

She shrugged. "They all want to see if I speak their

language. And it is quite exhilarating to get to practice again. I've only been stumped once so far—by one of the crew whose mother was an Iroquois Indian from the Americas. I must say, your brother has quite a diverse and interesting crew."

That was putting it mildly, Robert thought. He wondered if Olivia would still say that if she knew his brother's crew had been culled from the very dregs of the Royal Navy—some of the most nefarious and cutthroat sailors in the fleet. And she looked upon them as a London lady might greet her guests at an afternoon tea party.

There was no denying that Olivia Sutton was an unusual minx. Innocent one moment, defiantly maddening the next. It made Robert only that much more curious to uncover her secrets . . . her past . . . .

"How many languages do you speak?" he asked, trying to come up with some way to broach the subject he wanted to discuss, and finding only an idle question to bridge the silence.

"Speak?" She shrugged. "About sixteen. I can read many more. Speaking is difficult without someone to practice with." She paused for a moment, her expression turning wistful.

Robert could have kicked himself.

Her father. She was remembering her father. He could see the pain and anger on her face as clearly as it had been there when Chambley had told her about Sir Sutton's murder.

She seemed to shake off the unhappy recollection and settled down again on the coil of rope, where she'd obviously been doing some mending.

Robert sat on the deck beside her. While the subject

may not be a pleasant one for her, perhaps it would give him the opening he needed. "Did you practice your skills with your father?"

She nodded. "He and I used to speak in a different language each day, so neither of us would get out of practice."

"I'm sorry about what happened to him," Robert told her. "He sounds like a good man. I know he was highly respected. Well, before—"

Olivia glanced at him, her expression guarded. "Yes. Before." She paused for a moment. "But, thank you. He was a good man. And very intelligent. He spoke over thirty languages and was a master of codes and encyphering. I had hoped to learn them all from him . . . one day."

"Thirty!" Robert shook his head. "Wellington would have loved him. He's always looking for someone with a head for decoding the French missives we intercept."

"Perhaps I could volunteer for that duty," she suggested, glancing up at him from beneath her lacy lashes, a sly smile on her face.

"I'll make that recommendation when we get to headquarters," he told her, trying to ignore the wry twist of her rosy lips and the way his body tightened at the memory of them pressed to his.

She laughed, and then they settled into an awkward silence for a time, with only the creaking of the ship and whistle of the wind overhead.

Robert did his best to shake off his wayward thoughts—of the day in the park or when he'd awakened from his fever with her asleep on his chest, her hair splayed over his bare chest, her arm flung possessively over him.

For her part, Olivia plied her needle, her movements steady and sure, obviously unaware of the turmoil within him. As far as he could tell, her thoughts still dwelled with her father and Lord Chambley's revelation. She held her work out to examine it and sighed.

It was then that he noticed what she was sewing. "Isn't that Aquiles's jacket?"

"Yes," she said, holding up the tattered coat. "I told him he needed a new one, but he says this is his lucky jacket and will not part with it. Where have you two been? It looks as if you've taken on the entire French army single-handed." She turned it one way, then the other, revealing several long slashes and patches where the jacket had been mended before. "What happened here?" she asked, pointing to a long slash.

Robert laughed. "What did Aquiles tell you?"

She snorted, and then said in a perfect imitation of his servant, "That is like a little mosquito bite. A pesky Frenchie nipped at me, but I swatted him away like a fly." She shook her head. "It looks to me like the French have nipped at you often."

"You could say that the French are not fond of us."

Suddenly her head slanted to one side, and she cast him a sly, almost seductive glance. "Is there anyone who is fond of you, Robert Danvers?"

Her question startled him, for he realized she was not just asking about his enemies, she was also inquiring about his life. And his heart.

Once again, she'd pulled at that strange, tenuous bond that had a way of drawing him closer to her. Of making him forget everything that needed to be said . . . and what was better left unsaid.

Before he could stammer a reply or deny the answer

that clamored to be said, Jemmy Reyburn came bounding up to where they sat.

"I say, Major, 'bout time you and I had that match we've been discussing." The young man grinned at Olivia. "Unless you're still too weak and sickly."

Robert rose to the youthful challenge, only too thankful to be leaving the powder keg her question had opened. "Now is a perfect time. I wouldn't want to be back to full strength and completely humiliate you."

Olivia watched the two men posture and challenge each other and almost threw up her hands in disgust. She had just about been able to breach the walls surrounding Robert's well-guarded heart when Jemmy had interrupted them.

She wanted to know what he knew about Hobbe and why since she'd mentioned that name he had been holding her at arm's length—as if he suspected her of some heinous crime far beyond shooting Chambley.

What she really needed to know was that she wasn't just a duty to him, that he believed in her, trusted her, that he would give her his loyalty as he obviously had this Lando.

She glanced up to see Robert and Jemmy clearing a section of the deck. And not far from where they stood, two polished swords glinted in the sunshine.

Fencing? The man's arm was barely healed and he was going to fence? She rose from her spot and began to cross the deck, the crew clearing a path for her. For a moment, she sympathized with the French. There were times when she wholeheartedly shared their displeasure with Robert Danvers.

Halfway across the ship, Aquiles caught her by the arm. "Leave him be, little miss."

"I will not. I did not spend all that time seeing him healed only to see him hurt again."

Aquiles shrugged. "He needs to get ready to go back to the field. Why, the last time he was shot, I just stitched him up and we kept riding for the next two weeks."

"It's a wonder he has any lives left," she muttered.

"It is not so good for a man to be contained," Aquiles continued. "The major is a man who needs his *freedom*."

His freedom. Olivia suspected what his servant meant was freedom from her. From anything that would keep him from his work. From his duty to Wellington.

Aquiles kindly smile and shrug seemed to tell her— no, warn her—of what to expect. That in Robert's life, there was no room for her. No room for matters of the heart.

When she glanced back up at him, he'd stripped off the shirt he'd been wearing and was down to only his breeches.

Olivia took a deep breath and glanced away to avoid staring. Yet with her eyes shut, her memories gave her just as clear a vision, for she couldn't, nay, would never forget the sight of him as he'd awakened from his fever and what a truly magnificent spectacle his bared body was to behold.

And to touch. The warmth of his chest against her cheek. The tangy, manly scent of him, so close, so intimate.

It was one thing to have him gone with fever, naked and helpless, but a vital and alive Robert Danvers was a dangerous temptation. Even as she watched him take up his sword and stretch, flexing the blade back and forth in the air, Olivia imagined those same arms entwined around her, pulling her close and hauling her against the bare heat of his body.

She blinked away the image, but what she saw before her was just as sensual.

Robert paced back and forth, his long legs and muscled body moving with fluid elegance as he tested his weapon against an unseen foe, his every gesture showing his incredible skill and grace. A deadly grace.

Deadly?

"Those blades are blunted, aren't they?" she asked.

Aquiles eyed them. "Oh, they can't hurt themselves with those."

She relaxed a bit, but still she couldn't help but worry about him.

As the younger man drew his weapon and turned it right and left with a great flourish, the crew began to take notice. Soon men were dropping their chores and gathering in knots about the fringes, and from the looks of it, wagering with abandon over who would be the victor.

Jemmy, she knew, was a skilled fencer, so she didn't cast too much concern in his direction, but Robert was still healing.

Within a circle drawn in chalk on the deck, Jemmy and Robert faced off.

Her mending forgotten, Olivia watched, along with the crew, mesmerized.

The two men eyed each other, their intense focus only on their opponent. Neither of them seemed to notice the cheers and cries as their blades first hit.

The steel collided with a mighty crash, and Olivia flinched.

Those blades certainly didn't look dull to her. "Are you sure they're safe?"

Aquiles waved off her concerns. "They are just boys. What harm is a little practice?"

Without even realizing what she was doing, she edged her way along the deck, her back pressed to the railing, her gaze fixed on the combatants.

Back and forth the two men moved, steel clashing between them with deadly precision.

Deadly . . .

Despite Aquiles's assurances, she had a feeling there was more to this sport than met the eye.

Robert moved as if he were one with the steel, as if the blade were a mere extension of his arm. He followed Jemmy's every advance with a determined stance, and then just as quickly it was Jemmy who found himself on the defense, as Robert suddenly pushed forward.

Olivia took a quick breath at this swift reversal.

Slashing every which way to defend his position, Jemmy lost ground rapidly. Though the young man would probably have found it humiliating at his club to be beaten back with such ease, instead the youth grinned with unabashed pride, especially as the crew shouted encouragement to him.

That seemed to rally Jemmy's confidence, and he made a driving push forward, using Robert's wounded side to his advantage—something Olivia thought hardly fair.

But she learned very quickly that Robert had been just baiting his partner. Suddenly his arm arced over his head, bringing his sword crashing toward Jemmy.

Sparks flew as their blades hit, and then Jemmy's spun wildly out of his hands, going end over end until it crashed into the railing next to Olivia, the point imbedded a good inch into the polished wood.

It teetered and wobbled back and forth.

Olivia knew how it felt, for her legs were doing the same thing. She took several quick breaths, trying to find the air that had whooshed out of her lungs with the same speed as the blade that had nearly shorn her in half.

As she turned and surveyed the steel blade not a foot from her heart, it struck her—they hadn't been practicing with dulled blades. The sword could easily slice a man in half.

Or a woman.

"What were you thinking?" she said to Robert.

"Or you?" she said, turning the other half of her wrath on Jemmy.

They both turned sheepish.

Robert shrugged, while Jemmy blurted out, "We hadn't meant it to get out of hand."

"Out of hand? You could have killed each other," she scolded. Olivia crossed the deck until she stood toe to toe with Robert. "And you. I didn't sit up for a week just to see you throw away all my hard work. You'll put yourself right back in that berth, and then where will I be?"

Robert only seemed to have gained more energy from the exertion. He grinned at her, then leaned down and whispered into her ear. "Hopefully right beside me."

"Oh!" she sputtered. "You're impossible." She turned on one heel and marched back to the spot on the deck where she had been doing her sewing. Picking up her mending with new vigor, she wielded her needle like a small blade, stabbing the material and mercilessly sewing the frayed edges together.

Jemmy sidled up beside Robert. "The Queen is in rare form there. She'll be mad for at least an hour, then she'll simmer down. Never fails."

"The Queen?" Robert asked.

"My own name for her. She came to live with us when I was young. Hate to admit it, but I had nightmares and used to scurry to her room to hide from them. She would tell me the story of Queen Mab to explain them away. She said it helped her when she had bad dreams." Jemmy glanced over at Olivia again. "I took to calling her my Queen Mab. Silly, I suppose." He grabbed the hilt and pulled the sword out of the deck rail. "Go another round?"

Robert nodded and followed the young man back to the chalk circle.

So Olivia suffered from nightmares.

He wondered if they were from what she had witnessed or what she had done all those years ago.

"Hey there," Jemmy said, flopping down on the deck beside Olivia. "Did you see that last round? I very nearly beat him."

"I've been busy."

"Oh, don't be mad at him. His arm is fine. A man can't be cooped up and mothered for too long." Jemmy stretched out, his hands behind his head. "Major Danvers says I'm a fine hand with a blade and if my riding is as capital, I would fit right into one of the better cavalry units. He'd even recommend me for a posting."

She put down her mending. "Since when did you

become his admirer? Do you remember a few days ago when you were going to challenge him to a duel?"

Jemmy waved her off. "That was when I thought he was Bradstone." He leaned forward. "Do you know who Major Danvers is?"

"A kidnapper? A scoundrel? A beast of a man?"

He blew out an exasperated breath. "He's a demmed hero. Everyone knows who he is. If you and mother weren't so busy reading the social pages and gossip columns, you would know he was instrumental in saving hundreds, probably thousands of lives during Moore's retreat to Corunna. And I've heard his work behind the lines is legendary. Why, he once intercepted a packet of missives filled with directives signed by Napoleon. It enabled Lord Wellington to cut off vital French supply lines and drive an entire battalion across the border."

Olivia glanced across the deck to where Robert was cleaning up with a rough cloth and a bucket of seawater. He appeared, as Jemmy had described, the immortal warrior, muscled, unstoppable, righteous in his cause.

As she imagined her Hobbe would be in the same situation.

But despite Jemmy's assurances, she still wished she could trust Robert as she knew she would innately trust her imaginary hero. This living, breathing man, her occasional hero, was holding something back from her. He wasn't telling her the entire truth.

There was more to his search for the secrets behind The King's Ransom than just finding the treasure, and it had to do with her. And Hobbe.

But how they were connected she couldn't fathom.

And until she uncovered that piece, Olivia wasn't about to trust Major Robert Danvers.

For she feared he already held her heart, and that, she knew from experience, was perilous enough.

Colin had asked her to dine with him that night, not that she hadn't dined with him before, but tonight would be different, he explained, a small celebration. It seemed they were drawing near to Lisbon and their journey would be over shortly.

As Olivia made her preparations, as meager as they were with her limited toilet, she decided to wear the beautiful sprigged muslin gown she had found in Georgiana Danvers's trunk. Colin had offered her his wife's store of clothes, since Olivia had brought nothing aboard ship other than the bloodstained dress she'd been wearing.

The captain's wife was about her size, and her clothes were as practical as they were well made. Olivia liked the lady immediately, the more so when she found the most unusual article of clothing at the bottom of the weathered trunk. A small pair of unfinished britches that couldn't possibly fit the tall captain but certainly couldn't belong to his lady wife.

But when she'd taken them to Colin and tried to tell him of the additional clothes in the trunk, he'd laughed.

"Oh, the devil take my wife. She promised she wouldn't make another pair of those." Captain Danvers shook his head. "She wears those when she climbs the rigging and at home she has a pair she wears under her riding habit. She swears they are more comfortable than anything Bond Street considers fashionable."

Olivia regarded the woman whose clothes she'd in-

herited through fate with high admiration. And she'd
finished the twill britches at night during her shifts by
Robert's side.

She could well imagine what Lady Finch would say
about a lady wearing britches.

As she climbed the ladders between decks and
walked around the deck, secretly wearing her new ac-
quisition beneath her more matronly dimity gown, she
felt quite scandalous.

But tonight she decided to wear another treasure
she'd found in Georgie Danvers's trunk. A sheer dress
that was as daring as it was gorgeous. Cut low at the
neck, the fabric draped down to Olivia's feet; the white
embroidered leaves and vines decorating the dress
shimmered in the lantern light.

She tried to tell herself that with her very staid
chemise on beneath and with her hair done so matronly in a plain chignon, she wasn't *that* improper.
That is, until she entered Colin's cabin.

Gavin was there to serve the dinner, and he was the
first one to spot her. He let out a low and entirely indecent whistle.

His father frowned at him and bade him to go fetch
the soup. "Good evening, Miss Sutton," Colin said in
his most formal tones, bowing to her.

She curtseyed to her host. So he knew her real
name. She supposed she should be relieved that he
knew the truth, for she hadn't liked lying to him in the
first place. As she looked up, she spied Robert lounging across the room, his back to her. His head turned
slowly, and for a moment he stared at her as if he had
never seen her before.

A startled light flamed to life in his eyes. While it
blazed hot and fast, the look that followed told her that

perhaps she should have stuck to the more demure and practical dimity gown of Georgie Danvers's that she had taken to wearing during the day.

His gaze raked from the open neck of her dress over where it clung to her breasts, rounded over her hips and grazed slowly down the length of her legs until it reached the tips of the satin slippers she wore.

She took a slow, deep breath. The intimacy of his examination left her with the feeling of not just his eyes but his touch having inspected every inch of her. Her breasts tingled, while her legs faltered for a moment as an unsteady rush flooded her middle.

He too had taken some care with his preparations for dinner. His hair was brushed, he'd managed to shave and he wore what she guessed was Colin's second best jacket, though on Robert the coat cut tightly across his chest.

Robert made his bow, but his eyes never left her. "Olivia," he said, his voice deep and husky. "You look . . . lovely this evening." He took her hand and brought it to his lips. The moment they whispered over her skin, the heat of his touch burned and enflamed the already heated response he'd elicited from her with his scorching gaze.

"Thank you," she mumbled, hastily retrieving her hand and taking the seat Colin offered.

"I hope you aren't still angry over this afternoon," Robert said, his words teasing down her spine with their smoky fingers.

She paused for a moment, trying to still her wildly beating heart. "No, I can't say that I am. Especially since you seem quite well yourself this evening. Apparently there was no harm in a bit of exercise."

As awkwardness settled over the table, Colin made

his best attempts to diffuse it. "Do try this wine, Miss Sutton," he said. "It is from Portugal and quite nice."

She smiled as he filled her glass.

Robert waved the offer away. His own glass was half filled with a liquor that swirled in a chestnut haze.

Gavin brought in the soup and served them with little incident other than grinning at Olivia and filling her bowl more than the others.

"My wife will be quite vexed with me," Colin was saying.

"Why is that?" she asked, trying to keep up with the conversation and ignore the dark, heated looks from the other guest at the table.

Colin grinned. "I've always told her she was the prettiest lady that I ever beheld when she wore that gown, but I must say you do it ample justice."

Olivia blushed. She had the feeling that the color rose all the way from the tips of her breasts up to her scalp. Struggling to ignore her embarrassment, she tried to change the subject. "Tell me about your wife, Captain Danvers. I always wondered how it was that men of the sea found time to court a lady. How did you meet her?"

Apparently the subject was something of a family scandal, for both Colin and Robert sputtered over their soup.

"At a ball," he finally managed to mutter.

"Oh, how romantic," she said.

"Yes, it was very romantic, from what I've heard," Robert said, his tone teasing. "Do tell Miss Sutton all about it."

"It was just a regular sort of ball," Colin said abruptly, turning his full attention back to his soup.

Olivia wasn't really listening. She was watching Robert. And right now his eyes sparkled with a mischievous gleam.

"It wasn't a regular sort of ball, Da," Gavin said. The impetuous boy turned to Olivia. "They met at the Cyprians' Ball."

Robert burst out laughing as Colin's very proper features colored to the dark shade of a beet, while Olivia uttered a surprised, "Oh my."

Lady Finch had a two page sheet of advice on how ladies could keep their husbands from attending London's most scandalous event. The Cyprians' Ball was the annual fête thrown by the most expensive and illustrious demimondaines and Incognitas about town.

No decent, self-respecting lady of the *ton* would dare set foot in such company. Despite the fact that their men flocked to the event.

"That sounds quite interesting," she managed to say, while searching for a more neutral subject to raise and to keep her attention away from Robert, whose eyes danced with merry delight at his brother's discomfiture and her innocent surprise. When she glanced over at him, she found his amusement infectious and brought her hands to her lips to stifle the giggle threatening to spill from them.

And in that shared moment, their gazes met, and Olivia was mesmerized. This was a side of him he exhibited so rarely that she wondered if this was the real Robert Danvers—a man of warm humor and deep passions. She also couldn't help wondering, as she looked even deeper into his green eyes, if she'd ever be able to know the answer for herself. For the woman, she guessed, who could find the key to unlock his hidden side would discover a prize greater than all the gold in Spain.

She hastily dropped her gaze. There was no point in dwelling on questions she'd never find the answer to, so she asked his brother, "Captain Danvers, have you been to Lisbon before? I hear it is a beautiful city. Pray, do tell me about it."

Colin looked more than relieved to escape the scandalous subject at hand and leaped into a rapt discussion of Lisbon's good food and friendly people.

While Robert and Colin debated in friendly and familiar tones the finer points of the city, Olivia wondered at her own fate in Portugal. After she met Wellington, then where would she be?

Back on a ship home? And to what? A hanging?

What if news of Chambley had already reached the British officials in Lisbon? Would they be waiting at the docks with shackles and a confessor for her last rites or just transfer her to the nearest ship bound for Botany Bay?

She could only imagine what would happen to her if her translation of The King's Ransom's location turned out to be wrong. Robert would probably lead the hanging party himself.

She choked and sputtered on the bite of tart she had just taken.

"Are you all right?" Robert asked, reaching over to pat her on the back. His hand was warm and strong, his touch burning through the thin fabric of her gown.

For a moment, her gaze met his, and that strange, inexplicable fire between them blazed to life, drawing them together. In that second, Olivia could have believed the entire world consisted just of them. And she had no doubts that Robert felt the same—his gaze held her captive with unrelenting desire.

With temptation and a promise.

It terrified her to find that she wanted nothing more than to give in to his passionate, unspoken offer.

Just as quickly, as if he sensed her surrender, he pulled his hand away, breaking the spell.

"I'm fine, thank you," she told him. "I think I just need a little air." She rose from the table, Colin and Robert bounding to their feet as well.

She thanked the Captain for the excellent meal and left the room.

Robert watched her go, his body aching to follow her, to stay within the graceful shadow of her light.

He'd always thought her a beautiful woman, despite her penchant for widow's weeds. But tonight he'd discovered a woman he'd only seen hints of before.

Tonight the sight of Olivia had taken his breath away.

The gown had only revealed what he had long suspected lurked beneath her matronly disguises, the body of a woman meant to be bedded and bedded often.

He couldn't help himself. He started to follow her.

"What are you doing?" Colin asked.

"I don't plan on seducing the woman, if that is what you are worried about," he said, though the knot in his gut said very clearly he was lying.

"Harumph," Colin clucked like an old woman. "I'm surprised you had any room for the meal, considering you spent most of the evening devouring the luscious Miss Sutton with your eyes."

Robert made a step around the table, but Colin stopped him. "I wouldn't advise going after her."

Shaking off Colin's grip, Robert asked, "Why the hell not?"

"Because the last time Georgie wore that dress was eight months ago."

"So?" Robert said, his attention still focused on the now empty doorway.

"Our next child is due in a month," Colin warned, but he was saying it to an empty cabin.

Chapter 10

Robert followed Olivia up onto the deck, despite his lingering misgivings about her. That afternoon he'd had every intention of asking her how she knew about Hobbe and what she knew of Orlando's death, but then she'd distracted him with that damn question of hers and that sidelong glance that had nearly done him in.

While he wanted to agree with Colin that she had nothing to do with Orlando's death, there was no disputing the fact that she had been at the scene of the murder. And there was no arguing that she wasn't incapable of firing a fatal shot.

But most of all, he had to find a way to extinguish this fire she stoked in his gut with her every glance, her all too rare touch, and the constant memory of her passionate kiss.

Above deck, the night was still and black except for

the glittering of a million stars overhead and a tiny sliver of a moon that cast its thin beam of light across the endless waves. But even in the pitch dark of night, Olivia was easy to find.

Her white gown practically glowed like the moon itself, making up for the poor crescent above. And he found himself inexplicably drawn to her.

"We're getting close," he said, taking a sniff of the air. "Not much longer at all."

She didn't turn around. "So we discussed at dinner."

"There are some things I want to ask you," he said, faltering over just what he needed to know first.

Olivia shifted from one foot to the other, then slowly she turned to face him. The wind ruffled her hair, pulling those tantalizing tendrils of fire free from her carefully crafted chignon. "You already know all my secrets."

"I suppose I should first thank you for saving my life," he said, moving closer to her until he stood next to her at the rail. He gripped the polished wood and hung on, rather than give in to the temptation to take her in his arms.

"You already have. Really, I only did what anyone else would have done," she said, her face still pointed out at the empty sea.

Her profile revealed a woman with finely sculpted features, a delicate nose, and lips . . . lips he could spend a lifetime kissing.

Oh, how he wanted her. As much or more than he needed to hear her say the words that would set his tormented soul free.

Deny your involvement in all this.

Yet all he could hear was Chambley's taunting voice

when he claimed that Olivia had joined in Bradstone's treachery willingly and wantonly.

He wanted to sweep aside his doubts, but they twisted in his gut with tendrils that curled around his soul like Pymm's most poisonous concoction.

He faltered for something else to say. "My shoulder feels almost like new. However did you learn to tend a gunshot wound?"

He thought for a moment that she flinched, as if pierced by the steely hot kiss of lead herself.

"I never have," she said quietly. "Tended one, that is. But Lady Finch considers herself quite an expert on medical matters—she treats all the injured at the manor—and I've assisted from time to time, but never like what I had to do for you." She sighed and brushed her hands over her skirt. "You should really thank her ladyship. She has some rather specific instructions on caring for flesh wounds, and I've copied them so many times, I suppose I've committed them to memory." She glanced over at him. "Anything else?"

Robert shifted uneasily. "Well, yes. How did you . . . well . . . oh, dammit, it isn't every day you see a woman shoot a man. Where'd you learn to handle a pistol like that?"

She didn't flinch this time, but he watched as she came to the conclusion he had been drawing her toward.

"You don't want to know where I learned to shoot but *when*, don't you, Robert?"

"Even you'll admit it is rather unusual for a woman—"

"To be able to shoot a man."

He looked away, feeling an unfamiliar sense of guilt

over his doubts about her. "Yes," he finally said, unwilling to give up until he had his answers.

"What you really want to know is if Chambley is the first man I've ever shot or was he the second." She stood before him, so strong and sure, virtuous in her stance. She made him feel almost ashamed of himself for doubting her.

"I never said—"

"Oh, stow it, Robert. You don't have to. You've been trying to ask me since we first met." She turned and faced him. "You want to know if I killed that poor boy. You want to know if I had a hand in his murder. What do your instincts tell you? Better yet, what does your heart tell you?"

His gut? His heart? His gut told him she was capable of anything.

But murder?

That question he didn't want to answer.

"I don't know," he finally managed to say.

"You don't know? After all this time, that's what your gut tells you? How can that be?" There was an urgency to her question that went beyond the obvious—as if she needed his honesty as much as he needed hers.

How in that moment he wanted to tell her the truth, to open himself up to her so there would be no secrets between them—nothing between them but their damned need for each other—but he couldn't do it. Not just yet. Not when there was so much at stake.

"Because my first allegiance is to Wellington. You've forced my hand, so that I have to take you to him, but I'd be a fool to put you before him and not trust you. Especially given your repu—"

"What? My reputation as a murderess? Next you'll be accusing me of being a French spy."

When she said it that way, it made him feel ridiculous.

"I've never killed anyone, Robert. Contrary to what the newspapers said, contrary to what Chambley said, I never killed that man."

Her emphatic statement hit him at the heart of his doubts. Why couldn't he just believe—like Colin seemed to be able to, like Jemmy did when he looked at her with his youthful and approving gaze?

Years of spying had left him full of cynicism, unable to believe with his heart as he had no doubts she did. And she looked at him now, expectantly, as if she wanted him to scale the wall he'd put up between them—for there on the other side she was waiting, hopefully, willingly . . .

Just then a freshening breeze rustled at her hair, teasing more of it out of place, the long tendrils curling down to her shoulders and floating up as if coaxed to dance by the wind. They tantalized him with their undulating movements, beckoning him to free the rest of her tendrils from their matronly prison.

She brushed at the loose strands and tried to poke them back into place, but he stopped her, taking her hand and holding it in his.

"Leave them be. I like your hair as it is." He didn't let go of her hand. Unfortunately for him, his need for answers was only surpassed by his need to know *her*.

In an entirely different sense.

"When have you ever seen my hair loose?" she asked, tugging at her hand, but only half-heartedly.

Robert knew that if she wanted her hand back,

Olivia was not the type to take no for an answer. "When I was sick. I may not have seemed lucid all the time, but I do remember you leaning over me, wiping my brow, talking to me." He paused for a moment, re-calling when he'd awakened and found her asleep atop him, her hair spilling over him like a silken sheet. He also recalled one other memory. "Oh, yes, there was the time when your hair was loose and you kissed me."

"I never," she said, but her color told another story.

One thing about Olivia Sutton he had learned was that she was a terrible liar. Try as she might, when she told a falsehood, she blushed.

And right now, even in the dark, he could see she was turning a rosy shade of untruth.

"Are you sure?" he asked.

"Why would I want to kiss you? I've already had the pleasure and it was rather unremarkable."

Her color rose again. Another lie. Robert pressed his advantage by tugging her closer and wrapping his arms around her. "Are you sure you didn't press your lips against mine just once, just because you feared you might not ever have another chance?"

"Oh, you arrogant beast. That wasn't it at all. I kissed you because I—"

He grinned down at her. "So now we have the truth. You admit you did kiss me. You don't need to tell me why. Your secret is safe with me."

"Why you . . . I should have left you to die!"

"That would have been foolish," he told her. "Be-cause then you wouldn't have been able to do this." And with that, his mouth covered hers, where first a muffled cry of protest sputtered forth, but he pressed his advantage, teasing her lips with his tongue to open for him, and then swept inside like a conquering hero.

She melted into his embrace.

And responded with the same wrenching passion that had nearly been his undoing so many weeks ago in London. Her answering touch held all the boldness he had long suspected she possessed. Her tongue met his, taunting him into her lair and then stroking him with her fevered kiss.

Her hands pulled him closer and her body melded with his, the thin fabric of her dress seeming to melt away as breasts pressed into his chest. Her hips swayed against the swollen, taut hardness that had blazed to life from the moment he'd started this tempestuous kiss.

His hand went to her breast, where he found the nipple hard and poised, as if waiting for his touch. As he started to roll his thumb over the nub, she sighed with a longing and need that matched his own.

Olivia's senses reeled, her body coming alive under his skilled touch.

His mouth still bound hers in a kiss, one that she didn't want to break. His tongue teased her, stroked her, called to her to trust him, to open herself to him.

To let go with all the wanton abandon that he awakened in her body.

Yet some part of her still clung to a fragile bit of sanity. To the notion that Robert Danvers's involvement with her was more than just a treasure hunt and that he wanted something more from her than just her body. Something that could destroy any chance of honesty, of true feelings between them.

And if she went to him now, like this, she wondered

if she would ever learn the truth. And so if she was to find out if Robert Danvers was the hero of her heart or another villain come to steal her secrets, she did the last thing she wanted to do.

She broke away from him with every ounce of strength she possessed.

"I can't do this," she said, her words coming out in passionate, ragged gasps. "I won't do this." With that, she ran from the deck and was down the ladder before he could stop her.

Olivia sought the refuge of her cabin but found that the devilment from above deck only hounded her below. She'd kissed him. She'd not only kissed him, she'd let him touch her like some type of wanton.

She wasn't like that. But her body told a different story. She'd wanted Robert with a passion and fire that kindled her blood until it raged unquenchable and demanding.

She struggled to get out of Georgie's dress, tugging the confounded thing over her head and tossing it into a heap in the corner. She should never have worn the thing, should never have gone up to the deck, never have hoped and prayed that Robert would follow her and never have wished on one of those countless stars that he would kiss her again.

But he had.

Her hand went to her still swollen lips. They tingled with the remembrance of his touch. That wasn't all that tingled, but she chose to ignore those feelings.

She had to.

She didn't know Robert Danvers any better than she had known Bradstone when she'd fallen prey to his lies and deceptions. And while Jemmy thought the man a hero, she was still unconvinced.

Tossing herself down on the wide berth that took up most of the room, Olivia discovered that sleep was as devilish as Robert's kiss. At first it eluded her, and when it came, it was as unwanted and unnerving, carrying her into the nightmare she'd fought and lost for seven years.

At first she resigned herself to its reliable and unchangeable course, but this time the dream had changed. She knew that in an instant and fought to free herself from its dark grasp.

She tried to scream, tried to find help, but she knew she was all alone.

So instead, Olivia Sutton poised herself to fight the battle for her soul once again.

The first scream sent Robert straight out of his bunk. The second one had him out of his cabin, jumping into his breeches with the practiced ease of a man who'd fled the French with less time to dress.

He raced through Colin's cabin, noting that his brother was nowhere to be seen, and went straight to Olivia's room. He hesitated for a blink of an eye and then threw the door open, not sure what he was about to find.

Moonlight streamed through the portal, lighting the wide berth that took up the length of the narrow room. There Olivia writhed and twisted on the bed, the sheet and blanket tangled in knots around her. Her chemise rode high, her legs bare well up to her thighs. She kicked and flailed at her phantom assailants.

He reached for her without thinking, trying to catch her up and rescue her from her demons.

"Olivia, wake up. It's a dream." An unholy one, he thought, as he watched her lashes flutter open, a raw fear blazing in her eyes, revealing a hint of the horrors she fought in her sleep.

She struggled against him and with such fury that he let her go. The moment he released her, she turned her anger on the sheets and blankets trapping her, pulling and tearing at them until they too released her from their grasp.

For a moment she paused, her breath coming in wild, ragged pants, like a fox at the end of the hunt.

Her gaze then took in her surroundings in wild, quick glances, as if she were looking for any more hidden assailants in the pale shimmer of moonlight. She blinked several more times until her gaze found and focused on him.

Her eyes widened with horror, and she scrambled away from him as if he were the object of her fears.

Then it hit him. She thought he was Bradstone.

"Olivia, it's me, Robert," he whispered, trying to soothe the fear still riding high in her eyes. "You're safe, there is no one here who will harm you."

He crossed the room, climbing into the bunk beside her and pulling her into his arms. Olivia fought him for a moment, but then, as if all her strength faded away, she gave in to his embrace.

She nestled further into his arms, something about her simple, trusting movements touching a part of his heart rarely reached. And as she tipped her head to his, he could think of nothing but blotting out the past with just one kiss.

Just one simple kiss.

He should have known from experience that a kiss between them would never be simple.

Surely it started that way, with their lips caressing, but then she opened up to him, her tongue flicking over his teeth, offering an invitation that pushed aside his reluctance, his misgivings, his distrust of this woman.

It was all overruled as his body clamored with reawakened need.

His mouth welcomed her lips, their soft, inviting touch caressing him, stroking him, inflaming him. Her hands curled around his neck and pulled him closer, her breasts pressing against his chest.

Unable to resist, his hand cupped one of them, pushing aside the fabric there, so he could feel her, touch the satin of her skin, the pebbled flesh of her nipple as it hardened under the feathery touch of his fingers.

She sighed, an earthy cry of need, and arched her back. "Do that again," she whispered.

And so he did. And she made the same contented little sound that only served to encourage him to explore her passionate needs all the more.

His mouth moved over her neck, down the slope of her shoulder. Her hair brushed against his cheek; the rich scent of the sea and wind whispered from those errant, fiery strands. Beneath his lips, her pulse fluttered and beat, while her mouth sighed and whispered encouragement in his ear. His lips trailed over her breast, the one he'd teased to a hardened peak. Once there he took it into his mouth and suckled, his teeth grazing over her, his tongue stroking her as his fingers had done before.

When he looked up, her mouth had fallen open in a moue of pleasure and surprise, while her eyes, alight with smoky passion, revealed the depths of pleasure she was finding under his ministrations.

His own body had grown hard at their first kiss, but now his member strained against his breeches, throbbing and demanding. He wanted more from her, wanted to see all of her, and so he tugged and pulled and tore at her chemise until it was discarded and lost from view.

Olivia lay back in the bunk, her body thrumming with a life she'd never felt before. She felt so wanton, so free, so alive, that she cared not that she didn't truly trust this man.

And yet she did.

How many times had she wished for someone to come and vanquish her nightmares, consign her enemies to a place where they would never hurt her again? And he had. All with his kiss. Something inside her trusted his touch, knew that his heart belonged to her and her alone. And so she couldn't refuse him, not when her body sang and beat in a wild tattoo under his passionate guidance.

When his lips had found her breast, a new world had begun to uncoil. For while the *ton* thought her a ruined woman, the truth be told, she had never made love before. Despite her passionate letters that all London had read, she'd never given in to more than Bradstone's practiced kiss. Even when they'd been alone in his bedchamber, she had shied away from taking that one last step into complete ruination. A wary voice had urged her to wait until she was truly wed, and now she understood that it had been some deep, instinctive part of her that had known not to trust Bradstone with such a gift. For now as something raw and untamed uncoiled deep inside her, promising hints of the burning fires to come, she was beginning to see, to realize why someone could give up so much for something so fleeting.

Robert had turned his attentions to her other breast, and it too was hard and tingling. But even more disconcerting was the hot, demanding need coming from the juncture of her thighs, in a place so private she dared not consider what pleasure could be found there.

And then he showed her. With his tongue still washing over the hardened peak of her breast, his fingers began to stray lower over her belly, her hips arching and guiding him on their own volition.

Touch me there, her body begged. *Please touch me there.*

When he did, she nearly cried out in delight, but his mouth had found hers again and cut of her ragged sigh with a deep, penetrating kiss.

As he shifted, closing any remaining gap between them, his body covered hers, and she felt his own hard need. A length of manly flesh, aroused and waiting for her.

His fingers had begun to explore the intimate folds of skin at her very core. Like long-held secrets, he coaxed each of them to reveal their need to him, her legs falling open, her hips arching to meet each gentle stroke.

It was like he was teasing her awake, pulling her toward something deep and unfathomable. Something her body wanted more than breath.

If it felt like this for her, surely, she thought, it must be the same for him. So with that in mind, she tentatively reached for him.

The heat of his manhood, the hardened evidence of what she aroused in him, made her bold. Her fingers found the buttons on his breeches and flicked them open, anxious to touch the flesh beneath, much as he had tugged and pulled at her chemise some time before. When the last button gave, the member beneath pushed through, springing up into her welcoming hand.

Now it was Robert's turn to groan, and his hips followed the same dance hers had done. Like satin in her hand, she ran her fingers over and down it, and marveling at her own wantonness. And yet it seemed so natural to be holding him, so part of her own need to be touching him like this.

Her fingers explored him from the coarse curls at the base to the rounded, velvety tip where it was already moist, slick with his readiness for her. It seemed to throb with a willingness to please her, a heady promise to fill the ache his fingers were eliciting from her depths.

Robert's touch had opened her, discovering a nubby jewel that seemed to have been waiting all this time for his caress.

So when he began to tease her, stroke her there, Olivia thought he was pulling the very breath from her. All her senses, the passion he'd been awakening in a long sensuous trail from her lips now converged in that one spot, begging for his touch, begging for release from that coiled prison.

"Oh, please, do that again," she whispered, when his fingers dipped into her and slowly moved up and over her own blossoming need.

"Do you like that?" he asked as he did it again.

"Yes," she managed to gasp.

Over and over he stroked her, bringing her to the brink of something she didn't understand yet wanted with a staggering need.

His thick, hard sex pulsed in her hand, and suddenly she knew what it was that was missing, what her body craved to feel.

"Make love to me," she told him. "Robert, please make love to me."

He grinned at her. "I thought you would never ask." Shifting his body so he fully covered her, his manhood nudged at her thighs, hard and insistent.

Olivia spread herself open to him willingly, anxious to have this empty, throbbing need inside her sated with his hardness. And as he pushed inside her, she sighed, arching her hips to take every inch of his velvet stroke—until he came to that unquestionable barrier.

Robert stopped abruptly and began to pull back.

Her eyes fluttered open; her hands caught his hips and held him fast, kept him inside her. There was shock on every feature of his face.

"What is it?" Olivia asked.

"You're a virgin!"

It wasn't a statement but an accusation.

She had wondered if he would notice, but obviously he had.

He started to pull out further, but she continued to hold him. "This is what I want, Robert. Don't stop now."

"But I can't . . . I mean, I thought . . . You've never done this before."

With one hand still on his hip, she caught his head with the other and pulled him down to her. Her lips caught his in a kiss, one she hoped would divert his attention. Inside her, she felt his member surge again, and she wanted to smile.

"What difference did it make to you five minutes ago? Make love to me, Robert," she whispered into his ear, while her hips rode along his length, teasing him.

For a moment he felt caught—trapped between what was honorable and what he wanted. And when he gazed into her eyes, he also could see it was what she wanted, needed. He'd never had a woman look up at him with such smoke-filled passion in her eyes. Olivia's eyes always revealed the truth about her, and right now she needed him to follow her lead.

She was also right. It hadn't mattered to him before he'd discovered her secret, and now, if he was to tell the truth, it only made him want her more.

Besides, his body ached for release, while hers thrummed with life, urging him to carry her over that abyss as well. And so he did.

"This can hurt," he said, breaking through her virgin's seal and pushing himself completely inside her.

She flinched for a moment, confusion at this sudden pain misting the passion on her face.

Slowly beginning again, he started to rekindle her fires, stroking her back to the place where they had been before, where their passions collided and held fast in ragged, mutual need.

Her hips began to match his, and he knew whatever pain he had caused her was now a long-forgotten memory. Her breath was coming in quick, anxious pants, and so he hastened his pace, urging her on.

Olivia wasn't sure what was happening as her entire world spun into one narrow focus. She followed his lead, her hips rising and falling, her hands clinging to his back. And then suddenly her entire world exploded. It was as if one moment she stood teetering at the edge of the unexpected and then she fell, tumbling into the awareness of what a man and woman could do together.

The passionate spasms wrenched a surprised cry

out of her, which Robert caught with his lips as he covered her mouth. His body moved within her with a hard, fierce urgency she understood. And then as suddenly he groaned, straining to fill her one last time as she sensed he too had fallen into that heavenly splendor that enveloped her senses and left her dreamy and fulfilled.

For a few moments, they lay coupled, one body, two hearts beating a wild, exotic rhythm in harmony that only they could hear. He stroked at the loose tendrils of her hair and whispered soft kisses on her bare shoulder. Her fingers splayed over those rough curls on his chest, loving the differences between their bodies and how completely they complemented each other.

"Thank you," she finally managed to whisper.

He shifted off her and cradled her in his arms. "You shouldn't be thanking me. I just ruined you." He shook his head.

She waved off his words. "You forget, I was ruined years ago. You only gave me what I've never had."

"What is that?"

"The memories of what I was missing!"

He laughed and reached over to toy with the chain around her neck, her only remaining adornment. "You should have told me," he insisted. "Here all this time, I had been thinking that—"

His words stopped abruptly as his fingers came to the ring at the end of the chain. He turned the simple band in the light, examining it, while his eyes went from passionate and loving to cold, dark anger in a matter of seconds.

"Where the hell did you get this?" he demanded, catching up the chain from her neck and holding it up between them. It dangled and flashed in the moonlight, a simple gold band, yet Olivia could sense nothing would be simple between them again.

She snatched it back. " 'Tis mine."

"I didn't ask that," he said, clambering out of the bed and staring down at her as if she had suddenly changed into Medusa. "I asked where you got it."

"It was given to me. As a promise," she said. "And one that is none of your business."

His eyes darkened with rage, with anger, with misunderstanding.

Tell him the truth, that voice from the past urged her. *Tell him.* But before she could, the boom of a cannon drove them further apart.

A second report brought the sound of footsteps pounding over the decks and all around them, as the crew disassembled the partitions that made up the underdecks and moved the cannons into position.

Robert grabbed the blanket, wrapped it around his midsection and started from the cabin. "Stay here," he ordered, before he left her in the darkness.

Olivia fumbled for her clothes, finding her chemise and the dimity gown she'd hung on the hook when she'd changed for dinner. Next came the pair of boots that Georgie Danvers kept aboard.

She knew she should probably stay below and out of the way, but her curiosity and fears drove her above. Besides, she had no intention of taking orders from Robert Danvers.

Above deck she found the entire crew of the *Sybaris* aloft, far above her, scampering over the crossbars and through the lines, setting the sails and making the ship ready for flight.

Even as she searched the deck for any sign of Colin

or Robert, a flash of powder, followed in an instant by the booming sound of a cannon sent her gaze across the sea where there loomed a great ship. Three decks high, a ship of the line, she thought they called them, a great towering enemy capable of vast destruction.

Just then the ball it had sent their way splashed not far from the side of the *Sybaris*.

A little bit closer and they would be . . . Olivia shuddered, not wanting to consider the ugly possibility.

She climbed the ladder to where Captain Danvers was shouting orders at the men aloft. Robert was at his side, but his eyes were focused on the ship gaining on them with every moment.

"French," he told her. Robert turned to Colin, who had just ordered his crew to turn out to sea. "What are you thinking? You've got enough cannon to take him. Show him what you've got below."

Jemmy had joined them on the deck, his eyes wide with excitement, a pistol in his hand.

Robert spared a glance at the young man, then asked his brother again, "Dammit, Colin, what are you doing? This is war. When have you ever run from a fight?"

"I can't," came Colin's terse reply as he marched across the deck and barked another order up into the rigging.

Robert was right behind him. "Why the hell not? That's the enemy. When did the Royal Navy start fleeing the French? It doesn't even look that well armed. With the cannon you've got hidden below you could—"

Olivia stepped forward and caught Robert by the arm. "He can't."

Both men turned and stared at her. She squared her

shoulders and explained, "Your brother can't let them get close to us. His entire hold is filled with powder. One shot from that ship and we'll light up the entire coast."

Colin acknowledged her revelation with a tight nod of his head.

Robert's face paled for a moment, not from fear, Olivia knew, but from cold dread born out of an understanding of what would happen to all of them if the French found their mark. "How can I help?"

Colin nodded to the hatchway leading to the gundecks. "Get below, all of you," he said, indicating Jemmy as well, "and help Livett get the cannon ready. If we must fight, I want to disable that bastard with one run and then get the hell out of here. I've got orders not to lose this cargo."

Robert turned to Olivia. "Get below. It will be safer."

She shook her head. "No. I don't want to be trapped down there. I'd rather take my chances up here."

"Then keep your head down." With that, he raced off to join Jemmy, who was already halfway down the open hatch.

Olivia shrank into the shadows, getting herself as far out of the way as possible. Her body still seemed caught in the cadence of Robert's lovemaking, thrumming with wild abandon and trembling with the chaos of confusion at his sudden, blinding anger.

It was as if he had recognized her ring. Had held it as if it were his own.

As if he'd known the original owner.

The realization shocked her to her very core. Robert had known that agent. Of this she was positive. But how? And who had that boy been to Robert? If only she could find the mysterious Hobbe, then she suspected she would finally find the truth.

Then a series of powder flashes erupted from the other ship's gunports, the report of the cannon louder and closer than it had been before.

Right then, Olivia doubted she would ever gain the answers she longed to find, for the French ship was gaining ground with every second.

Seconds the *Sybaris* and her crew could ill afford.

Chapter 11

A cannonball whistled overhead, passing over the bow of the ship without hitting anything. Several of the men whooped in joy, but the others, the more experienced hands, only cursed.

They knew, as Olivia guessed, that the next round wouldn't miss.

Robert's words uncoiled in her mind.

When did the Royal Navy start fleeing the French?

The Royal Navy?

The *Sybaris*, a naval ship? Every time she started to think she knew the Danvers men, another mystery landed in her lap. What other secrets were they keeping from her? For she had no doubt there were any number of them about to pop out of the woodwork.

Colin continued to bark a steady stream of orders, and the sails, every inch of them, unfurled and strained in a noisy, flapping whoosh of cloth and rope.

As if in answer to the prayers of all on board, a fresh breeze found them, sending the *Sybaris* leaping ahead on her new course at a breathless speed, riding over the waves and into the narrow line of moonlight that earlier had lit Olivia's berth.

The French ship moved to follow but had missed the breeze and now had to turn to tack, sails flapping impotently, their momentum slowing until they were nearly dead in the water.

The crew of the *Sybaris* cheered and jeered at their enemy, sending the taunts across the water in a cacophony of languages and vulgarity. The French were obviously not happy, for several of their sharpshooters started to fire aimlessly at their lost prize.

Colin frowned as first one bullet, then another pinged through their sails and chipped at the masts. Olivia ducked behind the railing and crawled behind a large rain barrel lashed to the deck.

"Dammit, keep your heads. We aren't free yet," Colin shouted at his men. He kept directing new headings and minding the sails to ensure they got every bit of the available wind.

And when the dawn started to peek over the horizon, they discovered they had lost the other ship. It was then that Robert came and joined her on the deck.

"We have unfinished business, you and I," he said.

She nodded and reached to her bodice, catching the silver chain there and tugging it until the ring sprang free from where it nestled beneath her breasts. "Do you know this?"

His brow furrowed, but he refused to answer.

"You knew him, didn't you? Who was he, Robert? Who is this Hobbe he spoke of?"

"Do not speak of him to me. Not ever," he said.

"Nor will I answer your questions. Not as long as you wear *that* around your neck like some prize."

Olivia bristled. A prize? Some ill-fated memento from her past? Is that what he thought it was?

"How can you think so little of me, sir? After . . . after . . ." She faltered over the words, her hurt and anger holding any further declarations fast in her throat. Instead, she shook the ring at him, hoping to anger him enough to reveal what he knew. "I'll not take this off until I have my answers."

But she'd met her stubborn match in Robert Danvers. "Then, Miss Sutton," he said, his voice just as stiff and formal as hers, "we have a stalemate."

"If it is a game we play, sir, then it is one you will lose," she said, her tone as icy as the cold chill closing over her heart.

At dusk Olivia learned they would be sailing not into Lisbon but into a cove some miles to the north of the city, where Captain Danvers was scheduled to meet a business associate later that night.

She didn't bother asking why this meeting had to take place under the cover of darkness and some distance from prying eyes. Olivia realized that like his brother, Colin offered more questions than answers about his life.

Standing at the rail, her valise clutched in her hand, she looked out into the inky, moonless night around them and could barely discern the shore in the distance. Robert, Jemmy, Aquiles and Livett had already taken their places in the bobbing longboat beside the *Sybaris*, and now it was her turn.

Captain Danvers held out his hand to her. "Thank

you, Miss Sutton, for saving his life." He nodded for Gavin to take her valise down to the boat.

She nodded, feeling a little choked up. While she still suspected Captain Danvers's activities bordered more on piracy than legitimacy, he had been nothing but generous and kind to her during her stay. "Some day I would like to meet your wife. Repay her for the clothes I've borrowed." She held out the hem of the cloak Colin had insisted she take along with the sprigged muslin tucked in her valise.

She had almost refused the muslin, for it brought back too many memories of Robert's passion, but Colin had been adamant she take the gown.

He'd left her to her packing, muttering something about the "demmed thing being nothing but trouble." He had that right.

"You've been most kind," she said. "Considering the inconvenience Mr. Pymm and Robert added to your journey."

The man glanced over the rail down at his brother and then back at her. "I was glad to have met *you*. I have learned that Pymm's inconveniences are often lessons in happenstance." He glanced over the railing at Robert, who sat staring moodily into the water. "Give him time," he told her.

With that, he bowed low over her hand and then helped her over the rail. As they rowed out of the shadow of the *Sybaris*, her last image of Captain Danvers was of the man climbing back onto the fo'c'sle, his face turned toward the now very distant shores of England.

She puzzled over his words, hoping to find some re-assurance in them that one day she and Robert would find a way to give each other the answers they so needed. To once again find the fragile trust and intimacy they had so briefly discovered on board the *Sybaris*.

The journey to shore went off without incident, leaving Olivia almost disappointed. With all their whispered plans and this dark departure, she had thought at the very least they were going to run into a French picquet or some hotheaded Portuguese nationalist bent on saving his country from another invading force.

Instead they rowed the short distance to land, where the beach met the waves in a gentle slope and the low surf gently deposited the longboat onto the pebbled shore. Aquiles, unwilling to wait his turn, bolted out of the back of the longboat and splashed to shore, going down on his knees and kissing the sand.

"Jamás abandonaré mi tierra otra vez," the giant man muttered. I'll never leave land again.

Robert hoisted Olivia up and out of the boat, carrying her in his arms to dry land, but his touch was nothing more than that of a man carrying an unremarkable burden ashore.

The heat of his hands was there, but they conveyed none of the passion and flame she'd felt the night before. It was as if the cold water splashing up from his boots had invaded his heart. And when she tipped back her hood and looked into his eyes, all that greeted her was a cold, bitter reception.

He set her down as if he were dropping hot coals and just as quickly set her valise next to her feet.

"Thank you," she muttered.

Once they were all gathered ashore, she said a quick good-bye to Livett and Gavin as Robert started marching up the beach. Apparently he knew where they were going, and it was up to the rest of them to keep up.

At first Olivia caught up her valise, but always the gentleman, Jemmy took it from her and lugged it along.

They climbed a short hill and then found themselves walking down a dark, rutted road. A grinning Aquiles brought up the rear.

"Seems rather irregular," Jemmy commented, as he stumbled for the third time. "Hey there, Danvers, where are we going?"

"An inn. Not far," Robert said, without even glancing back at them or slowing his pace.

"Chatty fellow tonight," Jemmy said to Olivia, shifting her valise from one hand to the other. "Hope this inn has clean beds and a bath. I'd love a good bath."

"I wouldn't hold too much hope of that," Olivia said as they rounded a bend and a poorly lit building appeared in the distance. From it came none of the noise one usually associated with an inn—the chatter of patrons, a bit of singing, the impatient stamp and whinny of horses—but this wasn't your usual hostelry, Olivia soon discovered.

Nor was it the type of place she expected a member of Wellington's personal staff to be familiar with.

Then perhaps Major Danvers was no more an ordinary officer in His Majesty's Army than his brother was a regular captain in the Royal Navy.

When they got to the door, Robert finally stopped. "Wait here. I'm going inside to engage rooms for the both of you. You are to speak to no one, tell them nothing of how you came here."

"Well, of all the high—" Jemmy started to complain, until a rough-hewn patron, taller than Aquiles and if possible twice as fierce, for he was missing part of his nose and several of his teeth, came lumbering out the door.

He cocked a dark glance at them, and for a moment Olivia gave them all up for lost, until the fierce giant spied Robert.

"Roberto!" he said, hauling him into a bear hug of an embrace.

"Samsão," Robert replied with equal enthusiasm. "How the hell are you, my friend?"

"Oh, so right," he said, a shrug of his shoulder punctuating his words. "There is much afoot. We have missed your help. But it is glad and surprised I am to see you back here." This was followed by another hug. When he released Robert, he tipped his head at the inn's door. "There is someone inside who will be as surprised as I am to see you. I was just asking Rafe—"

"That will have to wait, Samsão," Robert told him. "I must see my friends settled for the night. Does Bathasar still keep rooms available for special visitors?"

Samsão gave Jemmy and Olivia a more thoughtful perusal and then nodded. "When you get your friends tucked in, come and we will share a flagon." He opened his coat to show a bulging goatskin pouch hanging inside. "Those French *bastardos* haven't stolen all the good wine in this country." He laughed loudly, slapping first his chest, then Robert's back with resounding thwacks.

Before they entered, Robert reached over and pulled Olivia's cloak further over her face and around her body, concealing her like a duenna would her young charge. "Not one word," he cautioned them.

The inside of the inn was no more promising than

the outside had been. The smells were entirely foreign to Olivia—none of the familiar odors of smoke, roasted mutton and beer washing over one, but instead, the sweet bouquet of wine, the tangy, sharp scent of grilled fish and the sad, low strains of a guitar.

The low conversation of the trio of men in the room stopped as they entered. Olivia felt a tide of speculation encircle her, and she pulled her cloak tighter around her as if to ward off their whispered suspicions.

Then recognition lit the face of one of the men. His low-slung hat tipped back, his guarded expression opening into a wide grin.

A warm welcome of "Roberto" sang out, and the other two patrons grinned as well before surging forward to greet him.

"I didn't recognize you without your uniform."

"Long time, my friend."

"Drink with us," came their friendly salutations.

Olivia watched Robert acknowledge them. Though his expression and words were filled with lively warmth, she wondered if they saw the wall he placed between himself and them.

She knew every brick and stone that Robert Danvers could toss up so easily to keep the world out . . . and his heart and soul locked within.

Soon the establishment's patrons were joined by the innkeeper, Bathasar, whose ample girth and white apron marked him as the proprietor. He hailed Robert with equal warmth, and after a short whispered conversation and a few nods in her direction, the transaction was completed.

"He has a room that ought to work," Robert told them. "Come along."

Olivia and Jemmy started to follow, but she paused

for a moment when she saw a cloaked figure step out of the shadows of a private room at one end of the common area. The man was tall, a good head above most of the Portuguese in the room. And there was something in his bearing that told Olivia he wasn't one of the regular patrons. While she couldn't make out his features, it was obvious the man was staring directly at Robert.

When she glanced over at Robert, he appeared to have also spied the mysterious stranger and sent the fellow a slight, curt nod.

The man responded in kind and melted back into the shadows. And for a brief flash, Olivia thought she saw his face, a countenance so familiar it nearly took her breath away.

But it couldn't be. *He was dead*.

Chills ran down her arms. She knew she couldn't have seen what she just thought she had, but then again none of this was right.

Why hadn't they gone directly to Wellington? If her information about *El Rescate del Rey* was so essential to the progress of the war, why would Robert insist on hiding her away in this forgotten and forsaken inn? The place was no better than a Cornish smugglers' haunt.

And why didn't Robert want anyone to see her or know of their arrival in Portugal?

Before she could come to any logical conclusions, they arrived at their room. From the rough-hewn benches and dilapidated condition of the outside Olivia did not expect much in the way of comfort, but the accommodations Bathasar provided pleasantly surprised her.

They entered a large sitting room, which Olivia

noted, with some relief, was clean and cozy. There was a table and chairs for dining, two more comfortable chairs near the windows and a desk with all the necessary implements for sending correspondence. As she moved further into the room, she spied that either end of the large room featured a small, separate sleeping chamber.

Jemmy immediately took possession of the largest chair and pronounced it "capital."

The maid bustled in, chattering in Portuguese, two large pitchers in one hand, and balancing a stack of towels in the other. She settled these near the washstand and then went about directing a young boy who arrived moments behind her with a tray laden with food and drink.

"*Obrigada*," Olivia told them when they finished their tasks. Thank you.

The girl turned a suspicious eye on her, then said in her native tongue, "You don't look Portuguese."

"*Sou Inglesa*," Olivia answered in kind. I am English.

"Bah! Not like any English I've met," she said. She sidled past Olivia and out of the room. "Except perhaps *Roberto*." She fluttered her lashes at Robert, who stood in the doorway.

Jealousy hit Olivia hard in the gut at the way the woman smiled with familiar ease at him. And it doubled its hold on her tormented soul when he smiled back at the girl and flipped her a gold coin.

The money was far more than what Olivia guessed was needed to pay for the room . . . or other services. And from the greedy and hungry flash in the girl's eyes, Olivia didn't want to know just what those other services might encompass.

When she was gone, Robert turned on Olivia. "I said not one word out of you. Not in English and especially not in Portuguese."

"I was just being polite," she shot back. It occurred to her to ask Robert who the stranger in the shadows was, but she knew he would only deny the encounter.

Especially when she told him who she thought the man looked like.

Instead she said, "There is nothing wrong with being well mannered." She hoped the broader hint of her words would fall somewhere between his ears.

"Well, don't be. English women who speak fluent Portuguese get noticed and remembered." He raked his hand through his hair and let out an exasperated sigh. Then he turned his sharp gaze on Jemmy. "Stay in here," he told the young man. "And don't let *her* out."

Now she was just "her." Olivia fumed. Especially as Robert continued issuing orders like they were soldiers in his regiment.

Or prisoners of war.

"Lock the door behind me and don't open it to anyone but me or Aquiles." He took a quick tour of the suite, checking the windows and ensuring that all was in order. When he finished, he turned to Jemmy. "Do you still have that pistol of yours?"

"Oh, aye," he said, drawing it out of his jacket. "Though it isn't loaded."

"Load it." He tossed him a pouch of powder and shot. "And if anyone tries to come in, shoot first."

"And if the Queen over there decides to leave?" Jemmy asked, tipping a grin in Olivia's direction.

Robert didn't even bother to spare her a glance. "Same orders."

Olivia opened her mouth to protest, but it was too

late. Robert had turned on one heel and left, pulling the door closed behind him with a moody slam. Jemmy threw the lock with all the enthusiasm of a boy on his first hunt, then eagerly set to work loading his pistol. Once he finished that task, he pulled a chair from the table and leaned it up against the heavy wood door, settling in, arms across his chest and the pistol at the ready.

Olivia knew that Robert was more than likely headed downstairs to meet with that stranger, and there was no way she wasn't going to be there as well.

She, of all people, had the most at stake in meeting him.

Looking around the room and at Jemmy's earnest, firm expression, she realized her only means of escape would require some subterfuge.

Having lived at Finch Manor for seven years, she knew one thing Jemmy and his father had a weakness for. Not entirely proud of herself, she walked over to the table and started to study the array of food and drink the boy had brought up.

And the first thing she did was pour herself a glass of port and take an appreciative sip.

"Oh, my!" she said, taking another drink. "This is wonderful."

Jemmy's brow furrowed, his jaw working back and forth.

Olivia smiled at him. "You must try this. It is simply divine. I doubt even your father has ever had such a bottle in his cellar."

The young man rose to his feet. "I doubt this shabby place could out-serve my father's cellar."

Olivia shrugged and took another sip. "I hate to say it, but I don't think I've ever tasted better."

"I'll be the judge of that," he said.

She almost smiled as the young man poured himself a large tumbler full of the potent port.

And three tumblers later, Jemmy had deemed the Portuguese vineyard adequate before his head slumped over and he fell fast asleep.

"I'm so sorry I have to take advantage of you like this, Jemmy," Olivia whispered to him, as she put a blanket over his shoulders. "Your mother always says, 'Reyburn men have no head for spirits,' and for once, I must say, I'm glad she was right."

When Robert got back to the common room, it was empty except for Bathasar, who stood behind the bar, cloth in one hand, a dirty glass in the other. The innkeeper nodded toward a back room, where only a single candle burned.

"He's waiting for you in there."

Then, as if in answer to his arrival, from out of the shadows a tall, familiar figure stepped forward. "What kept you?" his brother Raphael asked. "Or should I say who?"

"Maybe I didn't want to help unload your shipment," Robert told him, choosing to ignore the inquiry about Olivia.

"Now that I would believe. You officers never are much for hard work." Rafe walked back into the shadowed room and retook his seat. Before him sat a half-filled glass of wine, a flagon of the ruby liquid and an empty glass.

Robert took a seat as well and watched as his brother poured him a glass of wine.

"You've missed much since you left," Rafe said. "The rumors have run rampant."

"What are they saying?" Robert asked, taking an appreciative sip of the vintage.

There was something to be said for a smuggler's wine cellar. And Bathasar's was the finest in Portugal.

"That you kicked up a fuss when you were sent to London. Some even say you went after *El Rescate*."

"Sounds about right."

Rafe's brow cocked in surprise. Obviously it hadn't been the answer he'd been expecting. "So?"

"So what?"

He leaned forward. "Did you find it?"

Robert shrugged. "Depends on whether or not you believe in legends."

"And if one did?"

"Then I would have to say, yes, I suppose I did."

Rafe whistled. "That sure explains a lot."

"What do you mean?"

"The rest of the gossip. I've been plagued by every shady character from here to the border about your whereabouts. They seem to think that for a few coins I'd be willing to sell out my own brother."

"Wouldn't you?" Robert teased.

"Don't test me," Rafe shot back. "This is serious. The stake is already at five thousand in gold for you captured alive."

"And if I have the information they want?"

"If you know how to find *El Rescate del Rey*, you might as well double that."

Robert laughed. "Well by tomorrow I'll have delivered Miss Sutton to Wellington in Lisbon, and then she'll tell him where the ransom is buried, and I will no longer be a marked man."

Rafe looked up from his glass. "Who did you say?"

"Miss Sutton," Robert said, glad to have finally gotten to this portion of the conversation. He'd been wondering how he was going to tell Rafe about her.

Of all the Danvers brothers, Rafe had burned the hottest for revenge for Orlando's death. His mercurial temper, inherited from his Spanish mother, had nearly consumed him as he'd raged and railed against the fates and treachery which had taken his beloved brother and closest friend.

And now he, Robert, had brought the woman connected to that murder to within Rafe's very grasp.

But instead of the reaction he was expecting, Rafe laughed. "Oh, you had me going there for a moment. That chit died with our cousin and is probably still warming his bed in hell, if you'll pardon my pun."

Robert didn't return his grin. "It's no joke, Raphael. Miss Sutton lives."

His brother's eyes narrowed. "She's dead. As dead as that bastard lover of hers."

Shaking his head, Robert readied himself for the inevitable explosion.

Rafe didn't keep him waiting long.

He slammed up from the table and kicked at his chair, stomping back and forth in the empty room. A long string of curses followed.

Robert just watched and understood. He'd felt much the same way when Pymm had told him the news.

"And you brought her *here?*" Rafe asked. "How can you trust her after what she did?"

"I don't," he told him. And he meant it. He definitely meant it.

No, he couldn't, he wouldn't trust Olivia Sutton. Despite his desire for her soft curves, her whispered words, the body that fit to his. She wore Lando's ring like some prize—a token from a man she'd most likely watched die.

"Oh, this is bad," Rafe said, continuing to pace about the table.

"Like I said, after tomorrow she won't be my problem. I'm taking her at first light down to headquarters and delivering her to Wellington."

Rafe came to an abrupt halt. "To Wellington? But you can't."

"And why not?"

"Because Wellington pulled out weeks ago. He's in Badajoz by now."

Olivia slid the bolt on the door and eased it open. She half expected Aquiles to be stationed on the other side. But to her surprise and relief, Robert's giant servant was nowhere in sight.

The common area down below was empty, and the room was cast in shadows, the only light that of a single taper on the bar. She crept down the stairs, pausing at the bottom step, trying to discern where Robert had gone.

To her right, the muffled sound of voices caught her attention. With her back to the wall, her body swallowed in darkness, she eased toward the conversation.

She thought she heard Robert mumbling something, but the voice that answered him stopped her in her tracks. It was a voice she knew, had heard imploring her in her dreams to avenge him.

And now he was alive, here in this out-of-the-way Portuguese inn.

"Dammit, Hobbe, you can't mean to take her there," he was saying.

Olivia's heart froze. The voice . . . But he couldn't be. And what had he said?

Hobbe.

She shook her head, wondering if she had heard that correctly. Groping to steady herself, she bumped into a table, sending it rocking wildly.

The noise brought the occupants of the other room to their feet, and Olivia held her breath as first Robert, then his companion came barreling out of the private room, pistols drawn.

Robert caught up the candle on the bar and held it aloft, sending its thin light in her direction.

Olivia had witnessed many things in her short acquaintance with Robert Danvers, but the man standing next to him stopped her breath in her throat.

Like something out of a dream, out of a nightmare, he stepped past Robert and stood in front of her.

He was saying something, but what she couldn't discern through the unholy roar in her ears.

For never before had she come face to face with a ghost.

Chapter 12

Olivia faced the man who had died in her arms. "You're . . . you're alive?"

This living and breathing phantom had the audacity to grin. "I tend to like it that way."

"But how? I saw you . . . I held you . . . when you . . ." How could she utter the word "died" when he stood before her in such perfect health? She took a step closer to him and reached out with a tentative hand, prodding her finger into his chest, half expecting him to vanish into thin air.

But he remained before her, a living contradiction to the nightmare she remembered. Certainly he had changed some from the youthful Spaniard she remembered, but time had only given his promising sharp features a rugged, handsome quality.

"I don't understand," she said, touching him again. "How could this be?"

"How could what be, señorita?" he said, staring bemusedly over her shoulder at Robert.

Olivia had almost forgotten he was there. But nevertheless she tugged at the chain around her neck and pulled it until the ring sprang free. Holding it up for this man to see, she said, "*You* gave me this."

His reaction was much the same as Robert's had been. His eyes widened with shock. "I gave you that?"

Olivia shook it in front of him. "Yes! Don't you remember? In the library at Lord Chambley's. Right after you were . . . you were shot."

"What is this?" he asked Robert in rapid Spanish. "What is she talking about?"

"She thinks you are Lando," he told his companion. "Miss Sutton, I'm afraid you've made a mistake. This is my brother Raphael Danvers. The man who died in Chambley's library was Rafe's twin, Orlando."

She whirled around. "Your brother? That man was your brother?"

He nodded.

Everything she thought she'd known shattered like a dropped porcelain teacup at this revelation. His brother? Oh, dear God. No wonder he hated her.

As she tried desperately to put all the pieces back together, she realized Raphael had reached out to touch the ring she still held before her.

"You say Lando gave you this?" he asked, his fingers closing over hers.

She nodded, still taken aback by their startling resemblance.

"What did he say? What exactly did he say to you?" the man asked, his dark gaze burning into her.

She took a breath and struggled for a moment to remember. Then, as if it had happened yesterday, she told him, word by word.

Run, now. Go as far as you can. Hide where they cannot find you. Give this to no one but——Hobbe.

Rafe gazed at her, his lips mouthing the words silently as if he were weighing each one. And when he finished, he looked at her anew, but this time his gaze was filled only with sadness. "My apologies, Miss Sutton. If Lando gave that to you, then I owe you my deepest apologies."

Robert surged forward, pushing between them and coming face to face with his brother. "What the devil are you talking about? Are you out of your mind?"

Rafe bristled and met his brother nose to nose. "He would never have given *that* to her if he did not believe in her." His words came out in blistering hot Spanish so fast that even Olivia could barely keep up. As if to punctuate his words, he held up his hand to reveal a ring that matched hers. "Lando sent this to you as a sign of his faith in her. That is good enough for me, as it should be for you, Hobbe."

Hobbe.

"Hobbe?" she demanded. She caught Rafe by the arm. "You said that name earlier. Hobbe. Who is that?"

She sensed rather than saw Robert make a rapid gesture at his brother, but it wasn't fast enough to stop Rafe from saying, "You've already found him." He nodded at someone behind her.

She spun around, not knowing what to expect. And all she found in the empty room was Robert.

Robert.

He took a deep breath and straightened his stance,

looking every bit the hero she had always imagined her Hobbe would be. But a hero he wasn't. The realization howled in her ears like a spiteful banshee.

The man who died hadn't sent her to another agent or some larger than life hero. But to his brother. Robert Danvers.

Rage and anger surged through Olivia at this, his newest deception. Oh, how it stung! And she didn't know what was worse, that this lying, conniving bastard was her hero or that he had used her for his own means so effortlessly.

Why, he was no better than the cousin he had imitated so perfectly. No wonder he'd fooled everyone.

Including her.

"You lied to me," she said. "How you must have laughed at my stupidity. Used me, while all the time you knew the man I sought was you. What did you hope to discover from me in the meantime? My duplicity? The truth behind my *ruinous reputation*?" She paused for a moment. "Well, you did find a way to discover the truth about those *lies*, now, didn't you?"

"Olivia, there is more to this—" he began.

"Oh, yes, your sacred duty to King and country," she said. "Now I suppose you are going to introduce me to Wellington and tell me it is my duty to to lead *you* to The King's Ransom."

For a moment he flinched, as if she had stumbled onto something he didn't want her to find out.

"You are taking me to Wellington tomorrow, aren't you?" she demanded.

"That's exactly what I intend to do," he replied.

Olivia didn't believe him for a minute. "And I'll be presented to Wellington tomorrow."

On this he flinched again. "Well . . . on that there is a bit of a problem."

"Oh, do tell," she replied. "Let me guess, Wellington has conveniently left the country."

"She's got that one right," Rafe muttered under his breath. He'd settled down in a chair, his boots propped up on the table. "I like her, Hobbe. She's got fire."

"A few minutes ago you wanted to strangle her," his brother shot back.

Rafe grinned as he refilled his glass from a flagon. "I'll leave that pleasure up to you."

Olivia saw nothing amusing in their banter. "I will not be handed about like some Haymarket prize. Am I going to see Wellington tomorrow or not?"

Robert's frown creased even deeper, and he shot his brother a dark glance. "Actually, Rafe was just telling me that Lord Wellington has moved with the troops a bit east of Lisbon. We'll have to ride out to meet him."

"How far east?" she asked.

"Badajoz."

The chills ran down her arms. Had he just said what she thought she'd heard? "Badajoz?" she repeated.

"Yes. Do you have any objections?" he asked rather moodily.

Olivia didn't quite know how to answer. Was this a test? Did he truly know what he was asking her? "Why has his lordship gone there?"

Robert's lips pressed together, his jaw a solid line of impatience. "Madame, I'm not going to discuss the military implications of Wellington's strategies with you. Suffice it to say we are going to Badajoz."

Part of her wanted to hate him, to argue with him. Refuse to go with him. But she still found herself unable to let go of the dream that had sustained her all these years.

This was Hobbe. This was the man that boy—no, she corrected herself, Orlando—had asked her to trust. To give him the ring and to ask him to finish his lost mission. There was no reason for her to go all the way to Badajoz when she had promised Orlando she would entrust the secret of The King's Ransom to Hobbe.

And now she had found him. But the truth was, she didn't trust him. Yet if she didn't give him the information he wanted, she would be forced to travel the entire width of Portugal in his company.

With the haunting memories of their lovemaking tormenting her each step of the way.

"When your brother gave me this ring, he asked me to give you the translation of the parchment he carried as well. I can do that now. You can have the information you have sought, Major Danvers, and I can have my freedom." From you, she wanted to add. "You can continue on to Wellington with all due haste, and Jemmy and I can remain here in Lisbon until we can secure passage home."

Robert shook his head. "That is not possible. I'm afraid you cannot remain here."

"And why not?" she asked, her suspicions rising again.

"You wouldn't be safe."

Olivia laughed. "And I will be safer traveling across a war-torn country with the likes of you? Might I remind you that while in your protective care, I have been shot at, kidnapped and nearly sunk by a French corsair. I hardly see how I could be in more danger in Lisbon—without you protecting me."

Rafe coughed and sputtered, his hand covering his mouth. He swung his legs off the table and staggered away.

"Things have changed," Robert told her. "I would suggest returning to your room and getting as much rest as you can. We'll leave before daylight."

"I'm not going anywhere until I have some answers," she said. "You claim you want to finish your mission. I am offering you the final piece. Besides, you have made it clear that you want nothing more to do with this fool's folly, as you have called it, than to give Lord Wellington the information he seeks. Why this sudden change of heart?"

Robert didn't answer her, but Rafe did.

"He fears for your safety, Miss Sutton," he said. "Even now you are in grave danger. Do you know what happened to the last man who thought he knew the location of *El Rescate*?"

His dark intense gaze sent a chill through her blood. She shook her head.

"They tortured him for ten days. The man had been flayed, burned and dismembered before he finally found his freedom in death. And with him went the secret. Do not think eleven centuries of civilization will save you from such a fate. It has only whetted men's greed that much more." Rafe poured another glass of wine, rose from the table and pushed it into her quaking hands. "Have you not seen yourself enough death over its fabled gold?"

Olivia closed her eyes and took a deep breath. "No one knows I am here. No one knows I am even alive."

Rafe shook his head. "That is where you are wrong." He continued, pressing his point and underlining her obvious fears, "Lisbon, England, the open sea, there is no place that will afford you protection until the treasure is found and restored to the Spanish people." He glanced over at Robert and shrugged, as if in apology for revealing the truth of the matter. "Already there are whispers of your arrival."

"But why me? Why would anyone suspect me?" she asked. "Surely there are Englishwomen who arrive in Portugal every day." She was struggling to find a way to hide herself, much as she had after Orlando's murder.

"That might have been possible if you had kept your mouth shut earlier," Robert said, stepping into the conversation. "But you had to thank that maid in perfect Portuguese, something quite remarkable in this part of the country."

"Then I won't say another word," she offered, to which both men laughed. "I hardly think I am all that different from any other Englishwoman!"

"Have you ever heard the legend of *El Rescate del Rey*?" Rafe asked.

She shook her head.

"If you had, you wouldn't need to ask." He finished the last of his wine and gathered up his coat, which lay tossed negligently over a chair. "I have my men to see to and an extra mount to find for you, Miss Sutton." He nodded to Robert. "*Hasta mañana*." Until tomorrow.

Olivia knew the instant Rafe left the room and she was alone with Robert. A wretchedly uncomfortable silence settled between the two of them.

After all these years, she'd found her Hobbe, her knight in shining armor, her hero. And she hadn't the least idea what to say to him.

But then again, she had plenty to say. She turned and faced him. Rafe's words had left her scared.

No, she thought, frightened senseless was a better description. And she knew in her heart the only man who could keep her alive until she fulfilled the destiny Rafe seemed to think she was an integral part of was the silent, brooding man before her.

"All this time you thought I killed him. You thought me capable of murdering your brother." Olivia stared directly into his eyes. "You still do."

He shook his head, but with none of the conviction that might have redeemed him. "That's not true."

"Liar."

He had the decency to look away.

"I trusted you. I told you the truth."

His lips twisted ever so slightly into a smile. "Not always. You let me believe a number of things that weren't true. I think you were quite content to let me think you were a ruined woman. A woman capable of just about anything . . . including murder."

Olivia put her hands on her hips. He had her there. And she didn't like it one bit.

How the devil did he always do this—turn the tables on her when she just thought she'd finally outwitted him.

That, and the fact that her body still ached with a treasonous passion to know his kiss one more time. To feel his arms around her. To believe in the rapture he'd given her in that short time.

No, she didn't want to go to Spain with him. Not if it meant the risk of losing her heart to him again.

Her mutinous thoughts must have been plain on her face, because he turned away from her. "Don't think you'll escape me, Olivia. I will take you to Wellington. It is a duty and a promise I will see to the end."

With that, he caught her by the elbow and hauled

her toward the stairs. His firm grip brooked no resistance, and Olivia knew it was futile to try and escape him now.

When they got to the door of her room, she turned to him. "Why do they call you Hobbe?" she whispered.

He shrugged, then his features softened. "Orlando had a hard time saying 'Robert' when he was learning how to talk. When he did say it, it came out 'Hobbe,' and the name just stuck."

Olivia nodded. After another uncomfortable moment of silence, she asked, "What was he like?"

"I don't want to talk about him," he said, retreating behind his infamous wall.

But she knew it was not where he wanted to be. "Please. I've always wondered who he was. I have a right to know. He did save my life."

At this revelation, she could see Robert's eyes light with interest and the questions that had probably plagued him for years.

How had his brother died? Alone, and so far from his family.

Robert smiled, a wistful twist to his lips. And then he told her. Of Orlando's love of riding, of his serious nature and his desire to serve his countries—both of them, England and Spain.

When he finished, she had tears in her eyes, and he reached over and brushed them from her cheeks. When she hazarded a glance up at him, she found him staring at her, a look of emptiness and need shining in his eyes.

She thought he was going to kiss her, reach for her as she had sought him on the *Sybaris*, but just as she could have sworn his head was dipping down to kiss her, his arms were reaching to encircle her, he turned away and the moment was lost.

"You had best get a good night's sleep," he told her, his voice choked with emotion. "We have a long journey ahead of us, and there will be few comforts along the way." With that he opened the door and propelled her into the room, his touch both heated and all too brief.

And after he'd locked her in her room and she heard him settle his tall frame against the only door that led outside, all she could hear was one word in a never-ending refrain.

Duty.

Once again she was his duty. How she hated his honorable sense of obligation.

Before dawn, the sounds of restless animals and the voices of men brought Olivia fully awake.

After her argument with Robert, she'd intended to make her escape but found the windows covered with an ornate iron grillwork. Even if she could have gotten out, the height on that side of the building left her too dizzy to consider the window as a viable escape route.

She'd flopped down on the bed, and when she'd fallen asleep, she knew not. At first she'd been unable to rest, so instead she'd pulled out the paper Orlando had entrusted her with and her own journal, with her notes and research on *El Rescate del Rey*.

When Robert had accused her of holding back her own secrets, he'd been right.

The truth was, she'd lied to the duplicitous Marquis of Bradstone. Oh, she'd told him correctly that *El Rescate del Rey* was buried in the Tomb of the Virgin, but it wasn't in Madrid as she'd told him. For when she had gotten to that last word of the translation, she'd seen the agonizing truth for herself in the reflection of the window across the room—Bradstone held a pistol at the back of her head. In that one moment, she'd gone from a naïve girl in love to a woman scorned. And if the word she was about to translate was to be her last, then she'd do her best to send Bradstone on his own path to hell.

For according to the encoded message he'd given her to translate, the tomb was actually in Badajoz, the city Wellington meant to retake from the French. Was it just coincidence, or was she a pawn in a greater game that she could not fathom?

She glanced again at the parchment that had revealed so much to her and yet had cost so many lives. Her fingers traced over the coppery bloodstains that had all but obliterated some of the words.

Orlando's blood.

She felt an unshakable sense of guilt. She had promised him to get this information to Hobbe, and she had. But she knew that the young man had given his life to see the treasure found and restored to its rightful place—into the hands of the Spanish people and not the coffers of some greedy thief.

And by his blood, she would see this done—no matter what might come of her.

As for her heart, well, that was another matter, she thought, as she heard Robert's voice rise above the other conversations. He would be coming up for her soon, and so she finished packing her meager possessions and finishing her toilet.

The door to the main room opened. "Miss? Miss?" the serving girl from the night before called out.

Picking up her bag, Olivia left her sleeping chamber. "Yes?"

"Oh, good, you are ready. He wishes you to come down immediately," the maid said.

Olivia nodded and followed her. When she got to the door, she cast a look of regret at Jemmy's room. Robert had promised to see him booked on the next ship bound for London.

Out in the hallway, the girl's foot tapped a staccato beat. When Olivia joined her, she turned in the opposite direction from the main stairs. At first Olivia paused, and when the girl came to a halt, the glance she cast over her shoulder showed her impatience.

"He would have you come the back way. Hurry. You must leave now."

Sighing at all this exaggerated secrecy, Olivia followed her. They went down a narrow staircase and out a back door, which let them out into a small garden at the back of the inn. The morning had just dawned, but a light fog held the inn and the surrounding countryside in its ethereal, misty grasp.

Already well down the narrow path, the girl whispered at Olivia, "Come along."

They skirted the inn and continued down the road. The girl came to a stop near a pile of firewood. "Wait here," she told Olivia.

A prickle of unease ran down Olivia's spine. Why did Robert want her to wait for him so far from the horses and their traveling companions? She reached inside her valise and fished out her pistol.

The mist started to clear on a freshening breeze, and not far down the road, she saw a man coming toward her. Though she could barely discern him, she could tell from his height and the breadth of his shoulders it was Robert.

As she was about to call out to him, she heard a stick snap behind her and she jumped around, dropping her valise and taking aim into the swirling mist.

To her surprise, Rafe fumbled to a stop before her, his hands going up in the air in mock horror. "Come now, I don't think I look like Robert."

"Rafe!" Olivia said, lowering the weapon and letting the hammer slowly back down. "Oh, dear, I'm sorry."

"What are you doing out here?" he asked, picking up a piece of firewood.

"Robert sent that girl to bring me here." She nodded up the road, which was now deserted. Where the devil had he gone? She looked again and then back at Rafe.

"The maid came for you?" He shook his head. "I just saw Robert entering the inn. He said he was going to get you."

"But I just saw . . ." Olivia started to say, peering back into the dusky shadows of the early morning landscape and finding nothing but trees and an empty road.

"Come along, then," Rafe said, picking up her valise and taking a second hard glance down the road as well. "It is a good thing I found you. We are about to mount up."

"What were you doing out here?" she asked.

He grabbed several logs. "One of the loads is unbalanced, and this particular mule becomes very cranky when everything isn't to his liking."

"Is this mule another Danvers relation?" she asked.

Rafe laughed. "Robert is quite right about you."

"How is that?" she asked, almost afraid to hear the answer.

"You are a regular termagant."

Olivia followed Rafe to where the others were already waiting, most of them mounted on horses and holding ropes to strings of heavily laden mules. The men were a rough-looking lot, but they all to a man raised their hats in respect to her as she approached.

"*La Reina que ha vuelto*," they said to one another in quiet tones of awe.

"Why are they calling me that?" she asked Rafe.

"What?"

"The returning Queen," she said.

He laughed. "They all know the legend, and they know who you are. They are more than honored to be taking you to our homeland, and there isn't a man here who wouldn't protect you with his life."

"One of these days you'll have to tell me this legend," she said.

"When the time is right," he promised, "I will."

Rafe helped Olivia up onto the mount he'd found for her, a donkey who'd greeted her with a disgusted snicker and a great blowing snort and toss of her head.

"Sorry, this was the best I could do on such short notice," Rafe told Olivia as she backed away from the cantankerous animal.

"Can't she be used to haul your goods?" Olivia asked.

"She's too unpredictable," Rafe told her, grinning. "Robert assured me the two of you would get on well."

Olivia took a deep breath and climbed aboard the animal. As she gathered up the reins, she noticed a uniformed man coming out of the inn.

Out of instinct, she ducked her head into her cloak as the tall, imposing figure walked toward them. She could only wonder if news of her latest crime had reached the British officials in Portugal.

"There you are," Robert's voice called out. "I've been looking everywhere for you."

At first she stared at him, for while she knew he was a member of Wellington's personal staff, she had never considered what Robert would look like in his uniform.

He was utterly and completely changed before her eyes. In Bradstone's fashionable clothes he'd been the rakish man about town. Aboard the *Sybaris* he'd moved just as easily into the plain white shirt and breeches that most of the men wore.

But standing before her, his scarlet coat smartly tailored and pressed, his buttons and epaulets in perfect order and his glossy Hessians encasing his legs with elegant precision, Major Robert Danvers stole her breath away.

"I didn't recognize you," she managed to say. "I mean, I've never seen you in your uniform."

"Have I changed that much?" he asked.

She nodded, unable to put the words together. All his bearing, his commanding nature, his impossible honor, it all made sense now encased in this uniform. The scarlet coat and numerous decorations didn't make him what he was, but now that she saw him in it, it was hard to imagine him any other way.

"Now that I'm back on official duty," he said, "I'm required to wear it. Besides, it will afford us some measure of protection if we run—" He stopped in midsentence.

She knew what he meant. If they ran into any trouble. Glancing over her shoulder at Rafe's motley and fierce collection of men, she smiled. "I doubt anyone would dare."

"They do make an excellent guard, but if something does happen, get to my side immediately. I won't have you—" He stopped again, this time as if he didn't want to say anything more, much as he had stopped himself the night before. Then he bowed with all the precision that marked his uniform and strode over to where Aquiles was standing, holding the reins of a horse.

She smiled and watched him mount up onto a black beast of a thing that pranced and tossed its head with a noble disdain that put her poor donkey's antics to shame.

But Robert gave the stallion a sharp whistle and a nudge with his thigh, and the animal quieted immediately. Olivia had the sense that he could tame anything with his commanding manners.

Even her rebellious heart.

For a moment all eyes were on Robert. He nodded to his brother, and they set off in a solemn procession.

Rafe took the lead, his ragged lot of men following, with Olivia, Robert and Aquiles in the middle and a rather nefarious group of men bringing up the rear. These fellows, his handpicked guard, Rafe had called them, looked capable of taking on Napoleon's most battle-hardened regiments. All the men rode armed with a collection of rifles on either side of their saddles, and they had an ancient and wicked-looking array of *pistolas* stuck into their coats, belts, and crisscrossed holsters.

And as they went past the spot in the road where Olivia had thought she'd seen Robert earlier, a chill ran down her spine, as if she had just walked over her own grave. She had the feeling of being watched—but then told herself it was just her nerves over Rafe's ominous warnings.

For really, as far as she was concerned, her only enemy was the man in the scarlet coat riding ahead of her. He had lied to her, kidnapped her, brought her to this dangerous country.

And worst of all, he'd captured her heart.

Chapter 13

Olivia didn't give the laden mules much consideration until late in the first day. She had thought it quite a lot of provisions for what Rafe had told her would take a fortnight of travel. Then again, Robert and his brother knew better what their trip would require than she did, considering her only real outings had been hasty flights from crime scenes.

When they stopped by a stream to water the animals, before pushing on for a place Robert thought would be safe to camp for the night, Olivia learned the true nature of their journey.

The donkey Rafe had procured for her seemed to delight in braying at all the other animals around it, taking deliberate nips if they came too close and generally bedeviling everything in range with a well-aimed kick or a whip of her tail.

In short, the animal reminded Olivia of Lady Finch,

and so in deference to her former employer she called the opinionated little beast Evaline.

Evaline edged close to a nearby mule and gave the overladen beast a nip on its flank. The startled animal tugged and kicked at its restraints, all the while letting out a long string of loud, obnoxious brays, while Evaline looked on with wide, innocent brown eyes.

"Quiet, sssh," Olivia tried to tell the agitated animal. "Be still, you'll only encourage Evaline to misbehave more."

Her soothing words did nothing but irritate the mule further. She tried to catch its halter, but it jumped and tossed its head, sending the animal next to it into a frenzy of complaints as well.

Looking up for help, she realized all the men were staring at her in wide-eyed horror. Alamar, Rafe's second in command, was making the sign of the cross as he scrambled back from the mayhem erupting around her.

Evaline renewed her braying and kicking as if she were single-handedly attempting to perpetuate the mayhem.

Robert bolted out of nowhere to Olivia's side. "Get that animal quieted," he shouted at her, pointing at her donkey. "These packs are loaded with powder."

Olivia looked at the heavily laden animal he was struggling to control as it still bucked at its halter and lead, and felt her stomach drop to her toes.

Powder?

Then she remembered—the shipment on the *Sybaris*. So Rafe was Colin's business associate. Remembering how much explosive powder had been aboard, and considering that it was now surrounding her atop a group of agitated mules, Olivia froze.

In the meantime, Robert had waded into the frenzy, grabbing first one harness, then the other, barking at the animals as if they were disorderly soldiers in a drill. And the animals responded to his sharply issued commands by quieting into a docile line.

Olivia, however, was not so easily quelled. "What is the meaning of this?"

"The meaning of what?" he asked, his voice tinged with irritation, as he walked through the line of animals, checking the straps to the packs.

"This!" she said, waving her hands at the powder-laden bags. "We could be killed."

"You didn't mind when it was aboard the *Sybaris*," he said.

"I had little choice in that, I might remind you."

"And you have little choice in this as well." He tightened a buckle and gave the mule a scratch behind its ears.

Olivia's hands rolled up into balls. "And if I am killed and the information lost, then what?"

He leaned forward and grinned at her. "Then you can spend all eternity reminding me of how all this is my fault."

"See anyone?" Robert asked Rafe, as his brother rejoined their group after a little reconnaissance behind them. It had been nearly a week since they'd left the inn, and both Robert and Rafe were of the same suspicion.

Someone was following them.

Rafe shook his head. "I'll bet this store of powder that we're being followed, but I can't find anyone. We'll just have to keep a rear guard posted and keep a sharp eye out."

They rode for a time in silence.

"Why don't you just apologize to her?" Rafe blurted out.

"Apologize for what?" Robert asked back.

"For not telling her about the powder, about my men, about our real mission."

He turned and looked at his brother. "And why would I want to do that?"

Rafe laughed. "Because you want to. Oh, don't give me that black look. You've spent the last week staring at her. You never let her out of your sight. And don't think I haven't noticed that miserable expression when she goes to her tent . . . alone. So why not just talk to her?"

Robert ignored him. Ahead of them, Olivia rode with one of Rafe's men, the two of them chatting away in Spanish, the infatuated guerrilla pointing out the sights and landmarks around them to his avid audience. All the men had been taking turns riding beside Olivia, including Aquiles and Rafe—all of them except Robert.

He couldn't bring himself to bridge the gaping chasm that had opened between them since the night at the inn. His pride stood in the way. And that was a higher mountain than the ones looming in the distance, the ones that would lead them into Spain.

"I find it hard to believe that you of all people can so easily forget her involvement with Lando's death," Robert finally said.

Rafe shook his head. "She had nothing to do with it."

"How do you know?" Robert looked again up the line of mules and horses to where she rode. "She hasn't been honest about a number of things. Who's to say she's been honest about that?"

"Because she has Lando's ring."

When Robert said nothing, Rafe made an exasperated sound in the back of his throat. "And Wellington considers you one of his better officers? Bah, no wonder the British have spent so much time on their arses instead of fighting."

Robert's head swung around at this insult. "What the devil do you mean?"

"Think, man. If she had been in partnership with Bradstone and they had just discovered the whereabouts of a priceless treasure, do you think she would take the time to steal a worthless ring from a dead man's hand? You know the value of these rings—you gave them to us." Rafe spat to one side. "The only way she could have come by that ring is if Lando lived long enough to give it to her. She also knew that she was to take it to Hobbe. Just as you told us to do when you gave them to us, don't you remember?"

He did remember. He had been leaving for the army, and his young half brothers had been devastated that their beloved elder brother was going away, especially Lando, who had trailed after Robert since the day he'd learned to walk. So as tokens to remember him by, Robert had given them both rings and told them that if they ever needed him, they could send him one as a sign.

And Lando had. Dispatching his final cry for help via his own chosen messenger, Olivia Sutton. What he wouldn't tell Rafe was that he'd come to that very conclusion that night at the inn. And an even more staggering one—one he was unwilling to admit to anyone, not even himself.

Rafe pushed his point further. "Lando is the only witness we have from that night. Can't you see that he wouldn't have given the ring to her unless she had done something to instill his trust and faith. Obviously he didn't hold her responsible—much to the contrary. So neither should you."

Robert shook his head. "It really doesn't matter at this point. She wants nothing to do with me, and I certainly don't know what I would do with her."

At this Rafe laughed. "I think you know damn well what to do with her. And I think you've already done it." With that, he spurred his horse ahead and left Robert simmering in his own regrets.

As they drew closer to the Spanish border, Robert grew more and more distant. He often rode with the rear guard or up ahead to ensure there were no traps set for them along the narrow, seemingly forgotten trails that connected Portugal to Spain.

If only he'd been honest with her from the start. And she with him.

If Robert avoided her company, at least Rafe's band of guerrillas thought her worthy of their attentions. They took turns riding beside her, telling her of their families and misfortunes and of their dreams of a Spain free of Napoleon's stranglehold and treachery.

Just this morning, Paco, who liked to tease her about her red hair, had brought her a wreath of flowers he'd picked from the side of the road. Grumpy old Gaspar had come by and laughed at his young companion's offering and then shown her a small, tattered drawing of his wife. When prompted further, he'd told Olivia of his wife's bravery before she'd been butchered by a French cavalry unit she'd refused to feed.

But the one gift that she hadn't known what to make

of had come from Alamar. The second day out, Olivia had caught some of the men whispering about the possibility of someone following them. When she'd asked Rafe's second in command about it, he had denied it, but when she had pressed him for more information, he finally confirmed the bits of gossip she'd overheard.

They were being trailed.

Then he'd dug in his pack and handed her a small folded paper and told her to use the contents in case they were captured. In case there was no hope that they could save her from the cursed fate surrounding *El Rescate del Rey*.

He told her that the powder would give her a swifter and more humane end than what their enemies would offer her. And then he'd left her in stunned silence.

She'd tucked the powder in her bag and tried to forget they were being followed. Tried to forget that she was caught in the middle of a maze that went far beyond her own existence.

"Give him time, *mi reina*," Rafe said, as he suddenly rode up alongside her.

She turned to him. "What did you say?"

"My brother," he said, nodding at Robert, who was riding in the lead. "Give him time. He'll come to his senses."

"Colin said much the same thing," Olivia replied. She stuck her nose in the air and put on a nonchalant air. "I hardly see what that means to me. I am nothing more than a duty to your brother, an obligation he will happily be rid of once we get to Spain."

Rafe laughed uproariously, drawing not only the attention of all the men around them but Robert's as well, who cast an annoyed look back at them.

"You two are made for each other," Rafe said.

Olivia stared at him. "We are no such thing," she said, at the same time a small kindle of hope welled up in her heart. "Your brother is a dishonorable, lying, conniving—"

"Man in love." Rafe smiled at her. "And he doesn't know how to tell you." He tapped his heels into his horse's sides and said, "But give him time—he'll come around," before he trotted off to rejoin his men.

What had Rafe just said?

Robert loved her? While her heart thrilled at this disclosure, she reined in her tumultuous elation, telling herself it wasn't possible. Not with all the misunderstandings between them. Yet she couldn't help remembering the night at the inn, the look in his eyes, when she had thought that one tempting kiss might bridge the wide chasm separating their two hearts.

Perhaps he didn't need time, she thought, but rather a little prodding. At this, she smiled.

Along the way they had come into a number of sleepy villages that seemed to have escaped the ravages of war. Around noon, they arrived in one town that practically teemed with life. A market was in progress, and there were food and drinks and wares for sale. Rafe's party was welcomed in, and despite Robert's black looks and mouthed warning that she "not talk to anyone," Olivia happily waded into the crowd.

Robert, on the other hand, saw the entire situation as a disaster in the making. Especially when he lost sight of Olivia amongst the crowded stalls.

He rose up in his stirrups, his hand to his forehead to shield his eyes from the sun, and yet in this sea of dark heads, nowhere could he see Olivia's distinctive red hair.

This was the very reason he intended to deposit her into Wellington's care the moment they arrived in Badajoz. He didn't want the constant aggravation of watching over her when she refused to stay under his protection.

But his concern went far beyond his obligation to see her to Wellington. Rafe's words had cut to the very core of his pride. His stupid, misplaced pride and arrogance.

Orlando had sent her to him, and he'd been too blind to see it. And now that he did, it was probably too late.

"Are you looking for someone?" a soft voice asked him in Portuguese.

He barely spared the woman a glance, dressed as she was in a wide country skirt and white blouse, her hair and head covered with a bright blue shawl.

She sidled closer to him, hiking her skirt a bit to reveal slim tanned calves. "Perhaps you are looking for a woman?" she persisted. "I could help."

Robert shook his head. She was probably looking to make a few spare coins on the side, a practice the women of these villages had been driven to by the ravages of war. He twisted in his saddle, looking behind him to see if Olivia was with a group of women that had gathered near the well.

But she was nowhere to be seen.

His heart pounded even harder. Damn her.

For the past week, he'd remained increasingly vigilant, for his instincts told him they were being followed, being watched with each move they made.

Rafe's men had uttered the same sentiment—that

they felt they were being shadowed. Time and again, singly and in pairs, they'd taken turns doubling back, waiting and watching for their unknown enemy to appear, but the elusive shadow slipped their grasp each time.

This only made it harder and harder to watch out for Olivia, for she stubbornly refused to remain at his side.

"Sometimes you can find what you are looking for by just taking a closer look, don't you think?"

Robert dug into his jacket and pulled out a few coins, tossing them at the woman. "Take them, I really don't need your help right now."

"Oh, good," she said, switching to English. "Now I can pay the woman for my new clothes."

His gaze ricocheted back in the blink of an eye. "Olivia!" he shouted at the figure now skipping through the crowd toward the knot of women by the well.

She turned around slowly. Her head tipped back until her face peered out from beneath her shawl, a seductive smile on her lips. A pair of blue eyes, mischievous and dancing with amusement, looked back at him, cutting straight to his heart. "Yes?"

"What the devil are you doing?"

"You said I was too conspicuous, so I decided to look a little less English. What do you think?" She twirled one way, then the other in the full skirt, showing her boots and bare legs. The loose cotton top, gathered around the tops of her breasts, dipped as dangerously low as that cursed muslin thing she'd worn on the *Sybaris*.

The one that had driven him to distraction. And now she was going to wear something similar all day?

An old woman approached Olivia, and they began bargaining back and forth to come up with a price for the shawl the woman held up. The white wool length was adorned with embroidered roses.

The old woman's knowing gaze caught Robert staring at Olivia. A sly smile passed over her wrinkled face and she wrapped the shawl tighter around Olivia, so it covered her nearly bare shoulders and the tops of her breasts.

The old horse trader, he thought, trying to ignore his own relief at how well it covered Olivia. "How much?" he asked the lady.

She named her price, an outrageous sum that made Olivia gasp, but Robert saw the money as nothing but well spent.

He reached in his pocket and drew out the coins, dropping them into the woman's outstretched palm, while Olivia sputtered protests about the impropriety of his buying her such an extravagant gift.

He straightened in his saddle. "*You're* telling me what is considered improper?"

"I suppose that is rather like the pot calling the kettle black," she teased back, wrapping the shawl tighter around her shoulders.

Which is exactly what Robert had just paid a good portion of his monthly salary to see done. If that damned shawl kept her decently covered, then he wouldn't spend most of the day with his senses mired in speculative passion for her.

Rafe signaled for them to mount up, and Robert got off his mount and escorted Olivia to her beloved and wretched donkey. Now that he'd found her, he wasn't about to lose sight of her again. Not this close to the border, not ever.

Not ever? He shook his head and tightened his grip on her elbow as he steered her through the crowd. He had to stop thinking like that.

"You still haven't said what you think of my new outfit," she said, her toe nudging at a loose stone.

"I'm not really a good judge of women's fashions," he said, thinking that her skirt was too short and the top too revealing, but he wasn't going to tell the cheeky little minx that. "What would your esteemed Lady Finch say?"

"After I got done applying copious amounts of smelling salts to revive her, she'd declare me unfit for proper society."

Robert grinned. "I like your Lady Finch more and more."

"You would," Olivia said. "The two of you are a regular pair of drill sergeants."

They came up to Evaline, who immediately set up a fuss as Robert approached. She usually did save her best antics for him.

"I don't think she likes your uniform," Olivia said, eyeing his coat. "I believe the red frightens her."

Robert's horse had the good sense to stop a safe distance from the unfriendly and unpredictable little donkey.

Robert wondered if perhaps his horse had more wit than he did as Evaline started to snap at the braid on his sleeve. "What would Lady Finch say about having a donkey named after her?"

Olivia flinched, then laughed. "She wouldn't be all that amused until I told her of all Evaline's good traits."

"Which are?" Robert asked, as he swatted the impudent little beast out of reach of his buttons. This was his only good jacket, and buttons were hard to come by at the front.

Olivia patted Evaline on the top of her head and scratched her ears. The donkey gazed at her mistress as if Olivia were heaven-sent. "She's loyal and has good instincts about the people she chooses to like." With that, she lifted her hem and held out her foot, nodding at him that she was ready.

Robert nearly groaned at the sight of those trim calves. Just a glimpse of them reminded him what they'd felt like sliding down his legs, tangling with his feet. Besides, what game was this she was playing? He'd seen her climb up on Evaline any number of times without any help. He was starting to suspect she was deliberately baiting him.

First with her new outfit, and now her request for his help. His touch.

"Come along, Hobbe," Rafe called out.

With everyone watching, Robert caught hold of her foot. Olivia put her hand on his shoulder. He paused for a moment, then went to boost her up onto Evaline when the little donkey changed her mind about the entire process.

The beast sidestepped into Olivia, sending her crashing into Robert. All he could do was catch her as they both fell into the road, her soft form landing atop his, her breasts pressed into his chest, her hips grazing his.

For a moment, all he could think of was that dangerous moment back on *Sybaris* when they'd fallen into her berth, their lips locked and their bodies already heated with passion. The very thought made him harden, and as if instinctively, her body nestled closer to his quickly growing passion.

His gaze locked with hers. Instead of the shock or dismay he expected, she was laughing, her gaze holding an intimate recognition of how they fit—how they should be locked like this every night.

"I don't think Lady Finch would find this very proper either," he told her.

Olivia's gaze met his, and he could have sworn her eyes were filled with questions, and hope. "On some things," she said, "even Lady Finch hasn't the right instructions."

"If she did," he replied, "I doubt you would follow them."

"Would you want me to?"

Robert knew right then the only thing he wanted was this woman. This dangerous minx, who teased him, who toyed with him, who tempted his heart.

"If you two are quite through making a spectacle of yourselves, can we get moving?" Rafe asked, leaning out of his saddle and staring down at them.

Olivia scrambled up first, shaking the dust off her skirt and then quickly mounting the now docile Evaline without any further mishaps, or assistance, Robert noted wryly.

He stalked back to his horse and climbed into the saddle. "I should have had Colin find a deserted island somewhere and left you there," he muttered.

"I wouldn't have gone," Olivia shot back.

He didn't fail to notice that she deliberately nudged Evaline right next to his horse.

"You wouldn't have had a choice."

Olivia made no move to ride anywhere but by his side.

He supposed she intended to remain there the rest of the afternoon. He'd done his best to avoid this, though he hated to admit it, but he was glad of her company. He'd missed the intimate hours they'd spent on the *Sybaris* during his convalescence. And he'd never thought there would ever be a woman, especially an Englishwoman, who would take the same delight in the Peninsula and its people as he did.

And since he'd spent most of the winter in '10 mapping this area for Wellington, he knew the countryside well enough to share with her some of its history and landmarks as they rode.

And so it was that they spent the afternoon in companionable conversation until they came to a viable spot to make camp for the night. Nestled down in a valley by a stream, the water would mask the sound of their camp, and the steep hill around them would keep them from being visible at any distance.

Rafe and Gaspar joined Robert immediately.

"We've found our shadow," Gaspar whispered. "Leandro and Lacho are watching him as we speak."

"Then let's go catch him," Robert said, taking up his horse's reins and remounting without a moment's hesitation.

"I'll stay here." Rafe shielded his eyes with his hand and scanned the hills around them. "I still have an uneasy feeling about this."

"I agree," Robert said. "But once we have our traveling companion in custody, then we can determine how dangerous he is and if he has any friends. Until then, keep an eye on her, will you?"

Rafe grinned. "Only if that means you've finally come to your senses."

Robert didn't respond, but instead wheeled his mount around and with Gaspar on his heels rode down a narrow path along the stream that Gaspar said would meet up with the road and Leandro's and Lacho's hiding spot. With the noisy stream beside them, they rode as quickly as they could until twenty minutes later they rejoined the road and the spot where they were to meet them.

Riding up to a large rock, they found Leandro propped there, apparently taking a siesta in the warm afternoon sun. Lacho was nowhere in sight.

"Get up, you lazy dog," Gaspar called out good-naturedly.

When the young man didn't respond, Robert felt the hairs on the back of his neck stand on end. Suddenly nothing about the scene around them looked right. There was blood on the roadway, and the man's body leaned at an unnatural angle.

"Stay back," Robert told Gaspar, as he dismounted and approached the young Spaniard.

"He is making one of his jokes," Gaspar said. "Enough, Leandro, get up. You are frightening our good English friend."

Robert came around the young man and saw that Leandro would no longer be making jokes at the expense of his fellow guerrillas.

"He is not sleeping," he told Gaspar. "He's been murdered."

Gaspar scrambled off his horse and dashed to his friend's side. He turned Leandro around and revealed what Robert had already seen. The man's throat had been slit. Lacho they found hanging from a nearby tree, his fate just as tragic.

Gaspar let out a vicious oath, a promise of vengeance, while Robert's training went immediately into action.

He'd seen too many instances like this to take the

time for grief and anger. Carefully he walked around the scene and surmised that there had been a large party of men, the hoofprints in the dust easy to read.

What he didn't like was that the party had ridden off in the direction of his camp.

As they started to remount, a movement in the brush caught Robert's eye. He had his pistol out and aimed in the blink of an eye.

"I say, there," came a familiar voice. "Don't shoot." A man came stumbling out of the bush and up the bank to the road, his hands and feet bound with a length of rope. "I can tell you what happened if you would be so kind as to untie me."

Robert couldn't believe his eyes.

"Major Danvers, is that you?" called out none other than Jemmy Reyburn.

Chapter 14

When the hoofbeats came pounding in from the road, Olivia glanced up from the fire she was building, a smile on her face as she paused and waited to see Robert, Gaspar and the others come riding in.

But when the first horseman rounded the bend, sword raised, her breath caught in her throat.

A French picquet! Robert had warned her about this, but she had dismissed him time and time again as being overprotective.

Rafe and his men reacted instantly, calling out for arms.

Their scramble was to no avail, for the French riders encircled them in moments, leaving the Spaniards in a shower of dust and dismay.

Rafe stepped in front of Olivia, shielding her from them. "What is the meaning of this?" he asked. "We

are just merchants on our way to the fair in Portra-
legre."

A rider in the back nudged his horse forward. His elegant, albeit dusty, uniform marked him as the officer in
charge of the unit. "Merchants? I think not. I'll tell you
what you are—you are thieves and murderers. The entire lot of you. And from this moment on you are all
under arrest as traitors to the sovereign nation of
France."

"You are a long way from your country to be making
such an assertion, monsieur," Rafe replied in French,
his words polite but his intonation full of threat.

Olivia peered around him, trying to gauge what
would happen next.

"France is wherever I command, you insolent dog,"
the officer replied. He dismounted in a smooth motion, and Olivia took a deep breath as she surveyed the
man who now held their fate in his hands.

"And you are?" Rafe asked.

"Capitaine de Jenoure," he said. Tall and handsome,
the officer's bearing was as arrogant as the numerous
decorations on his coat. He strode directly up to Rafe,
his gaze never leaving him. He smiled with the deadly
charm of a snake, then with alarming speed and accu-
racy slammed his fist in two rapid punches into Rafe,
sending him staggering back.

"Oh!" Olivia squeaked, as she caught Rafe, holding
him up, knowing Robert's brother would not want to
fall to his knees before his men or this arrogant Frenchman. He staggered forward, only to have the officer
strike him again. By now Rafe's nose was bent to one
side, and there was a bloody gash on his lip.

She stepped in front of him and glared at the beast

of an officer who appeared to be coiling to strike again.

"Mademoiselle Sutton, get out of my way," the Frenchman told her.

Olivia's mouth fell open. *He knew who she was.*

It was no accident that this French force had stumbled upon them. The presumptuous light in the man's eyes told Olivia he'd found exactly what he'd been looking for.

"Step out of the way," he repeated.

"Do it," Rafe told her.

When she still refused to move, Capitaine de Jenoure nodded to one of his men, who dismounted and quickly caught her by the arm.

Alamar, always a bit of a hothead, surged forward. "Take your hands off her, you dirty pig."

Capitaine de Jenoure's gaze rolled upward, as if the entire proceedings were growing boring, and then in a blink of an eye, pulled a pistol from the holster at his side and shot Alamar.

The young man jerked in surprise, his eyes wide with alarm as a stain of red spilled across his chest. He tried to say something else, his hand outstretched to Olivia, but more blood spilled from his lips before he dropped to the ground.

Capitaine de Jenoure glanced over at the rest of Rafe's men. "Any more of these pointless heroics, and you shall share your friend's fate."

Olivia sank to her knees. She clutched at Alamar's sleeve, her fingers moving up to feel at his neck for a pulse, but there was nothing. No beat, no rhythm of life, just the emptiness of death. Tears spilled from her eyes as she realized there was nothing she could do.

"What do you want?" Rafe was asking.

"Why, that should be obvious," the Capitaine told him. "We've come for the treasure. We've come for Mademoiselle Sutton."

"Why you murdering devil," Gaspar said, as he surged toward Jemmy with a large wicked knife in his hand.

"No!" Robert said, catching the grief-blinded man by the arm. "Look at him? Does he look like he was capable of this?"

To aid in his defense, Jemmy tried to hold up his bound hands but only proceeded to trip himself up, landing in a dusty heap at Robert's feet.

"Besides, I know this man. He's a friend," Robert told the irate guerilla.

Gaspar muttered beneath his breath as he gave Jemmy one more suspicious glance. Then, as if he finally saw the harmless lad for what he was, he cut the bindings free.

"Thank you, sir," Jemmy said, as he rubbed his raw hands. "Your companions surprised me about an hour ago. Startled my horse, and the demmed hack left me in the dust. Good cattle are difficult to come by in this country." He rubbed at his wrists and then glanced over at the bodies. "Are they?"

Robert nodded.

"Thought so. Even though I wasn't too pleased when they tied me up, when the young one heard the horses coming, he shoved me down this ravine to hide me. He saved my life."

"What horses?" Robert asked.

"Why, the ones that demmed Frog picquet were riding. When I heard you two, I thought they'd come back."

"What French picquet?" Robert asked, a cold, icy river of dread chilling his blood. As if to punctuate his fears, a gunshot echoed in the distance.

"That one," Jemmy said, nodding up the road in the direction of their camp.

Robert cursed as he raced for his mount. The animal sidestepped his quick motions, but in a deft leap he was up and in the saddle, touching his spurs to its flanks and off down the road in a flash.

Near the stream, another horse whinnied, as if not wanting to be left out.

"I believe that is one of your friend's horses," Jemmy told Gaspar. "Mine's long gone. Rotten bit of cattle it was to begin with, skittish and not too reliable."

Gaspar whistled, and the horse trotted obediently up from the stream. "He is yours now, señor." Gaspar held out the reins. "Can you fight?"

"That I can, sir," Jemmy said, retrieving his pack from the ditch and accepting the proffered horse.

Gaspar tossed him a pistol, and Jemmy grinned as he tucked the wicked thing into his coat.

The two of them mounted and took off into the growing darkness after Robert.

The French dragoons quickly bound Rafe's remaining men. "Now Mademoiselle Sutton," Capitaine de Jenoure said, "where is this treasure all Spain is waiting for you to deliver?" He towered in front of Olivia, her arms still pinned behind her by one of his henchmen.

She answered by spitting at the Frenchman's boots.

Though outnumbered and bound, several Spaniards

snickered at her defiance. The capitaine vented his wrath on Rafe by pounding his fists into the battered man's ribs and face.

Robert's brother finally dropped to the ground, a bloody mess. This time Olivia was able to break her captor's hold and she rushed to Rafe's side.

"Don't tell him anything," Rafe managed to whisper. "They won't leave this place until daybreak—the French never move at night for fear of guerrillas." He paused for a moment, his eyes closed, his voice dropping even lower. "Robert will find you. He won't let them harm you."

Capitaine de Jenoure booted Rafe away from her. "Enough!" He scowled at Olivia as he caught her by the arm, dragging her away from Rafe and the others. "If he was telling you that your friends up the road would rescue you, rest assured they are in no position to help anyone. I'm afraid they died before they could go rouse the local sympathies."

Olivia's struggles to free herself from the loathsome man stopped as abruptly as the breath in her throat. The officer's words tolled in her mind.

Dead. All dead. Robert was gone. No, it couldn't be true. She looked to Rafe to see his reaction, but all she saw was raw grief mirrored in his one eye that wasn't swollen shut.

"Make camp," the Capitaine ordered his men. "Then search their packs. Let us see what kind of merchandise our friends purvey."

For the next half hour, Olivia watched from her lonely perch on a log as the French dragoons efficiently set up a tent for their commander, established a perimeter guard, lit several fires and proceeded to steal every bit of food and wine Rafe's men had stowed in their packs.

They hadn't even gotten to the dynamite and munitions, and Olivia wondered what they would do then.

Happy though with their current finds, especially the plentiful cache of wine, the Frenchmen settled about the fires, celebrating their success with toasts and boasts as to their eventual rewards for capturing Olivia.

"You must excuse my men," Capitaine de Jenoure said, coming up behind her as silently as a cat. "I fear we have been riding for nearly a week trying to locate you, and they are in the mood to celebrate."

"As I see it, you have little to celebrate, monsieur," Olivia said. "For you haven't the treasure."

He laughed. "But we have you, Mademoiselle Sutton. And you are enough for the emperor."

"Bonaparte?" she whispered.

"Oh, yes. Bonaparte. You see even the emperor has heard of you and this Spanish legend. And his gratitude for finding you and the gold will see me out of this godforsaken country and back home to France as a hero. A rich one, at that."

"I won't help you."

"Mademoiselle, rest assured, you will." He waved his hands over the fire. "For I have no intention of failing and remaining *here*."

He turned and starting walking to his tent, then stopped, casting a glance over his shoulder. "Come dine with me as my guest."

It was on the tip of her tongue to refuse him outright, but she saw Rafe watching her. His face was so swollen and bloody it was hard to recognize him. But he nodded for her to follow the capitaine.

"Your friend is right to send you with me," the Frenchman told her. "For you see, once my men are done imbibing the wine they have discovered, they will start looking for real sport, and I won't be in a position to protect you if you are not already claimed for the night."

"I won't leave these men," she said stubbornly, hugging herself, drawing her shawl tighter around her quaking shoulders.

"In the morning you will. For with no women about, my men will pursue other amusements, and I fear shooting your friends will be the first in a long night of entertainments that I doubt you will want to witness."

Rafe nodded to her again, emphatically gesturing for her to go with Capitaine de Jenoure. So Olivia rose to her feet. With slow, wooden movements she followed the Frenchman to his newly erected tent.

"A wise decision, mademoiselle."

He held the flap open for her and bowed slightly as she entered his private sanctuary. A small portable table took up most of the room, with a camp stool on either side. Atop the table sat her valise, a candle and a flagon of wine. In the corner there was a narrow cot.

Olivia chose to ignore it and walked purposefully over to her valise. Taking a mental inventory of her meager possessions, she thought of one or two things she could use to defend herself if she could just get to them.

Yet even as her hands closed over the handles, Capitaine de Jenoure's clamped down over hers. "And what treasures do you have in here?"

He shoved her down on a stool and opened the valise, his brow cocking arrogantly as he started to paw through her belongings. First to come out were the twill britches. He shook his head, muttering something about loathsome English fashions. The britches were dispatched with all due haste.

"Let those men go," Olivia said, trying to distract him from digging deeper into her valise.

"What, those thieves?" he scoffed. "I think not. They'd murder us in our beds before the night was over. Your concern for them is quite touching but most misplaced." He brought out her dimity gown, which elicited much the same response as the britches.

Next came her notebook. "Ah, now this might be most interesting." He settled down on the other stool, and poured himself a glass of wine. After taking an appreciative sip, he opened the book. Flipping through the pages, his expression was one of bafflement as he tried to decipher her notes. "I admit my English isn't perfect, but none of this makes any sense. Perhaps you would like to decipher this scrawl for me."

Outside, the dragoons' voices rose in a boisterous and rousing song.

Olivia smiled. "Not unless you let my friends go."

The capitaine shrugged and threw her notebook on his bed. "Yes, well, we have many nights ahead of us to discuss the contents of that and how best to translate them."

He returned to pawing through her valise, this time bringing out her pistol. "Tsk. Tsk. Such an ugly thing for a lady to carry. But considering the company you have been keeping, I can see why you might have found it necessary. I am sure by the morning you will agree that French hospitality is more to your liking."

Olivia had an entirely different opinion on that subject.

The next thing he pulled out was the sprigged muslin. It nearly brought tears to her eyes to see this loathsome man handling her beautiful dress, the one Robert had gazed upon her with such passion as she'd worn it.

Now he was gone, and they would never have another night like they'd had on the *Sybaris*.

"I would have you wear this for me," the Capitaine was saying. "It would be much more fetching than those rags this rabble has tried to disguise you in."

"I prefer these, thank you," she said, tightening her shawl around her shoulders.

He gave the sprigged muslin another leering glance and then tossed it on the bed alongside her journal. "You can wear it when I present you to the emperor." He reached inside her valise again and this time came out with a handful of items, including the packet of deadly powder Alamar had given her.

And it gave her an idea.

"As my friend out there said, monsieur, you are a long way from France. What makes you believe you can get me to Paris?"

Her sneering question elicited exactly the reaction she'd hoped for.

He slammed his fist down on the table, sending the various items fluttering to the floor. "You English bitch. By the time you get to France, you will be crawling into my bed, begging for my attentions."

Lady Finch had always said the French were a hot-headed lot. Happily, she was right.

In his anger and arrogant display, the paper filled with Alamar's murderous potion fluttered from the table and landed at her feet. She gulped, feigned dismay at Capitaine de Jenoure's display and let her shawl drop to her feet. When she bent to pick it up, she palmed the packet.

Robert surveyed the camp below calculating how best to liberate Rafe and his men.

And Olivia.

He tried not to think of her down there amidst these drunken French dragoons, who thought nothing of cutting up their victims for sport. He'd seen enough French atrocities during his time behind enemy lines to haunt his dreams for a lifetime.

"I count seven of our men," Gaspar whispered. "That means one of them is either missing and got away, or . . ."

He didn't need to finish his thought for Robert to know exactly what he was thinking. He'd already made the same difficult count and reached the conclusion that one of their group had probably died.

It also left Olivia unaccounted for. Where the devil was the little termagant?

Now, when he had finally gotten up the nerve to tell her how he felt—how much he cared for her, how much he needed her forgiveness.

"I say, isn't that the Queen?" Jemmy said, pointing toward the lone tent in the middle of the camp.

Silhouetted on the wall of the canvas was the figure of a man bent over a table. As he rose and held something up for examination, he revealed a second occupant in the tent.

Olivia, Robert's heart sang.

Suddenly he suspected this surprise attack hadn't been just happenstance after all. "Gaspar," he whispered. "Look there." He pointed at the mules that had yet to be unpacked, the poor animals hobbled together, but not unloaded. "If we could get down there and get our hands on a box of powder, do you think we could add some fireworks to their celebration?"

Gaspar grinned, then put his knife between his teeth and began a silent crawl toward one of the soldiers posted on the camp's perimeter.

"What do you want me to do?" Jemmy asked.

"Cover me," Robert told him, as he set out for the line of pack animals.

The bulk of the French force was getting drunk around the fire, while the few men who had been set to guard duty were spending more time watching their comrades with envy than attending to their duties.

Robert made it to the first animal, and to his dismay, it turned out to be Evaline. The horrid little donkey took one look at him and rolled her eyes, while her lips peeled back over her great yellow teeth. She let out a bray that could have alerted every single French soldier from Spain all the way back to Bonaparte's headquarters in Paris.

"Shut up," he whispered. "Be quiet. Don't you know I am trying to save you."

Evaline regarded him for one blessed silent moment

and then cut loose with another raucous chorus of complaints.

"How did you manage to find me?" Olivia asked. "The Spaniards hate the French, so I doubt one of them would sell me out to the likes of you."

The man laughed. "You underestimate the lure of gold." He paused for a moment before refilling his glass. "But if you must know, it was one of your own countrymen who helped us. A man who was quite willing to bring us to you for a portion of the reward." He held up the flagon to Olivia. "Would you care for a glass before we retire?"

"It isn't my vintage," she told him, trying without any success to find a way to distract him long enough to pour the powder into his cup and more importantly to avoid his bed.

If it came to that, she might be tempted to take the damned poison herself.

Off in the distance, Evaline made a distraught braying noise. It caught Olivia off guard because it was the same distinct protest the little donkey made every time Robert tried to make friends with her.

Robert?

The hairs on the back of her neck stood on end as Evaline protested again, while Capitaine de Jenoure covered his ears to blot out the discordant noise.

Olivia bit her lip. It couldn't be! But it had to be. Evaline reacted like that to only one person.

Robert!

Suddenly a new hope swelled to life inside her heart. Could he have escaped the fate Capitaine de Jenoure had described?

Meanwhile the capitaine crossed the tent and opened the flap, giving her just the chance she needed.

Olivia glanced over her shoulder at him to make sure he wasn't looking, then dumped the contents of Alamar's powder into his wine cup.

"Silence that wretched animal. Now!" he was shouting at one of his men, as Olivia watched the powder bubble for a moment then disappear into the ruby-colored wine without a trace.

Meanwhile Evaline continued to bray and protest as if the entire camp were filled with Roberts.

The capitaine stomped back to the table and picked up his wine. He waited for a moment until the report of a gun silenced her faithful little donkey's cry.

"There, that ought to be the end of that wretched beast," he said as he quaffed the entire contents of the cup.

And yours as well, you wretched man, Olivia thought.

Just then the camp rocked with an explosion, then another. A flurry of gunshots followed. The capitaine strode toward the doorway, reached for his pistol, but came to an abrupt halt.

He spun around, clutching at his throat, his eyes wild. Then his frantic gaze landed on his empty cup.

"You—" he managed to sputter, trying to raise his arm and aim his pistol at her. But before he could pull the trigger, his body went into a series of jerky spasms and he fell over dead.

Olivia jumped over his body and grabbed up her pistol as well as the capitaine's. Outside, men were shouting in several different languages, calling out orders, the replies coming in gunshots.

The flap of the tent flipped open, and Olivia

whirled around, a pistol in either hand. And in that instant before she made the decision to pull the trigger, Robert stepped into the tent.

"Don't shoot me, I'm here to rescue you," he said, as she came flying across the tent and into his arms. He glanced over her shoulder at the body of the capitaine. "Once again, it looks like you were doing fine all on your own."

Chapter 15

Rafe's troop had suffered the loss of four men in total, who they buried hastily, murmured prayers over their unmarked graves and vowed once again to rid the Peninsula of the French pestilence that had killed so many good people.

The dead dragoons they tossed into the ravine, but not before they had relieved them of their weapons and munitions and—almost as valuable—their boots.

After that, Robert and Rafe decided it was in their best interest to put as much distance as possible between them and the grisly scene in case Capitaine de Jenoure had not been working alone.

So with it still dark, they packed up and rode. Into the dawn and well into the next day they continued their flight through the barren, rough, mountainous spine separating Portugal from Spain. When the sun started to dip well into the western horizon, they stopped to make camp in an abandoned convent perched on a precipice and with the vantage of affording them a good view of the countryside around them in case they'd been followed.

After everyone took a few hours of much needed rest, the camp stirred to life. They were getting close to Badajoz, and most of the men were confident that by tomorrow they would see the banks of the Rio Guadiana and Wellington's camp.

The convent also afforded a luxury that not even Olivia had expected. In the former laundry there was a large cistern that filled and overflowed with water from an underground spring. The men left her to her privacy, so she was able to bathe and wash her clothes.

The brisk water and a bit of soap she'd purloined at the inn made for a heavenly bath, and she reveled in the unexpected luxury of it. With her regular clothes all hung out to dry, she donned the sprigged muslin and smiled as she pinned up her damp and curling hair.

She hoped Robert would notice . . . and remember the last time she wore this dress.

In the relative safety of their secluded hideout, Rafe's men built a fire and prepared a great meal to celebrate their last night on the road. When Olivia made her entrance, she was greeted with cheers and applause. With a shy smile at such flattery, she curtseyed quickly and then took a seat.

Cautiously, she glanced over at Robert, only to find that his gaze were very much upon her. He did remember, if the smoky fire lighting his eyes told the truth.

After everyone had eaten their fill, Paco began regaling them with tales of Spanish heroes and clowns, leaving his avid audience laughing and crying.

Finally Olivia spoke up. "Tell me the story of *El Rescate del Rey*."

All the men grew quiet and stared at her, as if she must be joking.

She shrugged her shoulders. "Truly, I do not know the story."

"How can that be, little Queen?" Paco asked. "You have Caliopa's heart and her daring. Yet you claim you don't know her story?"

Olivia shook her head and waited eagerly for Paco to begin.

Like a good storyteller, Paco let his audience wait for a few moments and then he began.

"In the dark first days when the Moors invaded our country, King Álvaro, a brave and wealthy ruler from the North, heard of his country's fate in the South, so he raised his army and went to meet the barbarian invaders, much against the wishes of his Queen . . ."

Spain, 712

"My Queen, there must be another way," the lady's confessor pleaded. "You could feign illness. You could flee. You could come with me tonight. There is a convent in Badajoz that would take you in. You would be safe there."

Queen Caliopa listened to Father Mateo's words and wished there was an alternative.

Damn the Moorish invaders for holding her husband hostage, and damn their enemies from within, she wanted to tell the gentle priest, but instead she shook her head, her hands already wringing the embroidered belt hanging at her waist. If she thought the silver and gold thread decorating the expensive piece would add to the likelihood of saving her beloved husband, she would have plucked every metallic strand from the design.

Already the small chest at her feet sat weighted with all the gold and silver she'd been able to wrangle from her husband's treasury. And when that hadn't been enough to satisfy the sultan's demands, she'd filled the remaining space with gems and jewels that had been in her family for centuries. Before she closed it, she pulled her betrothal ring from her hand and held it tightly.

"No, my Queen. Not your ring," Father Mateo said, his words more a prayer than a plea.

"It is so a part of me goes with you to him."

She closed the lid and turned the key in the lock. Handing it to Father Mateo, she said, "There is no other way. You must go. Without me. It is the only way to avoid our enemies."

"I won't leave you. Not now. Your husband would never—"

"My husband is a prisoner of the sultan's forces. I rule in his stead. The treasure goes with you and you alone. You must obey me in this." She reached over and touched his sleeve. "Take this ransom to Álvaro's captors and see my husband and your king freed." She smiled at him. "Who else can I trust but you, my cousin?"

Father Mateo nodded. He motioned to the two servants standing close by, two men Queen Caliopa and Father Mateo trusted as much as they trusted each other. The pair struggled to hoist the laden chest, but as they went to leave, Caliopa stopped them.

"Take the other stairs," she said.

"But Your Highness," one protested, "those are only for you and our King."

"Take them to avoid any prying eyes. I hear my husband's cousin in the courtyard and I would not want him . . ."—she paused, trying to find a way to phrase her next words without disparaging her husband's relative—"to delay your travels with added instructions," she finally said. "He has been overly attentive of late, and I do not want to tax his kindness any further." The men nodded in understanding and struggled with their load to the hidden entrance behind a large tapestry.

When the men left, Caliopa turned to Father Mateo. "Help me." She crossed the richly furnished solar to a bench and pulled a cloth away to reveal a chest, one matching the ransom chest in every detail.

"Help me put this in the middle of the room," she said, struggling to lift one side.

Father Mateo grabbed the other handle, and the pair of them hauled the heavy load across the room until it sat in exactly the same location as the first one.

"What have you got in here?" the holy man asked.

"A treasure of stones and lead," she said. "This will give Eurico no reason to follow you, for he will think I have not yet sent the ransom."

Caliopa's worst fear in the last month was that her husband's cousin, Eurico, would use Álvaro's imprisonment to stake his own claim to their small but prosperous kingdom.

"This is a dangerous game you play, Caliopa," Father Mateo whispered, no longer using her title or rank as he addressed her. In this moment, they were just Caliopa and Mateo, like the children they'd been when growing up on her father's estates near Madrid. "Your husband's cousin will not appreciate your duplicity in these matters. If he decides to strike, he may well take far more than just the ransom gold."

"Never you fear, good cousin. Eurico will not dare harm me. He fears Álvaro's wrath more than God's."

"As he should," Father Mateo muttered under his breath.

Caliopa hid her smile. Wandering over to the chess table she had set up in the corner of the room, she studied the pieces before her. The game was half finished, in the same position as it had been when she and her husband had halted their play at the news of the invasion of Moors from Africa. Her fingers stroked the proud king, standing as it was next to its queen.

Her husband was a fierce warrior, unmatched by any man she had ever seen. That he had been not only defeated but captured seemed beyond comprehension . . . and spoke of something that she did not want to consider.

That her husband had been betrayed by someone close to him. Someone who might have seen an opportunity in Álvaro's misfortune and the rest of Iberia in turmoil over the tide of Moorish invaders. In such chaos someone like Eurico might even be able to take a small kingdom if he played the game correctly.

But Caliopa hadn't learned the game of chess just to amuse her husband. She'd become a master of the game by watching the political machinations first of her grandfather, then of her father and now of her husband.

She may be a mere woman, but she knew she held the final piece to this checkmate.

The ransom for her King.

The door to her chamber flew open without a knock or even a by your leave. Eurico strolled in, arrogant and swaggering, as if the right was his to enter the Queen's private chamber at his own bidding.

He came to an abrupt stop when his gaze fell on the chest. Not even the duplicitous Eurico could hide the avarice in his heart at the sight of the ransom before him.

"My lord," Caliopa said, greeting him with a deferential nod, when in her heart she wanted to reach out and strangle the lout. "I was just at my prayers with good Father Mateo. Perhaps you have come to join us and pray for my husband's release."

Eurico spared Father Mateo barely a glance when he told her confessor, "Leave us."

Father Mateo glanced over at Caliopa. She nodded to him to follow Eurico's order. What better way to get Father Mateo out of the castle than on Eurico's own order?

The priest bowed his head to her and backed out of the room.

Godspeed, Mateo, she prayed silently.

The moment the door closed behind the priest, Eurico moved closer, circling her like a bird of prey. "I don't like you having men in your room." He glanced around, his eyes narrowing with suspicion. "And without even a maidservant present. What were you two plotting?" He moved closer still.

"Plotting with Father Mateo?" She laughed and sidestepped out of his orbit. "He is my confessor. He was hearing a confession of my sins."

"Lusting after me already, dear cousin?" he asked. "Wishing for me to warm your bed while your husband dallies with his enemies?"

Caliopa sent him an icy stare, one that matched the chill his words left curling in her veins. "How dare you presume what is not yours, Cousin."

Eurico's arm snaked out and caught her wrist. He yanked her into his embrace, his breath fetid against her cheek. "You're a comely bitch, Caliopa, so I will tolerate your insolence for now. But you had best learn to treat your new king and master with the deference I prefer or you will find yourself in grave circumstances."

"Let go of me," she said.

His grip only tightened. "I have come to claim my right to Álvaro's lands, his kingdom ..." He paused for a moment, wetting his lips with his serpentine tongue. ". . . and his wife."

In a moment that seemed to last an eternity, she saw the dementia in his eyes. A raging, twisted insanity, the madness of a rabid dog. "Never," she whispered. "Never will I come to you."

He laughed. "Oh, you will come to my bed, you little whore, and you will please me, or I will start killing everyone you love. Starting with that priest lover of yours, and finally with your dear husband, my cousin."

She broke his hold, desperation and fear giving her new strength. Backing away from him, she stumbled into the chess board, scattering the pieces, but the distance from Eurico gave her new courage. "What will you do?" she asked. "Challenge Álvaro when he returns?"

He shrugged. "Who says Álvaro is coming back?" With that he put his booted foot atop the chest. "I prefer to keep my treasury right here where it belongs, in our bedchamber, rather than give it to some insolent barbarian."

Caliopa looked down, hiding the triumph she feared might show in her eyes. To her dismay, the white king lay broken at her feet.

An omen. An evil one, her fears declared. A deepseated tremble sent her hands and limbs shaking. *No*, she told herself, willing her mind to focus, to stay attentive. *This is naught but my fears getting the better of me.* The board beside her was just a game, a trifling means to pass the time. But the man here in her chamber was the devil come to life, and she needed all her wits to check his intentions.

"Let us see what you have hidden in here, Caliopa," Eurico said as he knelt before the chest and attempted to open it. "I would know this chest's secrets before I attend to my next order of business."

"What is that, Eurico?" she asked, moving slowly toward the window. In one hasty glance, she saw a lone traveler leading a laden donkey pass unheeded through the gates. *Mateo.* Beyond the hills the sun was just about to finish setting, and soon the entire countryside would be cast in darkness. Welcoming, shielding darkness that would allow Mateo to gain enough distance from the castle to elude Eurico and his hired minions.

Her husband's cousin glanced up her. "Fetch me the key."

Caliopa smiled as she gave him her answer. "No."

She needed to gain as much time for Mateo as she could.

No matter the cost.

Eurico erupted with rage. "Give me the key right this moment, or I will have that confessor of yours brought up here and I'll consign him to hell with my very hands."

Time. Time. She needed time.

If he called for Mateo and found him gone, he would know she had deceived him. If he opened the chest with the key or not and found its worthless contents, he would know.

So she needed to keep his thoughts free of Mateo and free of the chest.

And she knew there was only one thing Eurico coveted more.

God may forgive her for what she was about to do, but she couldn't help but wonder if Álvaro would.

She threw her shoulders back and pressed her breasts upward, allowing them to strain against the velvet edge of her gown. Slowly she pushed back her hair so that it left her neck bare.

Eurico watched her every movement. His chest rose and fell in seizing heaves, as if he could barely control his need for her.

Pulling at the golden chain around her neck, she allowed a few of the links to pluck free from between her breasts. "At the end of this chain, my lord, is the key to that chest. If you are man enough to discover where it rests, then in the morning it will be yours."

The moment she'd made her pledge, said her desperate words, Eurico was across the room. He threw her onto her bed and was atop her before she could even manage another breath.

And in that moment, Caliopa knew that she had indeed consigned her soul to the devil and her body to hell.

The first stains of dawn began to paint the skyline when Caliopa was able to leave her bed. Thankfully Eurico had left an hour or so earlier, so she didn't have to share these few moments with his gloating boasts. Around her neck still hung the key to the chest that for now Eurico had forgotten.

For now.

Caliopa wasn't so foolish as to think she could hold his avarice at bay with her body forever. And soon he would be returning to take his treasure as he had her body. Pillaging and stealing what he had no right to.

She didn't dare look down at herself, for she knew the sight of bruises and marks marring the same fair, soft skin that had given Álvaro so much pleasure would only bring tears to her eyes.

And she wouldn't cry in front of Eurico.

Tugging on a light chemise, she passed by the chess board and caught up the pieces of the king in her hand. They were cold and hard and gave her little comfort, but still she had to believe that her king, her flesh and blood husband, would soon come home and make all this right.

And yet when she looked around, she still could not see where the white queen had fallen.

She put that thought from her mind and looked again out the window, thinking of Father Mateo.

"I have given you all the time I can, Cousin," she whispered.

As if on cue, the door bounded open, this time nearly tearing it off its leather hinges. "You deceptive bitch!" Eurico cursed. He stomped inside, stopping in front of the chest, followed by several of his henchmen. "Where is that priest of yours? Where has he gone?"

"He should be in the chapel," she replied, staring him directly in the eye. "You do know the building? The one with the cross over the door."

He came closer and slapped her hard across the face. "Insolent still. I see you need more lessons in humility."

"From you? You haven't the wit or the *weapon*," she said, casting a disparaging glance at his breeches.

His men snickered.

This only served to inflame Eurico further. He caught her by the throat and forced her toward the tall, open window. His grip cut off her air, and she gasped, clawing at him to no avail. The king in her hand fell, shattering into a thousand tiny pieces as it hit the tiled floor.

Then amidst her struggles she saw as well the fate of the white queen. The lady lay nearby, her head separated from her broken body.

Álvaro was dead, and she was lost.

It was no omen but the truth, the gut-wrenching knowledge that all her plans had been for naught.

She had lost more than the game. She had lost their kingdom, their life together—at least in this time, in this place.

Eurico pushed her further until the back of her legs pressed against the low metal railing that served as a small balcony outside the great window.

"Where has your confessor gone?" Eurico asked again.

She couldn't speak, for he still held her throat pinched tight.

His free hand ripped her chemise from her body, then his fingers scavenged over her breasts like a vulture picking bones until he found the key. With a quick jerk, he yanked the delicate chain, tearing it from her neck.

Eurico tossed his prize to one of his leering men. "Open it."

Caliopa closed her eyes. She knew she should pray, offer words begging forgiveness from God for what she had done, but all she could think of was her husband.

Forgive me, my dearest Álvaro. Forgive me, my love.

The key rattled in the lock, and for a few tense seconds the clumsy oaf Eurico had entrusted with it could not get the lock to work. Another of his minions, impatient to see the treasure they'd been hired to steal, cuffed the man out of the way and twisted the key so that it finally turned.

When the last tumbler fell with a distinctive click, Eurico and all his men took a collective, expectant breath. He relaxed his grip on her throat, and Caliopa took a deep breath.

She knew in a few moments it would be her last.

As the lid was flipped open, every man leaned forward, eager for the glittering wealth, their faces mirrored expressions of untamed greed. As each one came to the startling realization of the true nature of the contents, his expression changed first to disbelief, then anger.

No one more outraged than Eurico, his face mottled with madness, his lips flapping in speechless shock.

Caliopa broke their silence with laughter. So brazenly she mocked their folly, her delirious pitch rising to an unholy refrain, that one of the men crossed himself in fear of her and began backing toward the door.

"There is your treasure, Eurico," she said pointing at the worthless chest. "There is your legacy. Stones and lead. Just like your heart."

His grip tightened again, and this time Caliopa knew she would never find release. He brought his lips up to her ear. "I return your treasure to you, you traitorous bitch. Look upon it as your final *legacy*. For what you see will be your gravestones."

And with that, he plunged her out the window and released her. The courtyard below echoed with screams as her people watched her fall to her death.

She hit the rough stones of the courtyard, her body shattering like that of the fragile white queen. But unlike the hollow chess piece, Caliopa's soul found only freedom in her flight from Eurico.

And a chance to be with her Álvaro forever.

Olivia wiped at the tears falling down her cheeks. Poor Queen Caliopa. She had sacrificed so much and to no avail. "But the treasure, Paco? What happened to Father Mateo and the treasure? Surely Caliopa had given him enough time to escape Eurico's evil plans?" she asked.

Paco shook his head. "Eurico offered half the treasure to the man who found it. His henchmen swarmed out of Álvaro's castle like rats, moving southward as if the devil himself carried them. They found Father Mateo in a monastery in Badajoz. But the holy man no longer had the treasure with him. They beat and tortured him to no avail. He would not give up where he had hidden it. Eventually they left him for dead and returned to their leader empty-handed."

Olivia wiped at more tears. "But the note, the one the priest sent to Wellington to be decoded. How did that come about? Someone must have discovered the treasure."

"While they thought Father Mateo was dead when they left him, the nuns who came in to prepare his body for burial were stunned to find Mateo still clinging to life. With his final breath he whispered the secret of *El Rescate del Rey* to the Mother Superior, who'd been summoned to his bedside."

"And she encoded the secret," Olivia whispered.

Paco nodded. "Aye. Some say she had the sight, others say she was one of the most brilliant women who ever lived. The Moors were already riding north, so she knew there was no hope of saving Álvaro or Spain. At least not in her lifetime. But she knew that when God willed it, the treasure would be discovered, at a time when her homeland faced its darkest challenge. Its most evil invader."

Napoleon.

Olivia glanced across the flames at Robert. He was watching her, as he had through most of Paco's story, and she felt herself growing warm under his gaze.

Something had changed between them. Olivia could feel it with a certainty that left her trembling.

Hopefully they would not share the same fate as Caliopa and Álvaro and allow destiny to tear them apart.

And as the other men started to bunk down, Olivia bade them good night and made her way to the empty chamber she'd chosen for her room.

Chapter 16

"**O**livia, I—" Robert began to say.

She waited, and when he didn't speak again, she turned around and faced him. She offered him a smile of encouragement.

It was obviously the urging her proud lover needed.

"I've been so wrong about you. When I saw Lando's ring around your neck that night—I should have known. I should have understood what it meant. But I was determined to think ill of you. To hold you at arm's length. And now I know why."

She reached out and took his hand. "How is that?"

"When I heard that gunshot last night. When I realized I had left you in danger, I knew the real reason I'd been denying the truth about you. Very simply, because I love you."

She folded into his arms, relishing the warmth of

his body, the steady, welcoming beat of his heart on her cheek.

"I've been as mule-headed about this as that infernal Evaline of yours," he said.

Olivia laughed. "At least Evaline can be coaxed with carrots."

"Perhaps you should have tried that." He shook his head. "I made judgments about you, rash ones, ones born out of my anguish over Lando's death—over what I so willingly accepted as your intimacy and apparent duplicity with Bradstone. If only I'd believed what my gut was telling me instead of listening to all my old hatreds."

She couldn't help herself; she shivered. "We've both held onto long-held suspicions and foolish dreams." She glanced up at him, looking into those eyes and seeing now the true depth of his feelings, his belief in her.

The knight errant, the Hobbe of her imaginings could never equal the man before her. Now she knew, understood, that all their foibles, all their shared misunderstandings had been their true enemy, and now together they'd found a way to vanquish this once insurmountable foe.

"I would never have been able to keep my vow to your brother," she said, "if it hadn't been for you." She squeezed his hand. "I'm so glad I waited for my hero. Someone of noble and honorable spirit to restore the treasure to its rightful intent."

Robert didn't know if he fit that description. He'd hardly been honorable to her—taking her virginity, kidnapping her, bullying her into helping him. Yet one question remained. "But you did translate it—you gave Bradstone the location, for he set out for Portugal on the first ship leaving London that night."

Olivia smiled. "I may have translated it for him, but I didn't give him the right location."

At this Robert chuckled. "You sent him on a wild-goose chase."

"In many ways I sent him to his death." She looked up at him.

Robert heard the self-incrimination in her voice. This was what he loved most about Olivia—her deep-seated sense of honor, of noble integrity. Despite the fact that Bradstone had used her so ill, even murdered her father, she still bore in her heart a sense of guilt over what she believed was her hand in the man's death. The haunting light of her self-inflicted blame still glowed strong in her eyes, even after seven years.

If anyone should wish Bradstone dead, it was Olivia, and here she was looking at *him*, of all people, for absolution.

For if it had been him there that night in Chambley's library, he wouldn't have given a second thought about sending his cousin to his just reward, exacting the pound of flesh owed for Lando's death.

And yet as he found himself unable to look away from her troubled expression, he knew it was time to put the past behind them. It was the time for them to start a new life together, unhindered by their respective ghosts of culpability, recrimination, and most importantly, hatred.

"I killed him," she was saying, "as if I had pulled the trigger myself."

"You did no such thing. Bradstone's greed is what destroyed him," Robert told her.

"If only I could forget that night," she whispered. "You know I can still hear it?"

"Hear what?"

"The gun."

Robert didn't need to ask which gun. He kissed the top of her head and wondered just what she had seen that night.

Olivia snuggled tighter into his arms. "You know why I kissed you when you were so ill?"

"No, why?"

She turned her face toward the light of the portal. "I thought you were going to die. I didn't want to have another man die in my arms." He felt the chill race through her bones, her grief almost palpable.

"Like Lando?" His own grief, so familiar, so filled with remorse and a need for revenge, took a painful turn as he saw Orlando's death through her eyes for the first time.

She nodded.

"I never even learned his name," she said. "The papers just called him a French spy, but he wasn't. He was Spanish—I knew it that night, though Bradstone tried to tell me differently. But mostly, your brother didn't deserve what fate held in store for him. He was too young."

Too young. Her words ate at him. Orlando had been too young for the mission. But then he'd always been the most serious of the Danvers brothers and had always seemed older than his actual age.

"That night on the ship, you were dreaming of him, of that night, weren't you?" Robert asked.

Olivia shivered. "Yes. His face has haunted me for years. I hear the shot and see that look of surprise, of anguish, and of failure. You can't imagine it."

Robert could. He'd seen that image himself in more nightmares than he cared to count.

It seemed he and Olivia Sutton had more in common than either of them ever realized.

And yet he needed to know more.

Robert steeled himself and asked the one question that had consumed him for seven years. "Did he suffer?"

She shook her head. "I don't think so. When he died, he seemed almost at peace." Tears welled in her eyes, glistening as they rolled onto her cheeks. Robert brushed at them, catching and releasing them, fervently wishing they'd carry away the last of his own hatred, his own pain.

"I owe him my life," she whispered. "He saved me from Bradstone. That bullet was intended for me. Once your cousin had his translation, he was ready to consign me to my fate. But Orlando stopped him and died in the process."

Heroic to the end, Robert realized. How like his brother to think he could prevent Bradstone's evil plans all on his own.

Only the devil had been able to give Bradstone his due by sending him to the depths of the Atlantic.

"Robert, you have to believe me, I had nothing to do with his death. If I could have died—"

"Shh," he whispered into her ear. "That is in the past."

"Do you believe me?"

Did he? For the last month, he had turned his anger on Olivia. And now she was asking for his forgiveness.

"Yes, with all my heart." He tipped his head down and sealed his words with a kiss.

Olivia welcomed his lips, his words, as if she had been set free. Now, with the air cleared between them, she knew they would find the same passionate joy that they had found on the *Sybaris*.

Only this time it would last a lifetime.

His mouth covered hers, his tongue teasing open her lips. She opened to him, a soft moan slipping from her as his tongue dipped and caressed her own, stroking it, as she knew he would fill her and stroke other parts of her.

He backed her up against the wall, the cool stone a dizzying contrast to the heat of his body. The sturdy, solid presence behind her kept her knees from buckling as he deepened his kiss, his fingers tracing a slow, lazy line over the exposed tops of her breasts.

Another reason she could add to her list of things she liked about this dress.

That and the delicate fabric left her feeling all but naked up against him. A feeling she relished and couldn't wait to experience again.

His hand plucked at the tie that held the bodice gathered in front, and once he'd freed it, his fingers dipped lower, exploring the shape of her breast, curling around her flesh and moving ever closer to the nipple that was already taut and aching for his touch.

When at last his thumb plucked at the fevered flesh, she pulled her mouth from his and let out a long, hot sigh.

It felt so good to be touched by him.

He took that as an invitation to move south, his mouth starting first at her ear, his teeth nipping at her lobe. "What do you want?" he whispered, while his fingers continued to roll lazy circles over her tight nipple. "What would you have me do next?"

Her thighs tensed, that place between her legs growing wet with possibilities. She wanted him to touch her, she wanted him to kiss her, she wanted him to fill her with his manhood and stroke her to that place that left her breathless and wanting it all over again.

She wanted it all, and she wanted it to last the night.

"Take me in your mouth," she whispered, her back arching, her breasts rising like an offering.

His arm around her waist tightened, pulling her close, while his head dipped down to take her as she had requested.

When his warm, hungry mouth closed over her breast, she gasped for air, her mouth gaping and struggling to find the air that suddenly seemed to have left the room. The rough, nubby flesh of his tongue washed over her nipple, and she found only joy in his touch. Over and over, his mouth suckled at her, while his tongue lapped and teased her.

All the while, his hand was making much the same motions on her other breast, so that both came alive with longing, while at the apex of her thighs there seemed to be breathless little whispers, uncoiling with passion, clamoring for more, begging for his touch.

She caught his hand and guided it there. "Touch me, please."

He tugged at her dress, drawing it up from the hem until it bunched around her hips, leaving that heated place open and exposed to the cool night air.

At first his fingers toyed with her, teasing little brushes that barely answered the anguish growing there.

"Is that what you want?" he asked.

She couldn't speak, she only shook her head, arching her hips toward him.

His mouth slanted in a wicked grin. "I think I know what will help."

With that he knelt before her, his breath coming in hot intimate waves against her. And then his fingers were there, opening her up to him, to his lips.

She nearly buckled in shock when his tongue began edging her open. Olivia clung to his shoulders for support, her back pressed against the wall.

Over and over his tongue dipped and delved deeper into her, until it found the very source of her pleasure. Slowly he began the same dance he'd started on her nipples, the rough pad of his tongue rolling over her flesh. Her world spun out of control as her body rose up to meet him. She was standing on her tiptoes and felt as if she were being lifted even higher.

Her body began to quake with those now familiar shudders. He was moving her toward completion, and as if he sensed it, his mouth began to suckle her in earnest, pushing her toward that heavenly abyss.

When the first wave struck, she nearly toppled over, her hands grasping and kneading his shoulders, her legs wobbling. He reached up to steady her, his tongue never leaving her, instead matching each clenching wave with its own encouraging stroke.

At last, when the tempest subsided, she pulled at his shoulders, drawing him up from the floor.

Robert scooped her up and drew her into his arms, carrying her to the bedroll in the corner of the room. Tenderly he laid her down and then joined her in the narrow warmth of the blankets. She nestled into his arms.

"How is that possible?" she asked, her fingers tracing a line over his lips. "How did you do that?"

"Did you like it?"

She nodded. "Very much."

"I'll have to remember that."

Her lips came to his and teased him to kiss her again. Robert only too happily complied. His body was hard and throbbing to find his fulfillment in her, but he wanted nothing this night but to pleasure her.

But his little termagant had other ideas.

Her fingers splayed over his shirt, pulling at the ties, tugging at the length tucked into his breeches. Only too willingly he helped her free it, plucking it from his body and tossing it to one side.

She smiled and pulled her dress from her body. Stretching like a proud cat, she then nestled against him.

He swore she purred in deep satisfaction as her hands splayed out over his chest, her fingers bringing mayhem to his senses. They immediately went to the front of his breeches, tracing the outline of his only too evident erection.

With one finger, she traced the length of his encased flesh, up one side and down the other. As hers had done earlier, his hips arched to meet her touch.

" 'Twould be so much better if I could feel you," she whispered. Her hand moved over his buttons, unfastening them, one after another. "If I could hold you."

When she flicked the last one open, her hand was there to take him as he sprang forth from that prison of woolen serge.

Her fingers encased him, drew out the entire length of him and then slid back down. "Yes, this is much better," she told him, taking his lips to her mouth again and kissing him as he had done her, long and slowly.

All the while, her hand stroked him, teasing him, using the slickness she provoked to add to his pleasure.

Robert had never known a woman's touch to be so erotic, so tender and yet so masterful.

Then again, this was his Olivia.

And she was bringing him nearly to his completion.

He wrestled free from her grasp and rolled onto his back, carrying her with him, so she straddled him.

She gazed down at him, one brow arched in wicked anticipation.

"Take me inside you," he told her.

She rose up on her knees and caught hold of him, guiding herself onto his throbbing shaft. Her mouth opened in surprise, and then a passionate light started to burn in her eyes as she slid onto him, slowly, testing each inch of him as he filled her.

From the smile on her lips, she didn't need any further encouragement, for she began to rise again, drawing him up and out and then closing back down over him, a soft sigh slipping from her.

"Does it feel that good for you?" she asked.

He nodded. "Don't stop."

"I have no intention to," she told him. Her body was tight around him, but with each stroke, it was as delirious as it had been with his fingers, his lips, yet this time it was his manhood, stretching her, rubbing against her, rousing her body to passion's call.

The faster she went, the louder the din became, like a fury's cry in her ears, the roar of passion begging her to move faster, harder, closer to him.

His breath was coming in ragged gasps, his hips rising to meet hers with eager, hungry thrusts.

Around him her body began to tighten, throbbing for release, and she found it in a shower of lights and sensation. He bucked beneath her, driving his body into hers, his manhood pulsing as he too found his completion, his seed bursting into her in a hot stream.

She collapsed on top of his chest, and he wrapped her into his arms. They lay there entwined, still bound as one, for some time, neither willing to break the connection between them.

"I want to make you my wife," he said. "Though I have no right to ask."

"Why not?" she asked, her heart welling to life at the thought of spending every night for the rest of her life so joined.

"I have nothing to offer you. No home. No title. Nothing but the hardships of an army wife."

"I don't remember asking for more," she told him, rising up with her elbows resting on his chest. "But why would you want to marry me? I'll probably be transported for shooting Chambley when we return to England."

"That will never happen," he told her with fierce possessiveness that made her smile.

She had found her hero. Her living and breathing hero. And she knew that as long as Robert was beside her, nothing and no one would ever harm her again.

Chapter 17

The next day, at the top of the mountain outside Badajoz, Rafe and his men bid farewell to Olivia, Robert, Jemmy and Aquiles. They were turning in a different direction, their supplies needed elsewhere. Olivia was sorry to see their traveling companions leave.

Rafe gave her a hug before they parted, whispering into her ear, "Lando chose well. And so has Robert."

As they continued on down the mountainside, a steady rain slowed their pace, but the cold drizzle and rugged conditions did nothing to cool the heat in Olivia's cheeks each time she thought of her night with Robert.

He rode ahead, greeting outriders and messengers from Wellington's camp, who were scouting positions and watching the roads for any sign of French reinforcements for the now besieged city.

Olivia noted that Robert was met with deference and something akin to awe by most of the men riding past them. It was as if they had given him up for lost.

Once they made it into the camp, their horses and Evaline were dispatched to the makeshift stables for a well-earned brushing and feeding, while they were escorted directly to Wellington's tent.

As they waited outside, Jemmy fidgeted on one foot, then the other. "Lord Wellington, you say? We are going to meet Wellington?"

Robert nodded to him. Jemmy immediately set about polishing his boots on the back of his breeches and trying to brush off the worst of the dust from his coat and cravat.

Lady Finch, Olivia knew, would be in a rare fit if she had any idea that her son was about to meet his idol, let alone probably beg for a commission in the nearest regiment.

She should stop him, but Jemmy had proven in the fight with the French that he was capable of taking care of himself in a rough spot. He was a man now, not a boy, and he deserved to follow his dreams.

Shortly thereafter, an aide de camp bustled out of the tent, nearly bumping into Robert. "Major Danvers, his lordship will see you now."

Robert entered the tent, and after a moment's hesitation, Olivia and Jemmy followed him inside.

The great tent bustled with activity. Tables covered with large maps and drawings nearly filled the room, and men conferred in quiet knots here and there about the place.

In the center of it all stood a man Olivia would have

known anywhere as the Commander-in-Chief of the Allied forces in the Peninsula.

Arthur Wellesley, Viscount Wellington.

"Danvers!" he called out. "Good timing, man. You always do know when to turn up."

He greeted Robert warmly with a handshake and a good thump on the back.

Olivia held back, unsure of how she would be welcomed into such esteemed company.

"Come back with my information, I hope," Wellington was saying to Robert. "Once we take this city, it will be our toehold in Spain. I'll need every one of those guerrilla leaders behind me so we can drive the French all the way back to Paris. The Ransom will be just the glue to stick all their factions together into a workable army." Wellington paused just long enough to look over Robert's shoulder and directly at Olivia. "And who is this?" he asked, his gaze cutting an assessing course over her. "I send you for a treasure and you bring me back a jewel," He took her hand and kissed it with great flourish.

Though Wellington was rumored to be an adept ladies' man, Olivia hadn't prepared herself for the onslaught of his charm and personal magnetism.

"May I introduce Miss Olivia Sutton, my lord," Robert said. "A skilled linguist, she has decoded the directions to the treasure."

Wellington's iron gray brows rose into an arch. "This is good news indeed, Danvers. Well and good. Don't see that it was necessary to bring her all the way here. I asked you to bring me the translation, and you bring me the translator. You always do go the extra mile."

"Miss Sutton insisted, sir," Robert said. "She would

give her information to no one but you. She felt it her patriotic duty."

"Ah, one of those," he said, winking at one of his aides.

Jemmy had stopped at a nearby table covered with maps of fortifications. He was staring at them with awe.

"And that young fellow over there? Who are you, sir?"

Jemmy's eyes went wide. "James Reyburn, my lord. An honor to meet you." He held out his hand, and when Wellington took his in greeting, Olivia would have sworn that Jemmy was going to fall over.

Wellington clapped him on the back and glanced over the maps that Jemmy had been examining. "Yes, well, there, what do you think of our plans to take the city."

"Wonderful, sir," Jemmy said. "But have you thought of making a line here or perhaps over here. I think it would give your cannon better advantage to take this wall."

Wellington stared down at the map and then at the boy. "Brilliant. Good job, Danvers! You bring me not only a translator but a strategist." He turned to Jemmy. "Why aren't you in my army, Mr. Reyburn?"

Jemmy's jaw dropped, and he managed to stammer, "Oh, it's always been my dream to serve with you. The problem, sir, has been gaining the money for my commission."

"I have few opportunities to recruit good men onto my staff, Reyburn, and you look to be the right type of fellow. So consider your commission a thank-you from me for the lives you will probably save with your advice." Wellington turned to an aide. "Go see about get-

ting Lieutenant Reyburn a uniform, and in the meantime, Reyburn, you see to those other maps and come
back here in an hour if you have any other worthy
opinions."

"Yes, sir," Jemmy said, his chest puffed up so much
that he looked ready to burst.

"Now, let's see, where were we?" Wellington asked,
glancing around the room until his gaze landed on
Olivia. "Oh, yes, Miss Sutton. Sutton? That name is familiar. I just received the recent paper, and there was
some matter or other about a Sutton chit who shot
Lord Chambley." Wellington looked over her. "No relation, I suppose."

Olivia flinched. "Actually, it was me, my lord. And I
would like to turn myself in."

"You shot Chambley?" Wellington asked.

"Yes," Olivia replied.

"This true?" he asked Robert.

Robert nodded.

Wellington scratched his chin. "Should get a medal
for it, if you want my opinion. Damn nuisance, that
Chambley. I'd probably be inclined to give you a commission as well if you'd finished the job instead of just
winging the bastard."

An aide de camp came up and whispered something in Lord Wellington's ear. "Yes, yes. I'll see to
that presently," he told the man. "Now, what were we
discussing?"

"I was turning myself in for the attempted murder
of Lord Chambley," Olivia said, holding out her hands
for the shackles she was positive were about to be cast
over her wrists.

"Oh, that nonsense," Wellington said. "Put your

hands down. I haven't got time for that now. What I need is for you to tell me where The King's Ransom is hidden away, so Major Danvers and Aquiles can go off and retrieve it while I take Badajoz away from the French." He turned to another aide. "Lieutenant Parrage, fetch Major Danvers a fresh pack of supplies and two horses from my stable, as well as a—"

"That won't be necessary," Olivia said, interrupting Wellington. Obviously that just wasn't done, since the entire tent fell silent, every one of the men staring at her as if she had just grown another head. "There is no need," she told the viscount, who was also staring at her.

"No need?" Wellington asked. "My dear woman, there is a war out there. The location of that treasure you are so handily carrying around inside your head is the most important piece to beating the French I could hope for, and you have the temerity to tell me it isn't necessary to send Major Danvers out to fetch it immediately?"

Olivia swallowed and then shook her head. "No, it is not."

"And why do you say that?" he asked.

She went up on her tiptoes and whispered into his ear, "Because the treasure is buried in Badajoz."

An hour or so later, the chaplain was summoned to Wellington's private tent. The man wasn't too sure what to expect when he arrived. He knew full well that the entire army camped here outside the gates of Badajoz was about to launch one of its most important battles. In a matter of hours, his work would turn into an endless offering of last rites to men twisting and writhing in pain as they went to meet their final reward and hastily offered words for the dead before they were buried.

But when he entered, he found his commander standing with a proud looking officer and a bright-eyed, red-headed young woman, and he was asked to perform a marriage ceremony.

While he made a few token objections about banns and other rules, Wellington waved his hand at such nonsense, as he usually did. This was war, and everyone in the tent knew that the groom might not live to see another day let alone the three weeks for banns to be read.

Therefore a special license was produced, and the chaplain married Major Robert Danvers to Miss Olivia Sutton, a spinster from Kent. She seemed a respectable young lady, a bit shy perhaps for the hardships asked of a military wife, but then again this was war, and men couldn't be counted on to take such matters into consideration when they faced an uncertain future and sought the comfort of a wife.

And after they were wed, the major placed a rather indecent and demanding kiss on his new wife's lips, and to the chaplain's embarrassment, the lady appeared to welcome her husband's lusty embrace with the same enthusiasm.

The chaplain left the tent, wiping his glasses, and wondering if perhaps he should have paid more attention to his brother's latest letter. A vicar in Surrey, he had spent two pages decrying the growing immorality of society. If Mrs. Danvers's wanton display was indicative of the current mores back home, he may well just consider remaining in the army.

* * *

The hours after Olivia's wedding sped by in a whirl of activity. Robert had to report immediately to duty, since all hands were going to be needed to take the city. Wellington had confided to the couple that the battle would begin that night.

The weather had confounded most of the English seige efforts, so the trenches and lines were not what Wellington had hoped they would be, but if they continued working, they would only give the French the advantage of getting reinforcements there in time.

It was now or never.

Aquiles helped Olivia pitch a tent and settle their things into the cramped quarters. Not that Olivia had much other than her battered valise. By the time they had gotten everything organized and their stores from the quartermaster, it was nearly dark, and Robert returned to make a hasty goodbye.

"I'm going to have Aquiles take you to where the other wives are waiting," he told her. "They are positioned far from the action, and you will be well out of harm."

Olivia clung to him, barely listening. She couldn't stand the idea of him leaving her so soon.

He must have sensed her fears, for he cradled her even tighter. "I'll be back for you. I promise."

Rising on her toes, she offered him her lips one more time, and they kissed hard and fast, as if sealing his vow with the sudden urgency that seemed to be surrounding them.

Robert took one last look at her and then turned and left. Olivia stood her ground and watched his tall, proud form until he had disappeared into the growing darkness.

"Come along, missus," Aquiles said, leading her in

a direction that took her with each step further and further from her heart.

She found the other soldiers' wives a mixed lot. They milled around fires and sat on boxes, some sewing, some tending children, others pacing nervously about tugging at stray locks of their hair or worrying a handkerchief.

When the first cannon belched its terror toward the besieged city, a number of the women began to cry.

As the guns continued to blaze to life across the lines, Olivia felt nothing but useless . . . and helpless.

One woman in particular started wailing as if she had been shot herself.

"Oh, shut yer trap," a rough looking woman said to the distraught lady. "If your man dies, it's not like there aren't ten more only too willing to take his place." She plucked a pipe from her coat, filled the bowl with tobacco and lit it from one of the fires. After a long puff, she glanced up at Olivia. "And who are you?"

"Mrs. Danvers," Olivia said. "I just married Major Danvers. Today."

"Harumph," the woman muttered. "Been married myself. Four times. Right now, most people just call me Martha. First battle?"

Olivia nodded.

"Thought so. Got that scared look about you. Well, settle in, Mrs. Danvers. My Johnny said this was going to take some time." Martha rose and nodded at the crate she'd been sitting on. She gathered up a bundle of rags and cloths, hoisting them onto her sturdy shoulder, and started back toward the main camp.

"Where are you going?" Olivia asked. She had thought they were supposed to stay behind the camp.

"Canna ya hear those guns, Mrs. Danvers?" The lady puffed once again on her pipe. "Those sounds mean the men are getting shot at. The lucky ones die, but the unlucky ones, well, they either bleed to death on the field or they get hauled back to the surgeon's tent." A couple of other women, hardy, rough looking souls, rose to join Martha. "Those poor souls who make it to the surgeon's will be needin' tending. And we do what we can." She turned again to leave.

"Can I help?"

Martha glanced over her shoulder, assessing Olivia's worthiness with an experienced and weary eye. "You ever seen someone who's been shot, Mrs. Danvers?"

Olivia swallowed. "Yes."

The woman didn't appear all that convinced.

"I know a thing or two about medical matters," Olivia insisted. She opened her valise and began pulling out what remained of her powders. "I even have some things that may help." She held out the packets to Martha.

Taking one of them, Martha took a practiced sniff, and then eyed her again, as if she couldn't quite reconcile the idea of a rosy-cheeked bride experienced in tending war wounds.

But finally she tossed her head toward the camp. "Come on with ye, if ye think ye got the stomach for it. More hands make for lighter work, me mother always said. And from the sounds of it, we'll have plenty to go around."

* * *

Martha hadn't been exaggerating when she had told Olivia there would be plenty of work. The surgeon's tent was overflowing with injured men by the time they arrived, and soon the ground around the medical tent was littered in a sea of wounded men.

Hours into the fight, Olivia was helping Martha tend to a batch of newly arrived men when one in particular caught her eye.

Jemmy.

Her heart caught in her throat. Dear God, he was like a brother to her, and she'd all but forgotten that he too would be out in that mayhem. She rushed to his side.

His leg was covered in blood and twisted at an odd angle. His eyes were closed, and his breathing seemed labored and pained.

Martha took one practiced glance at the boy and shook her head.

"He *is not* going to die," Olivia told her, ripping at the shreds of Jemmy's pant leg to reveal where a piece of shrapnel was still imbedded in his flesh. Her stomach rose with a rolling clench, but she bit back the bile threatening to spill forth.

She owed Lady Finch too much to let the woman's only child die.

"Ya know him?" Martha asked.

Olivia nodded.

"Yer husband."

"No. A good friend."

Martha shrugged. "Well, that's gotta come out," she said, pointing at the piece of metal. "And it will need to be burned to close off the bleedin'. Then we'll have to set the leg, 'cause it looks like it's broke." She glanced over at the surgeon's tent. "Go fetch a hot iron. Don't let them see you do it, just get it quick like."

Olivia nodded and did as Martha instructed her. The surgeon's tent and his meager staff were in such chaos they didn't notice her come and go.

When she got back, Jemmy's eyes were open. "Glad to see you, oh fair Queen Mab."

"He's feverish," Martha muttered.

"No, that's just what he calls me," Olivia said.

The woman just glanced heavenward, as if to say it took all kinds.

"Olivia, your husband—he was right beside me when the mine exploded. Demmed Frogs got enough powder up there to blow us all to hell."

Her heart caught in her throat. *Robert? Hurt?* "Did you see him, Jemmy? Did you see what happened to Robert?"

He shook his head. "We were with the Fourth Division. Near the walls. I saw him go down, but if he was hurt, I don't know."

Just then Martha nodded to one of the other women, a sturdy-looking thing capable of lifting an ox, who was ambling by with a bucket in either hand. "Hold him," Martha ordered.

The woman set down her load and pinned Jemmy to the ground.

"Olivia?" he called out, his eyes growing wild.

"Be still," she told him. "She can help you."

Martha went right to work. Holding onto his leg, she yanked the metal shard out in one quick pull.

Jemmy howled in pain, but Martha ignored him. She continued her rough ministrations, during which, much to Olivia's relief, Jemmy passed out, his body falling back, limp and spent.

"What have you got left of those powders?" Martha asked, the bleeding now stopped and the leg set firmly in place.

Olivia dug into her pocket and pulled out the packet she'd used on Robert. Martha poured the contents onto the wound. "Bind it tight with the cleanest cloths you can find, then get him out of here before the surgeon sees our handiwork. He doesn't appreciate the fact that my patients outlive his."

The woman who'd held Jemmy down, hoisted him up in her arms as if he were no more than a child.

Olivia led her to the tent she and Aquiles had pitched earlier. "Can you stay with him?" she asked the other woman.

"You going after your man—the one he was talking about?"

Olivia nodded.

The woman shook her head. "You'll learn soon enough. If you don't get yer arse shot in the meantime. Well, if you gotta go, stay in the trenches, keep your head down and don't get in the way." Then she settled next to Jemmy, looking over at the unconscious boy with something akin to motherly concern. "He looks like a dear, brave laddie."

"He is," Olivia said, and left Jemmy, wondering if she would ever see him alive again.

The fighting was more fierce than even Robert could have imagined. Wellington had assigned him to lend the Fourth Division a hand and also to help lead the first parties that breached the walls into the city, since he had been to Badajoz on numerous occasions in his time spent behind enemy lines.

He had no idea how long they had been fighting, but it seemed they weren't making any headway in taking the high walls. Then suddenly the French seemed to back down from their position, their fire fading down to a few token shots, as if they had been called back to protect another portion of the city.

But something about the entire thing didn't seem right. Unease prickled at his neck as the captain in charge ordered his men forward over the open space between them and the walls.

Something wasn't right. But still he moved forward, charging with the men, when in the distance behind him he heard his name being called.

He turned around, and to his shock he saw Olivia scrambling through the trenches, turning over the dead and the wounded, as if she were looking for someone.

"Robert!" she cried out. "Robert, where are you?"

"Dammit, get back," he shouted at her.

Her head came up, and her gaze met his, relief in her every feature. "I thought you were lost."

"Just get back," he yelled.

But she couldn't hear him and knelt down beside a wounded man to start giving him aid. Damn her, she was going to get her fool head shot off.

Then he heard it. The sizzle of fuses. His gaze darted around his feet, and he realized the entire area was mined with powder. And the lines led directly to Olivia.

There was no time to warn her or warn his fellow soldiers, for suddenly the night erupted into a hell of

Chapter 18

Olivia awoke in a small room, curtains drawn over the single window casting the entire chamber in shadows. If it was day or night, she couldn't tell. Nothing smelled familiar, for the room had a smoky, dry air to it. And in the distance she thought she heard gunfire and loud, angry voices, but there was a buzzing din in her ears that made it muffled and hard to discern.

She reached up to her aching temple and found a cool cloth over her forehead, while the hand she'd raised was bandaged. Her fingers moved stiffly under the wrappings, and her skin seemed raw and afire.

She'd been burned, she guessed. But how?

For the life of her, she couldn't fathom where she was or how she'd gotten there. She couldn't even remember how she'd gotten hurt. Struggling to get up, she found her entire body ached, and when she glanced down at her arms and legs, she found them covered in cuts and bruises. It was as if she'd been trampled by the very hounds of hell.

Unable to get out of bed, she tried to call out to someone, for obviously someone was caring for her, but the words refused to come out of her parched throat and sounded more like the tired croaking of a toad.

Then in the shadows something stirred. At first he seemed to rise out of the darkness into a towering figure of fierce proportions, and she sank into the mattress to hide herself.

That is, until her caretaker spoke. "You're awake. That's good. I feared you might never come to."

The voice! She knew this man. Her memory started to flash with confusing images.

He bent over something, and then suddenly a light flared to life. When he turned, he held a candle in his hand. "Let me see about getting you some water."

The shock of dark hair, the green eyes, the strong jaw and bearing. They were all so familiar, so intimately familiar.

"Robert," she managed to whisper.

"Yes, that's it," he said, putting a cup of tepid water to her lips. "You remember me. I'm glad to see that."

The water helped, soothing the worst of the burning in her throat. "Where are we? What happened?"

"Shh," he told her, taking the cloth off her head and dipping it into a basin. He wrung it out slowly and then gently replaced it on her brow. "You were hurt. In the fighting. You should never have been there."

For a moment, only the briefest flash, she thought she saw something odd in his gaze. A wildness, a madness that she had never seen before. Not even when he'd been gone with fever.

Then she started to remember more. She'd gone to find him in the darkness and the blazing fury of the battle. And when she had found him there had been a great gulf between them as Robert fought his way toward the walls. He'd turned and spotted her, yelling something at her, but she couldn't hear his words through the bedlam of battle.

And then the night had erupted into a blaze of fire.

"The explosion," she whispered.

"Yes, the French had mined that area." He shook his head. "You should never have been there. What if something had happened to you? You are far too important to risk losing in all this." He waved his arm at the covered windows.

Outside, the voices grew louder, closer, and Robert quickly blew out the candle, casting the room into darkness again.

"Be still," he whispered, as he moved to the window and parted the curtain ever so slightly. He stood there for a time, peering out into whatever was beyond this room, watching, his body tense, his fingers drumming anxiously at the wall. Finally he let out a long, slow breath and let the curtain slip closed. "They've moved on."

"Who?" she asked, wondering at all these strange events.

"The soldiers."

She gathered every ounce of strength she could muster and rose up in the bed. "The French?"

He shook his head. "No. British."

"What have we to fear from our own troops?"

He glanced back at the window. "They've gone mad. The entire city is in turmoil. They lost so many men trying to get in, what with the powder mines and the time it took, they are taking their revenge."

Outside, there were drunken shouts, the sound of bottles being thrown against a wall and calls for more wine.

"You mean they're pillaging?"

Robert settled back into his chair. "Yes. We're safe enough. This building is abandoned, and there is nothing in the two floors beneath us to entice anyone to waste their time here."

"But why isn't Wellington doing anything to stop them? Why aren't you?" she asked.

He eased forward in the chair. "Why would I?"

There was something in the icy timbre of his voice that chilled her spine. That warned her something was terribly wrong.

"Where is Aquiles?" she asked.

He seemed not to hear her. "You shouldn't worry about anything right now." He got up and dug around in a bag that lay on the floor.

Her valise! How had it gotten here from the tent? How had they gotten into the city when everything seemed in such turmoil? How had Robert found this place? Nothing about any of this, about Robert made sense.

"I was able to get us some food, before everything went so terribly wrong." He held out his hand. "The bread is rather stale, not what you're used to, but it will have to do until we can secure the treasure."

The treasure. The way he said it frightened her. A wistful note of longing clung to his words.

He moved over and sat on the corner of her bed. "When we have the treasure, I'll dress you in diamonds, my dear. I'll make all the promises I made those years ago come true. You'll be my wife, and I will shower you with riches."

And when he reached out to touch her cheek, she backed away. For the man reaching out to touch her was not Robert, not the Robert she had married, not the man who had captured her heart, but the one who had nearly destroyed it.

For the man before her was mad. She could see it in his eyes, hear it in the way he spoke.

"Don't be afraid," he said, his fingers stroking her hair. "I've forgiven you for not waiting for me. For being so deceived by that insidious cousin of mine. Rest assured, dispatching him will be my first order of business in securing our happiness."

He got up and went back to the window, watching in the night, for what she couldn't fathom.

Olivia swallowed back her fears. Her worst nightmare had come back to life amidst the hellish battle for Badajoz.

For somehow, someway, the Marquis of Bradstone lived. And now he held her life in his hands.

Outside a tent on the field beyond the walls of Badajoz, a lone man hung his head and wept. This wasn't the first time he had shed tears in the last three days, and it certainly wouldn't be the last.

Robert Danvers's grief tore at those who heard his painful cries, so much so that most just ducked their heads and continued on past him. He might have helped win the battle, but he had lost his wife in the terrible explosion that had destroyed so many lives.

Why had she ignored his warning to stay well clear of the battle? he asked himself.

After the explosion, he'd climbed through the burning embers and remains, searching for her. And when he couldn't find her, he'd dug and clawed at the rubble, trying to uncover where she had been buried.

Then he'd gotten swept back into the battle, carried along by the next line of troops. He'd lost sight of where she'd been, and in the changing landscape, it was impossible to tell where she had once stood and where she had fallen.

He tugged at the flask in his jacket and took a long pull, emptying the contents down his raw and burning throat. He'd spent most of the last three days drowning his grief in port, and now he'd have to find another bottle before the pain renewed its assault on his senses. He staggered off in search of more alcohol, anything to numb his heart.

Aquiles glanced up from inside the tent and watched him go. He shook his head and sighed.

"The major's taking her death hard. Must be something we can do for him," Jemmy said. "Though I can't blame him for being beat to snuff. I still can't believe the Queen's gone myself." He turned his face toward the tent wall, fresh tears spilling from his eyes.

Aquiles glanced down at the boy with a new appreciation. It was obvious that he would probably never walk again. Martha and Olivia's quick doctoring had saved him from infection, and worse, probably, from losing the leg, but that it would never function properly again was most likely. And yet he hadn't grumbled a word about his own painful condition, more worried about Robert and his lost ladylove.

Olivia had no idea how much time had passed when next Bradstone roused her. For some reason she had slipped back into a dreamless sleep, and she suspected he'd been mixing some of her powders into the tea he'd offered.

"Come, wake up," he said. " 'Tis nearly dawn, and the city is all but quiet. The worst of them are passed out, and the few stragglers that are out there will be no match for us."

He tugged at her uninjured hand, the one that wore the ring Robert had placed on her finger not so long ago.

Orlando's ring.

The sight of it offered her a glimmer of hope that somehow Robert, her Robert, was alive and searching for her.

"Where are we going?" she asked warily, as he hurried about the room, tossing the remaining bit of bread into her beleaguered valise.

"To the cathedral." Impatience marked each word. When she didn't rise any further, he stopped and stared at her. "To get the treasure," he prompted. "There are four possible churches here in town, but I think we will start with the cathedral."

She smiled at him. "But don't you remember, my lord, the treasure is in Madrid."

It was the wrong thing to say, for the madness she suspected that infected his mind now sprang to life in full fever.

He crossed the room in two mighty strides and sent a stinging slap across her face. "You faithless little bitch. I don't know why I have forgiven you. But I shall. You'll see."

Olivia struggled to catch her breath and said nothing.

Bradstone didn't seem to notice. "If the treasure is

in Madrid, why did you bring *him* here? Didn't you think I would follow you? Learn of your treachery?"

"I'm sorry," she whispered, trying to appease him, trying to regain his trust. "He forced me to do this."

The man nodded. "I thought as much. That is why I sent Capitaine de Jenoure to find you."

"*You* sent him to find me?"

He smiled. "I would have you safe, my love. Safe so we could find the treasure together. That was why it distressed me to see you start off for the battlefield. I had hoped to take you during the battle while you were in the camp with the women. But as it turned out, after the explosion, I was able to carry you away through the smoke without anyone noticing."

"Thank you, my lord," she whispered. The memory of the explosion replayed in her mind. Had Robert survived the blast? She had no way of knowing, and her heart ached to know the fate of her husband. "It was kind of you to save me," she told Bradstone, all the while cursing him for taking her from Robert when he may need her.

"Yes, it was," he said. "Now, up with you. We must hurry."

This time she rallied what strength she had and got out of bed. If she was to escape him, it would be easier out in the streets. The bruises on her legs had turned to shades of green and black, while her burned hand still stung. She moved stiffly out of the bed, pulling down what was left of the dimity dress to cover her bare legs.

"There you go," Bradstone said, encouraging her progress by handing over her stockings and shoes. "Good as new. But we will have to get you something else to wear. Can't have my marchioness wearing rags." He held out her cloak, which looked to have borne the brunt of the explosion. It was blackened by the fire and had several large holes in it.

She forced a smile to her lips and took the cape, holding back the cry of pain that threatened to escape her lips as she cast it over her shoulders. She'd be damned if she'd have him help her—allow him to touch her.

"Why do you need me to help you get the treasure?" she asked. "You know it is here in Badajoz, so why take me? I'll just slow your pace."

He laughed, a twisted little sound slipping from his lips like the growling of a rabid dog. "And what if it is not?" he asked. He dug into her valise and pulled out her notebook. "I have had my fill of your treachery, and if we do not find the treasure here in Badajoz, you will keep translating these notes until you get it right." He threw the journal at her. "For every empty tomb I am forced to dig, I promise I will exact my revenge from your flesh, until you find your translation skills"—he reached into his coat and pulled out a wicked-looking stiletto—"as sharp as my knife."

If Olivia had held any hope of escape, by the time she'd finished dressing and tucking her hair into a quick chignon, it quickly vanished. For just before they were about to head out the door, he turned to her, his face once again twisted with the insanity that infected his mind and the anger she feared.

"Don't think you will leave me, my dear." He reached inside his coat and pulled out her pistol. "How resourceful of you to bring this to me. And since I don't as yet trust you, I fear I will have to use it to ensure your loyalty for now." Then he shoved her out the door, prodding her toward the stairs, the muzzle resting between her shoulder blades.

The trip through the predawn streets offered no hope for escape. As he had said, the looting had all but ceased. Soldiers were lying in the doorways and gutters, snoring off their excess of wine and rum. Glass from shop windows glittered in the street, doors had been kicked in, and goods and booty lay ravaged and torn in the streets.

It appeared the British had exacted a heavy toll on the poor city for its stubborn and deadly resistance.

"Ah, vengeance," Bradstone said, stepping over the dead and naked body of a woman. "What a lovely sight."

Obviously he had done some exploration through the city, for they went directly to the cathedral through a maze of streets. He moved through the city like a rat, born to hiding and cunning stealth.

"How did you survive, my lord?" Olivia asked. "Everyone thought you dead."

"Not with any help from you," he muttered darkly. "But if you must know, when the *Bon Venture* went down, I was picked up by the Frenchies who sank us. Luckily the captain was a man of some breeding and recognized that I would be worth something in ransom. Unfortunately before he could make the arrangements to send word home, he was killed in port, and for a time I languished in a French prison, where—" He stopped abruptly, for up ahead of them a small contingent of British soldiers was marching through the street, apparently gathering up their drunken and fallen comrades.

He caught her arm and wrenched her into a doorway, covering her body with his to shield her from sight. She would have called out, but he put the pistol to her head and placed one finger on his lips to indicate he wanted her silence.

Olivia dared not so much as breathe until the men passed by, yet even after they had, Bradstone did not move.

"You've grown comely, Olivia," he said, his voice purring over the words. "Who would have thought that seven years would give you a woman's body and charms?"

She stiffened as his fingers traced a trail over her cheek and lips.

"I should take you now. Show you what you missed," he said, pushing himself closer to her.

"It will be light soon," she said. "There will be time enough for your pleasures, my lord, after you have gotten away with the treasure."

He laughed and stroked the pistol down the neckline of her gown, the cold metal chilling her skin. "How impatient you are for the treasure. And for me, I wager."

She shuddered again and hoped he took her revulsion for something else.

Stepping out of the alcove, Bradstone looked right and left to ensure the street was clear before he dragged her down from their hiding place and onward in his frantic pace toward the cathedral.

Ahead of them, its beautiful medieval towers rose above the low buildings surrounding it. She had to find a way to make her escape, for she doubted that Bradstone, in his madness, would allow her to live.

"How is it that you came to Spain?" she asked, hoping to distract him with chatter.

"My jailer in Le Havre was a greedy man. Over cards I made him an offer. I told him of the treasure and said we would split it if he would get us the necessary travel papers to go to Madrid. The bastard did it, but when we got there and there was no treasure, the authorities arrested us for traveling with false papers and threw us in a hole of a prison."

He made a guttural noise, as if recalling that terrible place only fed his madness. "Four years I spent in that dark hole," he said. "Four years without any light. Just the scraping sound of my jailers when they remembered to feed us and the constant gnawing of rats."

"How terrible for you," she whispered. *And too bad you didn't stay there forever*, she wanted to add.

Instead she asked, "How is it that you escaped?"

"A new commander arrived, a French officer—your friend de Jenoure. He ordered an inspection of the prisoners, and we were all brought up to the yards. From there we struck a deal. He would release me, and I would help him find the treasure."

"But you had already looked in Madrid," she said.

"Yes, but there were rumors of Danvers's mission to London. I knew he would find you and then he would return—imagine my surprise when I saw you at the inn."

"You. It was you that I saw. You sent the maid to bring me to you."

He nodded. "If that half-bred brother of Danvers's hadn't come along, we would have been well rid of him. As it turned out, I had to return to de Jenoure and seek his aid in retrieving you."

Olivia's mind whirled at the events that had surrounded her without her knowledge.

They got to the steps of the church, but they found

the doors barred. Unwilling to take this as a deterrent, Bradstone caught her by the arm and dragged her around the building.

The cathedral was huge, and it appeared it also housed a large convent. The gates hung open at an odd angle, obviously having been forced so, and when they got inside the sanctuary, they found the convent held what must have once been a beautiful garden. It was now littered with overturned statues, empty bottles and the smoldering remains of a bonfire.

"It appears the good sisters threw the British a welcoming party," he joked.

Olivia said nothing, her eyes and ears sharp for anyone who may be able to aid her. And then she saw something that caught her eye.

One statue that had escaped the mayhem. The proud, tall stone effigy of a medieval queen. At the sight of her, chills ran down Olivia's battered limbs. Beneath it was a single word carved into the base.

"Caliopa," she whispered.

"What is that?" Bradstone barked, as he tried another door, but only found it locked. "What are you muttering?"

"Nothing," Olivia said, as they walked past the queen who had lent her life and fortune to a lost cause. She could have sworn the woman was smiling at her, offering Olivia a bit of her own legendary courage.

If that is Caliopa's tomb, Olivia thought, *then the treasure must be buried here.*

From the garden, Bradstone finally found an unlocked door into the sisters' haven. They went past cell after empty cell and continued through the maze of halls until they came to a chapel.

At the doorway stood a statue of Mary, her steady

countenance guarding the place. The floor was paved with pale stones, while carefully hewn columns rose on either side, each arching gently to the next one. There was a simple, modest touch to the place, an almost feminine quality to it. Incense hung heavily in the air, and the place was lit by candles, their flickering light illuminating old stained glass showing images of roses, which Olivia guessed must have dated back to the time of the Berber invasions.

She thought back to her translation. *The Tomb of the Virgin*. This was the place. A chapel devoted to the Mother of God, the Holy Virgin.

"Have you come seeking shelter?" a woman asked, coming out from behind the altar. She wore the habit of a sister. "For we have no food to offer and little in the way of comforts to help you."

"Where is the Tomb of the Virgin, you old hag?" Bradstone demanded, leveling his pistol at her.

The woman's face paled, but Olivia admired her courage when she stood her ground. "Go away with you. There is nothing left here for you English to steal."

"Tell me where the Tomb of the Virgin is or die," he said.

She shook her head. "My life is in God's hands."

Bradstone then turned the gun away from her and at a small boy who had darted out from behind the altar. "What about that whelp's?" he asked.

The sister gathered the boy in her arms and stared at Bradstone as if assessing his intent.

Please, Olivia mouthed at her. *Tell him*.

The woman's jaw set in a firm line. Then she nodded at an alcove to the left. "Over there."

"Show me," Bradstone said.

As they followed the sister toward the tomb, several more children came out of the hiding spot. The sister issued a sharp command for them to get back, but Bradstone only laughed.

"Bring them all out," he told her. "I have a task for them." He stood before the tomb and waved his pistol at the tallest boy. "Pull those stones up." He motioned to another child. "Go fetch shovels and a bar to move them with."

The boy looked at the sister for a translation of the man's foreign words, and she translated them and gave him an approving nod only after Bradstone placed the pistol to the head of a little girl, who immediately broke into sobs.

Over the tomb there was an ancient stone, and on it was carved a warning.

Only those pure of heart and intent will find what they seek.

So much for the warning, Olivia thought, as Bradstone began to supervise the work. Much to her relief he quickly became absorbed in finding his treasure, so Olivia could draw back from him. Discreetly she beckoned at one of the boys, a sharp-eyed lad who appeared quick and agile. Quietly she whispered to him in Spanish, "Go to the British camp. Ask for Major Danvers and give him this." She pulled Orlando's ring from her finger and tucked it into his grubby hand.

"How will I know what this major looks like?" the boy asked, the ring already stowed in his pocket.

Olivia pointed at Bradstone. "Exactly like that man, but with a heart that is good and pure."

The boy nodded and silently crept from the chapel and made his escape.

* * *

Robert's latest stupor was just starting to fade when a small hand began tugging at the sleeve of his jacket.

"Major Danvers?" a small boy asked in Spanish. "Are you Major Danvers?"

He opened one eye and gauged from the poor clothes and lack of shoes he was probably begging. "What do you want?"

"A lady sent me."

"Go away. I have no interest in ladies."

The boy remained at his side, as stubborn as he was annoying.

"Are you Major Danvers?" he asked again.

"Yes, now go away."

"But the lady told me to give you this."

A shimmering object clattered to the table, spinning to a stop before his nose.

A simple band of gold. Orlando's ring.

Robert's head rose from the table, and his hand shot out to catch it up. "Where did you get this?"

The boy backed up at his sharp words, his eyes round as he stared at Robert's face. "A lady," he stammered. "At the chapel. She said to bring it to you. She is in danger. We all are."

Robert caught up his coat and hollered for Aquiles. His batman came stumbling out of the tent.

"She's alive," he said, holding up Orlando's ring. He turned back to the little urchin who was still staring at him as if he were a ghost.

"Where did you say she was?"

"The Virgin's chapel at the convent behind the cathedral."

"Show me," Robert said.

As they started out, the boy glanced up at him

again. "She said you would look just like the other man, and you do."

Robert stopped for a moment. "What other man?"

"The one with the *pistola*. The one who brought her there. He looks exactly like you."

For one unholy moment, he considered what the boy was saying. A man who looked just like him.

Could it be? Bradstone was alive?

It was the only explanation, as unbelievable as the discovery that his beloved little termagant lived.

He turned to Aquiles. "Get my pistol."

Bradstone had the children digging in shifts, for they were small and tired easily, much to his annoyance.

Olivia had stepped forward and offered to help, but he had loftily informed her that was work beneath his marchioness and ordered the children to redouble their efforts.

"What is it he seeks?" the sister whispered to her.

"*El Rescate del Rey*," she told her.

"Here?" the lady said, genuinely surprised.

Olivia nodded, while the sister glanced back at the now open tomb and crossed herself.

She had no idea how much time had passed but glanced often at the door, hoping to find Robert standing there with a regiment of men behind him.

But then again, she hadn't considered another possibility.

What if Robert hadn't survived the blast that had nearly taken her life? The boy's errand would be for naught, and there would be no rescue from that quarter.

But like Caliopa, Olivia didn't know if she wanted to live in a world without her husband. Her Álvaro.

Just then, one of the shovels hit a hard object, the metal scraping against metal.

"It's there. It's there," Bradstone said. "Dig it out. Dig it out now."

Ten minutes later, Bradstone and the children hoisted an ancient box from the hole. It took six of the largest boys and the marquis to muscle the weighty chest up to the floor.

"Señor," the nun implored, "that could be the holy remains of our patron saint or some other good soul. Do not defile them by opening it."

"Shut up!" Bradstone snapped at her. He cuffed the boys out of his way and caught up the heavy metal bar one of them had brought in. He swung it at the rusted lock in front, which shattered at the first blow.

His maniacal laughter echoed through the nave like a blasphemous choir. He stared at the chest for a moment, and then walked over to Olivia, caught her by the arm and dragged her over to it. "Open the lid," he told her.

"Why me?" she asked.

"Because if it is cursed, I would have that honor be yours," he said.

For a moment she could only look at the chest in wonder. Then glanced once again at the words carved in the stone above and sent up a small prayer begging forgiveness from Caliopa.

El Rescate del Rey. Hidden for eleven centuries and now it lay before her. Her hands shook as she started to open the lid.

"Stop where you are," a voice familiar and pure rang out.

Olivia spun around. "Robert!"

He stood at the end of the nave, pistol in hand, with Aquiles and several others behind him. Including Wellington.

But Bradstone, his years in the solitary confines of the prison, moved as fast and treacherously as the rats that had been his cellmates.

He caught Olivia by the arm and drew her into his arms, then whipped out the stiletto from his boot top and put it to her throat.

"Not one step, Danvers," he warned. "One move, and I'll kill her before your eyes."

Robert stilled, his gaze locked with hers.

They both knew Bradstone, mad or sane, would have no compunction about murdering anyone who stood in his way.

But Olivia wasn't about to let him use her to get the treasure, wasn't about to die in his arms. This man had murdered her father, killed Orlando. And that left her to see that he paid for his crimes.

She'd vowed revenge all those weeks ago, and now if the fire in Robert's eyes was any indication, she would have it with his help.

The sharp edge of the stiletto cut a thin line at her throat, but she didn't even flinch. Somehow she had to distract him, to get him to let down his guard so Robert could make his shot.

"Let her go," Robert told him. "You have no need for her now."

Bradstone shook his head, pointing the tip of the knife at the base of her throat, the point where her pulse fluttered wildly. "But I do. I want her to pay for all my lost years. This bitch sent me to hell with her treachery, and now she'll get the same in return."

Just then a shot rang out. Loud and true, it caught them all by surprise, including Robert, who surged forward.

Olivia felt Bradstone jerk with enough force to send the knife in his hand spinning from his grip and her flying to the floor. She glanced up to find him staring at her, his mouth open and a trickle of blood oozing from his lips. A second shot erupted from high in the choir above. This time the bullet found Bradstone's heart and sent the man pitching to the floor beside her, dead.

Even as he fell, Robert reached her side. He shielded her with his body and called out, "Who are you? Who killed him?"

A shadowy figure rose from the choir above. A single man.

None other than Pymm.

"Fine shot, as ever, my good man," Wellington called out to his friend and spymaster.

"What the devil are you doing here?" Robert asked, as the man climbed down the stairs and joined them in the nave.

"I heard that Bradstone was alive and in league with the French right after you left. I came as soon as I could to warn you. Wellington's aid told me you had come here, so I followed. Seems I arrived just in time." He nudged Bradstone's body with the toe of his well-worn boot. "Better end, this. Save the Treasury a pole of money, what with transportation fees and trial costs."

Robert held out his hand to Pymm. "I thank you, sir, for saving my wife's life."

"Your wife?" Pymm sputtered. "You married this . . . this—"

"Termagant?" Robert suggested.

"Yes, exactly," Pymm said. "Are you out of your mind?"

"Completely and hopelessly," Robert told the man as he swept Olivia into his arms and kissed her thoroughly before one and all.

Epilogue

England, 1816

Another four years passed before the Marquis of Bradstone returned home for good. His second return to London was as triumphant as his first, but this time the man holding the title was Colonel Robert Danvers, late of Wellington's personal staff.

A distant relative of the deceased marquis, he had been awarded the title for his devoted service to King and country during the Peninsular War and his recent heroics at Waterloo.

The new marquis was accompanied by his lady wife, a woman as elegant as the marquis was handsome. There were rumors that the lady had a scandalous past, and there was rampant speculation as to who she was, but when Lady Finch and the Dowager, Lady Bradstone, declared the new Lady Bradstone the perfect marchioness, few in the *ton* dared snub her or question her qualifications or controversial breeding.

But it seemed the Marquis and Marchioness of Bradstone cared little for society or its opinions, preferring to spend time in the country with their children, which left the Dowager full use of the London house. The arrangement had gone a long way in changing the good lady's opinion of Olivia Sutton, since the arrangement had been Olivia's idea along with a generous allowance from the Bradstone coffers to keep the esteemed lady in the style and fashion of her peers.

As for his lordship and his lady, with four sons to their credit and rumors of the marchioness once again breeding, there was no doubt that the couple enjoyed their privacy . . . and their marital bed.

"Oh, Robert," Olivia said, looking up from her letter from Lady Finch, her eyes sparkling with mirth, "you are going to love this."

Robert didn't know what to expect, given whom the letter had come from. "What?" he asked hesitantly.

"Lady Finch has heard we are expecting another child."

He cringed.

"Oh, yes," Olivia said. "And she feels it is high time I took another room far from your lecherous advances. She says at my advanced age, 'bearing the burden of your insatiable lust' will be the death of me."

Rising from his chair, he crossed the room, snatched the letter out of his wife's hands and tossed it into the fire. "That is what I think of Lady Finch's advice."

Olivia rushed to the fireplace to save her letter, but it was too late. The flames had consumed it. "You didn't need to do that," she scolded playfully. "Besides, I was just getting to the good part."

"And what, pray tell, was that?" he asked.

His wife giggled. "She suggested I find you a mistress."

Robert caught up the poker and made several futile attempts to save the now charred remains. "Why didn't you say so? Now, that is advice worth offering."

She prodded him in the side with her finger, and he made a painful grimace, then they both collapsed in front of the grate in a fit of laughter.

When they finally found their breath, Robert leaned over and kissed her. After all these years, after four children, this was the only woman for him. She had stood by him through the remaining years of the war, braved the hardships of the final campaigns and had refused to leave his side when Wellington had recalled him to service to fight Napoleon one last time—this time on the field of Waterloo.

And each time he kissed her, whether before a battle or here before their home fire, safe under their own roof, his body stirred to life, his desire for her only growing with the passing of years.

Olivia Danvers, Lady Bradstone, was and would always be the other half of his heart. No mistress could offer him more.

Her arms wound around his neck, and she pulled him closer until they lay on the floor, entwined and entangled, their bodies falling together like pieces of a puzzle.

Olivia felt the familiar stirrings as his hands curved over her hips, down along her legs, and began pulling at the hem of her gown. The heat of the fire bathed her now bare legs in warmth, while Robert's touch sizzled them with passionate heat.

His fingers trailed a slow path to the very center of

her need for him while his kiss deepened, his tongue stroking her as she knew his hardened member would soon fan her own fires.

"Did you lock the door?" she whispered glancing up at the parlor entrance.

"An hour ago," he told her, nibbling at her ear.

"And what have you been waiting for?"

"You to finish your confounded correspondence with Pymm."

"He needed me to decode some messages one of his agents intercepted," she said, defending their lost hour.

"If I had done this," he said, drawing his lips to her breast and suckling at it until the nipple rose in a nubby peak, "would that have been enough to convince you that the British Empire would survive another hour without your linguistic aid?"

Olivia laughed, arching her back to his touch. "For that, I would have condemned it all to the fireplace."

"I'll remember that," he said.

His fingers dipped into her, touched the honeyed flesh, drawing the wetness over her raised nub and leaving Olivia breathless with anticipation.

She hurried to rid him of his breeches, her fingers quickly taking care of the buttons, including sending one bouncing across the hearth.

He looked up at her. "How am I going to explain that to Babbit?" he asked, referring to his valet.

"That is not my problem," she said, as she finally freed him, relishing the feel of his hardness, the satiny length that gave her so much pleasure. She caressed him, kissed him, drew him into her mouth and left him on the edge, as he had done to her.

Very quickly he divested her of her gown, his body

covering hers, filling her with him in one slow movement, just the way she liked it. Olivia was more than ready for him, and her body met his in an anxious thrust, her hips rising and falling, urging him to move faster to meet her need.

And Robert did just that. Stroking her depths, until that familiar light of surprise rose in her eyes, when her mouth opened to say something but nothing but a sigh came forth, when she shuddered around him, telling him she'd found that pleasured place of bliss. That was all it took to send him speeding along with her, his seed spilling forth, his body taking a final last surge into her to draw out every moment of that fleeting rapture.

He sighed and curled her into his arms, cradling her, surrounding her with the heat of his body, with the warmth of his love for her.

"You never cease to amaze me, my love," he said.

"I'm glad," she told him. "I want to be the only one you ever turn to with that 'insatiable lust.' "

"And you always shall be," he said, kissing her again.

His senses took in every bit of her, the faint scent of roses from her favorite French soap, the fullness of breasts now once again growing in anticipation of the coming child and the hard, rounded fullness of her stomach.

His hand went there. It was too early to feel the child moving from the outside, though she assured him she had already felt the faint flutterings of life within.

Another child. Another miracle in their life. Robert couldn't help but kiss her again.

"I want a daughter," he whispered to her.

"Whatever for?" she asked, her hand covering his, Caliopa's ruby betrothal ring sparkling on her finger. With the great treasure restored, the Spanish King had sent the ring to Olivia as a token of his country's appreciation. "What do we know of raising daughters?"

"I would want her to have your hair, your eyes and your bright smile." Then he grinned. "And my temperament, so she doesn't turn out to be a regular termagant."

Olivia's mouth opened in a mock insulted moue. "Then you had better hope for another son," she told him.

He ruffled her hair and pulled her close, kissing her deeply again. And when she wiggled closer, intimating that she was ready for him again, he laughed. She was right.

One termagant was enough for him. Enough to fill his heart for a lifetime.

Author's Note

Though *El Rescate del Rey* and the tragic story of Caliopa and Álvaro are products of my imagination, the horrible conditions of the siege at Badajoz unfortunately are not. The carnage and loss of British soldiers was so great that Wellington was reduced to tears when he saw the piles of bodies the next morning. He was also shocked by the horrible and disgraceful pillaging that the angry British soldiers unleashed upon the hapless city once it was taken. For three days the soldiers raped, looted and burned what was left. It turned what was to have been a triumphant start to the removal of Napoleon from the Iberian peninsula into a sad chapter in British military history.

Elizabeth Boyle

Next month don't miss

The newest Avon Romantic Treasure from

Bestselling author

Linda Needham

MY WICKED EARL

Pretty Hollie Finch is forced to live with her sworn
enemy—the forbidding Lord Charles Stirling, the Earl
of Everingham. He places her under house arrest for
her rabble-rousing ways . . . but she entices him as no
other woman has ever done. But the powerful earl
has a secret . . . one that could destroy him. . . .

"Linda Needham's novels are sheer delight."
Lisa Kleypas

TRE 0701

America Loves Lindsey!

The Timeless Romances
of #1 Bestselling Author

Johanna Lindsey

The WONDER of KATHLEEN E. WOODIWISS

A Season Beyond A Kiss
0-380-80794-7 $7.99 U.S. ($10.99 Can)

Ashes in the Wind 0-380-76984-0 $6.99 U.S. ($8.99 Can)

Come Love a Stranger
0-380-89936-1 $6.99 U.S. ($9.99 Can)

The Elusive Flame
0-380-80786-6 $7.50 U.S. ($9.99 Can)

The Flame and the Flower
0-380-00525-5 $6.99 U.S. ($9.99 Can)

Forever in Your Embrace
0-380-77246-9 $7.50 U.S. ($9.99 Can)

Petals on the River
0-380-79828-X $6.99 U.S. ($8.99 Can)

A Rose in Winter 0-380-84400-1 $6.99 U.S. ($8.99 Can)

Shanna 0-380-38588-0 $6.99 U.S. ($8.99 Can)

So Worthy My Love
0-380-76148-3 $6.99 U.S. ($9.99 Can)

The Wolf and the Dove
0-380-00778-9 $6.99 U.S. ($8.99 Can)